PRAISE FOR AUSTIN REHL

It's rare that I read a sweet romance with so much adventure, danger, intrigue, passion- albeit clean. It had elements to it that very much reminded me of Lord of the Rings - in part that it's a newly created world by the author. Loved it, daughter loved it... Bravo you have captured my admiration.

   - Canada

Great blend of adventure and romance. I was totally absorbed in the characters' struggles to reconcile their feelings with their sense of responsibility. I appreciate getting to see into the hearts and minds of characters with high morals. I agree with the reviewer who said this is movie material.

   - Rebecca

GUARDIAN OF THE EMERALD COAST

BOOK THREE OF THE SĪHALT SERIES

AUSTIN REHL

Edited by
JOEY QUINCE

LOCK10 PRESS

ALSO BY AUSTIN REHL

Guardian of the Sunshine Bride - Book 1

Guardian of the Golden City - Book 2

For my Family
—those by blood and those by bonds of friendship.

ACKNOWLEDGMENTS

This project has taken more time than the last. I appreciate the patience so many of my fans as I have worked to complete this next installment of the series.

My wife Wendy and our children have been so supportive and listened to my thoughts about the plot and character development. I'm grateful for their opinions on how the story should unfurl. My fiction is derived from living and my family gives me the wonderful gift of love at home.

Others have been a great help too. My mother, Anna Rehl, not only taught me to love books but shared in my progress of this series. My friends Luke Bauserman, Alicia Phelps, Bethany Atwood, Kimberly Lovejoy, and Jordan Allen were all instrumental in inspiring me to write this novel. Thank you for your insights into reader expectations, human emotion, and plot development.

I'm thankful to Joey Quince and his team for the editing, Kimberly Huther for her proofing work, Jared Blando for the spectacular world map, John Anthony Di Giovanni for the beautiful cover art, Shawn King for the typography, and B. J. Harrison for the spectacular audio performances.

These folks have have helped to turn my idea turn into a work of art.

You have my sincere gratitude,
Austin Rehl

REFOUNDING SONNET

Like a seed of the spring flower,
She was carried on the wind.
From sun-lit shores, to frozen lakes,
An Empire she would mend.

She would break the shining walls,
And many of those within.
Shower her light, and Talented might
On the darkness that descends,

When unions fail, and a people are frail
From the ailment on the winds,
And fear from the west, becomes a test,
As the will of the empire bends.

Attributed to
Emperor Heathron Dol Lassimer,
Third Age

NOTHING BUT THE BLADE

The Sīhalt Guardian pretended to focus on sharpening his blade. The thin sword that he always wore on his hip remained as keen as ever, but Jared needed a distraction. Every now and again, he glanced up and watched them. Across the deck of the yacht called *Marine Escape* stood Kathleen. Her fiery hair tossed in the wind as the gusts swept inward toward land. Heathron, exiled Prince of Tyath, stood beside her with his hands about her waist. She leaned into him and the sandy-haired prince shifted his weight so that her head could more easily rest on his chest.

Jared growled under his breath as he watched. He pulled up the black hood of the Sīhalt cloak and went back to his sharpening stones, repeating in his head the words he had heard her whisper just moments before— *"Everything will be okay."*

Kathleen had said them to Heathron, but Jared knew they had been meant for him. The ears of a Sensor missed little. But what did they mean?

Everything will be okay, he repeated again. But despite the craft skipping like a stone on the swells, and out of the snatches of danger, he knew...

Nothing would be okay.

As he thought this, he glanced up at the reason why. There, across from him stood Prince Heathron, holding Kathleen in his arms while Jared sat alone with nothing. Nothing but the blade.

He scowled and swallowed hard.

"Brother, are you alright?" came a voice. It was Seth.

Jared shifted his weight and raised his eyes from where he was seated on the deck. There was his brother, approaching him cautiously. Seth was his twin, though not a perfect match. Seth's eyes were blue, as if some current of the azure seas had dripped into them, while Jared's were duller, like the color of a storm on the horizon.

"You seem to have found friendship on this voyage," Jared said by way of greeting, his eyes flicking away toward Lilly across the deck. He spoke warmly, trying to add an edge of compassion to his voice. He wanted to be happy for the romance Seth had found in the Tyathian guardswoman, but his heart could not warm when it seemed his own hopes were being dashed to the rocks.

Seth's ice-blue eyes sparkled and his lips parted with an involuntary smile.

"Lilly is delightful, don't you think?" he asked, looking toward the dark-haired woman as she spoke with Kathleen.

"I am happy for you," Jared said.

Seth placed a hand on Jared's shoulder, sensing how his brother was feeling. Jared knew his twin recognized the melancholy he felt now.

Jared shrugged him off. "I will be fine. It was never more than a dream, or a whisper—a hope of something that can never be."

Seth, looking unconvinced, dropped to his haunches so his gaze might meet his brother's.

"I don't believe you Jared," he replied.

Jared flinched at the observation.

"Okay, fine. But at least indulge my resistance, brother. I am trying to reconcile my heart to the reality of never..."

The sentence trailed off unfinished.

"Of never having her," Seth finished for him, after a period of silence.

Jared stiffened and then nodded. The pain of expressing the thought tore at him.

"Yes," he admitted. "I want to fight it, to find some way around, or through this dilemma. Either that she may be mine, or that I can stomach it and move on," he said, frustration brimming from the deep well of his emotions. "Neither seems possible right now." He flicked his eyes from his brother to Kathleen and Heathron's embrace, and then clenched his fists and looked out to sea.

Seth studied his brother, the way a scholar might gaze at an artifact, or as if he was an interesting riddle than needed to be puzzled out.

"You want to win, Jared," he said seriously and after some time. "Winning for you means holding Kathleen in your arms. You want to smell her hair and feel her soft lips against yours once more. Winning for you means loving her and feeling that love in return."

Jared, digesting every word, slowly turned his eyes back to his brother. They were pinned wide, the way a zealot might look upon hearing the incantations of his teacher.

Yes... he wanted to say. *Yes, that's exactly it!* But before he could, Seth's features seemed to harden, and his face paled somehow as he added, "But brother, this is a war you *should* not win. You should not even engage in the battle!" Seth was shaking his head now, a look of concern gathering on his face like robes of shadow.

Jared deflated. He shrank and then grimaced, nodding. "You say this can never be, but I know your ways. You have always believed me capable of doing the impossible. But now you fear I will bring ruin to myself?"

"I fear you will do just what I have said. You will seek to win. You will fight to have her as your own, and nothing will stop you."

"She loves me," Jared said softly, "and I, her."

"Don't do this, Brother. Restrain your desires."

"I *know* she loves me, even if she would deny it." He took up the stone and resumed dragging it along the edge of his blade. "But don't worry. I will not destroy the world simply because I am unhappy in it."

Seth kept looking into Jared's eyes, trying to read them.

Jared looked down at his blade.

"I've tried that before, and it only leads to unhappiness," he added.

Seth placed a hand on Jared's shoulder. The brothers seemed to exist tall and imposing, even on their haunches. They were bold and true, honorable reflections of each other. The wind whipped about the tails of their long black cloaks, the hems curling and writhing about their feet like sea snakes desperate to return to water.

It was this reflection that seemed to spur a memory in both their minds: one of terror and blood and death.

"I was just as complicit as you. We made that decision together," Seth said defensively, his words now as stiff as he stopped short of saying the word they both thought, the word that repeated itself in their minds: *massacre*. He didn't need to. Both men understood.

"That isn't the way I remember it. I hold myself responsible."

"Of course you do," Seth replied. "You always want to look out for your little brother."

"Cedric accepted our repentance—after a manner of speaking," Jared said, managing a half smile. Then he steered his eyes up from the blade and back to his brother's face. "Seth, I am glad that we are united again. I never gave up hope that you would survive."

Now Seth had a flash of humor cross his otherwise serious face.

"There were days when I almost gave up hope. For all our years of training with Master Tove, who would have guessed it would be our games of *Chendris* that would prove most useful to my survival among the Delathranes?" Seth said.

Jared shook his head at the memory. "Master Tove used to get so frustrated with us when he found we stayed up late to play."

"Do you remember the third time he found us playing a game, instead of sleeping?" Seth asked. He laughed and looked up toward the sky.

"We both got Master Tove's cane!" Jared exclaimed. "Do you remember the bitter way he used to look at us when we were caught? His expression at our continued disobedience was scary. And yet afterwards, how he always took us to his private office and—instead of punishing us further—taught us how to master the game, as if he was mastering himself at the same time, too."

"Mastering his anger, you mean?" Seth intoned with a knowing look. Jared nodded, considering. "He looked much older now."

"It was good to see him and some of the others," Jared replied.

"How will the Windstall Hermitage be led once Master Tove is gone? Some of the Sīhalt initiates seem to use the Windstall Hermitage as merely a school rather than a sacred Order. Fewer still actually complete the training to become a full Sīhalt Guardian these days," Seth said.

"The knowledge of the those who wear the Sword and Crook must not be lost. Times change and the flow of history goes onward, but the wisdom found within the walls of the Windstall Hermitage must be protected," Jared said.

"What would our land be like today, if Master Tove and Girdy Frast had not provided leadership when the empire needed it during the last Delathrane War? How many more lives would have been lost, even before the Great Sickness?" Seth wondered.

The brothers contemplated this as they looked toward the shoreline.

"Look at that. The beauty of the land is on full display," Jared observed.

The dazzling panorama of green fell away to paler, mossy hues. Trees, deep in the valleys of the forested hills, remained wreathed in mist. Those closer to the rocky shoreline shivered in the warm wind and seemed to shine blinding bright in the sunbeams that bathed them.

"That is why it is called the Emerald Coast," Jared said, putting an arm around Seth's shoulder and pulling him close.

"I love you, Brother," Jared said, realizing he had not said such a thing in years.

Seth returned the forceful embrace. "Thank you for finding for me."

"You knew I would come."

"As long as there was blood in your veins, I knew you would ride to my rescue," Seth said.

"That's what brothers do. We look out for each other."

Suddenly, Jared heard soft footsteps padding over the deck behind him. His senses allowed him to hear and see with amazing precision, and as he turned around, his mind had already formed a perfect picture of the vision he was about to see, down to the finest stroke. When he focused, he saw the satin slippers first, the ones that belonged to Kathleen, the woman who held his heart.

"It is so good to see the two of you together," she said, the sunlight picking out the golden highlights in her auburn hair. She was beautiful to him—beyond belief.

"You must feel so happy. I cannot wait to see my sister again," Kathleen said, her smile making the day seem even brighter.

Jared swallowed hard and was surprised at the difficulty in bringing words to his lips. With Kathleen standing this close, he was forced to meet her gaze, but each time he did so, he felt a force that drew him closer. It was almost a physical force. The impulse made him want to touch her.

"It is good to be with my brother again, Highness," Jared confirmed in his deep voice.

Kathleen's eyes flickered. She seemed slightly taken aback.

"Do you mean to distance yourself from me once again, Lord Sīhalt? I noticed the use of my formal title."

Her tone was even, expressing neither anger nor pain. Her use of his title, in return, let Jared know what she meant. They had sparred like this before, long ago in Candoreth.

"We were just sharing some memories, Princess," Seth explained.

Kathleen felt the awkwardness in the air, but nodded. "Ah yes, well, sometime during our voyage I would love to hear more about your lives and adventures," she said, ignoring the formality of the Sīhalt Guardians.

Jared swallowed and nodded, trying to hide his true emotions from her. He couldn't help himself. He found himself reverting to formal speech and postures anytime he felt his duty as a Guardian weighing more heavily upon him, or if he felt himself being drawn in too close. In this case, he felt both.

"I am sure we will all get to know one another much better the more we travel together," Seth said diplomatically, his smile easy and assuring.

"I look forward to it," Kathleen replied softly then moved on, padding back along the deck as the wind tossed her long red locks, twisting them into corkscrews.

"She does have a great power over you. I can see it in your eyes. I can sense it in your exchanges," Seth whispered to Jared.

Jared nodded, his eyes never leaving her. "In this fight, I must be resigned to lose her—and if not, to fight to the death *for* her."

"That is why I am concerned," Seth said cautiously.

2

NEW FOUND POWER

The footsteps of Pilus Dol Lassimer grew louder as he entered the throne room in Tyath. Lord Lars Balfoest, the Steward of the City, twitched his ears at the sound. He then opened his eyes from his meditation and barely turned his head as he dealt his visitor a sidelong glance. Pilus stopped and squared his shoulders to stand a little taller—commanding the navy had evidently improved his posture.

"What is it?" Lord Balfoest asked without fully turning to look at the uniformed man. Instead, Lord Balfoest turned his eyes back to the graceful movements of the girl before him: his newest, favorite pet.

She is pretty, he thought.

"Your Excellency, the Sundiland Princess…she got away," Pilus reported curtly.

Balfoest blinked but didn't move. "And her friends?"

"They got away too," Pilus stated, adjusting the white collar of his jacket before standing at attention once more. His face has turned a sudden shade of scarlet, and it was causing him to perspire.

"What do you mean they 'got away'?" Lord Balfoest hissed.

"They stole a yacht from the Turlin girl. We were almost to board them, then the water...changed," he explained, or rather, didn't explain.

"The water *changed?*" Balfoest asked, wondering what in all of Abboth's creations the man could mean.

"It turned against us, in their favor." The man hesitated; Lars could sense the confusion the man was feeling. "I saw their sails go slack, and still their yacht moved faster! It rose on a single wave, like a sled going over the snow in winter. It ran away from us quickly."

"I don't want excuses, Pilus. We need results," Lars said. The excuses grated on his ears, but Lars was sure that if he touched Pilus he would taste the sweet bitterness of the loss in the man's throat, not to mention the aching fear he must be enduring at having to report it now. Lars wanted to taste the man's emotions. So he motioned with his finger, beckoning the man closer to him.

Pilus shrank a little and, taking a couple of steps, stooped close at his master's side. As he did Lars reached out and took the younger man's hand in his own, tapping it with his bony fingers.

Oh yes Lars could feel the surge of emotion within the naval officer: how anxious he was to gain his favor. How delightfully awed he felt being in the presence of the great and powerful Steward—even if Pilus was the son of the late Emperor. Pilus was a man who honored those in power, not those who claimed to be. Lord Balfoest liked him.

"We searched for them along the Straits. Their hull was damaged when one of our ships struck theirs. So, it is possible they went down in the higher waves," Pilus suggested.

Lord Balfoest drew in a long breath, rolling his eyes toward the expansive ceiling.

"We can't count on that. It amazes me that you and your men were within boarding distance and they *still* got away."

"The Sīhalt Guardians cut the lines we cast, and there seemed to be some sorcery in use. Their boat was pushed by a swell of water that hurried them onward, as if the sea wanted them to escape—"

"Enough!" Lars narrowed his eyes. The man spoke sincerely enough, he thought. Even now, in the peculiar and awkward situation of having his hand held. Yes, this one was true enough, he thought again. Despite the incredible claims, Pilus was conveying the truth.

"If they survived, the Princess will try to make it back home. The people of Candoreth, and their foolish King Lukald, will be able to do nothing," Lord Balfoest mused, dropping the man's hand casually as if it was a sash he had grown bored of.

"Shall I search for them further down the Emerald Coast, Your Excellency?"

"There is still a bounty on her head among the pirates. The Centian ships from across the sea have been in a holding pattern. They want a place to dwell permanently and I have indicated to Admiral Yamatsu that Candoreth is a rouge province. He may have already taken that city."

Pilus looked taken aback. Evidently the young man didn't like the idea of handing any part of Desnia to the pirates. Well he could get used to the idea. Balfoest had plans for them as well.

"Her ship may be captured by them already," he said.

"Certainly the people of Hestin will not take them in," Pilus remarked, stepping back now that the awkward hand-holding custom of the Steward had ceased.

"Keep your focus, Pilus. We have much work to do. I plan to make a visit to House Sarkkand. If what I believe is true, he will negotiate. Finish building the fleet we already have in progress. Tighten the security and we will go north to bring Addisfall under our sway. Only then will we turn our attention to Candoreth."

Pilus saluted Lars crisply. He stood tall and straight with his hand raised to his brow.

Lars returned the salute. When Pilus turned on his heel to leave the room, Lars Balfoest rolled his eyes.

The rigidity of military men is so juvenile, he thought, then turned back to the other figure in the room.

"Are you ready to Grow again, Iskabel?" Lars asked the girl on the floor beside him. The young Delathrane Plant Witch no longer fought the collar, or the leash that held her. She had been much easier to train than the red-haired sorceress from the south. This one, Iskabel, was young and impressionable. She had learned at an early age that she deserved the lash if she did not obey. The Candorethian girl, in comparison, was a liability.

She is still a liability! Lars thought.

He laid his pale hand on Iskabel's deep brown shoulder and caressed her soft skin. The girl did not recoil like she used to, nor did she hold any animosity for him. Lars probed her emotions through his touch, looking into the girl's honey-brown eyes and feeling in her soul no amount of the tiny knot of hatred she had initially guarded and nursed for him.

Lars Balfoest smiled. He could not find any trace of disdain within the Delathrane girl now. She had been tamed.

"You are a beauty," he said in his voice of *Empathy*, gently scratching her scalp and caressing her behind the ear with his skeletal hand. The girl whined, but not with fear or disgust. Instead, he felt a wave of appreciation wash over her at the compliment.

Lars looped the leash over his hand two times to draw Iskabel closer.

"You may speak," he whispered into her ear.

"Thank you, Lord Balfoest," she said, keeping her gaze downcast.

"Would you like to eat?"

"Yes, Lord Balfoest," she replied. Her voice was so soft, so faint, so childish.

Lars picked up a bit of the breakfast he had been eating and lifted it to her lips. The girl opened her mouth and Lars put the food in. She chewed and swallowed, but Lars kept his hand next to her mouth. Some of the red sauce had run onto his fingers.

"Get it all," he commanded.

Iskabel licked the red sauce from his fingers as he smoothed her hair with his other hand.

"Good girl," he said, reveling in the contact that allowed him to feel her emotions so completely.

He released the clip that held the leash to her collar. The girl crawled over to the mat and curled up on the floor like one of his Horming Mastiffs. The time she had spent in his kennels had done her some good, he thought, watching her with satisfaction. She was as obedient as any of his dogs.

"That's it. Get your rest, child. I have a lot of Growing for you to do tomorrow," he ordered. "We have to build up our stores of *Kabris*. Once we have enough, we will be able to buy the alliance of Addisfall."

The girl nodded with sleepy contentment, her honey eyes staring up at him through her long dark lashes. She lay her head on the small pillow and closed her eyes.

Lars watched Iskabel until her breathing became regular and deep. Then a twisted smile grew on his gaunt, narrow lips.

"What a pleasure to have someone so completely my own," he said to himself.

Her eyes fluttered open a bit, but Lars placed a thin finger to his lips.

"Shhhh," he said, gently, "You have a big day tomorrow."

Iskabel smiled, and then snuggled deeper into her pillow.

3

TWO MEN, ONE VESSEL

Down in the cabin of the *Marine Escape*, Princess Kathleen winced again as Larissa roughly pulled the strands of her red hair into a tight braid.

"Sorry about that," Larissa said, not seeming sorry at all. "The wind is so strong out there that I want your hair to stay tight."

Melva, the ancient Healer, lay on the small bed across the tight narrow cabin, half watching the girls and half napping. The old woman had earned whatever rest she could find.

"I wish my hair was this thick," Larissa said, using her fingers to tease out and comb a few stray stands and bring them into the next pass. She brought the braids together, where they met at the back of her head.

"I have always admired your golden curls," Kathleen replied.

Larissa smiled and tugged the braids even tighter as she finished.

"Ow!"

"Sorry. But that should help keep from getting your hair so tangled in the wind," she said.

Kathleen looked at herself in the small mirror mounted on the wall of the cabin. She saw faint lines in her skin, crinkling at the corners of her eyes which were now glistening from the tears that Larissa's rough hands had drawn. She wiped them and squinted at herself, which only deepened the lines.

"I think I've gained some wrinkles since I left home," she observed.

"I think we both have," Larissa agreed, leaning close to look at her own face beside Kathleen's. "And are you surprised, considering what we've been through? I'll be shocked if I make it to thirty with a single golden hair left." She gestured over at Melva. "It will be as white as hers!"

Melva made an involuntary grumble of annoyance, but didn't stir.

"I wonder what my father will say when he sees us," Kathleen went on.

"He will be so happy to see you, I'm sure," Larissa replied, only half-listening, her mind still on the fate of her hair which she teased in her hand now and studied with an expression of sadness.

"He'll be disappointed that I have not married Heathron."

Larissa let go of her curls and looked at Kathleen, her hands propped determinedly on her hips.

"Your father will be thankful to have you safe at home—married or not. Queen Renata on the other hand..." Larissa craned her head to one side and arched her eyebrows.

"I can't please everyone," Kathleen replied with an air of defeat.

"Can't you and Heathron be married in Candoreth?" Larissa asked.

Kathleen shook her head. "We must hold the wedding ceremony in Tyath."

Larissa shrugged and sighed, spreading her palms. "Well, no matter what you do, someone will find fault with your decisions. I've learned that about life. Best to just not care what anyone thinks, because you'll never please them."

Kathleen thought about this. "Some choices are better than

others, though," she countered after a few moments. "If we are married anywhere except the Grand Cathedral in Tyath, Heathron could be charged with illegitimacy. It could hurt him."

"I say if it hurts, it's a poor choice. If it feels good, it's a good choice. That is the rule I live by," Larissa said, smiling before the mirror now with her arms up above her head and her hands buried in her heaps of golden curls. She seemed satisfied with herself once more.

Kathleen shook her head.

"I don't know if I can fully trust *pleasure* to be my guide. If a choice causes you pain, is it wrong? I'm not so sure. Some decisions that are right can still hurt."

Larissa cocked her head and looked at Kathleen.

Kathleen blushed.

"Why do I get the feeling you are no longer talking about pleasing your father?"

Kathleen ran her hands over her face. "Well, we have many days of sailing ahead of us and that prospect holds little pleasure for me, with those two men aboard the same boat..."

"Yes, how terrible," Larissa said sarcastically, rolling her eyes. "Two men who are deeply in love with you. I'd say there might be opportunities for pleasure in that. I can count two off the top of my head..." She arched her eyebrows suggestively and then threw back her head and let out a high giggle.

Kathleen couldn't restrain her lips curving up at the corners, and felt herself blush even more.

"There certainly will be opportunities for pain, too. How do I help Jared understand why I have to choose Heathron? Whenever I consider what to say to him, I just seize up. It's as if ... Oh, I don't know— nothing conveys the depth of how I feel."

"Or, you're in denial—and the reason you seize up is precisely *because* you don't know how you feel." She was beaming in that self-satisfied way again, pleasured by her own mischief and pleased too by the obvious ripple this had caused within Kathleen, who stared back silently. "You haven't had a moment to speak with him alone, have you?" she added returning to the conversation.

Kathleen shook her head. "And it is driving me mad. I want him to know that it was not for some trivial reason, that I chose Prince Heathron."

"Jared was only your Sīhalt Guardian during the Wedding Procession. He has no claim on your heart," Larissa said, trying to help.

"He still is my Guardian though—until I'm married," Kathleen replied, a little too quickly.

Larissa put her hands up, "Fine. My mistake. You seem kind of defensive about that."

Kathleen relaxed. "Is it that obvious?"

Larissa nodded, Kathleen looked toward the small door, then back at Larissa.

Suddenly, Melva's old, cracked voice spoke. "The claim the Guardian has on your heart is one of flesh and emotion–not a contract of parchment and ink," she said, still not opening her eyes.

"An emotional claim is the best kind," Larissa said coyly.

"You are not helping," Kathleen complained, but she flashed a smile too.

Larissa went on, "I mean, how do *I* get a handsome, mysterious warrior—who would readily give his life for mine—to stop being interested in me?" She queried in an exaggerated feminine tone, tapping her chin theatrically.

"Stop it!" Kathleen protested.

"I *dream* of that!" Larissa added, turning her hand up and resting it on her forehead like a damsel in distress.

Kathleen looked to the old woman for help. "Melva? What do you think?" she asked.

"Don't wake me up with your silly questions," the ancient Healer said, relaxing peacefully on the mattress with her eyes closed. "I'm dreaming of a handsome warrior, who can't resist me." She grinned as she lay there, and a shot of celebratory laughter came from Larissa. Kathleen grabbed a small pillow nearby and threw it at the old woman who chuckled softly.

Kathleen sought to escape these two's teasing and walked toward the door of the small cabin. She stopped just as Lilly entered.

"Oh! Greetings, Kathleen." The Douser's eyes looked tired, but it was the only part of her that didn't seemed so intensely alive. Her skin glistened with salt, and her long black hair seemed to possess a soaked shimmer in every strand from her waterwork at the bow of the *Marine Escape*, just above the waves.

"Lilly, you look like a dish cloth that is worn too think?" Melva said from her place on the small bed, her old eyes taking in the water dripping from the Douser's grey uniform. The Healer immediately began to get up. "Are you okay?"

"I do feel tired," Lilly admitted.

Kathleen noticed the darkness beneath Lilly's eyes underscoring the fact that she had not slept in days.

"I just need a quick nap, then I can tie the rope on my waist and go over the side again. I have to. *We* have to. We don't want to see the Tyathian navy behind us."

"You don't need to do that. You've done enough," Melva said gently, placing a hand on Lilly's shoulder. Kathleen saw the tenderness in the gesture.

"Lilly, Melva's right—you need to rest," Kathleen added. "There is no immediate danger to us now, thanks to you. The wind can push us south. Save your strength. You have given us enough of a head start."

Lilly fell silent, thinking about this. "I hope so as I feel very tired."

"Good, then it's settled. You will rest. You can sleep here if you like," Kathleen offered, steering her to a little bed.

"It has just suddenly come upon me. At first it wasn't so bad, but all of this water work, perhaps it has left me feeling a little drained," she admitted.

"I could not have Grown plants for half so long as you have moved the water" Kathleen said.

"Yes," Melva agreed. "Each of us is different in how the Talents affect us. I fear we will have need of your abilities again, before this voyage is over, Lilly. So rebuild your strength. Rest and eat."

Lilly nodded. "I will rest."

"May I fetch you some food?" Kathleen offered.

"I ate some bread and salted meat before daybreak, but it did not satisfy me. What I really desire is fresh fruit," Lilly replied.

Kathleen looked out the small porthole toward the distant coastline. The trees colored the green slopes, where they spread up into the hills above the beaches. It was springtime, but she wondered what fruit trees she might find if she could just get to shore and search the forest.

"Rest now. We will see what we can do," Kathleen said.

Lilly nodded, her eyelids seeming to fall lower now that she had accepted she must rest.

"We may need to stop anyway," Lilly said. The larger water barrels in the hold were damaged in the collision. They have leaked and are mixed with salt water. Seth told me he could repair some of the barrels, and get fresh water too."

Kathleen drew closer to the porthole and craned her neck to look at the sky. It was darkening in the distance. A storm seemed as if it might break upon them soon.

"I will keep an eye out for a safe harbor," she said.

4

A FRAYED KNOT

Thomas Dagger adjusted the coarse fabric of his shirt as he walked across the deck of what used to be his ship. The Centian vessel had held up to the Sea of Storms and made the crossing to Desnia a way that made him proud. It had been a harrowing voyage, but now they were within the sight of the Emerald Coast of the western continent. They had been lingering among the outer islands of this new land for far too long. If he were still the captain of the ship they would have already landed and begun to gather what they might from the towns along the coast. This was not a densely populated land. Even if the people were poorer, they would make easy targets with the long stretches of isolation on the Emerald Coast. Thomas looked down at the rough clothes he was wearing. It was nothing like the crisp uniform that one in his position deserved—or had deserved. Long gone was his deep blue jacket, with large double-breasted brass buttons and the glinting medal given to him by the admiralty. He didn't have his high black boots anymore, either. Instead he stood barefoot on the deck, clothed only in a homespun shirt and worn trousers. He missed the tall boots and especially the captain's feather he had worked so hard to obtain. But fate had demanded that he now play the part of a simple sailor, and Thomas hated it—so much so that he resolved to fight back and convince fate that he deserved to play a better part.

He ran his hand through his brown hair, pushing it away from his eyes. It was getting longer, and in his frustration he grabbed the whole lot of it and tied it back behind his head with a piece of twine he carried at his belt. He needed his vision and his mind clear, especially now, as he looked out to sea.

At that moment, one of the Centian sailors he did not recognize brushed past him, throwing his shoulder into the former captain's back. The force knocked him with a jolt and he was sent skidding off balance along the deck. The man laughed and muttered something under his breath as he passed.

"This is not your ship anymore, Dagger."

Thomas leveled his eyes at the muscular man with the protrusive jaw. The sturdy sailor had a permanent crease in his brow, dug from endless days squinting into sunny ocean skies. He was deeply tanned from years at sea under the beating sun, his skin leathery and hard, and his calloused hands were powered by arms that had been sculpted by the hard labor aboard a sailing vessel. The man was clearly a leader among the men of his low station, and he was not about to have a young, demoted officer take away any of his authority. Thomas had also taken note of the concealed knife that was always tucked in the man's belt.

At least he isn't trying to gut me yet, he thought, then swallowed as the last word in that thought repeated itself like an omen.

Despite his demotion, Thomas had been allowed to keep his pistols. Unfortunately, he couldn't pull his guns out without drawing unwanted attention from their Sulian commanders. But all Centians would have caused a ruckus if any of their countrymen's firearms were to be taken away. To them, warfare at sea was their religion and weapons were their souls. The treaty they had struck to help the Sulians cross the Sea of Storms did not extend that far. The Sulians wanted the knowledge of cannons and powder—a knowledge that Centians had—but thus far, the men of Centia had guarded it fiercely.

Thomas Dagger may have been stripped of his rank, he might be poor and have barely escaped the hangman's noose, but he was technically still free. And a free man was an armed man in *Centia*. He leveled his eyes at the man who sought to intimidate him.

"You were never one of my men," he began in the most understanding tone he could muster. "I don't wish to offend, but what I do want is to—"

"None of us are *your* men now," came the derisive response, cutting Thomas off before he could finish. The sailor coiled a rope at his feet, winding it around a bucket. He twisted the rope as if his fingers were on someone's neck. Thomas tried to keep calm. "You're walkin' around like a peacock, treating us like we're all dirty chickens, but you ain't a captain any more boy, and this ship is no longer called *The Dagger*," the sailor said. Then he let out a grunt, searching for the approval of his peers.

Thomas wanted to lash out and put the brute in his place— maybe have him whipped! This insubordinate behavior was the kind that destroys the disciplined harmony aboard a ship, but Thomas had to remind himself that the man *was* right, at least on a couple of accounts.

It was true that the ship no longer carried his name, for instance, and that he no longer wore the uniform of an officer— let alone that of a captain. Still, he couldn't let the challenge stand. He would never retain any authority, never get back to his rightful place among the Azo Fleet if he couldn't hold his own with an old sea-dog like this one.

So, Thomas Dagger looked over his shoulder to make sure no officers were watching, then swiftly, with all his might, bent down for purchase and kicked the belligerent man square in the crotch.

The sailor crumpled immediately, furrowing his heavy brow in pain and surprise as he dropped to the deck, the rope falling from his hands. He let out a moan that drew the attention of the officers. But Thomas bent down, pretending to assist him.

"Easy there, mate. Careful on the deck! It's a bit slippery," he said, extending a hand to the man who snarled up at him through the pain of the assault.

"You there!" One of the officers said in a breathy *Sulian* accent. "Is that man alright ?"

Thomas didn't recognize the officer. He was rather tall for a *Sulian*, with straight black hair and narrow eyes. He wore the white uniform of the East, and carried two of the unmatched Sulian swords at his waist. Thomas quickly nodded.

"I believe so, Sir. He's just getting older and must have slipped. Struck himself on that bucket there as he went down."

The *Sulian* officer nodded, pausing slightly to take in the intonation and form of Thomas' words. They were not those of a common sailor.

"Very well. Carry on," the officer replied.

Once the officer was out of sight, Thomas leaned over the groaning man. "I'll pretend you didn't insult me, and you can pretend I didn't smash your nuts with my foot. Does that sound fair?"

"I can...crush the likes of you...throttle you in the night while...you are sleeping in your hammock," the man struggled to say. His teeth were locked together in pain.

"That's just it mate, I don't sleep," Thomas said.

"This isn't over. I'm not the only one who would like to feed you to the sharks."

"My own mother wanted to feed me to the deep," Thomas replied. "I'll regain my commission soon, one way or the other, and if you play nice I may not have you whipped when I do."

"I'll see you...at the bottom of the Nuvian Trench...before I salute the likes of you," the man sneered, struggling to get back on his feet. He half-righted himself, then fell back down under the weight of the pain.

Thomas watched him, smiling. And when the man eventually did get to his feet, Thomas was waiting. "Have it your way," he said, and picked up the free end of the rope with a large stopper knot. He flicked the heavy rope, snapping it back like a whip and smacked the angry sailor once more in his nether regions.

The man didn't fall again, but hunched down, enduring the recurrent pain with a shiver and a whimper.

"Is that man okay?" the Sulian officer on the foredeck demanded.

"Yes, sir. He said he had a bit too much grog after winning at cards last night. Not to worry, I'll help him do his duties. He'll be back to full strength in no time!"

The Sulian officer looked annoyed at the Centians and turned back to survey the horizon.

"Just because the ship is called *Enmity* now, doesn't mean we can't be friends," Thomas said in the man's ear.

"You will blow us all to the Hereafter, with fire and smoke! We don't trust you, Dagger. We've all heard the stories."

"I was doing a nice job of figuring out the guns before I was stripped of command."

"You killed how many men?" the man asked, distrust written on his face.

"That wasn't my fault," Thomas said. "I don't want to die anymore than the rest of them. However, if the Sulian Empire really does send their navy after our little fleet, we'll be glad we know how to use the cannons."

"They would never send their ships across the Sea of Storms. It's too dangerous. What could possibly make them take the risk? We will be safe in *Desnia*, and free of men like you," the sailor said.

"Don't bet on it," Thomas muttered, as he looked out toward the distant green coast, trimmed with white beaches. There was a beautiful harbor, a quaint castle, and a sturdy wall surrounding city. The town spread toward the water on the beautiful site.

"Candoreth and these other colonial towns might have enough

loot to keep us all fed for a little while, but we'll need to become legitimate in *Desnia* before too long. We'll never be allowed back to the Old Realm."

The older sailor spat and frowned, the thought of legitimate work on land was clearly distasteful to him.

"The world is getting too small," the man said sourly, "but we can plunder what is here—maybe find a city large enough for all of us."

"Will a man ever find peace, even if he sails the world over? Afraid not," Thomas said, holding up the rope, smiling at his own pun.

The sailor shot him a puzzled frown.

5

DANGEROUS QUESTIONS

Dallin Sarkkand carried a bucket of feed to the stall where Steed was held. The great black horse seemed impatient, ready to run.

"Easy there," Dallin said to the horse ,and the noble beast tossed his head.

Holding out the feed in his palm, Dallin wondered how he had ever felt pleasure at riding any other kind of horse. The Sīhalt Guardian had asked him to care for the stallion while he was away. But after days upon days of staring into his eyes each morning, Dallin had to admit, he did not look forward to being parted from this animal.

The horse whinnied in response to this thought, seeming to understand him.

It must be the Tamer bond he passed to me, Dallin thought.

Dallin looked around to make sure he was not being watched. He knew that Lord Balfoest was visiting the estate with a few of his supporters, so Dallin needed to be more careful this morning. He knew where his own loyalties lay, but he wasn't so sure of his father's heart. Political realities and alliances needed to be considered and recalculated now that Prince Heathron Dol Lassimer was far from Tyath—even if he was the rightful successor to the Imperial throne.

Dallin was just glad to be in the stables and among the horses, instead of scheming with Lars Balfoest.

Presently, he wiped his wet hand against his shirt and then poured the rest of the sweet feed into the bucket that hung on the wall. Then he watched the enormous black horse chewing the grain. Steed snorted with pleasure and Dallin smiled at the stallion from the other side of the wooden stall.

"Isn't that horse a Windstall stallion?"

Dallin jumped at the sound of that voice. It was the Steward.

"It…it is," Dallin said, hesitating.

Evidently Lord Balfoest wanted to see him after all. The man only ever engaged in small talk if he had a purpose.

"The Sīhalt Guardian named Jared DeTorre rode that beast, no?" Lars Balfoest asked as he walked up to Dallin, dragging his hand along the top rail of wood that ran along the stable door. The edge of the boards had a rough, rounded edge, because over the years horses had a habit of cribbing and gnawing the surface of the top board in a wave-like pattern. The boards would need to be replaced eventually.

"Yes, that is a fine animal," Dallin replied, restraining the edge of anxiety that now clung to his voice. Lord Balfoest was known to have a most uncanny way of seeing straight through to the heart of a man, and Dallin had no wish to reveal his heart.

"You have played this game since your childhood, young Lord Sarkkand," Lord Balfoest mused without turning to look at him. The black stallion had suddenly grown skittish in the Steward's presence. It was tossing its mane, flaring its nostrils. Its eyes were wide and threatening, and it cared no longer for the sweet feed in the bucket.

"I do have a love for fine horses," Dallin ventured cautiously.

"And a love for power? You are a capable leader," the Steward of Tyath opined. He cleared his throat and extended that pale, skeletal hand toward the Windstall stallion. The horse bared its teeth and lunged at Lord Balfoest's exposed wrist, but the old man pulled it back faster than the horse moved, and quickly stroked the forelock of the beast as it crashed into the front gate of the stall. The heavy wooden boards on the latch creaked under the loud impact.

"I wouldn't do that!" Dallin warned, as an image flashed in his mind: of the latch breaking open, and the horse pounding Lord Balfoest to death with fury. "That horse has a will all its own."

"So I see," Lord Balfoest mused, drawing his hand back and grinning at the stallion that whinnied angrily. The horse reared up and struck the front of the stall, crashing its flying hooves into the boards this time, and Dallin moved to place himself between Lord Balfoest and the enraged animal.

The Steward chuckled. "He would tear me limb from limb given the chance, wouldn't he? I've rarely felt such rage," Lars said with pleasure, still looking at his hand that had touched the horse.

"He's dangerous," Dallin agreed.

"Have *you* ever ridden that horse?" He asked the question so softly and delicately as if it held no weight in it at all. But when Lord Balfoest lifted his eyes and fixed Dallin with a piercing gaze, Dallin felt a chill run through him.

Why is he asking me that? Dallin thought frantically.

He needed to calm himself. He need to be nonchalant. He had nothing to hide.

The question hung in the air. A few flies buzzed in the horse barn. Dallin felt as if he could not maintain the shield of emotional distance much longer. Lord Balfoest seemed to pry into his mind, even as Dallin resisted.

"I don't ride that one," he answered eventually.

Lord Balfoest raised an eyebrow while lowering his chin to look at Dallin more intently, almost amused by the answer. Then he reached out and touched the hand that held the bucket.

Dallin pulled back at the gesture. It felt cold. Exposing. Violating.

"I wouldn't suggest it either," Lord Balfoest said, "The Windstall horses are Tamed by Cursed Ones who have a Talent for that kind of thing. Without having the unholy bond passed from its Master to you, the beast would surely seek to kill you, rather than serve you. But..." he paused and chuckled again, "I'm sure you already knew that."

Dallin nodded, not able to tease any words from his mouth. It was dry and barren and he knew that if he were to swallow at this moment it would reveal his guilt. The feeling was unbearable.

How is Lord Balfoest so familiar with the workings of a Tamer's bond? Dallin had only learned of it when the Sīhalt, Jared De Torre, insisted he take the horse and keep it for him. He had passed the link to him before he fled the city. And well he did, for it had been the only way Dallin had been able to handle the great black stallion. The horse would tolerate no one else, and Dallin had thrilled at the experience of riding the powerful Windstall stallion every day since. Few things in life made him as happy as being in the saddle of such a magnificent mount, with the clear air of morning rushing past his cheeks as he rode over the verdant fields of the estate.

"Honestly, I don't know how you managed to get the thing in the stall," Lord Balfoest observed.

"It wasn't easy," Dallin stammered, scrambling in his mind to regain his composure.

Lord Balfoest adjusted the sleeves of his rich robe then clasped his long narrow fingers together. "Every creature must recognize the hand of its new Master. Otherwise, what good is it?" he said.

He knows! Dallin thought, and almost grabbed the hilt of the sword at his hip. He stopped the urge; Balfoest's guards would made quick work of him if he drew it. He pushed the thought down and swallowed.

I am not in danger, he told himself, *I just need to remain calm, and think.*

He knew the point Lord Balfoest was making. The Steward wanted Dallin to show proper obeisance to him—the new Master of the Golden City. It was a bitter thought, but Dallin could not let it show in his face. So he schooled his expression and nodded intently. And when he looked back up into Lord Balfoest's eyes, Dallin had regained the tranquility that had kept him safe for so long.

"You can count on me," he said.

"Count on you to do what?" Lord Balfoest asked, not blinking.

There was powerful tension in the air.

"You may rely on me to be your loyal supporter."

"Will you make that statement publicly? I believe your father is willing," Lord Balfoest said. He raised a hand suddenly. "Actually, don't answer that yet. I must leave soon and make for my carriage. Come, escort me and let's walk and talk—stretch our legs, hmm?"

They were soon walking down the central corridor of the barn. Servants in House Sarkkand continued to go about their labors as the men walked toward the pool of sunlight shining at the eastern end of the barn. The large double doors were thrown open as stable boys with wheelbarrows hauled loads to the manure pile beyond the fence. Motes of dust danced and floated on the currents of air, and were visible in the slash of light slanting into the barn. Next to it, parked just outside, was Lord Balfoest's carriage.

"When do you wish for me to make my Affirmation before the Imperial Court?" Dallin asked.

Lord Balfoest turned to him and smiled. It was like seeing a skull come to life.

"I have a few more Houses to visit. I'll expect your Affirmation of support by the end of the week."

Dallin nodded. "I can manage that," he replied.

"Lord Sarkkand?" came the voice of one of the stable boys that passed, knuckling his forehead. "Shall I help you to saddle the great black horse again this morning? It is a fine sight to see you riding him each day."

It was a simple offer to serve, and yet the importance of that piece of information spelled doom for Dallin.

"So, you *do* ride the Sīhalt Guardian's horse."

It was not a question. It was an observation. Lord Balfoest smiled again, a ghoulish expression of grim satisfaction arranging itself in his features. And then he climbed into his carriage. He inclined his head to Dallin who stood transfixed by his naked lie, laid bare before him.

"Drive on," Lord Balfoest said, and the carriage rolled away.

Dallin turned to the stable boy and tightened his lips in concern.

"I would like your help saddling the Windstall stallion," Dallin said, "I believe I will be enjoying an especially long ride this morning."

6

SECRETS OF THUNDER

"Who is that man?" Admiral Yamatsu said, leaning close to his nearest officer. Captain Murikama was a lean man with straight black hair that wanted to stand up.

"He is Thomas Dagger. The man who used the guns at the battle of Avron."

"Hmmm," the admiral responded. Cyril Yamatsu did not like *Centians* but he found himself admiring this one. The man had shown courage, was willing to face enormous risks, and still he kept his sense of humor.

"He knows how to use the guns?"

"Yes, Admiral."

Admiral Yamatsu smiled inwardly. It wouldn't do to have his men see it, but he watched the *Centian* closely. He saw the man offer his hand to help the other sailor, his enemy, to his feet.

He is honorable, even as he is strategic, he thought.

The admiral removed the white cap from his head and wiped the sweat from his brow. Yamatsu's hair, once black as night, was now graying at the temples. He thought of his family briefly, whom he had brought with him to the continent of *Desnia*. What else could he do? His entire bloodline was in danger.

They had waited at the Islands for as long as they had dared, before sailing further westward. Beyond luck, much of the Azo fleet had made it—even the transports. Now that his eyes rested on the fabled Emerald Coast of *Desnia*, Admiral Yamatsu finally had hope that he would live out the remainder of his life in tranquility. Just one more war, to make space for his people among the forgotten colonies of Desnia, and he would lay down his swords forever.

"Admiral Yamatsu, the people of Marth Island have been subdued. We are allowing the weakest to disembark and set up a settlement on the northern end," Murikama said.

Admiral Yamatsu nodded understanding.

Are the people here so used to peace that they will not fight to protect their lands and home? He considered this.

"Very well, but let us approach the city with discretion. The defensive walls and catapults were not placed there for show. I do not believe these *Desnians* will all be so welcoming of our arrival in their capital."

"No, sir. We have already had some skirmishes with them in the months leading up to your arrival. They do have a fighting spirit."

Yamatsu grunted. "We will make our permanent home here in *Desnia*, no matter the cost." He displayed no other emotion to the man except determination and strength.

"We have no way to return to the Old Realm?"

The admiral shook his head. "We knew this when we set our course westward. Now we know for ourselves the ancients did not embellish their accounts of the Sea of Storms. It was every bit as bad as they described. The maps were true. Now we are here."

The admiral looked at the lush coast and allowed his slanted eyes of deep brown to take in the beautiful scene. He saw some trees he recognized from home, but much of *Desnia* was new to him.

"I pray to the Ancestors that we will not be followed by the ships of the Crystal Throne, " Captain Murikama added, looking in the opposite direction of the sea.

"They have no need to follow us here. We allowed the Dorgund to save face. We kept his honor intact—for the most part—when we silently slipped from his noose. I like to believe he *allowed* us to escape. He gave us the Coup of Flight. Now if we can hold together the rabble of *Centians*, and maintain order among our own people, well, then we will form a new nation in Desnia," Admiral Yamtsu said, smiling now.

"If we did not need the Centians and their cursed guns, I would have thrown them into the sea before we reached the Islands," said the captain bitterly.

Admiral Yamatsu laughed. "The wide-eyed devils are hard to control, I admit, and they could all use a bath."

"Why *do* they refuse to bathe?"

"I am trying to understand the Centians. They have many secrets, but I have learned that the powder they use in their guns can be made useless by water," he said in a lower tone.

The admiral surveyed the few *Centians* working on the deck. They stood taller than his own people, and their faces were heavy with thick beards which they did not shave. Many of them bore ink writing under the skin of their hands, arms and necks. Admiral Yamatsu did not understand this.

How could a man get a sacred tattoo and make it a written message? Words do not capture the beauty of the body, he thought, again shaking his head.

A few Centians had personal guns tucked into their belts, smaller versions of the larger cannons.

"They are a dangerous lot," Yamatsu said, to the officer, "but good to have as our allies. We would not have made it this far without their guidance. And we have at least one more fight."

"But once we *learn* the secret of their guns, we will no longer need them," the officer replied.

"Maybe not. But before that, with the guns, we will subdue the *Desnians*. We will take what we need. We are stronger. That is the natural order of things. It has ever been thus."

The captain nodded. There was a glint of anticipation in his eyes. The desire for conflict had not abated in him. "We are stronger," he said hungrily.

Yamatsu went on, "We must find our place among the people of *Desnia*. I do not expect that we will be welcomed, but eventually I hope to gain legitimacy among them. We are just as legitimate as any of the other nations or cities here. The centuries old manifest to settle *Desnia* was never rescinded by the Crystal Throne, so they will need to accept that we are staying."

Admiral Yamatsu stopped then and sighed. He was tired. Tired of the sea, of the storms, of the watch they had to hold over the Centians... And tired of speaking with this man. He wanted be with his family, to see his wife and their grandsons. But of course, women and children were not allowed on a military vessel. He smiled inwardly at the thought of seeing them again, too. Their ship was further back among the fleet. They were some of the lucky ones to make it through the storms. And he would be able to see their smiling faces once they secured a beachhead and took the city. Then he would cease to be the warrior and instead plant a garden around the simple house he would build on a hill in this green land that reminded him of his childhood home.

"Admiral Yamatsu, there is a colonial ship hailing us on the starboard side. Shall we allow them to approach?"

"No, keep them at bay. If they persist, blow them from the water. We will not take the risk of bringing any enemies aboard the *Enmity*."

"Yes, sir." The man saluted sharply, and turned to pass along the command.

"Ready the guns!" he heard the men say.

The ship from the Desnian city called Candoreth, did not carry guns. It was well-built, Yamatsu could see that, the ships were made for landing men aboard the enemy vessels. The heavy spar on the front was made to punch holes in enemy vessels, while instead of holes for guns this ship had oars that could be used to propel or help navigate the ship. It was an older design, too, he mused; it looked clumsy compared to the *Centian* ship he now commanded. The shipwrights of the Centian Isles knew how to build boats better than anywhere else! This one carried over forty large guns, not including the smaller swivel guns mounted in defensive positions.

The Desnians are in for a surprise, Yamatsu thought as he watched the ship slowly slide into range.

7

STORM TOSSED SEAS

Wind lashed the deck of the *Marine Escape*. They had not made the best progress when Lilly rested. And during this time the winds had grown weak for hours. Now, however, torrents of rain swept over the vessel as another storm approached. Although it was made for pleasure the yacht endured the lashing easily, righting itself when the storm broke across her bow.

"Get below!" Channing Dur Ruston said, waving his arm to push the others toward the safety of the shelter below deck.

"You've been out here long enough," Heathron said. "Let me take the wheel for a while."

Channing set his jaw against the storm and held on, fighting the force of the wind and the spray of the waves.

"I wish we had more distance between us and the shore. I don't like being this close without any lights to guide us," he shouted over the gale.

"Even Lilly would struggle in this weather. She can't calm the seas in every direction—not when it's this angry. She needs more rest, and so do you!" Heathron ordered.

Channing finally relinquished the helm. "Fine. Keep her that way," he said at the top of his voice, stretching an arm into the blackness.

Heathron looked in the direction Channing pointed. There was little to distinguish it from any other: dark and grey and stormy.

"Is the land on our righthand side?" he asked, in a shout.

Captain Channing reached for the wheel again, his eyes widening as he realized the import of Heathron's question. " I won't leave all their lives in your hands if you're that clueless!"

"I'm joking!" the prince said, pushing him away. "Now get below so you can rest. I will keep us away from the shore."

Channing grumbled, then relented and staggered on the swaying deck toward the ladder that offered shelter below.

Channing slammed the hatch shut and took off his slick outer layer in the warmth of the cabin. Water poured from his clothing and onto the floor, and he looked up to see Larissa gliding over to take the soaked overcoat.

"It's wet out there," Channing observed with an understatement to his group of friends.

"This spring storm certainly is fierce," Lilly agreed.

"How is Heathron?" Kathleen asked.

Channing began peeling off the sticky-wet undershirt as he answered. "He promised to keep us off of the rocks. If he doesn't, we will know about it."

Lilly and Kathleen gave a little laugh as Larissa clung to his side, ready to help him with the rest of his clothes.

"I can take that for you," she said.

Channing thought he detected a hint of admiration in her voice. He made sure that when he stood upright, his chest was full and his shoulders were back.

"Does Lord Turlin have something that will fit me?" he asked, using the edge of his hand to sweep the water from his skin.

Channing liked the way Larissa appraised him, looking over his torso, judging his size.

"He may have a jacket that would just about fit you. The shirts might be too tight, however," she said, chewing on her fingernail.

"Hand them over and I'll have a go. I'm soaked to the bones right now and anything dry would feel wonderful."

Maxwell tossed a bundle of cloth in his direction. Channing caught it and unfurled the cloth to reveal a luxurious robe that opened along the front and could be tied with a thick belt of cloth at the waist.

"Try that on, captain; it will keep you warm if you tie it up right. If you don't, I'm sure it will keep Larissa warm…" he said.

Larissa shot Maxwell a look of scorn, but the Shifter just threw his head back and laughed.

Captain Dur Ruston struggled to get his powerful arms into it so Larissa helped, pulling the robe up to his neck and shoulders, squeezing his muscles as she did so. She adjusted the collar, too.

"There you go, captain," she said, in a voice that confirmed Channing's suspicions. "Now you can warm up like the rest of us. Thank you for steering the boat in such foul weather," she added breathlessly.

Channing turned toward her as he tied the belt around his waist, folding one half of the robe across the other. Lord Turlin's robe certainly was a snug fit for him, so the robe lay open, fairly wide across his chest and revealing his bronzed complexion and two strange markings.

"What happened to you there?" Larissa asked, almost reaching out to touch one of the marks when she noticed. Channing saw Lilly roll her eyes and look at Kathleen, but Channing said nothing. Evidently he was not the only one to have noticed Larissa's admiration. He could understand though—why a girl might be impressed with his physique. Larissa wasn't the first, not by a long shot.

"Ask the Sīhalt if you want to hear that story," Channing said. Then he opened the robe a little more to revealed two U shaped markings on his chest. "These are my lucky charms," he said proudly.

Larissa's eyes never left his display of muscled strength, until Channing pulled the robe shut again.

"You don't want me to tell that story, do you?" Jared asked from his place in the corner. He sat with his legs crossed and his fingers laced behind his head, resting against the wall.

"Oh, come on, there is no modesty among friends!" Maxwell exclaimed.

"I doubt you keep modest amongst anyone, Maxwell," Kathleen chortled.

"I'm a Shifter. I lose my clothes from time to time. I can't afford to be modest!" he replied, changing himself back into the form of an old man, and then, just as quickly, to his younger, natural-looking self once more.

"It would be nicer if you looked more like the captain," Larissa noted.

Maxwell placed a hand on his chin, "Let me see what I can do."

In the flicker of the candle lights, Maxwell changed his form once more. He stayed in his natural identity, but had made his arms much more muscled. His jawline was also sharper, and his hair thick and swept back from his forehead like that of the captain.

"Just one more thing," he said, tapping his chin, and bronzed his skin to match.

"There! How's this?" he said.

"Not bad," Lilly remarked.

"You should go around like that more often," Melva offered.

"Even the old woman is impressed," came Seth's hooting voice.

Among all this, Maxwell was clearly enjoying the attention.

"I can even do this," he said and suddenly two U-shaped scars, mimicking those of Channing's, appeared on his chest.

"Now just a minute… I earned mine!"

"Tell the story," Seth said with a grin. "I recognize the outline of those as horse shoes."

"I was there that day, along with Larissa," Kathleen said.

Channing stretched an arm toward Kathleen. "Allow the princess to tell the tale and perhaps we will be further through the gale," he said, as if he were a bard in a popular tavern.

"Must I say it in rhyme?" she asked.

"It makes it more fun to pass the time," Jared added, "Are you up for the challenge of a story-teller's trade?"

Kathleen paused and looked around at the group of friends, swaying and sheltering in the warmth of the cabin, their faces bathed in swinging gloom and lamplight.

Channing felt love and a deep sense of belonging with the people with whom he had endured so much. The boat still tossed and the candles flickered, but Channing saw Kathleen smile and say, "This is the way that legends are made."

The friends smiled at her rhyme and leaned closer to hear Kathleen tell of Channing's lucky charms.

8

LUCKY CHARMS

Kathleen took a moment to compose her thoughts. Her small audience gathered closer around the flickering flames of the candles. Melva handed Channing a steaming mug, then sat with a satisfied smile, her eyes almost closed as she propped her head against a small pillow. The old woman looked content. Larissa found a seat next to Captain Channing who had braced himself, his right arm across her back as he leaned forward, eager to hear the story.

Maxwell lounged across a bench, uncaring when the movement of the boat sent a shiver through the room. The *Marine Escape* swayed with the wind and waves, but the Shifter rode the movements of the yacht as comfortably as a cat resting on a window sill. His deep brown eyes brimmed with merriment.

Jared and Seth sat upright, the flickering shadows outlining their chiseled features and the need for a shave. Except their eyes, they looked like a reflection of each other bent through time and suffering. Jared had almost died before the Healing. He was the older version of the twins, with faint gray in his hair and skin that was beginning to crease at the corners of the eyes. Seth presented the younger image, with features reminiscent of the boyhood they had recently left behind. Kathleen could see plainly that there was love between the brothers.

Lilly sat next to Kathleen, protective as always. However her eyes often lingered on the younger Sīhalt Guardian, while Kathleen's glances danced across Jared's face.

"I'll tell the story best I can," Kathleen said, and wet her lips with her tongue. She smiled, swallowed, and began.

The way I remember that day in my life
Was with banners flying, sunshine and strife.
My father had arranged all the fighting before
the Sīhalt named Jared brought the prospect of gore.

"I was gentle with those soldiers the day before," Jared said with a smile.

"Don't interrupt!" Maxwell said, "We all know you believe in 'fair play.'"

"I'll not have my daughter travel with him,
Unless he is worthy and proves he can win!"
King Lukald said with a grand sweep of his hand,
Inviting the people from across our land,
To watch the duel between Candoreth's best
And the curious stranger who stepped up to the quest
Of escorting a princess and new bride-to-be,
To the high looming walls of the Golden City.

Captain Channing raised his eyebrows and inclined his head at this point. Kathleen could imagine the plume of his audacious hat waving in the candlelight. Larissa seemed to shake her head at the idea of safety being found in Tyath. Kathleen nodded slightly in recognition and continued,

But here was the captain, willing to fight,
For honor and glory and red-blooded might.
The Guardian, for his part, seemed wont to engage,
He dallied when handing his clothes to his Page.
He seemed not to want to enter the fray
Although he did his duty that day.

"That about sums it up," Jared admitted. "You had to choose the Marth style didn't you, Channing."

The captain spread his hands out in a show of innocence. "That is my strongest style," he replied.

Jared shook his head and smiled knowingly.

"You certainly seemed like you were ready to take your shirt off."

"It is the traditional way of fighting in my homeland," Channing replied.

"I was glad you fought on horseback. It made it more interesting," Larissa observed.

"I'm sure it was the horses that held your interest," Melva intoned without opening her eyes.

Lilly laughed and Kathleen continued her story.

At his opponent's behest, the Sīhalt stripped to the waist
Although he was pale, he would not be debased.
So he mounted his Steed and rode 'round the arena,
With sand flying up from the hooves, between a
Couple of horses—

"Nice, I like how you did that," Jared said.

"You like my storytelling technique?" she replied.

"Would you be quiet, Jared. I'm trying to enjoy the story," Maxwell insisted. Jared held up his hands in a show of defeat, and gestured to Kathleen.

She continued.

That Man of Marth,
Twirling his sword, with the skill of a god,
Would take every advantage to see the Sīhalt on the sod.
He spanked the flanks of the stallion black,
Making the beast flinch when the reins were slack.

"You struck Steed with your sword?" Seth asked Channing incredulously. Channing took a sip of the hot drink he was holding and grinned over the rim of the mug.

"I can't believe you survived that!" Seth added.

"Oh, for the love!" Maxwell exclaimed, "Would you let the lady finish the story?"

Round and round the men galloped their steeds,
While the crowd grew more raucous with their glorious deeds,
Every man woman and child had placed their bets,
Knowing that this was as good, as good fighting gets.
They hung on every movement of their champion fair,
And at each encounter would offer a prayer.

"Amen," Channing said softly, following her words as if he had not lived through the contest himself.

The king and the queen thought the Sīhalt undone,
When he almost toppled from his horse, on the run.
But regaining his balance the warrior arose,
Despite all the grime on his neck, hands, and nose.
"Don't touch my horse!" the Guardian shouted,
but the captain believed he had him routed,
So he raised his sword and let it fall with a smack
That could be heard in the arena from front to back.
The people in the place thought their man had won,
On that blissful day in the southern sun.
Candoreth's own Captain Channing Dur Ruston
Was certain to see his own bust on
—the entrance.
To commemorate the skills of that glorious fight
And establish anew all of Sundiland's might.
The captain whirled his shining blade,
Certain he'd gain the victor's stage.
But Channing did not see the look in the eye
Of the Windstall stallion standing close by.
What he thought was a victory became sudden defeat
When the horse gathered himself with no place for retreat.
Each hoof was the size of a large dinner plate.
The captain of Marth was raised from his saddle,
When the giant hooves connected with him, in the battle.

He flew like an arrow shot from a bow,
Then came back to earth, as all arrows go.
The Sīhalt Guardian flew to his side
And made sure the captain was yet alive.
Channing finally rose from the dust, despite the harms,
left with not one but two lucky charms!

Kathleen gestured grandly with a sweep of her hand toward Caption Dur Ruston standing proudly in the small quarters of the yacht.

"Bravo, Princess!" Channing said, standing and showing off the actual marks where the hooves had stamped his chest. He held his mug high and smiled, enjoying the attention.

"That was fantastic," Jared said, and gave a nod and admiring glance at her.

Seth shook his head. "I trained and Tamed that stallion, and I know of his spirit," he said. "He is Tamed, for Jared, but not nearly docile enough go smacking him with the broadside of your blade!"

"I know that now!" Channing said with a grin.

"That was very entertaining," Larissa said, leaning closer to Channing. It was just the way I remember it too."

"You were there?" Channing asked.

"You don't remember?" Larissa replied in surprise.

Channing winked at her. "Of course I do, my lady. Even as I fought for consciousness, I still couldn't forget your face in the crowd. You were wearing a purple dress, were you not?"

"She was!" Kathleen confirmed as Larissa sighed. "Very good, captain. I'm surprised you can remember such a small detail from that day." She thought it was sweet that Channing had remembered a detail like that.

Jared leaned forward, catching Kathleen's eye.

"And your dress was blue, made of the softest silk. You wore earrings of pearl and a necklace to match. Your hair was pulled back to reveal your neck, and the cream-colored, broad-brimmed hat you wore that day shaded your face in the summer sun. I thought you looked amazing," Jared said from the corner where he lounged.

His comment was followed by a few heartbeats of silence as everyone took in the Sīhalt Guardian's words.

Maxwell and Melva looked at each other, as did Seth and Lilly. Jared's eye remains fixed on hers. Kathleen felt herself blush. She felt a tingle run up her spine and suddenly wanted to leave the situation.

"I do believe you are right, Lord Sīhalt" she said softly, as redness rose to her cheeks. "And now that the sea has calmed a bit, I will go check on Heathron."

Kathleen got up to make her way up the stairs. The group of friends exchanged several awkward looks, then resumed talking about how impressed they were at her storytelling abilities. Yet for her part, Kathleen remained shaken by the suddenly fierce and piercing gaze of the Sīhalt Guardian.

9

LADY SILVERBOW

Kathleen climbed the stairs, glad to be out of the uncomfortable setting. She walked carefully on the deck, careful not to slip on the wet wood. The salty air smelled clean in the wake of the passing storm.

"How is it going?" Kathleen asked as she approached Heathron. Though the storm had eased, rivulets of water still rushed and ran and dripped from the mast.

"I can see a few stars have come out. I recognize that one," Heathron said, pointing to the sky.

A few pinpricks of light managed to filter through the breaking wisps of the scudding grey cloud. "At least now I don't have to worry about sailing in the wrong direction." He smiled.

Kathleen came to a stop across the deck, leaning back against the handrail as Heathron stood stiffly at the wheel. She steadied herself by hanging on to a rope that tumbled down from the rigging overhead, her bare arms lambent under the sheets of moonlight that broke through the cloud, then vanished behind it once more.

Meanwhile, Heathron, wreathed in shadows once more, reached up and pulled on a rope to hoist more sail, now that the winds were fair and the danger of the storm had passed. From across the deck, Kathleen watched his every move: how his strong arms tensed as the rope ran through a pulley; how he delicately brushed away the hair that dropped over his eyes.

"We had fun below. I told a story about Channing getting kicked by a horse," she said.

"I bet that was fun. Is everyone still awake?"

"Yes, everyone was enjoying the humor of Channing's bravado, but Lilly seems exhausted."

"She did look tired. I'm thankful that she was able to help us escape."

Kathleen shivered, as if reading his thoughts. "I don't even like to say or hear his name," she said. "If the Navy had stopped our escape...I hate to think of what *he* would have done with us."

By *he*, she meant Lord Balfoest, and even the thought of that name brought back memories of what he had done to her before the escape.

"Yes," said Heathron awkwardly, bowing his head a little, and a second or two of silence ensued before he puffed out his chest and added, "but who would have guessed that we would find ourselves here, at this time, in these circumstances!" Heathron spread out his powerful arms, gesturing to the dark, wide sea now tranquil around them. He wheeled round to her, trying to brighten her mood now, for he saw how ill at ease she was at anchor in her memories.

"You're right. I wouldn't have imagined it, either," she said, her haunted features rearranging themselves softly until she was smiling again.

Heathron gazed out over the sea.

"Do you know, I pictured us sailing south like this, after we were married. We would have taken the *Passion Flower*, and left at this time of year, I think. I dreamed of sailing into the harbor at Candoreth and parading my wonderful new bride to the people."

"That would have been nice," Kathleen said, "I am sorry to

have rammed that beautiful yacht you made for me onto those rocks."

Heathron waved a dismissive hand through the salty air. "It wasn't your fault. Anyway, I'm glad you saved Eldin. I'd give a hundred ships for any of my friends...and a thousand for you."

"I know you would, Heathron," Kathleen replied softly, gazing up through her lashes.

She watched his hands, steadying the wheel now, and could see the power in them. It was a comfort to her to know he had regained much of his strength.

"If you want me to take the wheel, I'd be happy to do it," she offered.

"That's okay. I like having the helm, especially with you, here by my side," he said and flashed her one of his brilliant smiles. Even in the low light of a starry night it seemed to blaze.

Kathleen smiled in return and looked out at the endless waves.

"Can you imagine sailing all the way across the Eastern Sea?" she said.

Heathron followed her gaze and then pointed to the moon that peeked out behind the breaks in the clouds along the horizon.

"Looks like Lady Silverbow will be joining us as well," he said.

"Silver Bow?"

"It's one of my favorite poems by Za'han," Heathron explained.

"Tell it to me," Kathleen said.

Heathron extended his arm toward her. "Only if I can put my arm around you while I recite it," he said.

Kathleen, rising up against the handrail, seemed to consider the offer first, before allowing her head to fall into a series of coy nods, and then she melted across the deck toward him. She shivered as she did so, the cold air hitting her skin as she went. Heathron found an oil skin cloak and slung it around her shoulders. It was not at thick as she would have liked for the chill that still clung to the night air, but as she sidled up to him and sank into his embrace his body heat helped.

Heathron rested his chin on her shoulder, allowing himself to sway with her and the movement of the boat. "My mother used to tell me this one. It was only when I got older that I recognize how romantic it is."

"Oh?" Kathleen replied. "Now I really want to hear it."

Heathron adjusted the wheel of the yacht and pulled Kathleen to his front so that she too could reach the smooth wooden handles of the wheel.

"It is called, '*The Chase*,'" Heathron explained as he spoke close to her ear. Kathleen huddled nearer to him as he began to recite the poem.

I, the bolder sphere,
See her sheer and clear,
So dear, and never near enough.
Her bright light emboldens night.
Her silver bow I seek to know.
I arise and grow,
But I'm too slow,
As she slips to sleep again."

He said the last lines very slowly and deliberately.

"So Lady Silver bow is the moon?" Kathleen asked.

"That's right."

"It's kind of presumptuous of the Sun to say he is the 'bolder sphere' don't you think?"

"He is the bolder sphere," Heathron said.

"And how about you? Are you the bolder sphere between us?" she asked playfully.

"I don't know," Heathron said seriously. "I am rather bold."

"I'd rather be the moon anyway. It seems more feminine to me."

"Like her, you light up the darkness," Heathron said, "I've witnessed that many times, and I do feel that I am too slow, at times—unable to keep up with all that will be required of me to catch you. I guess that is what I love about the poem. It has a sense of longing, a metaphorical sweetness that makes me think of how we should always strive for what we want most, even if we never reach it."

"The sun does catch the moon, sometimes, doesn't it?" Kathleen asked.

Heathron nodded.

"It is called an eclipse. You're very lucky if you can see one in your lifetime."

"In Sundiland, we don't think of them as lucky. It's kind of a curse to be born near a sun-darkening or even to see one. As a child, my teacher told me there was a drought the last time we had an eclipse."

"Hmmm, maybe I should have chosen a different poem."

"Nonsense, I loved it."

"And I love you," he said.

Kathleen swallowed and kept looking out to sea.

"I know you do," she replied, allowing him to pull her even closer.

LOVE THE DESTROYER

L ater in the night, Jared came to Heathron. He heard Kathleen mention that the Prince sought a safe place to anchor the boat. Since Jared could see almost perfectly, even at night, he stayed on deck, leaning over the handrail and watching the shore.

"There is a cove where we can shelter over there," Jared said, pointing toward land.

"I can't see it. Are you sure?" Channing replied, having joined Jared on the deck.

The Sīhalt Guardian squinted, and saw again the subtle change in the surface of the water. It was deep here.

"I can see an opening in the breakers there, where the waves are calmed and they become more still."

Channing screwed up his face, first in concentration and then in confusion. "You can see that from here?" he said, shaking his head in disbelief.

Jared leveled his eyes at the captain.

"I'm a Sensor, remember?"

"Yes, but I can't see anything of what you are talking about," he replied, squinting into the distance where the land met the sea.

"Just trust me," Jared replied, and Channing shrugged.

"Fine. But this is on you." Then the captain steered the yacht toward the opening Jared indicated. The water did indeed deepen, calmed by the boulders that receded beneath the waves. Beyond the rocky barrier, the water swirled as it became even more still.

The natural harbor had a deep channel that ran diagonal from the trees. A small river swirled outward, the cool, fresh water from the highlands mixed with the saltwater of the sea. The surface of the natural harbor was as smooth as a frozen pool. The *Marine Escape* cut through the mirror-like surface, gliding gently to a stop on the furthest edge of the inlet.

"You were right again, Sīhalt. This will do nicely," Channing said, looking over the rail. He stretched his arms and yawned as the boat slowed its progress.

Now they were away from the open sea, a warmer breeze blew across the deck, and the sound of insects could be heard over the tree covered slopes.

"Set the anchor and I will take the rest of the first watch," Jared said. "Seth can take second, and Maxwell will cover the third watch of the night." The Shifter nodded and the other Sīhalt signed his agreement with a quick movement of his fingers.

"I'll take the fourth," Heathron offered, as he approached the two men.

"Keep your weapons at the ready," Jared reminded the group as he gauged the peaceful scene. "This area appears empty, but I wouldn't want to be surprised by anyone."

"We can gather water, and find food in the morning," Heathron said.

The company bid goodnight to one another. Jared walked around the edge of the yacht, considering the depth of the water on all sides, estimating their distance from the shore. He felt calm. The hidden cove seemed to be a safe place, and looking up at the green hills that surrounded them, Jared felt a contentment that he had longed for. The night promised to bring tranquility. He watched as Maxwell and Seth settled into each of their hammocks while the women disappeared behind the door that led to the cabins below deck.

It did not take long for the company to fall asleep. The night was peaceful and the *Marine Escape* rocked gently. The shrill cry of a bird hunting at night drifted across the water. Jared wrapped the thin black cloak around himself. The depth of night was not a hindrance to his eyesight. He could see quite clearly, even in the darkness. His ears, too, were keen as a fox's, and where others couldn't he could hear the smallest creak of the yacht, or the movements of his friends as they adjusted themselves in the hammocks. So there Jared remained, awake, enjoying the feeling of the wood pressing against his back where he sat that so reminded him of nights sleeping in the Windstall Hermitage, and keeping watch.

After some time, he heard a sound that was so quiet he almost did not notice it. In the stillness came the sound of slippered feet approaching. They did not have the rhythm of someone who intended to do him harm. Rather it was the quiet continuous sound of someone who simply wanted to move quietly. Jared's thoughts immediately turned to Kathleen. He imagined it was her. He hoped it was her—quietly coming to him in the night.

"I know you can hear me," the silent visitor said softly.

It was her.

In the darkness Kathleen stood looking toward him, hesitant, uncertain if she should take another step. Her hands were clasped in front as if she might ask, "May I approach?"

She did not meet his eyes because she could not see him in the darkness, but looked beyond the place where he sat.

"Come closer," Jared said in his deep, rich voice. He noticed his heart was pounding. He could hear hers as well, and it pleased him to know that she was just as affected by his presence as he was by hers.

"I do not want to wake the others," she whispered, turning to glance over her shoulder from where she had come.

"Then come with me," he said and stretched out his hand to take hers in the darkness.

Her hand was soft and warm, and he wanted to slide his other hand along her arm and around her back and waist and bring her closer to him. He wanted to press his lips to hers and unburden his heart. He wanted to tell Kathleen that his love had never faltered and that the time he spent away from her in the Delathrane lands had been torture for him. But he refrained. Holding her hand, he led her to the bow where they could speak quietly and not wake the others.

They sat knee to knee, at the point where the port and starboard sides of the boat met, leaning close. She spoke softly, hesitantly.

"I wanted to talk with you," Kathleen began. She took a deep breath and let it out slowly. "I just don't want it to be strange between us," she said, then stopped, looking up toward the heavens as if searching for the right words.

The faint light from the few visible stars fell on her cheeks.

How has nature assembled such beauty? Jared thought as he waited for what she would say next.

"I need you to understand why..." she finally managed.

She paused, and the silence extended for some time. He waited for her to say more, hearing nothing but the sea, but she didn't. There was only one question Jared had in his mind. It was the only answer he needed.

Why not me?

But he would not be so direct.

"Why?" he asked.

Jared wanted her to say the words, to explain why she was choosing Heathron instead of him. Perhaps if he could hear her say it he could accept it and move on, or otherwise it may make her feel pain at the thought of losing him. Saying it aloud might allow him to hear the emotion in her voice, and give him a clue to the truth of what the princess must feel for him.

"I wanted you to know why I didn't wait for you," she said.

Jared exhaled slowly. He did hear the anguish in her voice!

"You were imprisoned and tortured, Kathleen. I am so sorry I was not there for you in your darkest hour," he said.

"But you were, Jared!" she replied, then lowered her voice, "You were."

"What do you mean?"

"When I was at my breaking point. When I thought that life would leave me, it was you who visited me in my dreams. I remember crying out for you, and you came, even if only in the shattered remnants of my dreams."

Jared swallowed hard.

"Some comfort that is," he said, "to have a Guardian that can only protect you in your dreams."

"And yet the dreams came true. You returned!" she said.

"I have returned." He said it with conviction. He had returned and he would not leave her again.

Suddenly Kathleen realized how close she was now to Jared, so close she could feel his breath. She backed away and stared at her feet.

"But I promised Heathron that we would be married. He needed me. He still needs me, Jared. And I..." she raised a timid, reluctant glance up then, as if her eyes didn't want to meet his. "I was promised to him from the beginning," she finally said, the words softer, quieter now.

Jared swallowed and looked away briefly. "He reminded me as much, you know? When we were at Windstall," Jared replied, and let out a sigh.

"In the courtyard?"

Jared raised his eyebrows, surprised. "You were watching?" Then he softened his features again and smiled, as if it all made sense. "Of course you were. I thought I Sensed your presence."

"I'm sorry for that," Kathleen began.

Jared shook his head. "You do not need to apologize. Heathron meant every word he said to me. I can't blame him. If I had even the smallest chance to marry you, I would fight to the death any obstacle, any man or any beast that arose to keep me from having you forever."

"You scare me when you speak like that," Kathleen whispered.

"Love can be frightful. It is good to approach with some trepidation the power that can make us or destroy us."

"Will it destroy us?" she asked, her voice strangely caught between hope and fear. She asked the question directly. She wasn't being coy, but the way she had said *us* caused a current of hope to surge through his body.

Looking at her now, he was unsure of his answer, but examined every line and detail of her fine-boned face staring back at him. Every play of her questioning eyebrows, every curve of her sensuous lips.

"It could," he finally admitted, and as he said the words, a faint vision played out in his mind: the destruction that would come from a forbidden love. The thought passed through to her, too—he could see that now in her face. And together they were caught in a still posture, examining each other. In that silent storm, rage: Jared considered the jealousy he felt when he saw her in Heathron's arms, and the desire to have her all to himself. He swallowed the jealousy down to the pit of his stomach, hoping it would sit at anchor, hidden.

Kathleen too, seemed to be musing on the consequences, the thrill and destruction of an illicit relationship. Jared could see that. He felt her breathing quicken, shallow and fast, and heard and saw the subtle change in her respirations as clearly as he had seen the depth and safety of the water in the cove earlier on.

"Then we must control it. It is up to us."

She used the word 'us' again, he thought. But that seemed a preposterous concept.

"Control love?" he scoffed, unable to stop it. A long breath coursed out of his lungs, as if considering a chore too great to accomplish, and it sucked all vigor from his body. "I am not a perfect master of my emotions, Kathleen. But prudence is perhaps the weakest of my strengths," he admitted.

"I have a long road to travel in that virtue as well," Kathleen agreed, easing him, and laid a hand on his arm.

"But how can we help each other like this?" Jared asked, trying not to think of how her lips felt against his, and how he might kiss her neck now. Her smell, her touch, her voice—they washed over him like a tide he could not escape.

Suddenly, she rose up on her knees and hugged him, cradling his face to her chest.

"Just say the word, Jared. I'll do anything I can to help you. I'm sorry."

She squeezed him, then pulled his head up and shrank then into his chest and pulled his arms tightly around her. It was as if she was suddenly releasing some energy. She could barely breathe, and her eyes were wet.

Stunned, Jared could feel her body against him now, and he reveled in the warmth of her touch. But just as he placed his hands on the small of her back to pull her closer, and then her waist, Kathleen pushed him away.

"I can't," she whispered and untangling herself, slipped from his embrace. Her soft slippers made little sound as she retreated to her cabin, until all that was left on the deck was the light of the faint stars still shining in the quiet night sky, and Jared, alone.

He let out a breath that seemed to shudder as he exhaled, then pulled his black Sīhalt cloak closer about him.

LONG RIDE

Dallin raced into the house and down the hallway toward his chambers.

"There you are. I wanted to fill you in on the negotiations I just finished with Lord Balfoest."

Lord Sarkkand held up a document that was freshly signed.

"I don't know if I have time, Father," Dallin said. He kept walking and his father followed him into his room.

"The Steward seems to be acting reasonably," Lord Sarkkand explained. "He asked us to continue to serve on the Council of Nine and he even spoke of having you take on some duties with the Imperial Guard."

"I don't want to do that," Dallin said, as he grabbed a bag and began stuffing it with travel clothes.

"I thought you had an interest in serving the Tyathian Guard. Wouldn't you want to be an officer?"

Only half-listening, Dallin selected two of his favorite books and the bag of golden coins he kept hidden; he put them into the bag as well.

"I have always wished to serve the Golden City, Father. However, I have no wish to serve Lars Balfoest."

Lord Sarkkand sighed. "We need to be practical about these things, son. I think I have a new path for our House to follow. You know I would prefer Heathron as much as you, but that is looking less likely with each passing week."

Dallin tightened the scabbard that held his sword and added his dagger to his belt on the other side.

"Is there something I may do for you?" his manservant asked.

"Go to the kitchens and gather some food for me, I will be traveling so pack some cheese and dried meat that will not spoil."

"Yes, my lord," the servant said with a bow and melted away to the kitchen pantry.

"Where are you planning to go?" Lord Sarkkand asked. "Are you that upset by my meeting with the Steward? He is ruthless, and powerful. I could not just brush him off when he wanted to meet with me."

Dallin rolled up a blanket and threw it over his shoulder. "The man gives me the creeps," he said.

"I agree. He is always violating my personal space, wanting to touch me with those boney fingers of his. Maybe that is just his way, but I've never known another man to do that like him."

"He asked me about the horse, Father, " Dallin said gravely.

"He was in the stables?"

"He stopped there after speaking with you. He kind of surprised me."

"Did he seem pleased with our meeting?" Lord Sarkkand asked.

"He knows I ride the Windstall Stallion."

Dallin's father leveled his eyes at his son. "I told you not to keep it. And why would you ever reveal that to Lord Balfoest?"

"One of the stable boys said it. He didn't mean any harm."

His father nodded gravely. "Now I see why you are packing."

"Have I put you in danger, Father?" Dallin asked.

"I don't think so. But it would be a wise decision to lie low for a while."

"Tell Mother that I love her."

"You can tell me yourself," Lady Sarkkand said as she came into Dallin's room carrying the food he'd requested from the kitchens.

Dallin came forward and hugged his mother, who placed a gentle kiss on his cheek.

"Where are you going?" his father asked.

"Should I even tell you? Wouldn't it be better to be able to deny my location?"

"Now you are being dramatic. We won't need to tell anyone the truth of your whereabouts, but it would do us good to know."

"I'm just afraid Balfoest and his supporters will come for us," Dallin said.

Lady Sarkkand clicked her tongue. "Your father and I have known him our entire lives. Lars will not attack us. He may wish to punish you though, for helping Heathron and the Sīhalt Guardian."

"He knows the Tamer bond with that horse was passed to me."

"All the better for you to be far from this estate when he gets back to Tyath, then," Lord Sarkkand said.

"I'm going to Eldin's."

"Give our regards to Lord and Lady Stellat," his mother said. "And be careful on the road."

Dallin nodded, "I will," he said, then he picked up the bag and accepted the food provisions. "Thank you for understanding."

"We all need to make our own way in the world, Dallin. We are proud to be your parents," Lady Sarkkand said.

"And I am proud to be your son," Dallin replied and hugged them both at once.

~

The ride from the edge of the Clearwater Sea to Eldin's estate didn't take Dallin very long. The long strides of the Windstall stallion carried him over the land quickly. When he finally approached the guarded gate, Dallin was relieved to see how many of the guards Lord Stellat had placed on the walls. Someone must have recognized him, because the gates began to open for Dallin as he approached. He was not asked to stop and share his business. Instead, he rode directly through the gates and looked up to see Eldin waving.

The thin young man scampered down the steps so quickly that Dallin feared he might stumble, his gangly gait and awkwardness an ever present danger anytime heights were involved. Dallin remembered Eldin's fateful jump from the Fingers of Flint and didn't want to see any reenactment of any part of that fiasco on the stone steps.

"Dallin, how are you?" Eldin greeted him as he rushed across the courtyard, Steed whinnying and backing up a few paces as Eldin approached.

"Easy Steed, easy," Dallin said to the horse, calming the mount with a stroke of his hand against its mane. He got out of the saddle and embraced Eldin, then handed the reins to one of the liverymen who had drifted out of the stables toward them.

"I didn't know you were coming, but I'm glad you're here," Eldin said, "What's going on?"

"Lord Balfoest paid a visit to our estate. He heard from one of my servants that I like to take the Windstall stallion out for a ride every morning," Dallin explained.

Eldin immediately caught the meaning and the importance of that piece of information. He winced. "Yeah, you'd better lie low for a while," he said.

"May I stay with you?"

"Absolutely."

"I noticed you doubled the guards on the wall, or tripled them."

Eldin nodded gravely. "Yeah. My mother and father are very worried. We've brought as many provisions as we can into our home, and some of our friends from Tyath are here as well."

"Really? Who?" Dallin asked.

"Lord and Lady Aviella showed up not long ago. Hannah is spending some time with my sister, and there are others."

"Would Balfoest be so bold as to send his investigators here?" Dallin asked.

"If he does, I've got a great place for you to hide. Come with me. I've got to show you something." Dallin followed Eldin into the manor and up the stairs.

He opened a secret door at the back of wall revealing a small room with a bed and lamp stand.

"It doesn't have any windows, but it is secret. I stay here when I need private time in my laboratory," Eldin said as he gestured to the small space.

"By harboring me you are taking a risk," Dallin replied.

"We must do something to resist. I hope Heathron will be able to return soon. If not, I fear House Dol Lassimer may never have the throne again."

"Lord Balfoest may use Pilus as a pawn to get more Houses to support him. At least he can claim the Dol Lassimer banner."

"People know that Pilus doesn't even compare to Heathron," Eldin said.

Dallin bit his lip.

"Balfoest will destroy whoever and whatever stands in his way."

"I plan to go to the city tomorrow. Father Overbrook is there and I down know if the old man realizes the danger he's in."

"Father Overbrook may not even care. I've heard him say on a number of occasions that defending against villainy is the highest form of heroism."

"I know but he is more valuable to our cause alive. And I love the old priest," Eldin said.

"No one makes me feel the weight of Abboth's word like he does," Dallin agreed.

"You mean, Abbath?" Eldin chided.

"I'm sorry. It's just commonplace."

"I want to pick the right time. I'd rather not be stopped and questioned so maybe I can go to the cathedral on Holy day. Father Overbrook is bound to be there, and even Lars Balfoest would be hard pressed to justify apprehending someone at a worship service."

Dallin raised his eyebrows.

"The way he's consolidating power, I don't think he'd be hesitant to do anything."

"I know, but we've got to try."

12

SAFE HARBOR

The water lapped gently against the hull of the *Marine Escape* as she lay at anchor in the peaceful natural harbor. The morning sun made its climb above the horizon on the Eastern Sea. Kathleen was already awake and moving in its soft, deepening light—as were the brothers. They were on deck, practicing their movements in perfect synchronicity. She delighted in watching the display: so perfect, so like poetry, she thought. Jared's extra wrinkles were picked out by the sun, highlighting the age he carried over his younger brother. But apart from that, they were so alike. Kathleen remembered the first time she had seen him after he was Healed. Melva had worked her Talent magnificently to close so many of the wounds. She recalled the time she saw him getting dressed in the stable, and the many scars scattered across his back. She remembered especially his muscles, how toned and strong and broad they were...

She felt heat in her cheeks at that thought now of his arrival in Tyath all that time ago. It made her heart pound.

"There you are!" came a voice suddenly, snapping her back to the present. It was Heathron, marching from out of nowhere. He came and sat down next to her.

"Oh, Heathron…" she said, a little flustered, gathering the folds of her gown about her knees. "How was your rest?" she asked, resting a hand on his thigh as if to conceal the guilt of her thoughts.

Heathron stretched and arched his back. His sandy-blond curls had grown longer, and he brushed them away from his eyes.

"I feel like a new man! How about you?"

"I slept soundly—when I was finally able to fall asleep."

He crinkled his nose. "You look concerned Come, tell me what's on your mind?"

She couldn't tell him the truth, so instead she said, "I was thinking of how nice it will be to see Elayna again. Seeing the DeTorre brothers over there makes me realize just how much I miss my baby sister."

Heathron's features softened. "I can't say I feel the same toward my siblings," he admitted, then creased his brow again. "They may still be pursuing us, for all I know. How much longer do you think it will be until we reach Candoreth?"

"About six days of sailing, once we pass Hestin."

"Well, with better food and exercise I hope to be back to my full strength soon." Heathron jutted out his chin and puffed his chest. He seemed optimistic and full of cheer.

"I imagine you will be able to do all manner of your strength poses before too long." Kathleen smiled.

Heathron did too, then placed his hands on either side of her cheeks and kissed her.

"Now, I need to get back to my practice with the blade," he said, watching the Sīhalts preparing to train.

"Have you found any aboard?"

He pursed his lips. "There are some cutlasses, which are fine," he pondered, tapping his chin. "It has been some time since I trained with the curved blade, but I will remember my training before too long."

"I am willing to train with you," came Jared's deep voice from across the deck. Prince Heathron turned away from Kathleen in surprise, and faced the Sīhalt.

"Oh, Lord Sīhalt, I didn't know you could hear us from that far away," Heathron mused, elevating his voice in response. "Thank you for the offer. Shall I take you up on it after breakfast, or before?"

"At your pleasure," Jared replied.

"Good. Good," he repeated, not looking convinced.

"I'll go and wake the others," Kathleen said.

~

S he peeked her head into the small room she shared with Melva and Larissa.

"You are an early bird this morning," Melva croaked, her ancient voice not yet ready for the day.

"I thought I would get an early start," Kathleen said.

"No. You heard the ringing of steel and you wanted to see the men training, didn't you?" Larissa countered, leveling her eyes at her.

Kathleen flushed. "I...I felt rested," she replied unconvincingly. "There was no need to remain in bed."

"Hmm, I'm sure the anticipation was unbearable for you," Larissa said doubiously. "Anyway, I hope Channing joins in the training too," she added brightly, and sat up and stretched in her bed.

Kathleen shook her head and threw the blankets back over Larissa's head. "It's not like that. I just needed to get some fresh air!" she retorted defensively.

"I'll be right out too," Larissa promised from her sprawled position. Her hair was askew and her eyes were dark and tired.

"It looks like it would take a team of oxen to make that happen," Kathleen said with a laugh.

Larissa thought about this before saying, "No...just a few muscled men will do!"

"You are definitely getting back to your old self," Kathleen smiled, and climbed the ladder back up to the deck

❧

Heathron uncurled his spine and craned his neck in readiness for the joust. He rolled his head gently to stretch the muscles and beckoned Kathleen as she emerged back on deck. "I'm doing some stretching to warm up before my swordplay. Do you want to join me?"

He was dressed in fitted light blue pants and a shirt that seemed too large for him.

"Those pants seem to run on the small side for you," Kathleen observed.

Heathron looked down at himself. "Hmm..." he said, and scratched his chin. "These pants probably belonged to Jessica's younger brother, and this shirt..."—he pinched a piece of the silk garment away from his arm then watched it pull back as he let it go—"I believe was her father's," he guessed, his nostrils crinkling unpleasantly as he sniffed. "It certainly smells fusty enough!"

Kathleen laughed.

"Still, I think they will work until my own clothes dry. I washed them out and hung them from one of the lines." He took a deep breath, closed his eyes and exhaled. "And now I'm ready to go through my routine."

Kathleen brushed a strand of hair from her face and removed her slippers. She joined him, imitating the position of his body.

"What is this one called?" she asked.

Heathron reached upward toward the clouds. "This is called, *Warrior of the Sky*," he said.

Kathleen felt her rib cage expand and the muscles under her chin stretch as she looked up toward the heavens.

"That feels good," she said.

Heathron smiled at her and nodded his agreement.

"Here is the next one," he said, moving to fold at the waist and rise slowly. Rolling his spine as he did so, he spread his arms wide and rose onto the balls of his feet. Reaching upward once more, Kathleen echoed his movements and felt the core of her body relax. She closed her eyes and felt the morning sun warm her eyelids. It felt good, comforting. She smelled the fresh air and the smooth wood under her feet and suddenly felt a world away from Lord Balfoest and all those memories...

"Make sure to flex the muscles of your backside to support your back," Heathron cautioned.

Kathleen tensed her muscles and felt the reassuring support within her body.

At the other end of the deck came the ringing of steel against steel. When she opened her eyes to look she saw Jared and Seth moving through a series of routines that seemed like a slow dance. The brothers were silent, inhaling and exhaling deeply, and all in a rhythm that flowed with the music of their bodies. At times they would reach out and touch each other with the open edge of their hand, or even a curled fist—never actually striking a blow, but reminding their muscles of the punches and jabs that were often intermingled with their Sīhalt swordplay. Kathleen was reminded of the morning in the mist when she secretly watched Jared in the courtyard of Windstall Hermitage. She had been enthralled by his movements then, just as she was now in the light of morning.

"It's quite something, isn't it?" Heathron said, standing beside her.

The question jolted her out of her reverie and snapped her back to the present again. "Hmm?" she said, not realizing she had stopped following Heathron's lead. "What's something?"

"The way the Sīhalts move," Heathron replied. "They remind me of phantoms. They don't fight like mere mortals."

As Kathleen stood watching, Heathron moved closer to her

and slid his arm around her waist. She was glad he was not upset with how mesmerized she must have seemed for a few moments. And then Kathleen saw why...the Guardians had stopped and were approaching from across the deck.

"You are not planning to use the *impla* when we are practicing, are you?" Heathron shouted over to them.

Jared shook his head and answered. "No, it would not be fair." He then lifted the sword in his hand. "A common cutlass is no match for this Windstall blade. It would be shorn in two."

Heathron's eyebrows rose, "Really?"

"Really."

"Show me," the prince insisted.

Seth and Jared paused. Stripes of perspiration shone on their foreheads.

"All right, I can show you," Jared offered.

Seth picked up one of the cutlasses and held it out, presenting it to his brother.

Jared waved it away. "Let Heathron hold the cutlass," Jared said, "He is the one who asked."

Seth nodded, handing the cutlass to Heathron.

"Your Sīhalt blades are new to me. As slender as they are, I'm surprised they would hold up to a heavy cutlass."

Heathron extended the blade outward, holding the cutlass with one hand.

"You may want used both hands for this," Jared suggested.

"I'll be fine," Heathron assured him.

"Suit yourself." Jared moved the slender *impla* through the air in a clover-like pattern, making it sing.

Kathleen sported a look of concern. "Are you sure you don't want to set it on the edge of that barrel or something? I'd hate to see it glance off and hurt someone."

"Just stand back. I'll make sure you aren't harmed," Heathron said.

Lilly suddenly emerged on deck and said, "Don't worry, Highness, that is my job."

Maxwell approached now, too, rubbing his eyes of sleep. He looked as if he had rolled out of bed, with his short brown hair sticking up in patches at funny angles where it hadn't been matted by the pillow.

"Enjoying your game of 'whose sword is bigger'?" he asked, a crooked grin arranging itself on his lips.

Both Jared and Heathron leveled their eyes at the Shifter, and said, "I'm not trying to prove anything," almost in unison. They turned and looked at each other dumbly.

"Sure..." Maxwell said, laughing now.

"Heathron simply asked for a demonstration," Jared replied innocently.

"Go ahead and get it over with, then," Seth said with a grin and a knowing wink at Lilly.

Heathron and Jared both seem relax a little bit and the tension that had been building between them softened as the foolishness of their contest was made plain.

"I wouldn't mind seeing this either," Channing added, his heavy footsteps making the last wrung on the ladder from the cabin whine and creak. He rose up onto the deck and lurched towards them, folding two meaty arms across his broad chest in readiness. "I've wondered how such a slim blade can be so strong."

Jared began to swing the sword to the right and left in large circles. "The ancient secret of the *impla* is guarded by the swordsmiths at Windstall. Their work is legendary and has saved the lives of many Guardians," he lectured as he displayed the sword in all its glory. Then he lunged forward with the speed of a viper, toward Heathron, bringing the *impla* down perpendicular to the curved blade of his cutlass.

Heathron stiffened as blade met blade. The metal sparked and chimed like a bell. The high-pitched note echoed loudly from the masts and across the sea, and then was followed by the dull thud of the heavy cutlass hilt and half-blade dropping out of his hand to the deck of the ship.

Heathron blinked and looked at his open palm. "Impressive," he admitted, then bent down to pick up only the blade. Rising from his haunches, he examined the new edge of the cutlass, how clean it was—even sharper than the cutlass' original blade. This new cut shone under the sunlight as if it, too, had come from Winstall.

Jared, however, had lowered his blade, and was presently ignoring Heathron entirely. Instead, his storm grey eyes were fixed on Kathleen, studying her reaction.

For that reason, he didn't see Heathron lunge forward and steer the broken tip toward Jared's throat. There was a gasp from the onlookers, and the Sīhalt Guardian stiffened, unprepared for the sudden offensive. He remained still.

Suddenly Heathron stepped back, lowering the broken cutlass, and burst into laughter. "Oh, I got you there, Guardian, didn't I?" he bragged, twirling the broken cutlass. "Don't forget that even a broken blade can be dangerous." Then he turned and tossed the halved cutlass into the sea. "Come, Kathleen, let us continue my stretching ritual," he added, wrapping an arm around her waist and steering her toward the bow. She went with him reluctantly, casting glances over her shoulder.

Jared watched on furiously. "As can a broken man," he whispered.

BONE FISH GIRL

K athleen did not like seeing the two men at odds. She could tell Jared was angry, even if it was just a silly demonstration.

"It's hot to the touch," Channing observed, as he picked up the broken tip of the cutlass. "What kind of steel is the *impla* made of?"

"The swordsmith at Windstall Hermitage could tell you that, but even he did not make the original metal blanks for the interior of the blade," Seth replied.

"What do you mean?" Heathron asked.

"The beauty of the Guardian blade comes from its ability to be thin and lightweight, to bend without breaking, and yet maintain the stiffness needed to parry a blow."

Jared tossed his sword to Channing and he caught it by the hilt.

"So light!" he exclaimed. "A man could fight all day and not tire with a blade such as this."

"It is very difficult to sharpen—the stones needed are hard to come by—but once the *impla* is ready for battle it keeps its edge, too."

Heathron examined the length of Jared's sword looking for any sign that the weapon had just been used to cleave the cutlass in two.

"There's not a scratch on it," he said, and then whistled as he set down the broken cutlass and ran his fingers along the length of the Guardian's blade.

"Is it made with a Talent?" Channing asked.

Jared and Seth looked at each other considering the question.

"I suppose it is possible, as the blades of the Sīhalts are legendary. They are treasured and passed from one generation to the next. The myths says the first Maker of Swords in Windstall Hermitage found the blanks in a cave where the barracks now stand. They do not rust, and although they retain the heat of the forge, the metal requires extreme temperatures in order to be worked into a blade," Jared explained.

Seth drew his sword and held it in both hands horizontally, presenting it to Heathron.

"Upon being raised to the level of a Guardian, the apprentices at the Hermitage are presented with their own sword. New blades haven't been needed for many years, as the swords of the fallen Guardians are given to the ones newly raised. The Order has a surplus of swords, since the great Sickness."

Heathron handed Jared's sword back to him, and took steps to examine it as well.

"Have you ever known of one to break?" he asked.

"I've never witnessed it. I know of no one who has," Jared said.

"There is a legend of a Sīhalt Guardian from ancient times who got his sword wedged between some boulders on a mountainside. An avalanche of boulders fell from above, crushing him and changing the entire face of the mountainside. When the Brothers of the Order finally found his body, they looked for his sword in the area he was last seen. The *impla* was found wedged where he had left it. Numerous boulders, downhill from the blade, had been severed. Although the hilt was broken, the *impla* blade remained intact."

"What I would give to see such a weapon!" Channing said.

"You have seen it, Captain Dur Ruston," Jared said, "the Sīhalt Guardian named Girdy Frast, carries the blade named *Avalanche* in Candoreth."

"I didn't know that," Kathleen said, in surprise. "There is so much I don't know about him."

Melva smiled and nodded at this.

"Girdy is a man of many legends. He once told me the story of his sword," Melva said.

"If you would spar with me, would you be willing to use a weapon more similar to mine?" Heathron asked.

"That is no problem; I have fought with the cutlass before," Jared replied.

"Is there a weapon unfamiliar to you? Heathron asked.

Jared looked to Seth and Maxwell. The two Sīhalt Guardians frowned and shook their heads.

"He's good with almost every weapon," Seth admitted.

"He's got no defense against a bonefish," Lilly said, breaking into the conversation. She spoke softly, going about her business, her face smooth and tranquil.

Maxwell unleashed a laugh at the comment.

"What?" Jared said looking from Maxwell's grinning face to Lilly's pursed lips. She stood with hands on her hips.

Jared rose to his feet, his head tilted and he looked more closely at Lilly. She smiled and Jared turned to Maxwell.

"Did she say bonefish?"

Maxwell nodded, "That was perfect timing," he said to Lilly, still beaming.

"I recognized you immediately. As soon as I saw you in the tunnel during our escape." Lilly said.

Jared looked askance at Maxwell.

"If this is a trick of yours..."

"It's no trick, Lord Sīhalt. Your face hasn't changed that much since the day we first met," the guardswoman replied.

"I don't remember the girl of that day," Jared said, absently laying a hand on his cheek.

"Of course not!" Maxwell chided, "You were knocked unconscious. I wouldn't want to remember it either if I were you."

"If you are that girl, then tell me what I said on that day so long ago that made you upset?" Jared said. He looked at the guardswoman with a piercing gaze.

Lilly furrowed her brow and glanced upward, trying to recall the past.

Kathleen caught hold of Lilly's hand and asked, "You two know each other from the past?"

"We met once, long ago." Lilly said.

"I was there, too," Maxwell said, grinning.

"How long ago was this?" Kathleen asked, trying to hide the tension in her voice.

"A long time ago." Jared replied.

"I remember it like it was yesterday," Maxwell said.

"Do you remember me?" Lilly asked, turning to Seth.

"I remember the day," he admitted, "but I couldn't say for sure it was you."

Jared nodded. "Do you remember what I said that day?"

"What happened?" Kathleen said.

"I was helping my father unload the boat and clean the catch.You said, 'What is that awful smell?' Then your brother said, 'It smells like rotten fish.'"

Both brothers looked at each other, guilt written in their expressions.

"Then Jared said, 'It's probably her.'"

Maxwell nodded. "I didn't tell her that either."

"So I hit you across the face with a bonefish," Lilly admitted.

"Knocked him out cold!" Maxwell chortled.

Jared took a step toward Lilly, and took her by the hand.

14

SĪHALT HUMILITY

"Oh, this is delightful," Kathleen said, smiling as she watched Jared kneel in front of the guardswoman.

Jared held Lilly's hand, amazed that he finally had a chance to set this aright. He spent many hours in the chapel at Windstall, contemplating his life and where he might have gone wrong. He never dreamed he might find the poor fishing girl. It was a small thing but important to him. She had never completely left his mind

"What is your full name?" he asked.

"Lilly Dubae Sentara Delano Caprice Vinagru, the Third."

"Okay…" Jared said running the name through his mind again.

"You can just say Lilly."

"No I can't," Jared replied.

"He has to say the entire name, Lilly. You don't know how long I've waited for this," Maxwell said happily rubbing his hands together like a child that expected a sweet roll from his mother's oven.

"Take it easy on him," Seth cautioned.

"I just had to say this to him *so* many times. It's good to see him kneel in front of somebody else and say the *Sīhalt Humiliation*."

"I'm glad you're taking pleasure in this," Jared said.

"Oh, I am!"

He Shifted back and forth from the shape of a scrawny old man to the form of young man, then to the old, then back to the young again.

"You're so excited you can't hold your form," Jared said.

"I know, this is great!" Maxwell admitted.

Lilly began to blush, surprised by the response of the Sīhalt Guardian, and the attention of everyone on deck.

"I wish I had just kept my mouth shut. There is no need to-" Lilly began.

"It was you," Jared said cutting her off.

The Sīhalt moved with purpose. The sudden rigid, yet graceful formality of his movements told how seriously he held this moment.

"You were merciful when it was not required of you," he said.

"I don't understand," Kathleen said.

"It's part of our training and traditions. Proper training etiquette means that when you are defeated, the one who is vanquished must kneel and recite a simple ode to the victor. It makes the loss more bitter, and the victory more sweet," Seth explained.

"But Jared never had to do it, and he skipped out on this one a long time ago. This would've been sweeter back when Jared was younger, and more cocky, but I'll take what I can get," Maxwell said.

"I wondered how long it would take you to recognize me," Lilly said.

Jared held her hand and looked at her with eyes that pleaded for forgiveness.

"You could have finished me and you stayed your hand," Jared said.

"We were just foolish children. I'm not surprised you didn't remember me."

"I remember the day clearly. That is, until that fish connected with my jaw."

"My Imperial Guardswoman is certainly worthy of her position, if a Sīhalt Guardian is kneeling to her and thanking her for the mercy she extended to him on the field of battle," Kathleen said.

"Its been a long time in coming," Maxwell said, savoring the scene.

"Take it easy," Seth replied, "You never know when you may need to do the same."

"Maxwell isn't a Sīhalt Guardian, though," Larissa observed.

The Shifter shot her a dirty look. "I still follow the rules," he said.

"I'm just saying you don't wear all the black, and the *impla*, and the special cloak," she replied

"Maxwell took the same oaths we did during training. Master Tove thought he would better serve the Order if his talents were used in a different way."

"I'm no good at negotiations," Maxwell admitted. "I'm a fight-it-out-and-wash-the-blood-off-later kind of fellow. Master Tove wants Sīhalt Guardians who are both wise and charitable."

He said this last with an elevated tone of mock reverence, and stood to his tallest height.

"And Jared was made a Guardian?" Lilly asked as he knelt before her.

Maxwell laughed. "I know! Truly?"

"I'm trying to apologize properly and acknowledge my defeat," Jared said to Lilly.

"Go ahead, Lord Sīhalt. I'm sorry," she replied, trying to maintain a serious demeanor.

Maxwell slapped his thigh and forced out more laughter. "I didn't expect to have a court jester mocking me as I made amends."

Jared rolled his eyes.

Maxwell laughed again, this time intentionally embellishing it with snorts of pleasure.

Jared shook his head and continued the formal apology. He said the words slowly and clearly for all to hear, raising his voice.

"Lilly Dubae Sentara Delano Caprice Vinagru, the Third, I owe you my life and my sword. I am humbled by your skill, and for that my humiliation is complete."

Maxwell recited the last line in unison with Jared, relishing Jared's defeat as if he himself was the victor.

"*He who laughs at another's defeat exposes himself to vengeance replete,*" Melva said, raising an eyebrow at Maxwell disapprovingly.

Maxwell slapped his thigh again, still laughing. "At least my defeat won't be by a girl!" he said.

"*He who laughs, when the laughter of all has faded, makes himself a fool,*" Seth added, reciting a line from their primer on childhood etiquette.

"I don't care," Maxwell said wiping tears from his eyes. "If you could have seen his face when that bonefish slapped him upside the head!"

"A bonefish? That must've hurt," Kathleen said.

"You might be able to see a faint scar on my jawline, even now," Jared replied, turning and angling his cheek toward the sunlight.

"I do see it," Kathleen said ,then traced her fingers along the white smudge at the edge of his jawline.

Her touch sent a wave of emotion through Jared's body. He looked up at Kathleen from where he knelt to meet her eyes. The pleasure he felt was enhanced by the sudden increase he could hear in her pulse when she gazed at him.

"You may rise, Lord Sīhalt. I accept your humiliation," Lilly said finally.

"Make him do it again; you have the right!" Maxwell exclaimed.

"He's done enough. I accept it."

Seth started to laugh and then Larissa too. Lilly lost her composure and then Melva, Kathleen, and Heathron joined in. Finally even Jared, kneeling where he was, could not hold it in any longer. He pointed to Maxwell and barely was able to say, "This is all your fault," as his face reddened.

Heathron had to kneel down, holding his sides. "I can't," he said through laughter that seemed to cause him pain. But the sound of his voice was high-pitched, and it set off a new ripple of laughter from everyone.

The moment of simple humor bought the friends closer, and had a way of purging the stress and concerns of the past few months.

Jared managed to say the rest of his required statement, then got to his feet and hugged Maxwell and Lilly. "Is that sufficient for you?" he asked.

Both Lilly and the Shifter agreed that he had done enough.

15

TO STAY AWAY

"What is the matter?" Larissa asked, closing the door behind her. Kathleen caught Melva's gaze just before the door to the cabin closed.

The Healer tilted her head, giving her a look of reproof. Kathleen was not in the mood for Melva's axioms or aged wisdom. So she sat down on the bed and ran her hands across her face. She brushed away the wayward strands of hair nearest her temple, and exhaled with her lower lip protruding slightly beyond the upper. Then she turned to her friend and let out what remained of the air in her lungs.

"I need to stay away from him, don't I?" she said.

"The Sīhalt? I wondered what was happening between you two. What did he say when he spoke with you on the deck?" Larissa asked, excitement in her expression.

Kathleen exhaled again, considering if she should share her thoughts. She shook her head.

"I just need to be careful."

"We are in the middle of the sea. You will not be able to avoid him. Besides, he is your protector," Larissa said.

"I suppose I won't be completely free of him."

"That's not *really* what you want anyway," Larissa said with a smile.

"I told Jared that I had chosen Heathron. I will marry the prince."

"How did he take that?" Larissa asked.

"I hurt him, but he tries to hide his emotions from me."

"Was he angry? What did he say?" Larissa asked.

"I knew you would want the details," Kathleen said.

Melva cleared her throat and ran a wrinkled brown hand across her chin.

"Remember, there is a part of every man that is a beast. Be careful, Kathleen. You are playing with forces I do not think you fully understand or respect," the Healer said.

"Jared would never hurt me," Kathleen said with certainty.

The old woman blinked slowly and drew up one corner of her lips.

"You're not convinced?" Larissa asked.

"The Sīhalt would not intentionally harm you. He is in love with you. Unfortunately, people have a way of hurting those they love the most. You are right, you should distance yourself from him. However, that is impossible, right now," Melva said.

Larissa shivered with excitement.

"Ooh, I wouldn't want to run from him. You'd miss out on the fun," she exclaimed.

"That is exactly what I am talking about," Melva said.

Larissa flashed an expression of mock innocence at Melva.

"I'll be glad when I am back home among my people. I will be able to think more clearly in Candoreth, I am sure."

"Heathron plans to marry you there?" Melva asked.

"He does, but it would be better for him if we were married in the Grand Cathedral in Tyath. I think Heathron fears to lose legitimacy if he remains unmarried for any more time."

"Heathron fears he will lose you to the Sīhalt Guardian. That is his greatest worry," Melva said.

For a moment, Kathleen wondered if Melva, too, had overheard the men in the misty courtyard of Windstall Hermitage.

"Heathron has nothing to worry about," Kathleen said. "I have made up my mind."

"I haven't," Larissa said. She placed a thumbnail against her teeth and stared off into the distance, considering Kathleen's options.

"Things will turn out. I have confidence in you," Melva said.

"Thank you, Melva. I want your approval."

The old woman put her arms around Kathleen and hugged her, rubbing her head with one hand and gently patting Kathleen's shoulder with the other. Melva's thin body had gained some strength since escaping Tyath. Kathleen curled closer to her and relaxed as Melva held her.

"You still think of me as a little girl, don't you? But I've noticed you haven't called me 'Child' in a long time," Kathleen said.

The old Healer kept smoothing Kathleen's hair. She smiled with her wrinkled brown lips.

"I can't call you 'Child' anymore, not after what you've been through. Does that make you sad?" Melva asked.

"Mostly it makes me thankful that we escaped," Kathleen said.

Larissa shivered again, this time with the memory of the dungeon. "Lets not talk about that. Instead, let's focus in the Sīhalt Guardian. I can't believe you told him it was over."

She grinned broadly.

"Honestly, Larissa, I don't see any way that could work. Even if I weren't engaged," Kathleen said. "What am I to do? Run off with my Sīhalt Guardian to live in the wild, consuming nothing but the passion we share and the sweet berries we can forage in the wilderness?"

"That sounds amazing! Don't forget about bathing together beneath pure waterfalls and feeding each other wild honeycomb with your bare hands," Larissa added.

"It sounds silly, doesn't it?" Kathleen said, rolling her eyes.

Melva chuckled at the vivid exchange between the girls.

"Life and relationships do not usually meet such high expectations. If you are lucky, or blessed, you may experience a few moments when it seems the earth stands still for your love, and the pleasure of sharing your love is illuminated by a perfect sunset or a vibrant summer storm. Most days are not like that, and so you will treasure them, when they come," Melva said.

"I've had moments like that," Kathleen observed quietly.

"With Heathron, or Jared?" Larissa asked.

Kathleen paused, remembering the moments she had spent together with Jared on the road, and Heathron in the Golden City.

"I've had magical moments with each of them," she said.

"Then you are very lucky. Or you are blessed," Melva replied.

"I am blessed to have Heathron Dol Lassimer as my future husband. I will not encourage the Sīhalt Guardian from now on. It could only end in ruin," Kathleen said.

DAGGER AND THE GIRL

Thomas Dagger considered his options as he went about his chores. To think that he, a Centian captain, was made to do the menial tasks aboard the ship that used to be his own, made his stomach churn with the rage of a storm, and tighten like a seaman's knot. What had he done to gain Abbath's displeasure? He looked up into the sky above and shook his head. But who was he kidding? He already knew the answer to that question.

Thomas Dagger had left the Path when he was eleven years old. In the days and weeks and years since then, neither his father, the priest, nor his mother was ever able to set him back on it.

"I *will* go back to the Lighted Path," he muttered to himself. "Someday—just not today."

He grabbed a long-handled scrub brush and made his way down the ladder to get a bucket from the hold. The Sulians might be lacking in creativity, he thought, but they did know how to clean a ship. The *Dagger* gleamed like the day she was born in the shipyard, and still the Sulian officers wanted her scrubbed. But in truth, Thomas didn't mind it. Few things gave him greater pleasure than seeing his true love looking so pretty; he just didn't want to be the one doing the scrubbing.

"Can you help me?" came a soft, breathless feminine voice from the darkness. The hold was cramped and cluttered, and Thomas wheeled around to see where this voice had come from. "Please!" came the voice again, and Thomas found that it was coming from the shadowy gloom behind a stack of crates.

Thomas jumped back and reached for the heavy handle of his pistol. "Who is it?" he asked. "Show yourself now."

From the gloom emerged a pale face with dark almond-shaped eyes. There was a spill of lancing light coming through the crack in the hatch above, and the girl came into it. She had long straight black hair that fell past her shoulders, some of which she had gathered into a loose pile on her head that was held with two wooden sticks in the manner of the Sulian women.

"My name is Shīanya. Will you help me?" she asked, in a heavy Sulian accent.

He eyed her suspiciously. She had a slight build and wore white clothing that was simple and well-made. She had removed her outer robe and wore a long shirt and skirt, with sandals on her feet. She was sweat-stained and Thomas wondered how she had managed to hide aboard the ship for so long without more ventilation in her hiding place.

"Your name sounds familiar to me," he said, "but I've visited many ports in many nations and all the names and faces run together." He paused and looked around, then rested his gaze back on the woman with almond eyes. "My name is Thomas Dagger," he said, placing a hand against his chest. When the girl said nothing he extended his hand.

Shīanya, still and uneasy, looked at his extended palm and made no move to do the same. She kept her hands clasped in front of her, and he felt nervous at the way her eyes were glancing toward the gun he kept tucked in his belt.

"They don't know you are aboard, do they?" he said, looking

upward at the beams that held the deck above their heads. 'You are a stowaway."

The girl looked around, scanning the area behind him.

"Who were you talking to when you came down the stairs?" she asked apprehensively.

"It's just me," Thomas replied.

"I will defend myself if you try to harm me," she said.

Thomas bowed low.

"I have never harmed a lady before, and I do not intend to begin today. I give you my word."

"That is good. I need water," she said, accepting his promise.

"Well you've gone from a lady-in-distress to telling me what I must do, in less than five seconds. That's just my luck," Dagger said.

"You are a Centian sailor, you will help me?" she said. It was not phrased as a question. It was more of a command. Thomas recognized that. He used the same technique with his own subordinates at times.

"I am a Centian *captain*, I was an officer on my first vessel at the age of twelve and I have not been on land for a full year since. This is my ship—or it was my ship, before the Sulian fleet joined us. I plan to get it back."

The young woman nodded, seeming to understand.

"I am thirsty," she said.

Thomas reprimanded himself for his foolishness. Women didn't want to hear about his exploits, no matter how much he always wanted to tell them, and especially when she might be dying of thirst.

"I will get you some water," he said. "Sit tight, I'll be right back. I've got some questions for you when I return."

She blinked her dark eyes and the smooth skin of her face and cheeks seemed all the fairer for the contrast. "Sit tight? I do not know what this means," she said with a confused look on her face.

"Stay here. That is what it means." he explained.

"I will go where I choose, Centian," she replied in her airy accent. "However, it does make sense for me to hide here a little while longer I think. Tell no one of my presence here."

Now it was Dagger's turn to be confused. He shook his head a bit. and climbed the ladder to deliver the bucket and brush.

Thomas considered whether he should go right to the commanding officers and tell them they had a young woman who was a stowaway. But he was intrigued by the mystery of her being aboard and wanted to find out more.

I'm certainly not doing anything wrong by helping her, he thought.

"Dagger! Get a move on! You're taking forever!" came the call from the officer on deck.

Thomas knuckled his forehead humbly and picked up his pace, still thinking of the strange girl hiding in the hold. And when the officers were distracted as they consulted one another, he filled a small waterskin. Then he waited until there were no eyes in his direction.

"Abbath, don't let anyone see me," he prayed. Thomas could already feel the lashes he would receive if he were caught. "I promise to burn fifty candles in the Daicon Cathedral, if you'll help me on this," he said, adding a mental note to the growing list of obligations he'd made to Abbath.

He looked to see where the sun was in the sky. He still had some time before they rang the bell for evening inspection. *These Sulians and all their inspections!* he thought with some exasperation. *They'd inspect the ticks on a sow's ear, just to make sure they weren't sucking improperly.*

He quickly made his way down the ladder again. When he again stood in the hold, he quietly called out to the petite woman he spoke with before.

"I've got your drink," he said, holding the water skin in front of him. He looked to the corner where he had last seen her but she was not there, and he was tempted to climb on top of the crates to look for her when he heard her voice.

"With whom were you speaking?" she asked.

"No one; I came alone," he whispered.

"I just heard you ask someone to help you hide."

"No, I didn't," Thomas insisted.

She glanced up the ladder.

"You gave me your word!" she hissed.

"I brought you water. Just as I promised."

"Tell your friend to come down here. I must speak with those who know I am here. Is he *Sulian*?"

Thomas Dagger furrowed his brow. "I don't know what you're talking about!" He was beginning to wonder if the woman was sane.

"I clearly heard you speak to your friend. Abbath, was it? That is a Sulian name. Call him down here immediately."

Dagger tried not to smile too broadly at her misunderstanding. He chuckled. "I can't call him down here, and I'm not sure you would want him here if I could. Abbath is the name of God."

Shīanya had a puzzled look on her face. "You speak with your God? You are a holy man?"

"I speak *to* God. He never really says anything back to me," Thomas corrected, and she looked at him deeply for a moment, apprising his worthiness.

"You do not look like a holy man who could talk with God," she concluded.

"Well, Abbath hasn't struck me down yet, and I've never claimed to be holy. I'm more like the opposite. He doesn't talk to me, but I speak to him all the time. Mother always said I need to do more of that, not less—for all the good it has done me."

He uncorked the waterskin and handed it to her. She hesitated at first, then extended her hand receiving it gracefully before putting it to her lips.

As she swallowed the water gratefully, Thomas, half speaking to himself, said, "Yeah, I don't like to think about how much I owe Abbath, in tithes, offerings and candles for the church. I'm still alive though, and I keep a running tally right here." Thomas said, tapping his forehead.

"You have a debt? To God?" the woman asked, wiping the water from her chin and mouth. Her expression was strangely caught between one of curious disbelief and immense satisfaction.

"Don't we all?" Thomas said, looking around and wondering how it was that he had gotten into a theological discussion with this strange young woman.

"I do not believe God would extend credit—that you could negotiate with him," she said.

"I do it all the time. It works for me and I'm still alive."

"This is an interesting thought, Centian."

"You may call me Dagger, or Thomas," he said, growing annoyed at the way she addressed him.

Shīanya finished the water and wiped her mouth again, then handed the water skin back. "You are a strange person," Shīanya said to him.

"I was just thinking the same thing about you," he replied with a crooked smile. "What are you doing here?"

"I am escaping to *Desnia*. Now that we have passed the Islands of No Return, I am ready to reveal myself to the crew," Shīanya said.

"That's not a good idea. I'm not sure how the officers and crew will take it. In *Centia*, a woman on a ship is considered bad luck. I personally have never believed that, mind you. In my experience, women are good luck, for the most part—"

"I don't want to hear about your experiences with women, Thomas. The crew will be honored to have me aboard," the young *Sulian* woman said.

Shīanya spoke with such certainty that Thomas paused to consider how she could be so certain of herself. The few *Sulian* women he had known personally had been passive, demur and ready to please. Shīanya was different. She had a softness about her and a refinement too, but beneath that exterior he sensed a hardness that would make iron nails look soft. "You must be a woman of the upper classes, to have such confidence," Thomas said. "Most women I know would be hesitant to reveal themselves on a ship full of men on the vastness of the open sea," he said, arching his eyebrows suggestively. "Especially if her presence could be considered *illegal*."

This remark seemed to offend the girl.

"My life is not yours to know, Centian," she replied.

Thomas shrugged. "Suit yourself."

The girl named Shīanya wrinkled her brow in confusion then looked down at her own clothing. "What do you mean? I do not wear suits as a man might. I wear dresses."

Thomas shook his head, and waved his hand. "Never mind," he said. "We passed the Islands of No Return two days ago. We don't have enough supplies to do anything except to keep going to *Desnia* so it looks like you got the passage you wanted to the new continent."

"The storms have been fierce. The ship was groaning as if it might break in two," Shīanya said.

"It will be better from here on, or so the old charts say." He turned to the girl more seriously now. "Look, allow me to tell the officers of your presence here. You should not surprise them. It will not go down well. I can soften it."

She thought about this, her features hardening at first as if to object. But with some consideration she nodded in resignation. "Very well. Go and tell them. I will change into something more *appropriate*," she said.

Thomas crinkled his face in amusement. "You speak as if you have a closet from which to choose!" he said with a laugh, casting his gaze around the dark, damp hold. But to his surprise, Shīanya bent down and opened a small wooden trunk that lay near the crates behind her. He moved closer a few steps and stooped to inspect it. The lid was inlaid with a motif he recognized from *Sulia*.

The girl was rummaging through it.

"What kind of stow-away brings multiple changes of cloth-ing?" he quipped, amused. But the young woman ignored him, and began to undress, so Thomas turned to the ladder and took his leave, shaking his head as he did so.

Back under the bright light that spilled onto the quarterdeck, Thomas took off his hat. He held it in his hands behind his back. and lowered his eyes as he waited to be recognized by one of the officers. He still wasn't used to the demanding rules of the Sulian navy, but he had seen enough of his old shipmates left bruised, battered and bleeding for insubordination that he had fallen into line. He decided it would not be too humiliating to remove his hat and lower his eyes, and they did at least allow a Centian sailor to remain standing, and keep his weapons.

"Ho!" a junior officer grunted.

Dagger kept his eyes down, looking at the man's shoes as they shone like mirrors in the sunlight. It irked him that he could not look him in the face until granted permission, but that humilia-tion didn't sting as much as the actual lash, so he took a breath and waited to be allowed to speak.

"What do you want?" the man finally said.

"Permission to speak with the admiral," Dagger said, finally raising his eyes to meet the dark countenance directed at him. He felt more like a slave than a free man, and he had always wondered: *Just how do they get the average Sulian to endure such treatment?*

The officer evaluated him, obviously finding him wanting. "The first mate is over there," he pointed toward the nearest mast where a knot of men were conversing. Thomas placed a fist to his forehead and backed away without turning from the officer.

The first mate he had been directed to was Jung Zah, a man of crisp movements and a fierce look, owing to the deep scars that ran along both of his cheeks.

Approaching him, Thomas saw that he and the other men

were studying a map. Their opinions were obviously split as they were glowering at each other—their features tight—gesturing at the map and each other with sharp, darting movements. They all were pointing to differing locations on the map with possessive and frustrated vigor.

"May I be of some service, sir?" Thomas enquired, as he lowered his eyes and bowed at the waist.

Again he held this posture for a moment or two, waiting to be allowed to speak further.

"Ho, Centian," the first mate said, "What makes you think you can help us?"

"That is a *Centian* map, if I am not mistaken. They can be complex, especially if the map maker was trying to be sly. I've read many of them—perhaps I may help?"

"You are a common sailor. How do you know how to read?"

"Sir, I was once an officer. Although I am no longer," Thomas replied. He left out the part about commanding the ship on which they stood—no need to stir up the Sulian's pride.

"Hmmm," the first mate said, "I doubt that you know anything more than we have determined, but it might be fun to see what a poor Centian can do with this mess of a chart.

Thomas seethed at the Sulian's hubris, but showed only a thin crease of a smile as he put his fist to his forehead. Centian map makers were the best in the world, everyone knew that. Why else were they using a copy of the oldest maps to be had for the Sea of Storms? Centians were the ones who preserved what little knowledge was known of *Desnia*—the land of mystery. If they ever made it to the hidden shores at all, it would be because of the Centians...

They handed Thomas the map and he uncreased it, held it up to the light and rotated it so that the indicated corner was oriented upward.

"Why did you do that?" one of the officers asked.

"Because this map maker put an insignia on the lower right

corner that tells me he was religious. So he would have drawn the map to be read with this corner pointing toward the sky to honor Abbath.

"Hmmm, very strange," the first mate said.

Thomas scanned the map. He saw through the many inky lines designed to confuse and distract unwanted eyes. The detailed outlines of the Desnian coast emerged from the chaos of the map.

"Where do we plan to land?" he asked, then winced as soon as he had said it. The predictable response from the Sulian officer cascaded over him.

"It is not for you to ask. Trust your superiors and do your duty, as you are told. We will tell you *what* we want *when* we want, *if* we want. We know more about the sea and this ship than you will ever know!"

Thomas hated being treated as a slave. He seethed with the knowledge that the *Dagger* had been his, even if they called the ship *Enmity* now. The ship had been his before it was ever commandeered by a bunch of Sulians. He had won the ship fairly, and risked his life in doing it! He had walked her decks and allowed his hand to run across every inch of the ship. He knew her canvas and her ropes, and every line from bow to stern. Thomas wished that some enemy would arise to force them to reckon with the gap in their knowledge about the guns and powder. For all their vaunted order and discipline, the Sulians had not mastered the power of thunder and fire the way his people had.

"Ho, yes sir," he replied. "There is one thing you do not know about this ship, that I wish the admiral to know."

"Admiral Yamatsu has already agreed to learn the guns. Matheson will teach us over the next few weeks how to use them," the officer said.

Matheson? That dirty child of a Barselon witch! He never trained with the Earl d'Hayes to learn the trajectories and powder charges of smaller guns. How did he weasel his way into the good graces of the Sulian officers? Thomas thought, bitterly.

"That is not what I was referring to," Thomas said, trying to hide his contempt for the man called Matheson. "I found a woman aboard. She is hiding in the hold."

Suddenly the Sulian officers began to look beyond his shoulder.

They spoke to each other quickly, the Sulian accent making it hard for Thomas to keep up with them. As if she had heard the conversation, Thomas heard footsteps and turned to see the woman named Shīanya walking confidently toward them. The hem of the long crimson gown she wore blew around her ankles as she glided over the wooden deck. Her slender arms and hands were clasped disarmingly behind her narrow waist. and her straight black hair that fell loosely over her shoulders was tied with matching crimson ribbons.

Thomas was wide-eyed. In a matter of minutes, Shīanya had been transformed from a bedraggled stowaway into a creature of grace. The change was complete. He would have had difficulty recognizing her as the disheveled, young woman he'd met a few moments before, if he had not been certain this was the only female aboard.

And then, the strangest thing happened. There was a fervor of excitement among the officers. They looked fearful, and dutiful all at once. And then, after a few moments of stultified shock, the Sulians began to kneel!

"Princess Shīanya!" they said, almost in unison, extending their arms as they pressed their faces to the deck in a deep and reverent bow.

Thomas turned as Shīanya came to a stop. "Princess?!" he said.

Shīanya ignored him, her dark gaze now fixed on the faces of the men. Not all of them were kneeling. The lowliest sailors were still face down on the deck, but the Sulian officers were torn in their reaction to her presence. Some stood in awe, while others looked stricken with fear or anger—their fingers twitching to reach their sword hilts. The Centian sailors who were watching the scene looked surprised, but respectfully tipped their hats to this beautiful woman, and then tucked their thumbs into their wide belts and watched, waiting for the Sulians to take the lead in welcoming her.

"I call upon all of you to help me," Shīanya said in a crisp clear voice to the gathered men.

"Ho, Princess Shīanya," came the reply of the Sulian men who bowed deeply.

Thomas looked up toward the sky and slapped his thigh.

"Unbelievable," Thomas said to himself.

The first mate knelt as the girl, dressed in crimson, approached.

"Why do you kneel to this girl?" the admiral asked. He looked as if he might smite the slight woman to the deck.

"It is Princess Shīanya," the first mate replied, his voice heavy with awe.

"I know who she is, but this is a military vessel, and she was not invited aboard. We are no longer under the power of the Crystal Throne. Her presence here means that we are undone," Admiral Yamastu said.

"I come aboard and leave as I please, Admiral," the girl said, looking him up and down. "And you have very bad manners," Shīanya added. She spoke to Admiral Yamatsu in a proud, preening manner.

"I am the sovereign on this ship! I will not submit to you," Admiral Yamatsu replied, saying the words as the air crackled with his emotion.

"She the daughter of the Emperor Yotem! She has claim on our loyalty," the first mate said, his face finally rising from the deck.

"I do not recognize your family's claim to the Crystal Throne any longer!" Admiral Yamatsu told the young woman..

The first mate shifted his direction, angling himself so that he now was on the side of the girl dressed in red.

"Then we have a problem," Shīanya said softly, "Because the majority of your crew may feel otherwise."

Admiral Yamatsu drew his sword and immediately the whisper of dozens of blades being drawn from scabbards punctuated the tension that rose between the girl and the admiral. Some of the men gathered behind the admiral, whilst many others moved to the side of Shīanya.

"I have the Centians on my side," Admiral Yamatsu said, gesturing to Thomas who stood watching from a few paces to the side.

Thomas held up his open hands. He surveyed the sailors who suddenly had chosen sides in this drama.

"I'd rather not get involved in Sulian domestic disputes. I just thought you all would like to know we had a woman aboard."

"How dare you refer to the princess as a woman! Have you no respect?" the red-faced Sulian shrieked, looking as if he might shed blood at that very moment.

Thomas shook his head slowly.

"So sorry, but she is a woman…if I am not mistaken," Thomas said.

The blade was drawn, but just as quickly Shīanya held up her hand to stop the officer from attacking. Thomas was proud of himself for not drawing his pistols. He wondered if he would have been fast enough. The Sulians were like lightening with a blade, and this one was angry.

"Thomas means no disrespect. In his land the term is not considered crude," Shīanya said, then looked toward the admiral, "That one, however, has very bad manners."

"Yes, Princess," the officer said and turned his attention to his superior.

"We left Sulia to get away from the tyranny of the Emperor. Why would you listen to her now?" Admiral Yamatsu asked.

"I left because I had no other choice. Now we have a chance to demonstrate our loyalty to the daughter of the Dragon House. We could be forgiven for our disobedience. We could return home!"

"Fool! There is no chance we will be welcomed home again. And we only have enough supplies to go onward to Desnia, not back to the Old World," the admiral said.

"If we show her that we are loyal—"

"She is not even permitted to be on our ship. If I had known she was aboard, I would have thrown her into the bay of Guingolas we left!"

"My family has need of your small flotilla. You should submit before it is too late, Admiral" Shīanya said.

"Never!" Yamatsu shouted and the men most loyal to him cried out in support.

Each side advanced and the Sulian melee began. Thomas was forced to draw his cutlass and one of his pistols.

"Curse the tides!" Thomas swore, and pointed his pistol at the chest of an enraged Sulian swordsman. He fired before he even got a chance to make certain what side the man was on, and watched the smoke belch from the barrel of his pistol. He saw the man fall, dropping his blade and clutching his wound. Thomas climbed to the upper deck, joining some of his countrymen there.

"What in the name of the Southern Sea Witch happened?" a Centian sailor yelled when he caught Thomas' eye. He was trying to make sense of the bloodshed.

"The young woman is Sulian royalty and half the crew is willing to die for her. The other half wants to feed her to the sharks," Thomas explained.

"Amazing," the sailor replied. "These Sulians are out of their minds. We're almost to Desnia aren't we? I wish we'd never agreed to join them. "

"If we had a better way out of Sulia, we would have taken it," Thomas replied, shaking his head at the new development.

He looked down and saw the group of men fighting to

defend the young woman dressed in red. Their circle widened about them. The defenders fought with more zeal than the attackers, who seemed to waver as the fighting moved deeper into their ranks. The attackers began to break ranks and run to the end of the ship where they formed a new battle line. They stood shoulder to shoulder as Admiral Yamatsu shouted commands.

"Either way this goes, it isn't looking good for us," another of the Centian sailor observed. He crossed his burly arms and worked a toothpick between his yellow teeth.

A separation opened up between the two sides and it appeared as if the attackers might now become the defenders. They stood bravely at one end of the ship now, their sides heaving from the exertion.

Men lay dead or dying. Some of them called out in the relative calm. Others lay still, their blood staining the gleaming deck.

"I just scrubbed that deck," Thomas said quietly, shaking his head, but not wanting to draw too much attention them.

The young woman called out to her defenders.

"Stop!" she commanded in a loud voice.

The men stopped advancing, and those sailors with Admiral Yamatsu held their ground. "She will bring ruin on all of us, including our families!" the admiral shouted, pointing to the sting of vessels that followed them."

"My father does not know that I am with you. I ran away from him," Shīanya said.

"He will be searching for you. Will the emperor of the Crystal Throne not move the land and sea to get his daughter back? Would he not send dragons to retrieve his beloved child? Why are you fleeing from him? We wanted peace. We wanted a new start. Your selfish act of sneaking aboard our vessel has given us a death sentence from the empire."

The men on both sides of the conflict looked at each other, listening to the words between the admiral and the girl.

"If your father did not send you, why are you here?" Admiral Yamatsu asked.

"I will not be forced to marry the Dorgund!"

The men closest to her clinched their spears all the tighter in response to her emotion.

"If you are truly the Dragon Princess, why did you need to ride on a boat?"

"Who is the Dorgund?" a sailor whispered to Thomas.

"He's the emperor's right arm. He is a prince from one of the kingdoms of Sulia. A cunning fighter and power-hungry as the rest of them. No surprise he was the one chosen to marry the princess. I don't blame her for running though. I wouldn't want to marry the Dorgund either. We met once and it didn't go so well for me. He's a bad man," Thomas said, rubbing an old wound on his torso.

The Centian sailor looked at Thomas in some amusement.

"And what are you Dagger?" he asked.

"I'm a man of principle," he said. "I just don't like it when people stand in my way."

The sailor laughed and Thomas watched the back and forth between the Sulians. He measured the eyes of the men. They were divided in this exchange. Many of them were uncertain what to do next.

"Sulians!" Thomas yelled from above. All eyes turned to him.

He grabbed the rail in front of him and vaulted over it, landing on the deck that ran just above the scene of battle.

"We are almost to Desnia. We can never hope to run from the Dorgund on the open sea if he decides to follow us here. Look at your family-ships that follow us. They rely on us to lead them," he said.

A trail of ships spread out behind the *Dagger*. Most were vessels of Sulian design. The family ships that followed plowed through the waves in the distance.

"We do not know what enemies we will face. The earliest

reports say the Desnians are weak, and divided, but they will fight us. We will need every man we have to carve out a place for ourselves on that wild continent."

Thomas saw some of the men relax as they thought of a common enemy instead of fighting each other.

"Look to the west. There is our enemy, not those who share this ship! I honor Admiral Yamatsu, and I will respect Princess Shīanya, but let us arrive on the shores of Desnia with some fighting spirit left in our bellies. If we slake our thirst for blood and treasure amongst each other what will we have left when we need it to fight the Desnians?"

"You speak the truth, Centian," Shīanya replied.

Admiral Yamatsu nodded his agreement too.

"We must share leadership," Thomas insisted, striking while their resistance was soft.

"A three-way sharing arrangement?" Shīanya said.

Thomas realized she was including him in the factions of leadership.

"Why, yes!" Dagger replied, raising his chin.

Admiral Yamatsu frowned, but looked at the trail of ship that followed the flagship. A slight crease of worry seemed to grow across his brow. Was he thinking of loved ones, or the possibility that the Dorgund of Sulia was in pursuit.

"I accept," he finally said.

There was a general release of the tension that had twisted the air of the ship.

"As do, I," Thomas said, smiling and placing his hand on the polished wooden handle of his pistol. He was one step closer to regaining his rightful position.

17

PURGING THE TYATHIAN NOBILITY

"This is good," Lord Balfoest muttered aloud as he perused the list of noble families that had pledged their allegiance.

"The list is growing," Pilus Dol Lassimer said, seated next to him on the long silk couch, and let out a breath of satisfaction.

"You're hungry, Pilus. Do go and get something to eat. You need to maintain your strength," Lord Balfoest said without raising his eyes from the list.

Pilus nodded and beckoned a servant bring him the platter of refreshments. Among the breads and olives were a few crackers and some cheese. He had the servant place a thin slice of meat on it as well, then snatched it out of his hand and brought it to his mouth.

Lars Balfoest, looking up now, watched him, then leaned over and placed a hand on his shoulder. The man was muscular like his father had been, but more slim of build. He had a shock of straight dark brown hair, almost black in color. And while the sides of his head were usually shaved tight, it was apparent that Pilus had not visited the barber for some time, for it had grown out. The flow of emotion that Lars Balfoest felt as he touched Pilus was much more precise than if he was just reading his expressions—even if he had mastered that skill long ago, too. But in that manner, subtle but telling nuances were often lost—whereas, through contact, he was always and unfailingly attuned to his *subject*.

Subject... Lars had always told to himself not think of them as *prey*. For one day someone would feel what he did in return, and then he would have to manage it. *Subject* was a better word—less threatening, and more distant.

Pilus looked up at him and stopped chewing, for some awkward seconds had passed as the Steward had mused on these thoughts. "Were you going to say something?" he asked, his mouth full.

Lars Balfoest's subject felt hungry, and hopeful beneath his touch. The Steward had to admit, he felt hopeful too, and he lifted his hand. "I sent the request to Adisfall," he replied finally.

"So you think it is time?"

"They accepted our second shipment and the third. I think they are ready to acquiesce. The Northmen will need time to gather and make their way south, but they have already sent a small force. I sent the Northmen to deal with House Sarkkand who, I'm told, denied that they knew where Dallin had gone. So I ordered our new allies to do some *convincing* of the Lord and Lady of the house."

Pilus grinned at the thought.

Lars Balfoest went on, "I'd prefer they be here within the walls of Tyath when the fighting begins, rather than trusting them to flank the enemy. They will fight better when they have more blood in the game—so to speak."

Pilus chewed, considering the words, then asked, "You are sure they will respond?"

Lord Balfoest nodded. "Adisfall will respond," he answered confidently.

"I wonder what my father would have to say about inviting Northmen into the Golden City," Pilus mused, then he grinned. "I know just what he'd say, 'The barbarians to the north are no better than those Delathranes to the West!' Then he'd give me a three-hour-long, boring lecture on the history of the first settlements in Desnia."

Lars smiled. "He had no problem with your half-brother being promised to a daughter of the Northmen bloodline? Candoreth was settled by a branch of that family, you know."

Pilus made face of disgust. "I know," he said bitterly. "It seems Tyath is the only remnant of culture left in this world."

Lars Balfoest rocked back a little in his seat. "Yes, that's always been the problem. The Northmen of Adisfall have always promoted their own distinct culture, often holding it above all others," he said, choosing his words carefully.

"They have dragon-ships. That's it," Pilus said.

The door opened and Jason Dol Lassimer marched into the private study. He, too, carried the strong features of Kade Dol Lassimer. But his hair, though just as dark as his brother's, was curly, and tumbled and bounced over the high collar of his dark naval jacket.

"Dragon ships? Who's got them?" he repeated, striding across the room to join Pilus and Lars on the couch.

"Lord Balfoest was just telling me the Northmen have been invited into Tyath."

Jason raised his eyebrows and scratched one side of his head. Lars could tell he was concerned about the arrival of the ships from Adisfall. He didn't blame him. He would be, too, if he were a naval man. "They can help us, but the attack will be from the land. Delathranes don't sail."

"I keep waiting to hear the Straits of Windstall are crowded with pirate ships from the east. So far, they have remained in the warmer waters to the south. I think they want an easy target."

"Then Candoreth it is," Jason said. "I just want to make sure we come out on top at the end of this."

"Adsifall will swear fealty to the throne."

"You mean to you?"

Balfoest allowed the question to pass without addressing it directly. "If they become a vassal state to Tyath, we will have advantages that should make us irresistible to the remaining kingdoms," he explained.

"A united Desnia," Pilus said, nodding his approval. "We can do it."

Lars Balfoest turned the paper over—the list continued.

Pilus gestured at the list. "Those on the back are the noble families we need to eliminate. They can't be trusted," he explained, as he placed another stack of crackers, meat and cheese on his tongue and spoke in between mouthfuls.

"I'm proud of both of you," Balfoest said and reached out to the brothers on the back. As he did so, he could discern that Pilus was fully committed. He was not bluffing. The disloyal families would be eliminated. Jason, on the other hand, still held an edge that resisted the *Empathy* Lars infused into his touch. There was still a ball of resistance, however small, in the recesses of Jason's heart and mind. Lars Balfoest would be patient, for he was always patient when time allowed. This eldest of Kade Dol Lassimer's sons was a lot like his father. He would require a little more coaxing and that was fine—Lars rather enjoyed the challenge.

A dog that is easily trained has its place, but some of the most spirited beasts are also the most rewarding to bring to the leash, thought Lars, with a slight grin.

"We will take action, without delay. Send the new squads of imperial guards to round them up the disloyal," Lars said.

Pilus raised a finger. "Unfortunately, Lord Balfoest, most of them are holed up at the Stellat estate. I think some of the old guards joined them when they were disbanded—something about the old oaths, they said," Pilus reported, and then adjusted a pillow to support this lower back as he fell deeper into the couch.

Jason—sat more upright—appearing to be thinking a great deal about this intelligence, and scratched his chin. "I can't help you if their defenses are at Lord Stellat's keep. I'm happy to ensure they do not escape by sea, but the distance is too far inland for me to round them up."

"I know," Lord Balfoest replied, but looked at Jason, seeking to find any hint of disloyalty in the naval officer. He saw none but wished he could touch Jason's skin, without it being strange to the young man. That way, he would know for sure.

Lars reached out to place his hand on Jason's arm. He tried to do it in a nonchalant manner, but Jason drew back and looked at the Steward with an unsure expression, his brow furrowed deep.

"Why are you always touching us, Lars?" Jason asked.

"Well, for one I enjoy being close to people," Lars replied innocently, his skinny, skeletal arms retracting like the pincers of a praying mantis.

"And yet you don't seem to love any of them," Jason replied suspiciously. He kept looking at him, and for a moment it made Lars feel uncomfortable, like he wanted to lash-out quickly with a stabbing strike to the younger man's eye or throat. It was very rare for the Steward to ever feel like this, to ever feel so unbalanced under another's gaze.

Too bad I still need him, thought Lars bitterly.

"Don't ever touch me again. I don't like it," Jason said, a seriousness entering his tone that Lars had not noticed before.

Pilus started to laugh. "It's true, Jason always hates it when people touch him. He wouldn't even allow our mother to give him a hug most days."

"Indeed. Perhaps he is a bit sensitive this morning, I think," Lars added.

Jason stood and turned to his brother. "Don't speak of Mother while we are making plans to destroy the people who were loyal to her. Her memory deserves better of us."

Pilus raised his hands, palms spread and turned his head to the side. "At ease, brother. We just need them to be loyal to us, not our dead parents."

Jason fumed. His icy stare flicked between his brother and Lord Balfoest and, without responding, he turned and marched out of the room the way he had come.

"Can we count on him?" Lars Balfoest asked.

"We attended a service at the infirmary. It was supposed to be nothing more than a short, official appearance, but they gave a tribute to our mother and I think it has affected his judgment temporarily—got him thinking of what she would want of us," Pilus sighed, then said, "All very sentimental and, as I say, temporary. He will be fine."

But Lars Balfoest was not so sure. "It is hard for a child to lose his mother," he observed, but did not share his distrust.

"I don't remember her all that much," Pilus shrugged. "Rema became more of a mother to me, after Father remarried." He reached down for the flask at his feet and took a swig.

"Drinking again?" Lars asked.

"All this talk of Mother," Pilus said, and waved a hand to dismiss the question.

"She would be proud of you," Balfoest added, and Pilus leveled his brown eyes at the Steward without blinking, as he recalled the memories of the woman who had loved him most.

"I'm not so sure," he replied coldly, and took another swig.

18

DALLIN RETURNS

Only the night watch seemed to be awake at the sprawling Stellat Estate, but Dallin was leaving.

"Eldin, I have to go back. I must tell my parents of the danger they're in," Dallin said as he rushed to saddle the black stallion.

"I'm worried about you, my friend," Eldin replied, as he watched Dallin prepare the horse and place the bridle in its mouth.

Dallin looked up at him. "I don't think I have any other option."

Eldin flared his nostrils, took a deep breath, and nodded. "Very well. But be careful. The road is swarming with Lord Balfoest's minions. If they catch you, I would not like to think of what they would do."

"Why? Do you suppose I'd be treated as bad as Heathron and Kathleen?"

"At least that bad," Eldin replied, arching his eyebrows with caution.

"I'll ride quickly and return as soon as I can. I know I can't stay at home."

Eldin nodded. "I wish you safety on the road. We'll leave the back gate open. You know how to get in."

"Thank you. You have been a good friend, Eldin."

"Hurry along now," Eldin ordered. "We need you back here."

Dallin's eyes were suddenly drawn to a window high overhead. He could tell immediately that the silhouette in the soft orange glow belonged to that of Hannah Aviella. As she waved from the window, others joined her: Michael Carnado and some of the other loyalists who had joined the company at the estate of Lord and Lady Stellat.

Eldin gave his last word as Dallin guided the stallion out of the stables and into the clearing lit by the bright half-moon. "Ride hard and fast, Dallin. I fear Balfoest's wrath is soon upon us."

Dallin covered the distance in half the time that it had taken him on the way there. Speed was of the essence, and when he finally saw the gates of his home rising in the distance, he tapped his heels into the sides of the horse, encouraging Steed to go even faster. He never ceased to thrill at the feeling of being linked with this animal. The Tamer's bond made horseback riding all the more exquisite. He could feel and understand what the horse was feeling as they rode together, and never had Dallin seemed more at one with anything than he was with this animal—even himself. But the closer he got to home, the more a growing knot of doubt and concern tightened in his stomach. The gates were open and when he rode in, he saw that hordes of soldiers were lounging around the front portico. The front door was open, too, where a stick had been jammed to hold it. And as he approached, the men with long-braided hair, fair skin and cheeks that seemed chapped by the wind, stirred and rose from their haunches, throwing aside their flasks and bottles as if making to draw their swords.

Northmen?

Dallin brought Steed to a stop and dismounted uneasily. "What is going on here?" he said, his voice thick with anxiety.

"We were given this place to live. We've had a long voyage

from Addisfall and this is where we plan to rest and recuperate," one of the men said. It was only now that Dallin realized he had risen from a chair that was usually to be found in his mother's study.

"Where are my mother and father?" Dallin asked. The man hiccuped from the ale in his flagon, and shrugged his shoulders, gesturing toward the door.

Not delaying a second longer, Dallin ran through the doorway, calling out for his father. He made his way to the kitchen and from there to the living room. He ran down the hall calling, "Mother! Father!" but no one answered.

The men had tracked muddy bootprints onto the rugs. They had spilled wine on one of the tapestries that decorated the library. Dallin could hear more of them laughing down the hall, a medley of many voices. Lines of more men came walking by, stinking of ale, their packs slung haphazardly over their shoulders. He could hear one of them calling to the others, "Down here. I found they've got a cellar full of it. Bring up the bottles."

They must have found the wine cellar, Dallin thought.

"Where are my parents?" he said aloud as he ran to the courtyard, his calls echoing off the walls. His heart leapt when he finally recognized one of his mother's maids.

"Where are my mother and father?" he demanded.

The girl looked at Dallin, her lip quivering. She was hesitant to answer.

"Where are my mother and father?" Dallin insisted. "I will not ask again!"

He grabbed her by the shoulders and shook her. The maid made an involuntary cry of protest, and then extended a trembling finger across the courtyard and to the gate that led to the orchard beyond. A chill ran down Dallin's spine. He didn't want to go. He didn't want to see what he feared, and yet he placed one foot in front of the other. When he reached the heavy wooden gate that led from the central courtyard to the orchard behind his home, he opened it. The gate whined as it swung open, and there, he saw how many of the trees had been chopped down. Axes shining in the moonlight laid idle at their stumps. The last of the blossoms from some of the trees still clung to the strewn scattered branches. And as he advanced his feet kicked through unripe fruit that had begun to swell on some of them.

Two of the largest trees remained standing. Dallin looked up, and there they were... He recognized his mother first, the way her hands hung lifelessly at her sides. The way her head was tilted, as if in the process of straining to look down at her feet, which were barefoot and muddy. And then his eyes, moist now, drifted to the form of his father, only heavier somehow. So heavy he couldn't understand how the rope from which he swung hadn't snapped the bending bough above.

Dallin ran first to his mother. He wrapped his arms around her and despite his desire to lift her up, to somehow allow her to breathe, he felt the rigidity and the coldness. He sobbed and the maid came to stand beside him. "I'm sorry, Lord Sarkkand," the girl said, "There was nothing I could do."

Dallin looked at the maid. "Bring the ladder. We're going to cut her down." The girl obeyed, bringing a wooden ladder and setting it up beside the tree.

The maid scaled the ladder and used the small knife to cut the rope. The weight of his mother fell into Dallin's arms, and the weight of his loss settled upon him. Dallin collapsed to his knees, not because he couldn't hold the body of his mother, but because he could not stand the grief poured over him. He lay her in the grass. The maid brought the ladder to his father. The man was big, larger than Dallin, but the grief and determination gave him strength so that when the rope was cut, Dallin was also able to lower his father to the ground gently beside his mother.

They lay in the grass. Their faces were ashen. The rope bit deep into their necks behind their jaw. Dallin worked his fingers in the loop. He would not have them desecrated by the rope. He cut the ropes loose and arranged their clothing so that it settled gently over their bodies. He stood and looked down at them, his nostrils flaring, his lips pursed, his lips creased in tension. A quivering frown twitched at the right corner of his chin. Dallin felt his hand clenching the hilt of his sword. He knelt before his parents and laid his hand on each of them. "I promise you, Mother and Father, justice will be served on your behalf. I promise you," he repeated again.

"What shall I do?" the girl asked, laying a hand on the shoulder of the young man who was now master of the estate. Dallin turned to her, "I can't stay here, but I would have them buried or at least covered." The maid nodded. The walls of the orchard were stacked stone, and Dallin began to grab one stone off of the wall. And the maid helped. Dallin carried them one by one and stacked them around his mother and father and then on top. After a time, they were completely covered. Dallin turned and asked for help ion gathering branches of the trees to be piled together as well.

He ignored the sound of the men singing in his home. It was a song he was not familiar with, probably a song made for the drinking halls in the cold North of Addisfall, but as the fire took hold of the wood and the flames reached up as the sunlight began to fade, Dallin saw the sparks rising towards the heavens and hoped that the souls of his mother and father were rising as well. Perhaps they were winging their way to the halls of Abboth, where they would find peace and rest. He knew there would be no peace for him, nor rest. His life would be devoted not only to the city and the empire that he loved, but to the good that he could establish to carry on what his parents had left him and to defend what was good and true. He knew he needed to hide, but not forever.

"Shall I stay her to watch over them," the maid offered. He shook his head. She was a pretty young woman and probably had already suffered greatly at the hands of the Northmen. She had every reason to runs and yet offered her devotion to his family.

She must be of the olden type—servants who took the oath to serve, and meant it. There was every reason for her to run. She had every reason to fear. Her life was just beginning. "I appreciate that," Dallin said. "But I cannot leave you here. You will go with me. My mother would have wanted that." He heard glass breaking and another loud laugh from within the house. The maid winced, knowing that the sound of destruction was painful to Dallin, not because of broken material things, but because of what it represented and the loss of the sanctity of his home.

"What is your name?" Dallin asked.

"I am Thema," she said.

"Thank you again for serving my family, and … for helping me to bury my parents."

The maid nodded, "It's been my pleasure, and my duty to serve them."

"Yes," Dallin replied, "we all have our duty." He motioned for the girl to join him as he walked back to Steed. The horse was quietly grazing at the corner of the orchard. The flames of the firelight illuminated the walls, and the shadow that was the dark horse remained hidden.

Dallin led Thema and Steed to the orchard gate in the distant wall. The horse shook his head and blew out his breath through his nose. The dark, intelligent eyes looked at his own and blinked. Dallin patted his neck and lifted the maid onto the horse's back. Then he put a boot in the stirrup, swinging his other leg over to settle into the saddle. "We head back south, Steed. We're going to ride all night." The horse always seemed ready to ride. He blew another breath out of his nose and picked up the pace as they rode down the long drive away from House Sarkkand.

19

SIGNS OF AFFECTION

Despite her best efforts Kathleen found herself on the deck, taking in the fresh air. She told herself Kath she did not intend to be close to Jared. She just needed fresh air and sunshine on her face. Still, her glances turned more and more often to the Sīhalt Guardian, whose rugged appearance kept drawing her eye. He no longer had the youthful look that Heathron and Seth still shared, it was true. Jared was aged, but the decade and a half he had lost from the Healing had not harmed the picture he made against the backdrop of the Emerald Coast. Kathleen watched as Jared's fingers danced. The day was calm and the deck rocked gently as the *Marine Escape* lay protected in the natural harbor. Seth replied to his brother's sign language with swift movements of his hands.

"I saw what you said," Lilly said, watching. The cream-colored dress she wore contrasted with her shiny black hair.

Seth looked at her, disbelieving. "Surely you are not familiar with our hand-talk."

"We were making the plans for the day—to get food and make some repairs before we continue our journey," Jared replied.

"I know some of the sign language used by the Sīhalts, yes," she said, her lips curving with a hint of smugness.

Kathleen, watching on, thought she could see Seth blush faintly.

What were they saying? Kathleen wondered.

"I don't believe you," Seth said, but the color in his cheeks made him look as if he did believe her, very much. Surely they were discussing more than hunting for food.

Had they been speaking with their hands in a way that perhaps he did not want Lilly to see?

"Prove it," Jared said in a friendly tone.

Lilly held her hands up in front of her, not at all trying to be discreet with the movements. She concentrated and worked her hands in broad strokes. "I'm trying to remember if this is the exact way to do it," she said, concentrating.

"It's true. The lady does know how to sign," Jared confirmed after watching for just a moment. When Lilly was finished, Seth blushed even more furiously.

"I saw it, too," Lilly said to Jared.

He raised his eyebrows in surprise. "Oh really?"

Kathleen couldn't stand it anymore. She made her way closer to Lilly and the Guardians.

"Lilly, I'm dying to know what you signed."

"Ask *him*—he's the one who doubted me," she said, leveling her eyes at Jared.

Kathleen looked at the Sīhalt Guardian. "Lord Sīhalt, what did Lilly say with the hand-talking that has made your brother so uncomfortable?" she asked primly.

"Lady Lilly signed a message that said something to the effect that 'she liked the compliment and would return the favor' if I understood her correctly," Jared said.

"Oh? What was the compliment?" Kathleen asked.

Jared looked at Seth, not wanting to answer her. "I'll allow my brother to answer that question. The sign language is not always accurately translated into speech. There can be multiple meanings with any given set of movements."

Seth looked at Jared. His expression was one of a puppy caught stealing from the table. He blushed a deep red on his neck and cheeks, visible despite his tanned skin.

"He said I looked nice in this dress," Lilly replied, seeking to save Seth from further embarrassment.

"That's not all he said," Maxwell added. His skinny frame hung from the rigging above them. Kathleen had forgotten the Shifter was up there.

"Maxwell, don't you dare..." Seth began.

"He said he likes the way the white dress clings to Lilly's body and that she looks way better in it than the blonde girl ever would have."

Seth shook his head. "I can't believe you," he said.

Maxwell smiled in return.

"By 'blonde girl', I suppose he means Jessica Turlin? That is quite a compliment. She is very shapely," Kathleen said.

Now Lilly blushed, turning her eyes aside.

"And Jared's response was just as interesting," Maxwell said.

"You can stop there," Jared said, immediately looking up at Maxwell.

The Shifter turned his head to one side and examined Jared as if he was in his eagle form.

"Jared doesn't want you to know what he said."

"Well, if Seth's secret language is going to be revealed to the world, wouldn't it be unfair to allow his brother to get away, unscathed?" Kathleen suggested.

"That's what I say!" Maxwell agreed.

Jared warned the Shifter. "I will climb that rigging and teach you a lesson,"

"You know I can just fly away if you come after me," Maxwell replied with a snort that threatened to turn into full laughter.

"What did Jared say in return?" Kathleen asked.

"He said Lilly looked like a Sīhalt bride in that dress."

"That is sweet of you, Lord Sīhalt," Lilly said, choosing not to make a big deal of any meaning behind the compliment.

Kathleen felt disappointed. She wanted more. She nodded in agreeable understanding.

"And…" Maxwell said dramatically.

This time Jared didn't try to stop him. Instead he pursed his lips, cocked his head and waited for Maxwell to spill the secret.

"Go on," Kathleen prodded.

"Jared said, as beautiful as Lilly is, she does not compare to how beautiful you were when dressed as his bride in the wilderness. He said you were like an angel descended from the heavens."

Kathleen looked at Jared and the Sīhalt Guardian surrendered to the truth. His eyes met hers, nothing guarded or restrained in his expression. He was like a child resigned to the truth of his desires and it touched Kathleen's heart. The excitement of holding his gaze passed through her, and she began to feel her body responding.

"Then he said your butt looked better in your dress, too," Maxwell added.

Both women turned to Jared, aghast at the comment.

The Sīhalt raised his hands in defense. "That, I did *not* say!" he exclaimed.

Maxwell's laughter from the rigging above was the only thing that kept Jared from enduring a torrent of indignation.

"He didn't say that," Seth said in defense of his brother.

"Clearly, we need to learn more of this sign language," Kathleen said, folding her arms.

"We would be happy to teach you, if time allows" Jared offered in an attempt to smooth the discomfort brought on by Maxwell's revelations.

"Lilly and I accept the invitation. Perhaps, we could begin tomorrow," Kathleen said, wrapping her arms around Lilly's. The guardswoman nodded, looking especially pleased as they made their way further down the deck.

20

IWYWM

The next day, Jared stood along the rail of the ship. The wind made his cloak ripple and dance. Captain Channing Dur Ruston stood with a wide stance at the helm, piloting the *Marine Escape* southward. Watching him, it was as if the man from Marth seemed to be gaining energy as they sailed closer to his homeland. He seemed to stand straighter. His eyes shone with excitement. His muscles tensed with longing.

Jared wondered if he would ever feel that way about a place. He wondered just where it might be that he would come to make his home. The Windstall Hermitage, perhaps? It had been his place of training, the place he had felt most comfortable. It had also been the place which had molded the boy into the man he had become—even if his place of birth was deep within the realm of Adisfall.

Will I ever call a place my home? he wondered to himself then. *Will I ever find a place to plant a garden or raise a child?*

As the words repeated themselves in his mind, his thoughts turned his gaze to Kathleen. He saw her walking on the foredeck of the vessel, her hair shining around her heart-shaped face. She looked like she belonged there: an ornament herself of the ship's prow, sculpted in beauty.

Jared walked up behind her quietly, and placed his hands on the rail to her right and leaned toward her.

"I've missed you," he told her. "I can tell you have been avoiding me."

Her hair was just an inch from his nose now, and he could smell the freshness of her scent.

Kathleen didn't turn around

"I've missed you, too," she replied, adjusting her balance a little, so that her body made contact with his. "Will you really teach me the Sīhalt hand language?" she asked.

Jared considered this, and returned her question with a question.

"Why do you want to know?"

"Well, it could be helpful to communicate more..." she hesitated and looked around before saying, "...silently."

He stiffened a little, his eyes widening as much as hers, which were looking through her lashes suggestively.

Jared looked around and saw only Channing watching them. The captain tipped his hat, and inclined his head in acknowledgment of their privacy. As Channing's liege, Kathleen had his unending loyalty.

Jared nodded to the captain in return.

"There are feelings in my heart I dare not vocalize. Can you show me how to say them in another way?"

Jared understood. There were things he wanted to say to Kathleen, too, but had held his tongue because of the company they kept. If she could hear his thoughts, through the silent movement of his hands!

He stood facing her now, leaning against the railing to brace himself as the yacht sailed onward, rolling though the waves.

"The best way to teach you would be to show you. You'll need to learn all the symbols for all the sounds. Then you can learn your letters and numbers. After that, whole words and ideas can be combined to speak in the hand language."

"Show me," she said, holding her elegant hands out to him.

"Sing with me and mimic the movements I make," Jared said with a smile.

He began to sing a nursey rhyme—a common song that children used when first learning to read and write. Jared moved his hands slowly in the graceful movements of the Sīhalt signs. Kathleen tried to follow him. Her movements were not as practiced, but they were still graceful. She laughed at her inability to follow, despite how slow ly they were singing and reached out to touch his hand in resignation. Jared caught her hand in his and lifted it to his lips. He kissed her hand between the knuckles of her first and second finger. He raised his eyes to hers as her singing trailed off.

Jared continued the words of the song.

'Next time won't you sing with me?'

"Did I get that right?" she asked.

"The K is made like this," he demonstrated, "And a J is more like this," he said as he turned his hands and fingers.

"It will be good when I don't have to spell everything out."

She made the letters to her name K-A-T-H-L-E-E-N

"Well done," Jared said, with a smile. "We don't spell out every word. Sometimes we just abbreviate. Once you gain more skill, you will be able to do it with motions and gestures. Your facial expressions can be very important to communicate nonverbally too. It is all about context and the situation for the communication. Abbreviations can be fun to work out, too."

"I'll practice with you during the day and then I'll quiz you each evening to see what you were able to learn."

"All right, give me my first homework lesson," Kathleen said.

Jared thought for a moment, then moved his hand, making letters from the alphabet.

"I-W-Y-W-M," she repeated aloud, and looked up at him.

"Very good."

"That isn't a word. What does it mean?" she asked.

"Think about it today, and at supper, you can tell me what *you* think it means."

Kathleen wrinkled her nose. "I do like mysteries," she said.

"What are you doing?" Heathron said, reaching the top step to the foredeck. His eyes flicked from Jared to Kathleen as he approached. Jared saw a flicker of jealousy in Heathron's eyes.

"Jared was just giving me a lesson in the Sīhalt hand language," Kathleen explained.

"Hmmm, I supposed that is good to know," Heathron replied.

"Let me know if you figure it out," Jared said and excused himself.

～

Heathron watched Jared go and then turned back to Kathleen.

"He is still in love with you," Heathron said. "But, I suppose you knew that."

"Jared is honorable," Kathleen said. "He respects my wishes."

Heathron met her gaze and searched her eyes.

"He will respect your wishes, Kathleen. That I do believe," Heathron said.

She swallowed, not wanting to look away for fear that he might see it as a lack of confidence. "We will be in Candoreth soon. This ship is beginning to feel entirely too small," Heathron added as he encircled Kathleen's waist with his arms.

Captain Channing tipped his hat to the prince when they looked toward him.

"Yes, I am ready to be back home, too," Kathleen said.

～

K athleen spent all day considering what the hand-talk abbreviation could mean.

I-W-Y-W-M

It could mean anything.

She thought that she might ask Lilly or Larissa for help to interpret the message, but in the end, Kathleen decided to keep it to herself.

She sensed that Jared wanted it that way. She thought the message might be intimate to them, and she had to admit that the prospect of having a secret message from Jared made her feel a tingle of excitement.

All throughout the day, she considered what the letters represented. She and Lilly practiced all the numbers and the letters of the alphabet. They passed them off with Seth and Maxwell smiled in approval at the progress they made.

"Well done, Princess," he said, "It took me a lot longer to learn. Of course, I was younger then. Now it's second nature to me."

Kathleen smiled but her thoughts remained with the letters Jared had given her—

I could stand for "I"

W could stand for will or won't or even want

Y could stand for you or yell or yank. Not yank, certainly he wouldn't use that word.

W could stand for won't, were, or willing

M could stand for mother, Maxwell, or mine.

She ran the words through her mind arranging them one after the other trying to decide what the Sīhalt Guardian could possibly desire to express with his encoded message.

I will yell... I want you... Kathleen took a breath.

Kathleen worked through the possibilities of the letters.

As evening came, the friends shared a meal. Melva did the cooking, and it smelled excellent.

"This is the last of the Turlin food. Since we're near the forest,

I thought we should resupply by gathering what we can over the next few days," Melva said.

"I hope Candoreth will have plenty when we arrive. I can't wait," Kathleen said, as she passed the food to Seth.

"I am sure Sundiland is doing better this year," Heathron replied. "I can't wait to get there and meet your family."

Kathleen looked at her own hands, realizing that she had been repeating the dance Jared had made with his fingers:

IWYWM, IWYWM, IWYWM...

The sun was warm on her face, and she wanted to be alone with her thoughts. She looked out at the endless sea.

IWYWM—her fingers moved gracefully as she thought.

Jared had not changed, after all. Yes, he was older, but was she not also older?

The ease with which he left her alone in the Golden City had hurt. She had tried to understand.

Kathleen wasn't sure what to do with the powerful emotions she felt for Jared. She half expected her attraction to him to disappear in the months he was gone. She had been able to tell herself that he would not come back until Midsummer. The days spent with Heathron allowed her to glimpse what life would be like at his side. If so much tragedy had not befallen them, to be Heathron's wife would a good life—a happy and peaceful one. Kathleen saw herself growing old with Heathron. Before their capture, the dream of building a life and a family with the prince seemed so possible.

So why did she feel a tingle up her spine when Jared walked close to her?

"Will I ever resolve this?" Kathleen wondered aloud.

What would Melva say? she wondered.

Kathleen saw the old woman sitting, busying her fingers by carving a small, round wooden bead. She held it up to the sunlight and blew a breath of air across the surface to remove the bits of wood that she had trimmed with her knife. Melva smiled in a self-satisfied way and began to untie a string she wore around her neck.

"Making a new necklace?" Kathleen asked as she approached.

"A proper Healer shouldn't be without her beads. They took mine from me in Tyath, but I'll just make more," she said.

Kathleen watched her work deftly, despite her age.

"If you keep your hands moving, they won't stop working. You've got to keep moving," the Healer explained.

Melva held up her wrinkled, brown hands. Her fingers were twisted by age and use. Although they were no longer straight, she moved them, flexing them as she opened and closed her hands.

"If only my eyes worked the same way!" Melva added humorously.

Kathleen offered a hand. "Let me help you." She took the wooden bead and threaded the hemp string through it, pulling the bead onto the line.

Melva's eyebrows arched slightly, and her face seemed to brighten and warm. "Your eyes are much better than mine. That would have taken me forever," she said.

"I'm not so sure I can see better than you. When it comes to people, you read them better than most."

The old woman nodded warmly. "What's on your mind?"

Kathleen thought about dismissing the question and smiling as she normally did. But instead she felt her shoulders sink involuntarily, and she sighed and saw in an instant that it was impossible to hide what she was feeling. So instead, she nodded to herself, looked around, and then said—"Melva, which is the stronger kind of love—is it this carnal passion and pull that I feel in my desire to be close to Jared? Or is it the honorable and dutiful love that I feel toward Heathron?"

"Do you feel respect for the Sīhalt Guardian?" the old woman said.

"I do respect him… but in some ways I fear him, too. Not that he would harm me… but he is wild in a way that can be dangerous, I think."

"You mean he is untamed?"

"Yes, but he *is* a gentleman."

"With a man like Jared, you must be willing to except his strength and forceful nature. He has a spirit that can be kind, but friendliness is a veneer for him. Caring he may be, but the howling wolf lies at the core of his being," Melva said.

"So why would I want to run to the forest when I hear the cry of the wolf? Shouldn't my desire be to stay indoors, by the hearth, where it is safe?" Kathleen asked.

Melva looked at the Princess of Candoreth, and raised one of her hands to Kathleen's cheek. "That, my child, depends on whether or not you, too, are a wolf."

The comment made her stop and although the old Healer continued her work, carving another bead, Kathleen was grateful that Melva did not see the look of fear in her eyes.

Like a lamb, I have always tried to do what others wanted of me, but maybe I am a wolf.

The thought made her spine tingle, and she shivered it away.

21

PART OF THE BARGAIN

"You seem so divided," Heathron remarked. "One moment you are on my arm walking peacefully on the deck as if we were strolling the gardens in Tyath. The next moment I see you look at him with what I try not to see as longing. It is difficult for me," Heathron said.

It was true. In her heart, Kathleen knew that what the prince noticed had merit. She did feel divided. Melva's words had caused her to consider her true feelings even more deeply the past few days. She did not like to think of herself as a 'wolf'. It was very strange of Melva to use such a way to describe her situation.

"These are difficult times," Kathleen said, placing a hand on Heathron's, trying to show him how much she cared.

Kathleen felt her passion for Jared working its way deeper and deeper into her heart. It was like the taproot of a tender sapling growing on a mountainside. The tendrils of the roots made their way through rocky soil of her resistance. No matter the obstacle, the young tree pushed ever deeper. Imperceptible at first, she felt sure the constant living force would eventually move great boulders on the mountainside as it reached for a deeper hold. In moments of time, in flashes of experience, Kathleen gloried in knowing that the growth of their shared love had not died during Jared's absence, only gone dormant. She was shocked at the strength the growing force still held.

Kathleen tried to examine the reality from every perspective, considering how she might train the tree of their love to a helpful and noble purpose. Could she direct the growth of their passion in a way that would bring joy? She had no desire to kill the beautiful thing. She recoiled from the idea of crushing it, but worried that the growth of the relationship would eventually send a boulder tumbling down the mountainside with an avalanche of destruction for the lives of everyone on the slopes. Kathleen wanted to shield Heathron from the dangerous truth. She wanted to protect him.

"It's the money, isn't it?" he asked.

"What?" Kathleen was shaken from her thoughts, and the image of the tree, by his question.

"I no longer have wealth, at least not immediately. I do have a claim on lands and titles and a portion of the Tyathian treasury, but not like I did when you agreed to marry me."

Kathleen was confused for a moment. She gathered her thoughts quickly.

"Heathron, do you believe that I care deeply about your wealth?"

He shrugged, his demeanor cold and his gaze distant, refusing to meet hers.

"I don't know—it was part of the bargain, and I'm not so foolish to think a lady would not consider these things. She must try to marry int he best way that she can manage," he added.

It was the way he said *manage* that made Kathleen's stomach give a little jolt, like missing a step in the dark. She felt the knot harden into anger and fear all at once.

"You think I agreed to marry you because of the luxury you could bring into my life?" she demanded.

Heathron shrugged again.

"Why else would you agree to marry a man you barely knew from your childhood?"

"When have I ever given you the impression that access to your wealth was my motivation for marriage?" she said.

Kathleen was shaking now, his words biting deep. It seemed like he was describing Renata—her materialistic step-mother.

"I suppose you were looking out for your family as well. So, there is that," Heathron reasoned, in a superior manner.

"Well, at least you've granted me a *sliver* of virtue in my treasure seeking," Kathleen replied sharply, crossing her arms.

Heathron sounded pathetic, and it made her want to recoil. How could he believe such things of her?

"You have given me your word, and I will hold you to it," Heathron snapped, "I always dreamed of a loving relationship, but if my marriage must be one of political expediency, of convenience—so be it."

He crossed his arms now, too, and turned to look out to sea.

Kathleen could not believe what she was hearing. "So now I will become one of your royal accoutrements? That's what you want? Your future bride exist in some reliquary like a little trinket you bring out to show your court and visiting emissariesis. Shall I live as nothing more than some bejeweled scepter of your power instead of a companion, a confidante?"

Heathron wheeled around and scowled.

"No, that's what you want! I no longer have the jewels, but I must be married to regain the throne in the Golden City," Heathron said.

Kathleen felt the sinking feeling she remembered from the day she signed the documents agreeing to the royal wedding. She was fulfilling a requirement.

"When you say it like that, it hurts me," she said.

"How much do you think it hurts me, to know that I cannot give you what you really want?"

"I don't care about the wealth, Heathron! You know this about me!" she exclaimed.

"Then what do you really want, Kathleen?" Heathron asked.

She looked out to sea, southward to Candoreth. Kathleen fought down the images of the Sīhalt Guardian that rose to Heathron's question.

What do I really want? she asked herself silently.

"I want to see my home still standing when we pass Turtle Island. I want to see Elayna, and Father. I miss Sam and Girdy, and I want you to meet them," Kathleen said, and ducked under his arm to embrace him tightly. "I am just thankful to be alive," she added.

Heathron returned her embrace seemingly half-heartedly by placing his arm across her shoulder. She could feel his disappointment and wondered how she could make him feel better.

"I don't care about your money," she said softly.

Heathron swallowed, nodding his understanding, but Kathleen wasn't sure of his conviction. She slid her hands around his neck and stood up on her toes, stretching her neck to reach his lips. Heathron responded and Kathleen was comforted but he kiss they shared. His lips were warm and soft and she felt herself respond to him. When she opened her eyes he was looking at her.

"You are so beautiful. You really are the only jewel a prince could desire."

He said it sincerely and it melted some of the bitterness of his previous words.

"That's the Heathron I know and love," Kathleen said, and followed it with a hug that was just as passionate as the kiss they had shared. Heathron didn't let go, so she didn't either. They stood like that for a long time, watching the waves pass. They reluctantly released their embrace.

"I need to prepare some letters for the nobility of Candoreth and some to send some to Tyath. I need to shore up my support in the Golden City. Lords Aviella and Cornado will want to hear from me. The nobility in Candoreth will be disappointed we have not wed. They deserve an explanation."

"They will be elated you have come to visit. We will be married soon enough," Kathleen said.

22

THE TORRENT

After Heathron took his leave, Kathleen moved to the yacht's stern to look out on the ocean. The boat's wake trailed out behind them. Small air bubbles in the water rose to the surface, leaving a temporary chain where the *Marine Escape's* hull had sliced through the foamy water.

Kathleen wished her soul could heal as fast as the surface of the sea, as she watched subtle crest off the vessel's rudder fall into itself and summon a helix of foam that stretched behind the stern. As she closed her eyes, and listened to the whisper of the surf, she breathed a sigh of heartache for all the challenges she felt.

Then came the pace of footsteps, heavy and true, advancing across the deck. She turned to see Jared approaching purposefully. He had shaved since she had seen him last. The seaman's stubble was gone, replaced with a clean, sharp jaw that shone like a freshly polished blade. He wore a look of understanding mixed with slight hesitancy. His eyes were keen, and no doubt he could tell that something was wrong. Still, Kathleen smiled sadly, glad to see him approach.

"I overheard your conversation with Heathron," he admitted, laying his heavy hands on the rail and cornering his gaze at her.

Kathleen let out the breath she had been holding, unable to speak. She bit her lip and shook her head.

"I'm sorry," he went on. "I wasn't trying to listen, it's just that in such a place as this, it is hard for me not to hear everything people say."

Kathleen raised a palm in understanding.

"I know. It's not your fault. Sometimes the *Marine Escape* doesn't seem big enough, and feels like it has no privacy."

Jared rocked back and half-turned.

"I will leave you alone with your thoughts, if you wish? I don't mean to intrude."

She stiffened, shaking her head as she smoothed down the folds of her gown.

"It's not that, Jared. I should be thankful for a sailing vessel such as this. We are making good time on our voyage, and I appreciate your strength. You don't need to leave."

"I don't always feel strong," Jared replied.

"What do you mean?"

"I feel like something is broken inside of me," he said softly.

She considered all that the Sīhalt had endured. Despite the Healing that had required so many of his years, perhaps there was still a part of him that needed to be fixed.

"Perhaps Melva can help you." she offered.

Jared shook his head.

"Throughout my life I have always been able to decide for myself what will or will not be.

He paused. Kathleen was going to respond, but waited.

He continued. "But not with you. I am broken inside, and I have not been able to mend it."

"What is broken, Jared?" she asked, unable to resist the question.

"I—it's hard to explain. Not 'broken' in the way of destruction, so perhaps this is not the right word." He paused again and frowned slightly as he concentrated on finding the right words. "I feel a torrent within me, a release of energy that flows from my heart."

He looked down and swallowed, and Kathleen gave a sigh of relief. "You're glad?" he asked, turning to her confused.

"No. It's just... I was worried you might have an untreatable illness, or something," she said foolishly. "It's stupid, I know. It just scared me. What with the Healing and what it took out of you."

He smiled a little. "Whether or not this is a flaw of my physical heart, remains to be seen. What is broken is my resistance to you. I don't want to pull back from you. I feel such a painful loss when you draw distant from me, as you have done these past days."

"You know—" Kathleen began.

"I know that what I desire, cannot be," he finished.

Kathleen listened, her heart pounding and eyes glistening. She motioned for him to sit with her on the warm wooden bench beside them. Jared sat close to her, not touching her, but less than an arm's length.

"I'm sorry. I do not mean to place a heavier burden on you..." he began to say.

"Shh... Be still." She placed a finger to his lips. "We are of the same mind," she whispered, her eyes shining now. "Have you ever read the story of King Nupara?" she asked.

Jared nodded.

"I have," he said, but frowned as he tried to understand the intention behind the question.

"Well, last night I was reading that tale and was struck by the story of Paetros the loyal servant. He was the most loyal of friends, sworn to the service of the good King Nupara, and yet *he* was the one who almost destroyed the whole kingdom."

"What is your point?" Jared asked, leaning closer to her.

"My point is that we are all part of something greater than ourselves, Jared. I have thought of this many times since leaving my home in Candoreth. So often, I wished I was not a princess. I wished that I was not a Daughter of the Realm, even. During my wedding procession, I wanted nothing but to run away with you into the wild, and live without the expectations of everyone else. But during this past year I have had time to contemplate the nature of my duty. I have been able to watch Heathron, as he too was required to make decisions that considered the well-being of the many before himself. I guess what I'm saying is that I am beginning to understand myself now, to trust that I'm conflicted because the recklessness of youth still clings to me, but it is shedding..."

When she was finished, she waited a second for the nature of her words to land before looking up to search his face.

Jared squinted into the light as he contemplated the words, repeated them, arranged them. But no matter how hard he tried, how many different combinations his mind interpreted and rein-terpreted, the answer was always the same: she was saying that her future did rest with him, but in duty with Heathron. He felt his stomach sink and churn.

"Is it impossible to have our duties coincide with our desires? What game is Abbath playing to illuminate a path of love, for a beautiful woman and then ask that man to walk another path?"

"This isn't a game. It is serious, and I want both of us to be safe. It is true that you ignite a fire within me as well, whenever you are close to me. But fire may destroy as much as it can purify," Kathleen said.

"How can I keep you safe, Kathleen?" he asked sincerely, his training as a Sīhalt Guardian never far from the surface.

"When I chose to marry Heathron, I announced it to all the noble houses of Tyath. He needed me, and I freely reaffirmed my promise to him. Heathron will not have a chance to regain the throne without a wife at his side."

"Do you regret it? Is there any part of you that would still dream of living a life with me?" His deep voice was even, but the tremors in it betrayed him, failing to hide the emotion behind the question.

"I wish I had known myself better before I came of age. I would have known better, what I want—what I need" She paused, then hurried to finish. Feeling the weight of what she was expressing to him. "That knowledge would have helped me negotiate the demands of life and love," she explained sadly.

"Would you have chosen me if you had known yourself better?" Jared asked.

She knew the answer to his question, but didn't reply. What good would it do? The choice was never offered to her before the decision of her marriage was made. Jared nodded in understanding at her silence, and let out a world-weary sigh. He even afforded himself a sad little smile.

"I suppose I have grown to know myself better, too," he said finally, "even if I have been hiding from it myself."

"It is too late for us," Kathleen said, sensing he finally agreed. But when she looked up, Jared was gazing at her with that familiar fierceness in his eyes. It made her tremble. His look could be terrifying and it reminded her that she was treading on dangerous ground.

"Knowing that you will remain with Heathron, while loving me, is a bitter thing. But it is made sweeter by knowing that you *do* love me."

With that the Sīhalt Guardian turned sharply and walked away.

23

THE WATERFALL

"What are you going to do?" Larissa asked.

Kathleen shrugged. "I don't know. I'd kind of like some time alone. It's been months since I've had a chance to walk in a forest. The terrain here looks like it would be good for the Gilded trees and if I can find one, you will enjoy the fruit. It's like eating sunshine dipped in honey."

"That sounds wonderful," Larissa replied. "I'll stay here with Melva and get things organized."

Jared strode by, walking with purpose. He wore his sword and black cape. The footfalls of his boots were incredibly silent when he wanted them to be. The man always moved like a dancer.

"How about you, Jared? What is your plan?" Kathleen asked.

"I want to scout the forest, up to those ridges," he replied.

"Maxwell flew over the area. He saw no sign of anyone besides us," Kathleen said.

"I'd like to make sure that there's no trouble lurking in the woods beneath the canopy. It would be surprising to find anyone this far from a settlements, but it is possible."

"No other people in a place this beautiful? Seems like a waste. You could build a city here," Lilly said.

Kathleen nodded her agreement and looked around at the hills that rose sharply from the narrow beach and shoreline. It seemed like a dream the way the mist hung on the forest canopy.

"Shall I accompany you?" Lilly asked, worry slightly creasing her brow as her eyes flicked to the emerald hills.

"I don't plan to go far," Kathleen said.

"Be careful out there while you're walking," Jared said.

"I'll call for you if I need you," Kathleen said.

Jared nodded then left, Larissa watched him go.

"Which way are you headed?" she asked in an innocent tone.

Kathleen eyed her friend. She knew what the girl was getting at. "I am headed in the opposite direction, toward the waterfall," she said, with a turn of her heel.

"Be careful," Larissa added, stretching out the words to add meaning to them.

"I always am," Kathleen replied with a look over her shoulder.

Lilly was smiling and Melva was waving.

As Kathleen walked through the forest, she recognized many of the plants that she had seen as a child growing up in the land surrounding Candoreth. She considered how beautiful they were. She missed being able to commune with living things, and the forest was perfect. Not since she had left the Golden City, had she been alone and she relished the idea of it. Besides, many of the plants seemed like old friends. Her thoughts turned back to the previous day. She hummed to herself and replayed in her mind the conversation she had with Jared.

"Would you have chosen me, if you had known yourself better?" he had asked.

Kathleen picked her steps carefully and lifted the hem of her dress when she stepped over a branch that had fallen onto the path.

If things had been different, I would have chosen him.

But then she had a difficult time creating a scenario where they might have become acquainted.

"He could have come to Candoreth on assignment for the Sīhalt Order," she said to the ivy that climbed the trunks of the towering trees. The leaves seemed to nod their agreement as she passed by.

"I was promised to Heathron, and I always have thought of myself as loyal, but perhaps I would have entertained Jared's admiration back then." She shook her head as she imagined it. "No, he was not impressed by me, when he first met me. He made that clear," she said aloud, then smiled at the memory.

"You are nothing more than a package to be delivered," she muttered in a deeper voice, mimicking Jared's statement from so long ago.

She smiled at the memory, ran a hand through her hair and looked up at the sky through the foliage.

"Well, certainly he got the whole package," she sighed, laughed at her own comment and looked down at herself. She was sweating now. The humidity had increased, but if felt good. There were fewer insects to bother her now, and she decided she wouldn't even mind if a late morning rain shower swept through.

"The truth is," Kathleen said, to the plants around her, "I don't know if it really would have worked. We made a good show of it it on the road though."

Kathleen wondered just how keen Jared's senses were. How soft of a whisper could the Sensor hear? If she spoke his name, calling out to him in the forest, would he appear?

Kathleen held her hands close to her mouth cupping them to mute the words she would say.

Then she spoke softly—"Jared. Come to me."

She waited a few moments, listening even though she knew that even if Jared could hear her invitation, she would not likely hear his reply.

"Come to me, Jared," she said again, only slightly louder.

No answer came, and she shook her head at the silliness of her experiment. Kathleen walked on. She gathered a few interesting leaves and flowers into a bouquet as she walked.

Presently she came to a small clearing where a stream ran through a meadow. She spread her arms and twirled her way through the green grass. It was soft under foot. As the world spun about her, she suddenly saw a dark figure of a man standing at the edge of the clearing. Kathleen stopped, regaining her balance as she half-crouched on the ground.

"You called for me?" the Sīhalt Guardian said. His head tilted to the side as if he were still striving to hear a faint whisper.

"I did," Kathleen replied. Her hands smoothed her dress where it had twisted around her waist. The bouquet of flowers lay forgotten on the grass as she stood and faced him.

"I almost didn't hear you over the sound of the falls. I ran but you didn't sound afraid so I didn't think you were in danger."

"I'm not in danger," Kathleen said, but wondered if perhaps she had created a dangerous situation for herself after all, with the handsome warrior standing before her.

"Would you like to see the waterfall?" Jared asked. He pointed to the stream. "It flows down from up above."

Kathleen nodded and took a few steps in his direction. Jared smiled and offered her his arm. She took it and there walked through the glade just as if they were on the narrow streets of Altrastadt.

They walked near the waterfall. Kathleen could hear the sound of water tumbling over rocks.

"Why do you think people are drawn to waterfalls? They are treated differently from other features of nature. Men and women seem to revere them—treat them as holy sites."

Kathleen considered the question.

"I suppose it is because they are so rare. We are surrounded by trees and rocks that do not speak, but falling water can have a joyful sound. It draws us in and begs us to ask the question, 'River, why do you sing?'"

Jared smiled at her reply and extended a hand toward her.

"Let me help you up," he offered, "The rocks here are slick."

Kathleen placed her hand in his and began to lean forward, taking the large step up to the boulder where he was standing.

All of a sudden Jared lost his footing. His black boots found no traction on the wet, mossy rock. He windmilled his free hand in an attempt to regain his balance, not letting go of her hand as he tilted backward. Instead he pulled against her, trying to use her stability to regain his own. In the end, he had to let go, and fell to his back with a thud on the rocks. The Sīhalt grunted with the sudden impact, a surprised look on his face. Kathleen let out a high-pitched laugh at the comical look on Jared's face, but her laugh was cut short when she too lost her footing. She spun her arms in the same way, tilting as her body fought to regain her balance. Finally, Kathleen collapsed directly onto Jared's chest. He caught her but grunted with the force of the impact. The two of them slid down the steep incline of smooth boulders. Kathleen felt Jared wrap his arms around her protectively. Their sudden slide came to a halt when they landed on the cold, shallow water at the river's edge.

"Ooh! That's cold," Kathleen exclaimed.

The chill water lapped at their sides, where they lay, but neither she, nor the Guardian made a sudden move to shore. They lay for a moment in the clear water, looking into each other's eyes. Kathleen rested on her elbows, propped against his chest. The rest of her body was pressed against his, and she found herself not wanting to move.

"Are you okay?" she asked him, slightly concerned that he might have hit his head on the rocks when they slipped.

Jared took a deep breath, and although she was not the Sensor, Kathleen felt the beating of his heart and felt the rise and fall of his chest as his breathing increased.

"I could lie like this forever," he said, holding her waist firmly.

Passion swept over her like a flame igniting birch bark. The river's cool water could not quench the fiery desire Kathleen felt rising within her. It swept upward from her body and tingled both sides of her neck, dancing across her spine. She breathed deeply, letting it move her forward. Kathleen felt herself falling deeper into him. She closed her eyes as her lips sought his. Jared caressed the back of her neck She felt the warmth of his kiss, his nose beside hers and the touching of their foreheads together. The physical expression of her emotions reignited the love she felt for Jared.

She felt him move and then she was on her back, pressed into the shallow of the crystal clear stream. The water flowed around her as Jared kissed her repeatedly. She reached for him and pulled him closer. Kathleen allowed her emotions to consume any thoughts of resistance, in her desire for him.

She was still trembling when he finally stood and offered his hands to help her stand as well.

"You must be cold. You are shaking like a leaf in the wind."

Kathleen smiled. "I assure you, Lord Sīhalt, that I am not cold at all, right now."

"Neither am I," Jared admitted with a grin, "But I'll help you out of the water."

Kathleen, still tumbling with emotion stepped onto a large, level rock. Jared followed her, dripping water as he stepped up beside her.

He hugged her again.

"I need to catch my breath," she said, leaning against him and enjoying the sweet smell of the blue water flowers they had crushed as they stepped ashore.

"I think that I know what the river is saying, now," Jared observed, tilting his head as if to listen to the sound.

"What is that?"

"He is laughing at us. The gurgling of the falls is his song of playfulness. And now we are the victims of his spritely tricks. Look at us," he said, gesturing toward their sodden clothes.

The sun was warm, and so were the dry rocks where they stretched themselves. Kathleen twisted her hair, wringing it out as much as she could. She looked into Jared's gray eyes and wondered what she was going to do now. She felt some distress at what little remorse she felt for having fallen into his arms—for having kissed him, and allowing him to return the kisses so passionately.

What am I going to do now? she thought.

"Kathleen, is that the tree you were looking for?" Jared asked.

She followed his outstretched finger and saw a Gilded tree.

Jared turned quickly, as if he heard someone approaching from across the river. "What is it?" Kathleen asked. His eyes scanned the tree line in the distance. "Someone's coming," Jared replied.

24

WATERFALL CLIMB

J ared moved Kathleen towards one of the giant boulders that were scattered among the falling water. They began to crouch down behind it when Jared heard a voice call out. He looked over the rock and saw Heathron approaching. The prince approached with his sword was on his hip and he was dressed in brown leather. In his right hand he carried what looked like a harpoon. The tip was pointed and barbed, and a length of rope was coiled along the shaft.

The prince walked with determination. As Jared looked at his features, he noticed he did not turn to the right or left, but walked directly towards them. Heathron didn't raise his hand to wave or display any other sign of friendship and, given their recent situation, Jared wondered how much Heathron had witnessed. Was he angry? Was he furious at having seen them kissing in the waterfall?

"It's Heathron." Jared said to Kathleen where she crouched behind the rock.

"Oh…" she replied. She too must wonder how much he'd witnessed. Jared stood up to his full height and took a step from behind the boulder.

"I wasn't sure who it was." Jared replied in explanation.

Heathron kept walking. He stepped quickly and bounded over the wet ground where the water ran across the rocks and landed on the dry side. He hoisted the javelin-like harpoon above his head and made his way directly towards Jared.

Jared didn't want to draw his sword. He had no shield, and was trying to make sense of what Heathron's intentions. Would he throw the harpoon at his chest and try to impale the man who'd stolen a kiss from his betrothed? Was there some danger with the other group that made him want to rush to speak with him? Jared's mind ran through the possibilities. In an instant he tried to evaluate the expression, to get some clue as to whether or not there was danger from the prince.

"Is he angry?" Kathleen asked. She looked up at Jared with eyes that were pleading for forgiveness.

"I don't know," Jared said.

Heathron didn't slow but kept his eyes forward. When he crossed the distance at which it would have been most effective to throw the harpoon, Jared felt some relief. But then, he quickly, considered how Heathron might be intent on hand to hand combat instead. Would he try to shove the barbed point through him instead?

Jared turned his body to hide the fact that his hand went to the hilt of his *impla* and presented a smaller target with his left shoulder pointing towards Heathron.

"What news, Heathron?" Jared asked, keeping his voice even.

"I finally found you. I saw some tracks in the woods and thought that perhaps you and I might go hunting. There are wild pigs in this forest."

Jared exhaled relief, flooding through him. "I saw Princess Kathleen slip in the waterfall and came to her aid," Jared said, as an explanation for the soaked clothing.

Heathron waved to Kathleen as he approached, a smile

breaking across his face when he saw her sitting safely on the ground.

Heathron took the last few steps and smiled at both of them. "I see you're both soaked," he said. "The water is cold. You'd better get dried off."

Jared nodded and turned to Kathleen, and noted an expression of relief on her face. He imagined his was a mirror of that relief.

"Shall we walk you back to the ship? Jared asked.

"I'll be fine,"

Kathleen said, looking down at her dress, avoiding his gaze.

"You are positively glowing, Kathleen. I think this waterfall must be invigorating," Heathron said.

Jared had to admit. Kathleen did look vivacious. A drop of water traveled down her cheek and she brushed it away with her sodden sleeve. Heathron was clearly unaware of their recent encounter. He bent to give Kathleen a gentle kiss on the cheek.

"Oh, don't worry, Lilly and Larissa were right behind me. The ladies can walk back together after we gather some of the gilded fruit."

"What do you say we go on a hunt?" Heathron asked Jared, slapping him on the back.

Jared nodded. "That sounds good."

Heathron gestured to the thick trees that ran along the river. "I followed the pigs through that ravine and I think they went up that way through the forest."

"I think the easiest way would be to climb up the falls. That way we don't have to deal with the underbrush," Heathron explained. His expression was one of avid anticipation. His brow glistened with the sweat of his exertion and he smiled broadly. Jared had not seen the prince so happy since they had left the Golden City.

"Very well," Jared said. "I'll join you."

"Lead the way," Heathron replied. They bid goodbye to Kathleen and the other two ladies who had just joined them at the water's edge. Lilly removed her cloak and gave it to Kathleen in an attempt to help ward off the chill from her soaked clothing. The men watched the ladies leave the clearing and head back into the woods, toward the camp.

"She is simply wonderful," Heathron said as they watched them walk back toward the forest.

Jared nodded. "She is," he said curtly, then began to climb the stones that led up the waterfall. He felt embarrassed at the way he had reacted at the sudden appearance of Prince Heathron. He didn't like having to pretend that he was something that he wasn't. The heat of their passionate kiss still hung on his lips and Jared considered what he might do.

"This is a beautiful land, isn't it?" Heathron said, speaking of the forest, the river and the wooded Emerald Coast. "This continent is full of resources. There is no reason for any people to be poor in Desnia. I keep thinking of all the poverty stricken folk in the Golden City. The beggars, the swindlers, as well as the wealthy houses that own most of the land. Wouldn't it be wonderful if we set up a project to settle this part of the Emerald Coast to build a new city? Perhaps a new nation? Do you think there would be leaders within the ranks of the Tyathian merchants who would be prepared to form such a venture?" Heathron asked.

Jared's thoughts still swirled around Kathleen, but he listened to the musings of the prince and found wisdom there. "I think it would be a wonderful endeavor." Jared said. "When peace time comes again, I believe there would be many talented men and women who would be willing to accept that kind of responsibility." Jared was reminded once again that Heathron was a good man and a leader with enough vision to bring his people peace and prosperity. And yet he was his adversary. He was the challenge to Kathleen's affection, and there was a part of him that hated the prince for it.

"Be careful on this narrow ledge," Jared said, as they climbed further up the falls. Looking back behind them, he realized that the steepness of the rocks made it a precipitous drop. The sound of the water falling had gotten louder as they'd climbed the falls. They looked over the green canopy of the forest. It spread below them and they were just able to peek out over some trees to see the blue water of the Eastern Sea.

"When we climb all the way to the top, we'll have quite a view. This is almost as high as the tower wall," Heathron said, breathing heavily.

Jared nodded. He grunted with the force of pulling himself up to the next ledge. The mist from the waterfall made the rocks slick and Jared found the need to face the rock and turn his feet sideways, allowing the toes of his boots to hold to the ledge. Once Jared was at a secure location, he called down to Heathron. "Trying to carry the harpoon won't be easy. Toss it up here and I'll hold it until you make your way."

"Okay, here it is." Heathron counted to three and tossed the harpoon in the air over the rock that Jared had just climbed. Jared reached out and snatched the harpoon and the rope out of the air.

"Coming up," Heathron said. He began to climb. Jared saw the sandy blonde hair of the prince. It was wet from the mist of the waterfall. He saw his fingers grip the edges as he moved along the face of the rock. Suddenly a piece of the rock wall slipped away. Heathron lost one part of his footing. His fingers clawed at the edge and he caught himself on the thinnest of holds. His right foot dangled in the air and his left toe was extended, trying to support a portion of his weight. The prince struggled to pull himself up. The sheer drop below him and the many levels of stone would mean certain death if he fell.

Jared winced at the danger that the prince faced. "There's a foothold just above your foot. Move your right boot up," Jared called loudly. The prince scrambled, his toes pushing against the rock. He felt with his foot for the foothold that Jared had described, and finally placed his toe into the rock wall, stabilizing himself.

"That was close," the prince grunted, still trying to preserve himself. Heathron moved his boot from the left foothold, and inched his fingers along the wall. Jared's immediate instinct was to find some way to save him from harm, but he realized to his extreme shame that there was a part of himself that wanted to see the prince fall, to eliminate the competition for the love of Kathleen.

"What am I?" he asked himself.

Suddenly the last remaining foot hold crumbled beneath Heathron's boot, and he was left hanging from nothing but his fingertips. The roar of the waterfall rolled beneath him, promising an unconscious landing and a shattered skull or certain drowning.

"Heathron!" Jared called. He took the harpoon in his hand.

"Help!" Heathron gasped. Fear filled his voice as he wriggled to try to hold himself with the barest of fingertip holds.

Jared knew he could not throw Heathron the rope. The prince would fall if he tried to turn and grab it.

"Hold still!" Jared commanded. "I'm going to throw the harpoon into the crack beside you. You must hold still!"

"Where?" Heathron cried, frantically moving his head from side to side, trying to see the crack.

Jared raised his arm and took a few steps away for the edge. "Hold still, Heathron," Jared said as he ran forward and launched the harpoon at he rock wall. Jare's eyes and hands were steady and the iron tipped shaft flew across the divide and buried itself in the seam that ran in the stone along Heathron's right side. Sparks flew as the iron tip buried itself in the rock.

Heathron let out a yell and his fingers clawed at the rock as he lost his grip and began to fall. The prince threw his arm wide and the wooden shaft of the harpoon caught him under the arm. He turned his body as he began to fall and with his other hand and grasped the harpoon that remained lodged in the cliff. This broke his fall and the iron tip of the harpoon creaked as the full weight of the prince settled upon it.

"Ooh!" Heathron exclaimed as he looked down at the rocks below.

"I tightened the rope! When you're ready, grab it. I have it secure," Jared called.

"Okay," Heathron called back. The watery mist sprayed from the waterfall. "Letting go now," the prince said. He pushed himself away from the rock face and scrambled to grab the rope that stretched across the chasm.

Jared felt a sudden tension and jolt from the weight of the prince. The rope grew taut, the harpoon shivering as Heathron's entire weight was born up by the rope.

"I've got you!" Jared called, leaning back against the load. Jared could see the rope move as Heathron climbed, hand over hand, back to the top of the cliff. Jared closed his eyes and offered a silent simple prayer to Abbath.

"I am sorry." Those were the words that came into his mind.

A wave of contrition washed over him. Jared felt sorry for the jealous desire he had to let the prince fall to his death. Jared had been the cause of many a man's death, but not like this. This was different. There was a weakness, and a deception about it. The bitterness of that truth took away the pleasure he had felt in holding Kathleen in his arms.

When one hand reached over the top, Jared kept holding the rope with one hand and reached with his other to grab Heathron's grip in his own. He hauled the prince over the top of the precipice just as the harpoon tip scraped free of the rocks. The shaft fell until the rope ran out and smacked the side of the cliff, dangling from the rope Jared still held.

"That was a close thing!" Heathron said.

Heathron finally caught his breath. He stood again, leaning with his hands on his knees. Jared patted him on his back, unsure of how well he was doing. Heathron stood upright and took another deep breath. Then they both began laughing.

Jared was glad that the prince did not see the pain that flashed across his face. In recognition of the temptation, he had to violate his oath as a Sīhalt Guardian. He might have done nothing. He could have simply let the prince fall. It wouldn't have been his fault. He wouldn't have killed the man—imply not aided him.

"You saved my life, Brother," Heathron said and threw his arms around Jared in a fraternal embrace. Jared returned the hug but felt the guilt at the moment of indecision he experienced while Heathron hung on the ledge.

"I'm glad you were able to hang on to the rope."

"Without you, I'd be lying on those stones at the bottom of the falls. I owe you my life," Heathron said. He offered his hand to the Sīhalt Guardian.

Jared hesitated only an instant before clasping Heathron's forearm with his hand a feeling himself being drawn into a brotherly embrace by the man who made him feel so conflicted.

"I won't forget this. As soon as I am able to return the favor, I will," Heathron said sincerely.

As the prince spoke, Jared recalled the teaching of Master Tove, during his training as a Sīhalt Guardian. *"Is it just as evil to withhold your help, when you can save someone, as it is to cause that person to fail?"*

He knew the answer. Jared knew that his duty was to protect the innocent and to honor what was good, and the prince was both.

2 5

A CHOICE TO BE MADE

"What is this?" Lilly asked.

"This," Kathleen said turning to them, "is a Gilded tree." Larissa placed her hand on the smooth bark. It had a golden tinge to it.

"I can see why they call it gilded," she said.

"This tree," Kathleen continued, "has the most delicious fruit in all the world."

Kathleen pushed her sleeves up. They were still damp from her frolic in the water.

"This is what you were hoping to find in the forest and you found the Guardian instead?" Larissa asked. Kathleen shot her a glance, "And I'm grateful I did. I lost my footing over there."

"Yeah, I saw he was soaked as well," Lilly observed.

Kathleen shot her a withering glance. Then she looked at both of them with innocent eyes.

"He was just doing his duty," she stated.

"Right…" Larissa replied.

Lilly kept her face stoic, but Kathleen knew that behind her brown eyes, she too had a grin. Kathleen placed her hands on the trunk of the tree.

"There is no fruit or blossoms on it," Lilly said.

Kathleen walked to one of the branches that hung low. "There will be soon," she replied.

Cupping her hand around the end of the branch, Kathleen smelled the fragrance of the Gilded tree. The spring leaves we're soft and delicate and still hadn't expanded to their full breadth. Kathleen allowed herself to become tranquil of mind. She began to hum and watched as the Gilded tree leaves expanded and darkened at the end of the branch where she touched it.

She smiled as a blossom formed on the end of the branch and opened. Kathleen gently shook the branch, brushing her fingertips across the open face of a number of the blossoms. Then she began to hum again. The buds became swollen and heavy. Kathleen supported the branch with one hand, as she continued to touch and caress the forming fruits with the other.

Before long, Lilly stepped forward and stretched out her skirt to receive the Gilded fruit. When Kathleen finished chanting, she plucked the large fruit from the tree and handed them to her friends.

"Gilded fruit tastes like a mix between a pineapple and a strawberry," she said.

"What is a pineapple?" Lilly and Larissa asked in unison. Kathleen looked at both of them. "You've never had a pineapple? It's a fruit with a top that looks kind of like a cactus, and the bottom is scaled like the back of a lizard."

Lilly pursed her lips and shook her head. "I've never tried one."

"You're in for a treat," Kathleen said. "It's smooth—the most heavenly fruit you could ever taste. Let's carry these back."

As they made their way back to the camp, Larissa brought the subject up again. "So what will you do, Kathleen? Clearly, Heathron is as smitten with you as the first day you met, and the Guardian loves you." They walked quietly until Kathleen decided to respond. "I don't know what to do for sure. My plan is to keep my commitment to Heathron. I will marry him."

"Is that what is in your heart?" Lilly asked.

Kathleen considered the question.

"I do love Heathron, and he is worthy of my love."

"And that's not really answering her question," Larissa said.

Kathleen stopped walking and shifted her with to one foot. Her two friends paused as well. "What would you do if you were me? Would you choose the prince and go forward with the marriage that has been set on your path since childhood, or would you choose the warrior, the Sīhalt Guardian?"

Now, it was Lilly and Larissa's turn to remain silent for a time.

"Jared's voice and manner are irresistible," Larissa observed. Lilly nodded.

"And yet I've known Prince Heathron for many years. There isn't a better man, you could wish for in a husband. He's true and good," Lilly said.

Kathleen found herself twisting the stem of the Gilded fruit she held in her hand. "With time, I think the fires will cool. The passions will subside."

"Do you mean that you will eventually feel less passion for the Heathron in your marriage?—or less temptation to be with Jared as time goes by?" Lilly asked. Kathleen could see that her friend cared deeply about the answer and it was a comfort to Kathleen to know that Lilly was so concerned for her well being.

"I don't want the passion to subside in my marriage. I want it to grow and deepen, and yet the people I trust the most say that a marriage ought to be first, a friendship."

Larissa raised her eyes to this comment. "I don't know about friendship being the *first* thing," she intoned.

"It is important," Lilly said. "I watched my father and mother and they always had a relationship based on mutual respect. They worked together very hard, catching cleaning and selling the fish each day to provide for our family, and although I did not see great passion in their relationship, I know they loved each other. They found happiness together in their lives they chose to live."

"My father has been miserable with the woman he married, after my mother's passing," Kathleen said.

The three women began to walk again.

"Who do you know that has it all in their marriage?" Larissa asked. "I think of my parents. Their marriage was one of convenience. I think they're happy, in some ways, but I'm certain my mother would not have married my father if he didn't have lands and titles, meager as they are now," she said.

"I really don't care about the wealth," Kathleen said. "My husband doesn't need to be wealthy for me to find happiness with him."

"That's easy for you to say, Kathleen," Larissa replied. "You've been raised as a princess in Candoreth. All of your needs have been met. I know that you felt the struggle of your father with the greater economic burden he faces as a monarch, but you haven't had to be worried about sustaining a life. You've only ever had to consider what would bring you the most pleasure and delight."

"The advantages come with a cost. There are many times when I've considered how nice it would be to be a commoner—to make my own decisions regarding love and life without having to please the crown or the throne. I remember on my way through Altrastadt. I met a woman named Cara and her husband Richard. She made the dress that I wore as a disguise when I entered the Golden City. They had four children. She was still young, and I believe she and her husband had both passion and friendship. That's what I want," Kathleen said, "but I don't know if the decision I face right now is a challenge to the good that might be, out an opportunity to have it all."

"What do you mean?" Lilly asked.

"I wish I felt nothing for him, but I do." Kathleen admitted

"You mean the Guardian?" Larissa said, more of a statement than a question. Kathleen nodded. "I don't think I can extricate him from my heart. Is it wrong for me to go forward with

Heathron, if there's a man that I love in addition to my husband?" she asked.

"My mother always said that after we die, we are held accountable before Abbath for our behavior, our words, and even our thoughts. How soon do you expect it to happen? Are you really planning to marry Heathron as soon as we get to Candoreth?" Lilly asked.

"I don't even know," Kathleen replied. "Candoreth may be burning for all I know."

"Don't say that," Lilly said, placing her hand on Kathleen's shoulder to comfort her. "I have hope that we'll see your family and perhaps by being once again in the presence of your father, and your little sister, and your people, you'll have clarity on what you should do."

"I've already made up my mind as to what I will do. The question remains. Is it wrong to go through with it, given how I feel? How do I manage the emotion that I feel?"

"If I were you," Lilly said, "I would marry the prince."

"That's ironic for you to say that," Larissa replied. "You've got your Sīhalt Guardian wrapped around your little finger. Seth prowls around you like a saber-toothed cat protecting its next meal."

Lilly smiled and blushed.

"If you feel passionate towards Jared, I would say be very careful. If you feel passion towards the Sīhalt Guardian that has not been quenched by the travails of the dungeon, or the beauty of the throne, then you should reconsider the promises that you've made to Heathron," Larissa offered.

"There I have my two best friends giving me opposing advice!" Kathleen lamented.

"It all goes back to your heart, Kathleen," Lilly said. Larissa nodded her agreement. "I know," Kathleen replied, allowing her eyes to look up at the sky. "I know," she repeated.

26

BOAR HUNT

After they rested and regained their breath from the close catastrophe at the waterfall, the two men found their way along a game trail in the forest.

"I can hear the sounds of swine. They are not far. Look at all the acorns scattered about," Jared said.

The mature oak trees shaded the hills in front of them, and they were laden with nuts. The shells crunched underfoot as Jared and Heathron stalked their quarry.

"I wouldn't mind having some bacon, and this should work on a boar as well as it does a fish?" Heathron said, holding up the harpoon.

Jared examined the shaft. "Boar spears are much heavier than this. This harpoon doesn't have the cross-bar on the shaft, to stop a charging boar."

Heathron winced at the thought. "I wouldn't want be on the receiving end of those tusks. Let's choose a smaller pig," he suggested.

The wild pigs grunted as they foraged for roots and nuts among the leaves on the forest floor. The men move silently through the trees and eventually found them.

"Since there are two of us, one of us can get in position and the other one can push the pigs in that direction," Heathron said quietly.

Jared was impressed with how well the prince moved among the trees. Although Heathron was raised in luxury, he definitely put forth effort to develop not only his martial skills but those for the wilderness as well.

"Have you hunted wild boar before?" Jared asked.

"My father first took me to hunt wild boar when I was only eleven years of of age," Heathron said, "but I didn't make my first kill until I was thirteen."

Jared raised his eyebrows. "That's impressive. You must have been very excited to do that."

"I was terrified. If it had not been for my father coming to my rescue, I would have died that day."

Jared smiled, imagining the scene form Heathron's childhood. It was good to know the man had known and overcome fears at a young age. Jared respected that.

Jared and Heathron advanced deeper into he forest, until they found themselves some time later in an area where the contours of the forest made a broad basin.

"Go over to that side where the ravine narrows. I will circle around and keep moving in their direction. When they come through, that is the time to strike," Heathron said.

He handed the harpoon to Jared.

Jared nodded, somewhat unaccustomed to having someone gives him directions. He had always been the one to create a plan and direct Seth and Maxwell, or the other guardians. Heathron's plan seemed like a good one, though, and so he complied, walking quietly to a small pile of rocks where they anticipated the animals would run.

The wind was dead, and that was an advantage to the hunters. Jared was certain their scent hung in the air, but the hogs had not yet reacted to their presence.

The swine began moving towards him. Some of the pigs were obscured by branches and brush, but Jared counted fourteen of them. There were a number of large sows and some juveniles and a massive boar. The beast was wary and he followed the herd of pigs carefully, grunting when he found new acorns. Bristles of hair stood up along his back and shoulders, following a line down its back toward the short curled tail that flicked rapidly, alert to danger. His front legs and shoulders showed signs of many scars from battle with other hogs, and his sharp tusks curled danger-ously, protruding at the corners of his mouth.

Jared wanted nothing to do with the large boar. He placed his boots firmly in the earth, preparing for when he would stand and throw the harpoon at one of the smaller animals.

Meanwhile, Heathron continued to follow them. Finally the hogs caught his scent, and with a snort, and a whuffing sound, one of the sows warned her offspring. The wild hogs began to move faster, their mottled coats blending in with the surrounding brush. They ran on sharp cloven hooves and despite their rounded shapes, moved swiftly along the forest trail.

Jared tightened the grip he held on the harpoon, drawing it back. His right hand held the distal part of the shaft. He singled out a good-sized sow and decided she would be his target.

Just as she passed the rock pile, Jared stood and raised the weapon. There was a moment of indecision among the herd as the pigs rotated about. The sow jumped as Jared hurled the shaft. Instead of hitting her, a smaller pig, running beside the sow took a direct hit from the harpoon.

The forest erupted in squeals of terror. The young pig lay on its side, pinned to the ground by the harpoon. It kicked dirt into the air, spinning in an arc of agony around the iron tip. Its pink snout opened wide, the pig sounded the alarm.

The sow turned on Jared - detecting his movements. She huffed, and snapped her teeth together. The squeals of her offspring, inspired her to attack. She charged the Sīhalt Guardian.

Jared drew his *impla* and pierced the sow between the shoulder blades. The narrow sword passed through the animal with little resistance, but the cacophony of snorts and growls increased and Jared struggled to pull the blade free as the animal twisted and sought to continue the attack. Just as he was getting this angry sow under control, he looked over his shoulder to see the giant boar bearing down on him with blinding speed.

He had no time to react. The boar slammed into him, smashing him into the rock pile. Before he could stand, the boar was on him, tossing its head from side to side, gouging the air with razor sharp tusks. The hog was heavy and angry, and the squeals of the younger pig inspired the attack.

Jared rolled to his side to protect his face and neck. Saliva dripped from the dirty mouth and curved, sharp yellow tusks gouged at him. He reached for his knife, as his sword lay out of his reach. The Sīhalt lashed out with his knife, cutting a a gash in the hog's shoulder. Jared felt the weight of the hooves pressing into his upper arm. He tried to shove the beast away, but the hog pushed harder. Jared gritted his teeth when he felt the gashes in his forearms, and saw the blood spilling over his hands. He curled up and tucked his chin as he sought to protect his neck from the tusks.

Then Jared heard Heathron bellow. The smaller hogs scattered. He saw Heathron coming at a dead run. The prince ripped the harpoon from the earth, and corpse of the dying pig. He turned the shaft in his hands like the baton of a court jester, spinning it so the tip was aimed at the boar. He took two more quick steps, rotating his torso to take aim. Jared winced as Heathron released the harpoon. It flew through the air toward him. For a moment it seemed it would skewer him and the boar alike. Instead, it slammed through the red-rimmed eye of the wild boar. The iron tip came out below the ear on the other side. Heathron's aim was perfect. The shaft paralyzed the boar. It dropped immediately, it's entire body quaking in death. The beast slumped further, and Jared felt the weight of the immense beast settled upon him—dead.

Jared looked to Heathron and coughed painfully.

"I can't breathe," Jared managed. The full weight of the boar was collapsing his chest.

Heathron quickly looked around to make sure there was no other danger. The remaining hogs were running through the trees, with snorts and grunts.

"Let me help you," Heathron said. With his shoulder, he pushed the body of the boar to one side. When he was able, Jared used his boot to help push the carcass further away. "How bad is it?" Heathron asked, looking at the tattered blood-soaked sleeve of Jared's shirt.

Jared knelt feeling pain in his side. He seated his knife and examined his bleeding forearms. "I may have some broken ribs, and he cut me to ribbons," Jared replied. Heathron cut strips of leather from his own shirt and used it to bind Jared's arms. "Now you may have saved my life," Jared said, as the prince finished binding the wound. "I didn't expect you to return the favor so soon."

"Nor did I," Heathron said with a smile, and stepped back to wipe the sweat from his brow. "You probably would have gotten the best of him, in the end."

"I don't know, my knife didn't seem to do much to that hog. I could have stabbed him all day and still not killed it."

"And it would have been such a bore, in the meantime," Heathron replied, his eyes glinting.

Jared shook his head and looked at him. They stood for second in silence.

"That sounds like something Seth would have said." Jared said, unable to resist the broad grin on his face. They were both a little high on adrenaline—then Heathron released two full-throated round of laughter.

"I bet that looked kind of funny, me fighting off that huge hog," Jared admitted.

"Your legs were kicking like a baby rabbit in the jaws of a fox," Heathron said with laugh, "but don't think you will escape of helping me to carry this meat back to camp just because a little piggy gave you a few scratches."

Heathron retrieved the *impla* for Jared.

"I can carry a pole on my shoulder without too much trouble," Jared replied and used the Sīhalt blade to cut a sturdy wooden pole from a young tree.

"Did you mean to hit him in the eye?" Jared asked.

"He wouldn't have stopped so suddenly if I hit him anywhere else."

Jared nodded his head, "I might have held him off," he said, "nevertheless, thank you."

He extended arm towards the prince, and not for the first time Jared felt that the two of them might've been great friends is their paths had crossed earlier in life—under different circumstances.

Heathron smiled. "We set out to hunt one pig, and got three."

"We might be able to take the sow and the smaller one back, but this beast will have to stay were he lays." Jared said.

Heathron walked in front of Jared, carrying one end of the pole that held their prize. The sow was heavy but the two men were able to carry it without too much trouble. Jared felt a brotherhood growing with Heathron—like men who had known battle together, he felt a kinship with the prince. Jared shouldered the burden, switching it to the other shoulder when the weight became too much. Jared considered the dilemma of his situation. Heathron was a man who was courageous, a worthwhile leader for the people of Desnia. Jared saw him as talented and virtuous—in many ways better than him. How then, could he in good faith compete with him for Kathleen's hand, knowing that she rightfully and legally belonged to Heathron as his betrothed? His heart was heavy as he thought of distancing himself from Kathleen, her radiant smile, smooth skin, and soft lips. The memory of their recent kiss, as alluring as it was, made him feel sick in that it represented a betrayal to Heathtron. Jared knew he would never offend Seth in such a way, by competing for Lilly's attention. And yet, he had been unable, and unwilling to distance himself from Kathleen, because he loved her.

"The others will be happy to see what we bring. We can have a feast tonight. We haven't had food this fresh since the Hermitage," Heathron said.

Jared nodded. "I was thinking there same thing. Although what I look forward to the most is having Melva give me touch of Healing," Jared added.

Heathron slowed and set down the burden as Jared did the same.

"This has been good," Heathron said.

"Thanks for inviting me to hunt with you," Jared said.

"I want you as a friend," Heathron replied.

Jared swallowed and glanced down at the ground, then leveled his storm-like gray eyes at the prince.

He searched Heathron's face, feeling the sincerity in the man's plea.

"You have my loyalty…and my friendship," Jared said.

"And Kathleen?" he asked.

The Sīhalt could not bring himself to apologize for pursuing Kathleen. He had loved her sincerely and treated her virtuously. If his life had been different, he would have asked Kathleen to be his wife—she was the only woman who had captured his heart in a way that made him feel complete. And yet she was not his to rightfully hold—and he knew it.

Heathron held Jared's gaze, waiting for his answer.

"She is rightfully yours. I will remain as her Guardian, nothing more," Jared said.

27

BROTHER'S SONG

When Jared and Heathron entered the camp, Kathleen stood up in concern. Jared's shirt was covered with blood but she was relieved to see a smile on both of their faces. They grinned like two boys who won a pie at the village fair. They brought back a wild pig, strung on a pole between them.

"We will feast tonight!" Heathron said.

"Indeed!" Channing said, "Larissa and I have been gathering wood for the fire."

"I've flown over the hills in every direction. There are no people within many miles of our position—on land or sea. We can rest easy tonight," Maxwell said.

Kathleen was delighted to find that she and her friends all had some success while foraging in the forest.

In addition to the various fruit she gathered, Melva found savory mushrooms and Lilly filled the barrels on the yacht with cold, clean water.

The clouds parted, and the last sun rays of the the afternoon, warmed the earth. When the moon rose, and the flames from the fire flicked upward into the night, the travelers were gathered together in comfort, with satisfied stomachs and full hearts.

Melva sat quietly by the fire looking into the flames after they had eaten the savory meat and shared the sweet fruit and quenched their thirst.

They moved some logs closer to the fire to keep away from the night's chill. "Now is the time for stories," Lilly said.

Seth nodded, enthusiastically and moved closer to her. Lilly began by sharing the stories her father had told her about the early founding of Tyath—passed down through generation of her family. Then, at Kathleen's urging, Melva sang a brief song about the trials and triumphs of her people. Afterward, Kathleen shared the epic poetry that spoke of her distant ancestors coming from Addisfall on long ships to land on the warm beaches of Sundiland. Jared and Seth took particular interest in the poem, recognizing stanzas within the story that matched what they had learned as children in the north.

The the Sīhalt Guardians took turns telling stories from the years they spent in training as boys at the Windstall Hermitage. Lilly clapped her hands at certain parts and exclaimed how she remembered some of the tricks they played on the townsfolk and fishing point.

When Jared began to sing in a deep, resonant voice, Heathron moved closer to him and put his arm around the Sīhalt Guardian, like a brother. The men sang together, their voices harmonizing in the night air. Kathleen watched them from the other side of the fire. Noticing the true friendship that seemed to be forming between them. Heathron looked happy, with his sandy blonde curls and dark eyes, he sang without hesitation. When a particularly vigorous portion of a song arose, he looked at Jared and they matched their pace encouraging everyone around the fire to join in.

Their voices carried high into the night air, emphasizing the elevated notes of the song. They sang of battles won and lost, of kingdoms saved, some parts of their ancient song must have come from before the founding of Tyath.

Jared looked more at peace than she had ever seen before. His face was calm. Gone were the lines of intensity in his brow. His mouth turned up in an easy smile as he laughed with Heathron, Maxwell and the others.

Kathleen blinked back tears, feeling the softness of the moment, seeing two men that she admired greatly united at this time together—on this night. She imagined her father would have greatly loved to hear them sing. She felt a deep longing to be with Jared, to be held his arms, to sit with him and feel his strength about her.

Channing noticed her expression. He sat with one arm around Larissa, but moved closer to Kathleen to place his other arm around her shoulders.

"They sound good, don't they?"

Kathleen nodded, "You should join them."

Channing smiled. "I wouldn't want to dominate the performance, right in the middle of their song," he said. "I could show them both up."

Kathleen nestled into Channing's friendly embrace.

"I believe you, Channing," she said with a smile. Larissa rolled her eyes, but it was in admiration for the captain.

"It's nice to be together on land for an evening of peace and enjoyment," Larissa said. "I wonder what we'll find when we get home," Kathleen replied.

Larissa reached over and patted Kathleen on the knee. "Whatever we find, Kathleen, we'll help to make it better. I'm excited to see Elayna too."

Kathleen smiled at the thought of her little sister. "She's going to be so excited to see me. It feels like it's been many years since I've seen her, even though we just left a little over a year ago." Larissa agreed. "I feel like I'm a completely different person," she said.

"We both are," Kathleen opined.

Suddenly, Channing stood up to join Jared and Heathron in their song. They were coming to the end of the epic saga of which they sang. And in the crescendo, Channing stood up and raised one hand toward the air. He, too, was illuminated by the fire light. And as they held their note, Seth joined in, and so did Maxwell—much to the chagrin of the group.

Kathleen winced a bit when Maxwell added his voice. His tone was somewhat of a screech.

"I think you've spent too much time as an eagle," Lilly said. But Maxwell paid her no mind. He sang out even louder as he joined the other men in song. When the final note came to an end, everyone clapped, and a greater sense of friendship could be felt among the friends around the fire.

"You didn't tell us that Gilded fruit could make you inebriated," Channing said to Kathleen.

Kathleen laughed. "It doesn't. I guess we just need to let loose a little," she replied.

Maxwell got up, and in the flickering fire light. He danced with Melva. Melva held her skirt up, revealing her scrawny ankles. They danced, kicking up their heels. Kathleen clapped and laughed along with the others. Seth sat beside Lilly on one edge of the fire, while Jared turned his back to the flames, keeping a look out into the darkness. Now and again, he would turn to watch the antics of the friends. Kathleen decided that she would try out some of the hand signing Jared had taught her.

There's no one out there, she signed to him. *Why don't you join us at the fire?*

His sharp jawline and angled brow was illuminated by the flickering flames. Kathleen watched his hand as Jared slowly signed a message back to her.

I believe Maxwell, that we are here alone in this wilderness, but it would be unwise to get out of the habit of maintaining a sentry, just in case.

Kathleen saw his response, but carried on her conversation with Larissa and Channing—keeping Jared in her peripheral vision. Heathron chopped more wood and brought it to the fire, tossing it on the flames, and sending a shower of sparks into the night sky.

It was nice to see you and Heathron singing together, Kathleen said with her hand. She saw the Guardian taking a breath and smile with a subtle laugh.

I haven't sung those songs since I was a boy, he responded slowly, allowing her time to make out the words he created with his hand.

I enjoyed our walk at the waterfall, Kathleen signed. *It was worth getting soaked*, she added,

He didn't reply.

She knew that Jared had seen the sign she wove, even in the darkness, but he hesitated.

I should not have kissed you, he replied.

It's okay, Kathleen quickly signed in the darkness. *I'm not sorry about it at all.*

She watched as Jared took a sip of water from the cup that he held.

Heathron saved my life today. I was attacked by a wild boar and it would have gone very poorly for me had he not been there.

I'm glad you weren't injured, she replied.

I saved his life too, Jared continued.

Oh? How? she asked, feeling exhilaration at the freedom to converse with Jared in the darkness, with no one knowing the better.

We climbed the waterfall after you left. When we were high up, he slipped. For a moment his life hung in the balance. I was able to ge the rope to him at the last second. He almost fell to his death.

I heard him say something about that, Kathleen replied, *I am glad you were there to help him.*

I almost didn't help him, Jared signed. The words struck like a bolt of lightning through Kathleen.

Why? she signed.

Because there was an instant when I cared more about being the only man you loved than being an honorable Guardian.

Kathleen paused. Not sure what to sign next.

But you did save him, Kathleen responded.

Heathron did not hesitate to save me—when I was in need. He's a better man than I, Kathleen. He deserves you.

I-W-I-W-Y, she signed, knowing he would make out the meaning. She saw him take a deep breath and look off into the darkness, turning his face from hers. When he turned back, and she knew that in his peripheral vision she might see her hand work another message, she signed to him again this time making the entire word of the message. *I wish I was yours.* Her heart was pounding heavily in her chest, as she waited for his reply.

Jared brought his hands up.

Never say that again, he signed. *I will never be yours, and you will never be mine.* He turned his back to her and looked out into the darkness.

At first Kathleen was unsure if she had understood his message correctly. Then she felt a stab of emotional pain. Why would he react so abruptly, and so harsh? Had he not also enjoyed their recent encounter? He had. What changed in so short a time? What had transpired between Heathron and Jared to make him so resistant to her?

"Kathleen, come and dance with me." Heathron stood in front of her with his hand extended. His eyes shone in the firelight and he smiled broadly. His expression was one of tenderness and joy. Kathleen fought through the pain of Jared's message. She wanted to reply to him, she wanted him to believe they could be together —somehow, but he had walked into the darkness of the surrounding trees. She placed her hands in Heathron's.

"Kathleen, are you all right?" Heathron asked. His brows furrowed in concern and his brown eyes looked concerned as he brought her to her feet.

She looked down to compose herself, then looked at Heathron.

"I'm just so happy to see everyone enjoying themselves this evening. We've been through such hardship," Kathleen said.

"Then let us share in the happiness of this evening. Dance with me!"

He lifted her to her feet and twirled her around, guiding her to the area where Channing and Larissa sang together and Seth danced with Lilly, to keep up with Maxwell and Melva as they stepped quickly in the firelight.

J ared watched as Kathleen danced with Heathron, from the edge of the forest. The flames flickered, illuminating their shapes. Her red hair flowed as she twirled. Heathron laughed and placed his hand at the small of her back, guiding her to the next step. Jared remembered when he had once been blessed to have her in his arms, on the dance floor.

Jared didn't feel jealous. He was mostly happy for them. He knew in his heart he loved Kathleen deeply—even as he still wanted her as his own. For the first time, he found himself capable of feeling happiness at her relationship with Heathron.

Kathleen laughed when Maxwell cut in and traded dancing partners with Heathron. The old Healer was not be the most beautiful trade, but she was dancing as vigorously as her old legs could manage. Heathron didn't miss a beat. He twirled Melva as smoothly as if she were a young noblewoman. Jared found the corner of his mouth rise.

"Her life will be good with Heathron. I will remain her Guardian, nothing more," he whispered.

2 8

HESTIN REJECTION

In the following days, Jared avoided her. They were back at sea, sailing in south. Again the yacht felt small, especially with the awkwardness between them. When they passed by each other Kathleen didn't attempt to break their silence. She refused to be the one to ease the discomfort. She had spoken honestly to him. She replayed their brief interaction at the fireside again and again.

He treated me like a child, telling me what I must not say!

He can have it his way—until he asked for it to be otherwise, she thought.

Kathleen redoubled her efforts and focused on Heathron, and home. Soon the *Marine Escape* entered Hestin's territorial waters. Kathleen sat on the deck as Channing pointed along the horizon.

"They don't want us here," he said.

Kathleen squinted across the shimmering water, trying to pinpoint what the captain saw.

"Do you see the three white triangles—the sails just on the horizon?" Channing asked.

"I don't see them," Kathleen said. "Your eyes must be better than mine."

"They're right below that cloud, shaped like a pineapple." Channing replied. He pointed to the cloud, then moved his finger vertically toward the horizon.

"I see them now," Kathleen said. "They're close together."

"Do you think they've seen us?"

"I'm not certain, but they want to have a word with us."

Soon the Hestin ships were coming alongside. Channing responded by slowing the *Marine Escape*, Lilly stood ready to move water in case there was any trouble, while the other men were tensed and ready for action. When the ships finally slowed, matching their speed on the swells of the ocean, Hestin sailors threw ropes across to the *Marine Escape*. Jared and Seth and Maxwell secured the ropes and invited the Hestin officers to come aboard.

The Hestins were bare to the waist. Their white linen shorts contrasted with their dark skin. Each one wore colorful fabric twisted into a belt and wrapped around the waist. A tall man walked past the others and approached Channing.

"What are you doing?" Their officer asked. His tone was forthright and direct.

Kathleen stepped forward. "I am Princess Kathleen Dal Sundi." Kathleen said.

The man tilted head and examined her as if she was an unruly child speaking when she shouldn't. Kathleen fumed. The people of Hestin could be insular when not acting as a merchant.

"What is your business here?" he asked in a tone that was more accusatory than inquisitive.

"I'm returning home after a visit to Tyath. We will not be in these waters long," she added.

"I am sorry," the man replied. "We are extra cautious. The entire coast of Desnia to the south has ships of a strange origin. The pirates pay no heed to our sovereignty and we have had to chase a number of them as they scouted along our coast."

"We mean Hestin no harm." Kathleen said. "And we will not delay. We have plenty of supplies, we don't need to stop."

"That is good. No one is permitted to stop in Hestin. Our council has closed the gates of the city and the harbor is made available only to our own people. Many of our merchants are being recalled home. War is at hand. This isn't good for business, but what can we do?"

"Has Hestin declared war on the pirates?"

"No." The man shook his head. "But it is clear from our reports from Tyath and Horming that the empire has yet to decide what to do next. is making up its mind what to do next. They face barbarians on the land and now pirates on the sea."

"Will Westin join in the fight to establish order? Channing asked.

"We have no desire to be involved in the wars of other people. We will make our peace with the victors—whomever that may be."

"Could we not rely on Hestin for some neighborly support in cleaning up the lawlessness?"

Candoreth is under siege. Tyath is in turmoil. Horming may be the next city to have the barbarians at the gate," he said.

"Candoreth is under siege? How do you know this? Have you sent them assistance?" Kathleen asked.

"We do not believe in becoming involved in foreign entanglements," the man said. "Our council is very adamant about this."

"You know, Renata is married to my father."

"Although it brings us no joy, we know this," the man said.

Kathleen wanted to say that it hadn't brought her very much joy either, but she held her tongue.

"I suppose an alliance with Hestin is too much to hope for."

"If Candoreth cannot defeat them, why would you think that Hestin could do any better?"

"If we join, we will be stronger together."

"Our people were slaves once. We have prepared for such a day as this. I do not believe it will be worth the price of blood for the pirates to try and conquer Hestin."

Kathleen heard the words and they struck deep her in heart knowing the weakness that her nation faced when she left the previous year. She feared that perhaps Candoreth was just the sort of target that invading people might desire, the rich farmland, the plentiful waters and a city that was beautiful and insufficiently defended.

"I am trying to get home. Now I feel even greater urgency. May we sail through instead of going around?"

"Go out to sea and go around. We have no wish for visitors."

"We will do as you request, "Kathleen replied bitterly.

The man placed his hands together and bowed slightly. "It is good."

It was as if he had negotiated the purchase of trade items at the market.

"It is good." Kathleen replied, in the traditional phrasing of Hestin, although she felt that nothing at all was good.

The man turned on his heel and returned to his ship. Kathleen saw that Jared had remained close the entire time the Hestin sailors were on board. He kept quiet but his Sīhalt blade was ever close by. She wanted to hear his opinion but did not speak with him.

"I'll make sure we sail quickly. I am feeling strong again," Lilly said.

The wind was strong, but Lilly was stronger. The Hestin ship moved parallel to their position—keeping a defensive posture.

Lilly tied the rope harness around her waist.

Jared secured the other end of the rope to the mast as Lilly prepared to go over the side.

Maxwell climbed into the rigging and began to wave at the Hestin ship.

"See you later, boys!" he called in anticipation of Lilly's talent.

The waves behind the yacht rose up, swelling into a roiling

mound of churning water. The Hestin sailors saw the mountain of water, folding in on itself like a pile of gigantic eels fighting for the surface. The men made symbols of religious fidelity—seeking to ward off the evil they saw rising from the ocean.

But there was no evil, only water under the hand of a Douser. Lilly's fingers slid across the surface of the water as she braced her feet against the hull and leaned backward. Her dark hair fell over her shoulders and brushed the water like her fingertips. Larissa let out a gasp of delight as the yacht surged forward. Lilly responded with a delightful laugh and shouted for joy.

The Hestin ship caught the wave on the side of their vessel. It tossed them to an angle away from the *Marine Escape.* The sailors scrambled to steady their ship as it rocked dangerously close to capsizing.

"That will teach them, Lilly!" Maxwell shouted

The Shifter looked like a child's doll caught in a web as he was tossed about in the rigging. Maxwell's laughter never ceased as Lilly added to their speed. The sails were full of wind, but the yacht sliced as quickly through the waves as the white seagulls cut through the air around them. The white birds swooped past their bow for the small fish that rose within diving distance.

Everyone aboard the yacht braced themselves, holding onto anything secure. Melva grinned leaning against the rail. Channing held on to the rudder with one hand and Larissa's waist with the other. While Seth and Jared managed to appear stoic, for the most part, but Kathleen caught a smile that creased their lips too. They were caught up in the exhilaration of the moment as well.

"On to Candoreth!" Kathleen shouted into the wind as Heathron steadied her with his strong arms. She smiled at him.

She knew she would be home soon.

A BURNING CITY

They sailed through the day and into the evening hours. Eventually Lilly needed to rest. When she came back aboard the yacht, their speed slowed to a more natural rate. The night passed without event—Kathleen lay awake, listening to the water spraying away from the prow. She got up early to walk the deck and take in the fresh air. As the dawn approached, pinpoints of light shone in the darkness of early morning. Heathron saw her and secured the rudder to step away from the wheel and join her at the rail. The *Marine Escape* sailed closer, to Kathleen's home. Fires burned along the shore. The glimmer of their flames reflected on the water.

"This is what I was afraid of," Kathleen said, the flames now dancing in her eyes.

"Master Tove's manuscript warned of a city on fire," Heathron said.

She sucked in a breath of air and steadied herself.

"Elayna must be terrified," she said.

In the distance, ghostly spirals of smoke rose from the towers closest to the harbor. It appeared that the defenders of Candoreth had been unable to push the enemy ships further from their shores. Two of the large dark ships, outlined by the dawn, were turned broadside to the harbor wall.

Suddenly, there was movement, and a great thunderous noise rang out across the water from one of the two ships that—both now belching fire from their sides—looked as if they were great beasts felled on a king's hunt, their innards falling from their stomachs. One resounding crash came after another, and then another, until the thick stone of the harbor walls shivered and cracked beneath the force.

"Dear Abbath, what are those?" Channing cried.

"I have never seen the like," Heathron said, and moved closer to Kathleen to comfort her.

A dim murmur of men's voices floated across the water. The trebuchets mounted on the wall, closest to the ships, crumbled into the water, trailed by screaming men who had been stationed to operate them. Other machines of war were set in motion, but the boulders they threw into the air, dark against the dawning sky, arched upward with menace, but splashed harmlessly into the harbor— far short of the enemy ships.

"I hope our navy is not trapped in the harbor," Kathleen said. The foreign ships besieging her homeland gathered like wolves surrounding a kill.

"Where do they have come from? I don't recognize them," Heathron said as he scanned the scene. Channing and Jared joined them as the bow of the ship.

The masts of the pirate ships were stacked in ranks among the outer islands. They were anchored as if they intended to stay forever. These were not undisciplined seamen. These ships, although many were in need of repairs, were clean and their flags ordered.

Squinting, Channing said, "I don't recognize the emblems they carry. They are not from the south."

"They do not bear the markings of raider ships, with intent only to loot and leave," Jared said darkly.

Seth shook his head. "This is more than a pirate attack, this is an invasion."

"An invasion?" Kathleen gasped. She thought of there father and what this must be doing to him.

"I'll take a closer look," Maxwell offered. He ran the length of the deck before springing into the air on metallic green wings.

Jared turned to Seth. "We cannot sail into the harbor, we will have to go ashore north of here and make our way on foot. It's too dangerous."

Lilly, listening nearby, mused on this, rubbing her chin. "We could… Or we could sail around them, come in from the south if needed. Then we will have a better idea of their numbers."

"I'd like to see if Marth Island is still free," Channing said. "At the very least we could speak with some friends to find out what is going on before we rush headlong into a trap."

The slow, shuffling footsteps of Melva approached behind them. She had climbed up from the cabin.

"Melva, you shouldn't be up here. You're not well enough," said Lilly, noticing her first.

But Melva, lips-pursed, waved a dismissive hand through the air and said, "Candoreth Castle still stands. The Passionflower flag of House Dal Sundi is still flying from the ramparts. King Lukald will fight to the last. We still have time."

All eyes turned to Kathleen now. Candoreth was her home, and she was under the most duress. It would be her plan that they followed.

She turned to Channing. "Captain Dur Ruston, you will sail to Marth and see what friends we have there," she commanded stiffly.

Channing bolted upright, and fell into a series of dutiful nods. "Yes, Your Highness," he piped, and wheeled around to take up the helm of the *Marine Escape* at once.

Then Kathleen turned to Lilly.

"Lilly, you will help us to sail on the water with the most swiftness you have ever summoned—think of a stone being skimmed across it by the hand of a giant. We must not be caught by the pirates."

"I will make sure of it," Lilly said.

Next, she turned to the brothers of Windtsall. "Guardians, if the enemy should try to come aboard—make them pay dearly!"

In a synchronized response Jared and Seth placed their right fists across their chests in a show of devoted service.

"This vessel carries the Sunshine Bride of Candoreth, the rightful heir of the Desnian Empire. We will defend it with our lives, Your Highness," came Jared's reply. Seth nodded gravely as well.

Kathleen was biting her lip in determination now. "Good. Then let us sail south," she said, looking out to sea, and at once Channing tugged hard on the helm, angling the *Marine Escape* in a new direction.

"Rig up the harness for me to go over the side, if you don't mind," Lilly ordered Seth. He nodded and expertly looped the rope into a shape that would hold her waist securely. "I'll be ready to touch the water at a moment's notice."

The *Marine Escape* nosed southward.

"We can circle back to my home on the North Shore," Channing said. "We have a private dock hidden among the marshes of the island. Our plantation overlooks the waters to the west. We will be able see for miles."

He was nodding with determination, but as Kathleen listened, she could see through Channing's optimism. Though his words were bright and direct, there was no hiding the tension in his features.

She walked briskly to his side and dropped a delicate hand on his shoulder, smiling softly. "I know you are worried about your home and family too, Channing. I hope all is well on the Island of Marth."

He swallowed and forced a smile to his lips. "A few pirates are not going to subjugate the proud people of Marth," he replied bravely and looked in the direction of the largest of the Turtle Islands.

"I hope you are right," she said, considering the vastness of the pirate fleet. Their ships were numerous and Kathleen wondered how any of the communities within the kingdom could hope to withstand the onslaught—even Marth.

They sailed toward the northern edge of the island. None of the pirate ships moved to intercept them and the wind was blowing in a good direction so there was no need for Lilly to go over the side.

"I want to save my strength just in case they decide to try to come after us," she explained.

Channing nodded in understanding. "We have a good wind," he said, but swallowed and blinked away the deep concern that flashed across his face.

"Tell me about this private harbor," Jared said, walking toward Channing where he steered the boat.

The captain pointed toward a peninsula that jutted out, with a commanding hill surrounded by a lowland valley.

"My home is on top of that hill. We farm the fields of the lowlands, and those marshes have many pathways for the tide to roll in and out. I know the back waters and given the hour, I should be able to take us right up to the closest dock."

"Don't worry about the tide, Channing. I'll make sure we have enough water to get in and out," Lilly said.

"We do have that advantage," Channing agreed. "I want to know that the pirates haven't commandeered the place."

He held his hand above his brow, shading his eyes as he looked out over the marsh grass.

"There is a ship moored over there," Jared observed.

Channing squinted. "Does it carry the Dur Ruston plume?"

Jared shook his head. "Its flag is black, with a red border."

Channing's face hardened. "That isn't ours," he replied.

Larissa placed a hand on his shoulder, seeking to comfort him.

When the *Marine Escape* got closer to the Dur Ruston dock, they saw two men dressed in white pants. They were bare to the waist and had cutlasses at their belt, watching as the boat came to rest along the dock.

"They don't seem very concerned at our presence," Channing noted.

"I was thinking the same thing," Heathron said. "They are very confident. I wonder why…"

"Bring her alongside," one of them called in an accent that sounded drawn out and strange to their ears. The sailor rolled the r as he said "bring".

"What goodies do you have for us today?" the other asked.

High above their heads, an eagle circled on the wind. It screeched and began a slow decent. The sailors looked up.

"There is that green bird again. Must have a nest here close by," he observed.

Seth tossed the lines to the sailor who quickly tied off the *Marine Escape* to the dock.

Channing, Jared, Heathron, and Seth made their way down the gang plank.

"I saw the ladies onboard. Are they for the admiral or might they be saved for us common sailors?" one of them asked, attempting humor.

"The admiral doesn't need to know about them," Channing said and doffed his hat, winking knowingly at the man.

He laughed and Channing patted him on the back.

The other sailor paused, looking at Channing and the others men seriously.

"I am a man of the Bactan Fleet, body and soul," one said seriously.

"He's joking, Daim! Can't you take a joke?" the other sailor said. The serious one eased up a bit.

"He's uptight. It's been a long voyage and things have gone

better than we expected. Some people can't seem to accept good luck even when it smacks them on the cheek!" he laughed again, and finished with a cough.

"Where is everyone to help us unload this cargo?" Channing asked, gesturing to the vessel.

"You'll have to do it yourselves. The others are all at the wharf helping to organize things there."

Channing nodded. "I see," he said slowly.

"How about the master of this place? Has he been—compliant?" Channing enquired.

"Lord Dur Ruston? Of course! I've never know a more hospitable man. He welcomed us with open arms and even offered his own rooms for the admiral to use. Then he helped to gain the compliance of some of the village folk when things got heated early on."

"Good to hear!" Channing lied. "I'd like to see the old sea dog if I might."

"I don't see any problem in that. Maybe you could bring the boat around to the wharf afterward. It'll be easier to catalog the haul there rather than here on the backside—oh, look, there he is now." The pirate pointed up the hill to a man who stood with hand raised in welcome. "That's Lord Dur Ruston there."

Channing raised a hand of greeting to his father.

A STRING OF PEARLS

"I need you to take the people to safety," King Lukald said forcefully. "Horming City will welcome our most vulnerable—at least the women and children."

Surely King Dareson wouldn't turn my people away in such time of need, King Lukald thought.

Queen Renata might as well have been deaf for all the attention she paid him. She kept directing two of her maids to pack her things. No matter how much they tried she always found a reason to criticize their efforts.

"Abbath save me! I told you to fold it along the lace," she said, yanking the article of clothing out of the hands of the older maid, and handing it to the younger.

"Maybe you can do it right," the queen said. "Your hands might be more nimble—even if your mind isn't."

"Your Majesty," the maid replied humbly and curtsied.

"Oh, hurry up!" Renata snapped.

The maid bowed her head and tried to make herself smaller as she folded the fabric to the edge of the lace.

"The people need me to stay here, to defend the city," Lukald said.

Queen Renata rolled her eyes and Lukald felt his blood begin to heat. His face reddened and his nostrils flared.

"I do detest it when you roll your eyes at me."

Renata responded by rolling her eyes again.

"I'm tired of this—fighting you *and* the pirates," the king said, falling mutinously and with a great sigh into high-backed chair.

Queen Renata shrugged her bare shoulders in the red satin gown she wore. "You had problems long before I came along. Now it appears you are losing the war on both fronts, Lukald. I'm leaving, but I am not going to Horming...I plan to go back to Hestin."

Her words cut through the irritation that was so common in her presence. Lukald leveled his eyes at his wife, daring her to continue. She matched his look with her own fiery gaze and raised her chin defiantly.

"Your father said you were banished from his presence. He said you could never go back—unless you went back to stay," the king reminded her.

"I should have never left my homeland."

"You are choosing a fine time to leave me, Renata. I am trying to hold together a kingdom, fend off invaders, and protect our family and people."

"Oh Lukald, you always wanted this. You enjoy the thrill of a crisis. That is why you create them. You always want to be the hero and you don't love me—not like you love your daughters."

"I loved you...when you loved me," he replied.

Renata pursed her full lips tightly and looked toward the ceiling, considering his words. Eventually, she said, "Then, you never loved me," she added curtly.

Lukald was surprised that her words still caused him pain.

She never truly loved me? he thought.

"I came here to escape the limitations of my father's demands. I hated the way I was treated in Hestin. 'Renata, cover your hair. Renata, your brother must accompany you. Renata, your dress must cover your ankles. When will you marry and have children, Renata?' That is all I ever heard."

"I gave you my heart. My conscience is clear in that," Lukald said.

"I made a mistake in marrying you, and now I am going to fix it. If Kathleen could have formed the alliance with the Golden City, we would have all been better off."

"You are leaving me because I am financially ruined? Because we are at war? This is not my fault!"

"No, but because I always had to compete with your dead wife. And now I have to compete with the memory of your dead daughter too," she said.

His hand almost flew. Lukald held his fist at his side. He had never struck a woman, nor had he ever conceived that he might do so to his very own wife. But in the moment she felt like his enemy, and he would strike his enemies.

She did not recognize the depth of his anger or perhaps she was accustomed to his restraint. Regardless, she did not see him as a threat to her safety. Renata despised him and he felt the cold cutting blade of that reality.

"You know I'm right. Don't you?" she goaded him.

Lukald clenched his jaw, unwilling to leave and let her win with his retreat, but unwilling to become something he despised— a beater of women.

Renata swept earrings and many decorative combs into the jewelry case she was packing. She poured a tray of golden, jewel-encrusted rings into a bag and dropped it unceremoniously into the case as well.

Lukald heard the clinking of precious metal and thought of the sacrifices the Sundiland people had made. The famine and subsequent conflict left them destitute, and yet they supported him as their king.

How have I come to this? he asked himself, as the woman who had once taken away his loneliness now made him feel more isolated than ever.

She pulled open another drawer full of necklaces. The fine chains of silver and gold were laid out on black velvet. A simple string of soft, white pearls lay among them. Diamonds and sapphires, rubies and emeralds shone in the lamplight. Intricate charms with delicate workmanship in every part made them a treasure beyond anything else to be found in the royal chambers.

"If I had known you'd amassed such a treasure, a few more children in Candoreth would have slept with a full belly these last few years."

"And that is why I did not tell you," she replied avariciously.

Renata raked the necklaces up with her red lacquered nails, like the claws of a greedy mountain troll.

Then Lukald's hand flew. There was a high, piercing scream. He did not hit the queen, but grasped her wrist and held her hand upright between them. Her fingers curled and for a moment he thought she might try to claw at his face. Priceless jewelry hung from her fingers like the parasitic silken strands that the sack worms weave in the springtime fruit trees. Her fingers writhed like the black worms, disgusting and profane.

"What are you doing!" she cried, her dark eyes finally widening with the recognition of the threat he posed. His vise-like grip pressed into the ebony skin of her slender wrist and his blue eyes narrowed.

Lukald pulled her hand closer to him. She fought in vain to pull it back.

"That one..." he said as he looked closer at the jumbled, glittering mass, "does not belong to you." Lukald lifted the simple pearl necklace from her hand and held it up to the light. The faint swirl of an iridescent rainbow, on the surface of the pearls, caught his eye. "Yes, I thought I recognized this one. I gave it to Annalise the day Kathleen was born."

He put the string of matched pearls in his pocket and released Renata's wrist.

She spat at him when he turn his back to go.

"I never liked that one anyway, but I'm taking the rest!" she declared with a tone full of venom.

Lukald felt his anger ebb. He turned at the door and faced her again.

"Take it, Renata. You worked for it," he said before closing the door.

She screamed something unintelligible to him but he blocked it out and allowed his hand to caress the pearls in his pocket. He focused on the day he'd brought them home to his loving Annalise - the day of their first child's birth. By the time King Lukald rounded the corner of the long corridor, he realized that despite the deep pain, he was whistling.

STONECUTTER

E layna frowned at the smoke rising into the air. It colored the sky far out to sea and made the white clouds in the blue sky look black.

"We've lost another one," she heard her father say. He sounded so sad. Ever since Renata left, Elayna saw her father be both very happy and very sad. She worried about him.

"Can I help them, Father?" she asked.

King Lukald turned toward his daughter. "No my dear, this war against the pirates is one that must be fought by the grown-ups."

"But we are losing, right Father?" she asked.

"Now, what makes you say that?" King Lukald asked, pulling his youngest child closer to his side.

"I'm not allowed to play on the beach anymore. That means we are losing."

The king didn't immediately respond.

"Is that right?" Sam asked. "Well, maybe I can get you some lunch to take your mind off of all this fighting."

"I'm not hungry yet," Elayna said, patting her belly.

"She did eat well this morning. Princess Elayna is growing so tall!" Sam said.

"I'll be as tall as Kathleen soon."

Her father hesitated. Whenever she spoke of Mother or her big sister, she noticed a change in his voice - an uncertainty and sadness. Still, Elayna determined never to stop. She would say their names until Father became so used to it he would not flinch anymore.

Besides, thought Elayna, *Kathleen is going to come back.* She just knew it.

"Are you done with your studies for the day?" King Lukald asked.

The princess nodded. "I finished mathematics and history. Did you know the first ships to Candoreth came from the Far North?"

"I did, Elayna," the king said, "Our forefathers came from a place of ice and snow. Aren't you glad they didn't stay there?"

The girl shivered. "I am," she said, "but I would like to build a snowman sometime. One of Kathleen's letters told me how to do it. You take a ball of snow. It's white, kind of like sand, but fluffy and very cold. Then you roll it on the ground, and more and more of the white snow gets packed together until it gets bigger and bigger," she explained, eyes wide with the thought.

"And then what?" Sam asked.

"Then you make a another one and stack it on top." She held out her fists and demonstrated how a snow man would be built. "Finally you make two eyes with black oyster shells and a carrot on the face for a nose!"

"You like to build things don't you Elayna?" Sīhalt Girdy said.

She nodded again. "It's all I think about—almost everyday," she admitted.

"Since you can't play on the beaches anymore, perhaps Sam will take you to the harbor," King Lukald suggested.

"Where they're fixing the wall?" she said excitedly.

"The workers finished the first two sections and masons are beginning to lay up another course of stone."

"We will be careful with all of the ropes and cranes in use, Your Majesty," Sam said.

"Of course you will. I can't have Little Squirrel getting squashed on the pier!"

Elayna frowned playfully.

"Don't call me Little Squirrel anymore, Father, I don't like it."

"Would Big Squirrel be any better?"

Elayna crossed her arms, squinted her eyes at him, and shook her head, her auburn hair bouncing as she did so.

"All right, all right," the king said. "What shall I call you now?"

"Just call me Elayna," she said defensively.

"You sound so formal, and grown-up, Princess Elayna," King Lukald said and he bowed to her formally.

The girl giggled and ran to her father for a hug before joining the servant Sam on the way to the harbor.

~

Owen, the Master of the Guild of stonecutters in Candoreth, guided his workmen with an urgency born of war.

"I don't know where these blasted pirates came from, but they're not from South of Horming," his journeyman, observed.

They both wore leather aprons and carried the tools of their trade. All hands were needed. The Stonecutter Guild rarely had an opportunity to be heroes. The pirates with their strange new weapons had changed that. The men worked feverishly to repair the city walls.

"I don't care where they came from," Owen said, "but I know where I would like them to go."

The journeyman, named Simon, smiled and wiped the sweat from his brow. The moisture mixed with the stone dust left a cream-colored smear across his forehead.

Owen looked up at the sun, evaluating its position in the sky.

"The work isn't going as fast as I hoped. The old stone walls needed to be repaired even before we had enemies on the horizon."

Simon nodded. "I've heard the rumors, too. The smoke and fire laid waste to our strongest ships, shattered the masts and hulls with impact and burned others to the waterline."

"It's hard to believe, isn't it?" Owen said, as he secured the tips of the lifting tackle into the divots he cut in the heavy stone block. He waved to the men operating the tall wooden crane, motioning to them that they could safely take up the slack in the ropes.

"The men keep working, despite not being paid," Simon observed.

"Patriotic duty stokes the fire of their willingness," Owen said, "I just worry that since the food shipment stopped, the poor ones will be weak from hunger, before we can bring in the next harvest."

"These are hard times," Simon agreed.

The stone block began to move. First one side, then the other, rising slowly into the air. The block of stone was medium-sized, and Master Owen could just reach each corner if he spread his arms as wide. The stone would be used to repair the ancient harbor wall. The structure had gone into some disrepair, but with the new-found threat to the city, people were reminded of the wisdom their forebearers had shown in building it.

"Now, lift the other side and level it out," Owen called.

The crane operators adjusted the tension on the pulley. The metal teeth bit into the stone.

"That's better," Owen said.

Men on the platform used an iron pin to hitch the draft horses to the wooden beam that served as a lever to rotate the crane. The horses bent their necks and settled into the harness as they moved the next block through the air toward the rising harbor wall.

"Look who's come to visit," Simon said suddenly, noticing a figure advancing.

He pointed toward the wooden portions of the pier.

"That looks like Princess Elayna," Owen said.

"At least she's supervised this time," muttered Simon.

"She was always getting underfoot, but how do you tell a member of the royalty to leave the job site?" Owen mused.

"I've never seen a girl with so much energy."

"She's a lot like her sister, and her mother for that matter. Poor girl," Owen said as he tucked a chisel into his leather apron.

"Still, she's always cheerful. I can see her smile from here," Simon said.

The stone block passed overhead, and the little princess pointed to it, watching it arc through its pathway toward the wall.

Watching, Owen said, "Go and make sure they put the final dressing on the block. I'll find out what the girl wants."

Owen climbed down and made his way to the pier, dusting bits of stone from his clothing.

"What can I do for you today, Your Highness?" the master mason queried, appraising the girl and her company.

Princess Elayna stood flanked by two men. On her right was a servant in castle livery; Sam was his name, if Owen recalled correctly. And on her left stood the white-bearded Sīhalt Guardian who never left the girl's side, Girdy Frast.

"What are you doing today Master Owen?" the girl asked in her high-pitched tone, as she watched the block of stone swing through the air. The ocean breeze ruffled her light blue dress as she swayed playfully.

"We are cutting stone to fix the ancient wall—just like the other day when you asked," he answered.

"I wish to go up on the wall and watch them set the stone," she replied.

Owen looked at Sam. The servant shrugged and the Sīhalt was looking out to sea, as if he expected to see a pirate ship immediately on the horizon.

The white-bearded warrior spoke without looking at them: "If it will not be too much trouble. The girl has been cooped up for days, but all she talks about is your building project."

"I suppose it can't hurt for a few moments," Owen reasoned after musing on it awhile. "Just follow close by me, and watch your head as we go under the scaffolding."

Owen led the trio along the twisting path that wound its way among the workers. Wherever the little girl walked, workers doffed their hats and paid respect to Princess Elayna. The exhaustion Owen saw on so many of their faces was dimmed at the little girl's presence. After paying their respect, the men stood a little taller, shouldering their burdens with greater determination. The little red-haired girl reminded the men of why they worked and fought so hard.

If her presence inspires the men to their duty, maybe I should request to have Princess Elayna visit every day, Owen thought as he pondered the ripple of energy flowing through his men.

"Usually you are full of questions," Owen said. "Why are you quiet today, Highness?"

Princess Elayna ran her hands along the stonework leading to the section of the wall that was being repaired.

"Because today I want to help, so I've decided to listen."

"You want to help, do you?" Owen said as he chuckled. "Well, look at all these men. I've noticed that as you walk by, they all seem inspired by your visit. Just walking the ramparts, and looking down at them as they work, is enough to help them do their best."

"It's true. You are helping, Elayna, just by being here," Girdy added in his gravelly voice.

They approached the workmen as they directed the setting of the stone that had been hoisted into the air. The great block twisted gently, held by numerous ropes as the men turned it and lowered it into position.

"That ought to keep the pirates out," one of the workmen said with a wink toward Elayna.

But something had gripped the princess. Her brow was furrowed, and she was squinting up at the stone with intense concentration. "The stone isn't set right," Elayna observed, looking at the joint between previous course, and the new block.

Owen inspected the setting with his practiced eye. At first, all seemed well. Then, upon further inspection, he saw it—a flaw at the joint. It would've been no problem if these were joints with mortar, but the repair of the harbor wall was intended to mimic the methods used in the past. They weren't using mortar, and there was an imperfection on the block that needed to be fixed.

"Excellent eye, Your Highness!" Owen said in admiration, "My, you are right! I do indeed see a place where the stone must be trimmed." Turning to the crane operators, he motioned for them to raise the block once more. When the block was suspended above the wall, Owen spoke to one of the masons.

"Jed, use your fine chisel and smooth off that corner a bit," he said.

The man held his hammer in one hand, and reached for the chisel with the other.

"Can I do it?" Elayna asked.

The mason looked to Sam. "Is she allowed?" he asked.

"Princess Elayna is heir to the throne of Candoreth. She can do just about anything she desires," the servant replied.

Mason offered the little girl his hammer and chisel. She took them in her small hands and hefted them, feeling the weight. She frowned and shook her head.

"These are pretty heavy," she said. "How do you use them all day without getting tired?"

"I do get tired," the mason replied, "but it's my duty to repair the wall."

Elayna handed the tools back to the mason. "I think I'll just use my hands," she said.

The men smiled and humored the child as she approached the newly cut stone.

"Steady that block, Jed. Secure it so it's safe for the princess to work on it." He winked at the mason who made a show in preparing himself for whatever work the little girl might pretend to do.

Elayna approached the stone. She laid her hand on it, and stroked it softly as she might have done a puppy. Next, the little girl began to hum, and then leaned in and whispered to the stone.

"I am your friend," she said, caressing it, running her fingers to feel every etch and chip.

Owen furrowed his brow. He had never seen a child behave like this. He often felt a kind of love for special pieces of stone himself and that was why he chose to dedicate his life to masonry so many years ago. The rock had always seemed to speak to him, at times, but he rarely spoke back like the girl was doing now.

The princess approached the corner of the block that was in need of adjustment. She tilted her head, examining the contours while humming a simple tune. Then she grabbed the corner of the stone with both hands and began to smooth the block in opposite directions. Owen was puzzled by her actions, as were the other men. The girl closed her eyes. The afternoon sun shone down and a cool spring breeze passed over the wall. Owen watched as the shadow cast by the stone danced with the slight movement of the rope, still suspended a few feet off the ground. Had it changed —slightly?

"Okay, I'm all done," the girl announced brightly.

Owen smiled. "All right, Jed. Get in there and dress the stone so we can set it. Thank you for visiting, Your Highness."

"But it is done," Elayna insisted.

"Right, I'll just give it a touch," Jed said.

Elayna's small hand shot out and stopped the mason in his tracks. She held him by the arm. "You'll mess it up. Don't touch it."

"Yes, Princess," he said with a bow, now taking her seriously, due to her tone.

Owen looked from the block to the girl and back to the block.

He reached for his calipers.

"I think it is okay, Jed," he said, taking a closer look at the block. The shape seemed to be perfect for the space and he was not totally sure, but the chisel marks on the surface seemed to have been softened as well.

"Set it into place again," he commanded.

With the creaking of the ropes the block was once more lowered onto the wall. It fit perfectly.

"Maybe we didn't need to adjust it after all," Simon suggested.

"No. It was not shaped correctly—before Elayna touched it," Owen said reverently.

Elayna smiled. "Now look at it. It fits!" she beamed.

The master mason and his second looked closely at the stone. A tingle ran down Owen's spine as he appreciated the artistry of the well-set stone. His calloused hands passed over the block, examining every inch of the joint. It was seamless and made all the other blocks that had been set previously look like they had been done by an apprentice mason in his first year.

He turned slowly toward the girl and knelt in the dust. Owen pulled his well-used hammer and chisel from his leather apron and held it up to the girl.

"Will you touch my chisel?" he asked reverently, "I have always dreamed of having a Builder of ancient days bless the tools of my trade," he said with moisture brimming in his eyes.

"Then put down your metal tools and let me touch your hand, Master mason," the little girl said, " for those are your true tools." The little girl smiled and laid her delicate hand in his.

"Is there any other way we might improve our work?" he asked her sincerely.

"I would put some flowers on the stone to decorate it," she said.

With that she reached up and placed her hand on the stone block once more. Tiny lines creasing the stone spread out from her fingertips. The indentations widened and deepened as they watched, and the rock seemed to mold itself to a new shape as the man of the block changed to accommodate the decorated surface. Now carved stone flowers linked by stems and leaves adorned the edges of the stone block.

"I would be hard pressed to do that in an afternoon. That is stone work of the highest quality," Owen exclaimed.

"I think it's prettier with the flowers," Elayna said.

"How did you learn to do that?" Sam asked.

"Yes, who taught you?" Girdy added.

Elayna shrugged nonchalantly. "I just practiced when I was making sand castles. Even the littlest rocks moved whenever I would ask them to," she said.

"Can you move a big rock?" Owen asked, pointing to a large block of stone newly cut for the wall.

"I don't know. I never asked one that big to move for me."

"Try to move it," Girdy suggested, excited now. "It is okay if you can't."

Elayna nodded and then walked toward the large stone block. Simon removed the ropes that had been laid across the surface. The stone was larger than the one that had just been placed; it was longer by almost double. Simon shook his head in amazement.

"This is a miracle," he said.

"Even if she can't move it, I can die happy. I have witnessed the return of a Builder to Candoreth!" Owen added.

Elayna put both hands on the massive stone block and placed her cheek next to it.

"Will you move for me?" she asked with child-like innocence.

Then she began to push the stone across the ground toward the wall.

"It slid as if it is no heavier than a down pillow on a polished floor!" Simon exclaimed, pointing to the moving stone.

"The rocks and debris gathering at the leading edge tell a different story," Owen observed. "That stone is as heavy as it ever was—and yet she moves it without effort."

"Let me try, Elayna," Sam said.

The servant pushed with all his might but the stone did not budge. "I can't move it at all," he said.

Elayna smiled. "You have to ask it to move," she explained.

"The rocks don't listen to everyone, Your Highness, but you are special," Owen said.

The little girl's eyes squinted with her broad smile. "I can put it in place for you if you want," she offered.

"You can lift it?" Owen asked.

"I will put it right in place," she offered.

The men stood in amazement. The teams of masons and their apprentices stopped their labors and watched as the youngest daughter of their king moved a stone worthy of the strength of fifty men or two teams of oxen.

She pushed the massive block to the top of the wall without any harnesses, wedges, pulleys or ropes. The stone dropped, with a resounding thud, into place. Following her adjustments to the surface, it fit as neatly as the previous stone. Some of the workers dropped their hammers, their fingers forgetting their strength as their eyes witnessed the impossible.

"She's a Builder!" Owen shouted to the men under his command. "Candoreth has a Builder!"

The men began to shout for joy and their voices made Elayna draw back. She looked to Girdy, unsure if she had done something wrong.

"Don't worry," Girdy said, "You've given them hope that they can finish the wall before it is too late."

Elayna looked up at the men on the scaffolding. They cheered mightily for her. She waved and another surge of shouts washed over them.

"Do you think Father will let me help them tomorrow?" she asked.

Girdy and Sam nodded vigorously. "I am sure of it," Sam said.

A KING'S RANSOM

K ing Lukald slumped in the gilded chair and passed his hands over his face and through his fiery red hair. His temples were tinged with white that blended with the auburn shade. He was no longer a young man and today he felt much older than his fifty-five years.

"What do the reports say, Girdy?"

"It isn't good, Your Majesty," the old Sīhalt Guardian replied.

Girdy didn't look at the report in front of him as he recounted their losses. The man had a memory like a steel trap. He never forgot anything once his eyes had latched onto it. Lukald wished he could forget what he was seeing now—the wholesale slaughter of the entire Candorethian Navy.

"Have the pirates told us what they want?" he asked finally in resignation.

The Sīhalt shook his head. "They have made no effort to negotiate."

"They are desperate, like us," the king said. "They will fight to the death. Where else can they go? Where else would *I* go, given their situation?"

"Their ships look like they have taken a beating. The reports say they have arrived with their women and children," Girdy explained.

"When they showed up on our eastern horizon, many of the sails were in tatters. But if they have brought their families, they intended to stay in Desnia all along."

"Those were my thoughts, Your Majesty."

"Imagine how many they started out with. They must have lost many ships when they crossed the Sea of Storms. They cannot go back in the shape they are in. They must see us as the weakest, most susceptible kingdom on the coast, and I suppose they are right." He sighed gravely.

"Hestin has made no move to help us," Girdy added.

Lukald shook his head. "I didn't expect them to reply. They keep to their own and look after their own interests. I asked Queen Renata to send for help, but she would not even do that."

Girdy drew back the corners of one side of his mouth. It was an expression of disapproval Lukald had come to recognize many years before. Usually the old Sīhalt Guardian would say little else when he made that expression. It meant he didn't think a person would change their course of action. When Girdy looked like that, it meant he would soon leave, or fight, but not continue to discuss things.

"If I had to strike a city on the Emerald Coast, it would be Candoreth. The very islands that have protected us are being used against us now," Lukald observed.

Girdy nodded in agreement. He adjusted the thin black cape of his Sīhalt cloak.

"We do have some reports that Marth has been taken over," he said.

Lukald jerked his head up. "Marth?" he repeated, shocked. "They have already subdued the people of Marth?"

"That is what the reports say."

"Then we are lost, Girdy! If we cannot command the sea, what hope do we have? They will hop from island to island until they have a foothold at our gates. Not even the harbor walls will keep them out."

"They are attacking the harbor walls, as we speak. They have some strange and powerful ships that spew fire and thunder. The men are doing their best," Girdy said, but his tone, dropping down at the end of his statement was another bad sign.

"Fire and thunder?" Lukald repeated, and, as if to punctuate the question, a diminished *boom* could be heard in the distance.

The king leveled his eyes at his trusted Guardian.

"That is the thunder ship I speak of," Girdy confirmed.

"Father! I'm frightened!" Princess Elayna said as she ran into the room.

"Where were you hiding?" King Lukald asked, changing his expression to hide the worry in his heart.

"Over there," Elayna said, pointing to the short hallway that led to the private office.

The girl had the run of the palace since the horrific letter came from Tyath and her subsequent Talent for Building had been revealed. King Lukald insisted that his last remaining child be able to visit him any time of the day or night. Lukald pulled his daughter close to him, wrapping his arms around her and holding her head against his chest.

"They are breaking the walls," Elayna said, her tone tinged with anger. She might have been speaking of a foolish boy, being a bully on the beach, the kind that finds joy in destroying the play of smaller children. But this bully was no child and the stakes were so much greater than a sandcastle on the beach.

"You did a good job fixing them. I am proud of you," Lukald said, still holding her close.

"You made them very tall and thick," Girdy added. "They will have a difficult time breaking though."

"As soon as one ship hits the wall, that one sails away and another takes its place. The trebuchets cannot reach them, but they can reach us with the thunder," Elayna explained, as if tattling on her older sister.

"You shouldn't be watching all this," Lukald said, struggling to control the tone in his voice. He swallowed his sadness and raised his chin.

Elayna folded her small arms across her chest and stood frowning, her nostrils flaring as she breathed.

"I don't like them," she stated.

"I don't like them either," Lukald said, "they want to take our city and make Candoreth their city."

Elayna frowned. "They are not allowed to do that," she said, as if the pirates, or whatever they called themselves, should know the faulty morality of their invasion.

"We are trying to stop them, but if they break through, I want you to ride with Sīhalt Girdy to Horming. We have relatives there."

"They are *not* going to break through," Elayna said adamantly.

Lukald wished he felt the same certainty as the eight year old girl.

"Our sailors and soldiers are dying to protect us, Elayna. This is a war," Girdy said. "And sometimes you don't win at war."

Elayna closed her eyes, as if by doing so she could close off the words that entered her ears. She didn't like what she was hearing and Lukald knew that although she had the sweetness of her mother, the little girl had inherited his temper.

"Go with Girdy now. And don't look out the windows anymore. You have done your part Elayna, and we are all very thankful to you."

She stood obstinately and shook her head sharply.

"Elayna..." Lukald said, softening his voice, calling to the child's heart.

Still, she stood with eyes closed against the tears that rolled down her cheeks, and shook her head defiantly.

"Take Princess Elayna to her chambers and have the maids

pack her things. I will not have my daughter taken by these ruffians, should they win the day."

Girdy nodded and walked toward Elayna. The little girl shifted her weight and removed the slipper from one foot and then the other, so that she was now barefoot on the stone floor.

Girdy bent down and put his hands under Elayna's arms as if he would sweep her up and carry her out the door, but when the Sīhalt Guardian began to lift, he grunted and let go of the girl.

The look on the old man's face was one of surprise, and that was not an expression often seen of the face of Girdy Frast.

King Lukald looked at the Sīhalt and then at Elayna.

"I can't pick her up," Girdy said.

The king furrowed his brow. "Did you throw your hip out again?"

Elayna looked satisfied as she glanced toward her father and then the Guardian. Her small frame was dwarfed by the two powerful men that stood over her.

"I might as well try and lift a horse!" Girdy exclaimed.

"Elayna, what have you done?" Lukald demanded.

"I'm not letting go of the stone until you say I can help them," she said, wriggling her toes. Her small feet seemed to sink into the granite under her feet as if it was mud softened by a spring rain.

"Help who?" Girdy asked.

"The pirates like to break things, and I like to Build. So I will build the wall faster than they can break it!" she said with a determined smile.

King Lukald turned to Girdy.

"Who would have guessed that the Kingdom of Candoreth would ultimately be defended by a child?"

33

MARTH ESTATE

Channing resisted the urge to run up the hill to his home, perched above the sea, on the edge of Marth Island.

"Well, I'll be," he forced himself to say slowly as they disembarked. "He's still alive."

Lord Our Ruston stood high not he hill, surveying the process of the men below. Channing Dur Ruston patted the foreign pirates on the back and gestured for his friends to follow as he walked up the pier, past the swaying marsh grass to the path that led up toward his home. Heathron and Jared followed him but Seth declined.

"I'll wait here with the others," he explained. "I can have the boat ready to cross to the other side as soon as you return."

Lord Dur Ruston stood planted on the path. His red cloak caught the breeze that blew over Marth Island and was tossed full length behind. The large polished buttons that ran from collar to hem of the garment glinted blindingly in the sun. He was tall, like Channing, but heavier built, with a plump stomach and a thickness to his neck and shoulders that made him bristle like a bull. He wore a well-trimmed mustache and his hair was long enough to cover his collar when the wind wasn't tossing it like his cloak.

Channing strode forward and embraced his father and turned a few steps in a circle as they hugged.

"Checking to see if any of them are around?" Lord Dur Ruston said.

"And I'm glad to see you alive!" Channing replied.

"We can speak freely. I've gained their trust," he explained.

"Allow me to introduce you to my friends, F?ather," Channing said, turning to Heathron and Jared.

"This is Heathron Dol Lassimer, Heir to the imperial throne in the Golden City, and next to him, Jared De Torre, a Sīhalt Guardian of Windstall."

Lord Dur Ruston bowed formally to the two visitors. They returned the honor with an inclination of their heads.

"You've improved the company you keep, son," Lord Dur Ruston said. "Before you joined the military it was all gamblers, miscreants and whores."

"The cream rises to the surface given time," Channing replied, shaking his head at his friends and rolling his eyes a bit. His father chuckled and repeated the saying, "'The cream rises to the surface--given time.' Very good," he acknowledged, and hugged his son again, impressed with his development.

"Now, come, your mother will want to see you."

Channing seemed to hesitate. "Are you sure about that?"

Lord Dur Ruston waved his hand as if to swat a fly. "She forgave you before you even rode past the south lawn. You should have seen her pining for her little Channing every day you were in training, and then how proud she was to hear that you had served so well and made the rank of lieutenant.

"I'm a captain now," Channing said.

"Then even prouder still she will be. Come, let bygones be bygones," Lord Dur Ruston said, and draped an arm around his son's strong shoulders to lead the way. They began walking up the long path toward the house.

"I must say, Father, I am surprised at the welcome the pirates have received at your hand. What game are you playing?"

"No game, son. If I had resisted, there would be nothing left of our Grand Primrose. I heard the reports of what they had done to plantations on the other islands. The entire length of Shrimstock is burned black. All of the boats that tried to escape were burned or sunk. I shudder to think of all the people that died."

"How did you convince our island to comply?"

He took a deep breath before answering, his broad chest expanding, and raised his eyebrows in that customary way he did when delivering contestable news. "The people in Marth wanted to assemble a resistance, and I don't blame them. I did too. But the numbers that sailed over the horizon..." He took another deep breath. "All I could do was throw open my gates and welcome them, to give us time to plot a course to freedom. We have all had to deal with raiders at one point or another, but nothing like this."

"Their fleet is vast and they are attacking Candoreth," Channing said.

For the first time since their introductions, Jared spoke. "Have they been respectful to your family, Lord Dur Ruston?" he asked, eager to form a picture of the pirates' ways and customs of warfare.

"They are an ordered lot—thankfully. They seem to be a mix of races. The officers are all shorter and stockier, with straight black hair and fierce eyes that constantly squint. The other men look as if they could hail from Tyath, Candoreth, or Hestin. They told me they sailed across the seas from the Old Realm—Sulia, I think."

Jared nodded and rubbed his chin as he absorbed all of this. "We truly live in unsettling times," he said.

"But with Lilly to help us, I think we could go out to investigate," Channing suggested. "I know nothing about the speed of their ships, but I doubt we need to worry. They won't be able to catch us if we have Lilly helping us to sail."

"We should go to Candoreth first and find out what communication, if any, King Lukald has had with the pirates." the Sīhalt said.

"I know Princess Kathleen wants to see her family too," Channing replied.

Jared nodded. "We will go to Candoreth first. Do you plan to stay here?" he asked.

"If the Marthian militia was being raised, I would be among the first to draw my sword, but if the strategy here is to comply until the opportunistic day arrives, to throw off the yolk of the invaders, then I will go with you to help bring it about," Channing said.

He forced a smile and tipped his plumed hat to a group of bearded pirates walking by. They tipped a bottle of rum in return and laughed, staggering on.

"They are unloading families and have taken over the Marso Estates on the north shore," Jared said. "One of the farmers told me as much in town. He said the boats were full of women and children."

Channing squinted at the sun and swallowed. "We need to take action soon, I don't want to lose my homeland without a fight."

Lord Dur Ruston placed both of his hands on his son's shoulders and squeezed them. "Indeed, but the answer to all this, to our survival, lies in freeing Candoreth. We are outmatched, son. Do what you can for the king and return to fight here with honor."

"I will, Father."

34

THE SUNSHINE BRIDE RETURNS

"I do not believe what my eyes tell me!" King Lukald stood and took a shaking, tentative step toward them. His voice trembled with the possibility of truly seeing his daughter alive.

"Am I dreaming? Is that why I was not told you are here?" he said.

Before him stood two Sīhalt Guardians—one reminiscent of the man who escorted Kathleen—and there was a tall, handsome nobleman with golden hair. Heathron? It seemed so long ago. Even Melva stood there, just behind them. She was thinner than ever but smiling nevertheless.

"The immense stress of my current existence has certainly caused me to see, or want to believe things that are not true. How often have I imagined that my harbor is free of the enemy ships? How many times have I looked out this very tower window and thought I saw gentle blue waves slapping the docks, with merchant ships loading and unloading their trade goods, bringing prosperity to our shore once more? I've had countless dreams that the woman I love most in my life is brought back to me."

He took another step forward. Then Kathleen stepped out

from behind the protective stance of the Sīhalt Guardian. The king inhaled deeply.

"I knew that I was daydreaming then, as much as I might wish it to be true. But now, with *you* here... Tell me, are you a figment of my imagination, or an infinite blessing in my time of need?"

Lukald still was not convinced he could trust his senses. He wanted to rush to embrace her—but feared she would vanish like a vision of the night, like the flicker of firelight, or wispy sprites in the mist.

"Are you my dearest Annalise or my sweet Kathleen grown to look even more like her mother?

"Father," Kathleen said, and took step, coming toward him.

King Lukald's feet obeyed his heart, not waiting for his mind to make sense of the beautiful dream. She ran to him with arms outstretched.

"Oh, Katie," Lukald heard himself say as she folded into his arms. His hands sought her cheeks and pulled her face away from his chest so that he might look into her eyes.

"They told me you died," he said, pursing his lips as the tears flowed into his matted beard. Kathleen hugged him again and sobbed just like she had as a child, when he had gone into her room after a nightmare. They stood like this, swaying—each one silent, then sobbing, silent, then sobbing—as a gentle breeze might move a branch's new spring growth. Lukald felt his heart full to overflowing.

"Dear Abbath, how did you manage this?" he muttered, not sure if the question was for Kathleen, the Sīhalt Guardians, or the God from whom he was estranged.

The two Sīhalt Guardians advanced, surveying the room as if it too might be full of the enemy. One of them Lukald recognized, but he had aged significantly in the year since he had seen them last. The handsome nobleman with blond hair that brushed his shoulders, bowed to King Lukald. He looked youthful, but carried an air of weighted pain. Lukald thought he recognized that look—one of a conscientious monarch.

"You must be Heathron. You have grown since I last saw you," Lukald said, as he grasped Kathleen's hand, not wanting to let go of his newly returned child.

Prince Heathron stepped forward and suddenly embraced King Lukald, too. His strength, and the surprise of the more intimate greeting made the king exhale suddenly, and then he returned the hug with a series of strong pats on his back. Both Sīhalt Guardians looked at the king and the prince and then at each other, inquisitive expressions flickering across their otherwise stoic faces.

"If hugs are the way of greeting in Candoreth, I embrace it," Heathron said emphatically as he held the king.

"Very well," Lukald replied, patting the prince on the back in a subtle sign that the embrace could be concluded.

Through her tears of joy, Kathleen let out a laugh, looking at the two of them. "Heathron, we don't *always* hug as a greeting in Candoreth," she explained, wiping her nose with handkerchief.

The prince stood, and looked from Kathleen to Lukald, embarrassment coloring his cheeks.

He chuckled humorlessly, as if to check himself. "I am sorry, I have assumed too much, Your Majesty," he said, and backpedaled several steps.

"No you haven't, lad!" Lukald replied, "You brought my daughter back to me, and if it weren't for you, our people might have starved over the winter! So if I might..." The red-bearded king grasped Heathron's hand and pulled the imperial prince back into a rib-crushing hug of gratitude.

"It..was...my...pleasure," Heathron managed to reply, despite the strength of the embrace.

Lukald let go of Heathron and then embraced Kathleen again, still unable to contain the joy he felt knowing she was yet alive. Then he froze, his eyebrows arching up in sudden realization at something. "Elayna needs to know you are here," he said to Kathleen as he held her tight.

"Of course! I want to see her, too," Kathleen replied, spinning around as if she might see her sister in the hall.

"She's not here. She's probably in one of the towers that overlook the harbor. I told her not to look out at the devastation, but she has refused to listen to me. She wants to help. So instead of sending her to Horming, I've kept her here."

"How could she possibly help?" Kathleen asked incredulously. "She is just a girl, Father."

The king raised an eyebrow and grinned, then wagged a finger. "That was once said of you too, Kathleen. I may have even thought it myself a few times, but take a look out the window with me."

Confused, she let her father do it, and King Lukald led his eldest daughter to the window. There lay the expanse of the harbor. Beyond, they could see the Turtle islands scattered along the blue horizon. Foreign pirate ships lay at anchor, just beyond reach of the castle's remaining trebuchets. What was left of the Candorethian Navy was bottled up at the north end of the harbor, unable to maneuver or defend its city.

"I suppose the only reason they have not burned our remaining ships, is because we don't pose a threat by sea anymore," Lukald frowned.

Kathleen gave a long shuddering sigh and turned to looked to Jared and Prince Heathron. She waved them over to the window as well, as if to give them permission, for they had been standing very still and subservient in the presence of the king—and the father of the woman each of them loved.

"What can we possibly do against such odds?" she asked them, after a few moments of allowing them to gauge the harbor. Channing and Seth had moved over the flagstones to join them, too.

The prince was the first to react, whistling softly as he

surveyed the horizon, taking in all the pirate ships that threatened Candoreth.

"They haven't broken through the wall yet," Captain Channing observed.

"That is what I wanted to show you," Lukald said. "Do you see the new stone, where they join the old ones—close to that grove of trees?"

Kathleen and the others nodded, looking in the direction Lukald pointed.

"That is all new. Every last stone was cut and shaped and put in place over the last few weeks."

"That must have been a monumental task," the younger of the two Sīhalt Guardians said.

Lukald nodded.

"How did you manage to recruit so many masons to work on the walls while also fighting a battle for our shores?" Channing asked.

Lukald shook his head. "I wouldn't believe it myself, if I had not seen it with my own eyes."

"Elayna did this?" Melva tottered forward, laying her delicate old hands on the ledge and craning her neck to lean slightly out the window to get a better look at the enormous harbor wall. A gust of wind blew her gray hair away from her face, and Lukald saw the old Healer smiling with pride.

"How blessed you are, Lukald, to have two daughters of the Talents."

Kathleen furrowed her brow, confused. Then it hit her. "Wait...she did that? Elayna?! But...the enormity of the task... the city walls...it's just not possible, is it?"

Lukald, smiling now, nodded. "I assure you, daughter, it is. She can move the stone no matter how big the block. It is magical to watch."

"Your sister is a Builder," said the Sīhalt standing closest to

Kathleen, as if to help the source of amazement settle on her. But even his tone was reverent, filled with awe.

"But I thought she was only seven years old," Prince Heathron said.

"I'm eight," came a child's voice from across the room. "I just had my birthday."

35

A GOOD HUSBAND

All the heads turned to see Princess Elayna walking toward them, accompanied several steps behind her by the servant, Sam. The curls of her auburn hair bobbed as she swept her gaze right and left, taking in all the new faces.

After a moment of shock, Kathleen ran to her, falling to her knees, hugging the child. Elayna put her arms around Kathleen's neck, returning the embrace.

"It was your birthday the other day, wasn't it?" Kathleen muttered through her tears. "I thought I would never see you again—never see you older than you were."

"Well, now you do," the young princess replied, and everyone laughed. "I knew I would see you again. It's okay if you forgot my birthday. There's been a lot going on," Elayna said in a comforting tone.

Lukald felt his heart swell at the sight of his girls together once more and he could not fully hold back the emotion.

Melva came and leaned over the two of them, placing a hand on each of their heads, as a grandmother might do.

Elayna's small hands clung tightly to her sister.

"You've grown so much!" Kathleen said as she knelt, looking into her little sister's eyes.

Elayna smiled and looked around at the group of adults that surrounded them. Her eyes danced across the new faces she didn't recognize.

"Is he your husband?" Elayna asked, pointing to Heathron. Kathleen felt surprised by the suddenness of the question, and did not immediately respond. "He's really handsome," Elayna added, smiling up at the prince with dreamy eyes.

"Yes, he is," Kathleen managed to say, somewhat embarrassed by the dynamic of the audience and the urgency of the setting.

The prince bowed formally to Elayna.

"Heathron Dol Lassimer, at your service, Princess Elayna," he said. His movements were practiced and graceful, the tone of his voice filled with its usual regal air. Seeing Heathron for the first time though the eyes of her family, Kathleen appreciated to a greater degree the handsomeness of his features, and majesty of his bearing.

"I bet he's a really good husband," Elayna said, not taking her eyes off the prince.

Kathleen's face reddened, especially when she noticed Jared's eyes glance toward her, despite the Sīhalt Guardian's defensive stance on the perimeter.

"We are not married...yet, Elayna" Kathleen said.

The little girl furrowed her brows and turned to look at Kathleen. "But I thought that was the whole reason you went to the Golden City in the first place."

"It's a long story," Melva said, placing a hand on Elayna's shoulder.

"Will *you* tell me the story?" Elayna asked.

"We'll all hear the story, Elayna," interrupted King Lukald. "But we must all eat and have something to drink first. You have seen hardship on your journey here, no doubt," he added, flicking his eyes up to his eldest daughter.

"That sounds wonderful," Kathleen agreed, glad to have the subject changed to something other than the status of her relationship with Heathron.

∾

The meal was not grand, but it was wholesome and nourishing. They sat around a large wooden table bearing silver platters,

"We will give thanks to Abboth or your safe return," Lukald said.

It was the first time in many years that Kathleen heard her father offer sincere gratitude to the Creator. He held her hand as he prayed, and Kathleen opened her eyes to see him with bowed head and furrowed brow. She felt grateful to have a good man for a father.

After the prayer, Kathleen wondered where Renata might be, but decided not to risk the question, and ruin the moment. She savored the sweetness of the potatoes, and especially enjoyed the familiar seasonings of her homeland: the rolls were topped with bits of rosemary and the butter was mixed with honey and a dash of cinnamon. Kathleen closed her eyes and smelled the food in a long luxuriant inhalation. Even in its simplicity she felt a great sense of thankfulness. From the look on Channing's face, he had missed the Candorethian cuisine as much as she had.

While they ate, King Lukald told of how the strange pirate ships first began to appear along the coast and then increased in numbers rapidly: "They seemed to arrive overnight, waves of them. We fought them back initially, but they kept coming. We were outnumbered and truthfully, out sailed. These pirate ships are more agile than our own, and they use a system of rigging unknown to us. Genius, really."

"You say they come from the East?" Jared asked.

Lukald nodded. "They are not all one people. I've gathered

that," Lukald explained. "Some of them have speech that is very fast and deep in the throat. They use words we do not know, and have eyes that are sharper in shape, almost as if they are squinting."

He mimicked the look by pulling the corner of his eye, tightening the skin around it.

"Others look and sound like us, but their speech is somewhat thick and slow. They all refer to us as the 'colonies.'" He threw up his hands in frustration. "*The colonies!* Anyway, we don't know very much about Centia, or Sulia, or the ancient nations that make up the Old World, but that is where these people lived. I do not yet know why they have come to Desnia, or why they are making war on us, but they intend to stay."

The seriousness of the observation settled on the gathering. "I wonder if they could sail home, even if they wanted to do so," Channing agreed.

"Then we are left with few options," King Lukald observed. "We can fight to the death, and try to destroy them, or we could seek to make peace with them— in some way."

"They came as aggressors! Many of the island dwellers have been killed. I do not desire peace with them, " Channing said.

"Who leads them? Even pirates have a leadership structure," Seth said.

"We saw a ship that might have been a flagship of some kind, off the northern coast of Marth. They are using the island as their headquarters. Some of their men spoke of an admiral," Channing offered.

"If we could get in contact with their officers, perhaps we could negotiate with them. There is land available in Desnia, but they must not take our homes," Kathleen agreed.

"Why not sail out to the flagship and speak with them. If they have a supreme leader, we could kill him."

"Or her," Lilly added.

"Or her," Maxwell agreed with a smile. "Although I don't like killing girls, especially when they are pretty," he added.

Lilly rolled her eyes. "Then leave it to me, Maxwell. I wouldn't hesitate."

"I believe that about you!" he chortled.

"So if we can get a team on board that ship to open negotiations, we might be able to forestall the house to house combat that is certain to descend on Candoreth. Even a short truce would help us to get the supplies we need for our soldiers. They have been demoralized."

"Who can go, and who should stay?"

"Maxwell and I should certainly go. He can do reconnaissance and I can help the ship to sail where it needs to go," Lilly said.

"I want to be there," Channing said adamantly. "Especially if we are going back to Marth."

"Prince Heathron's presence here in Candoreth will give hope to the soldiers. They're not all aware of the coup in Tyath. The men will rally knowing House Dol Lassimer is with us."

Heathron nodded. "I wish I had eighty thousand men-at-arms behind me, to shore up your defenses. If my presence will help in Candoreth, then I will don some armor and stand with you in the city's defense," he exclaimed.

"I don't want you to go, Kathleen. I just got you back," her father said.

"No, I should go to negotiate. If we do it on Marth, I believe I could be safe," Kathleen said. "If we do not gain some advantage our whole nation will be lost. I love you, Father. You were willing to let me go before, to save our people, so let me help in this way. I can speak for you in the negotiations if we have any, and the people will still have their king."

Lukald nodded slowly. "I can't stand the thought of losing you again, but I see the wisdom in your words. I insist that the Sīhalt Guardian go with you. He has shown his skill in protecting you and his willingness to fight fiercely in your defense."

Jared inclined his head toward the king. "Thank you, Your Majesty. I will accompany Princess Kathleen, and defend her on this endeavor."

And I will help to rally your men," Heathron said.

The old Healer spoke next. "If it is okay with you, Kathleen, I'd like to stay with Elayna and your father. I've missed them greatly, and my help may be needed among the wounded."

"Of course, Melva—I want you to stay here." Kathleen hugged the old Healer and felt the thinness of her torso. Her ribs and backbone stood out beneath her clothing. Kathleen was reminded that, for all of Melva's spirit, the old woman was physically frail and the poor treatment in Tyath had weakened her constitution.

"I think I should stay here, too," Larissa said, to which Kathleen and the others nodded.

"Hopefully we can be there and back, to simply open a dialogue with them."

"Be careful," King Lukald said.

"We won't force it. If the pirates are willing to talk we will do so, but if they seem to be false in their actions, we will return immediately," Kathleen said.

"It is decided then," King Lukald said gravely. "You will leave in the morning."

HAVE SOME CHERRIES

"**I** am sorry for the meagerness of the meal," King Lukald said.

The long wooden table in the great dining hall was set with food for the royal guests. Servants hurried to bring bowls of steaming porridge.

"We thank you for your hospitality," Heathron said.

"This food is fit for the peasants, but does no justice to the talent of my cooks!" Lukald exclaimed.

"There is no dishonor in it Your Majesty," Jared said as he lifted a spoonful of the hot cereal to his mouth.

"I wish I had some sweet berries for mine," Elayna said.

"I like it just the way it is," Heathron replied.

Elayna smiled at Heathron.

"Are you going to marry my sister?" the child asked coyly.

"We are going to marry," he replied.

"Because if she doesn't marry you, I will," the little girl offered.

"Elayna!" Kathleen said, "that is no way for a princess to behave."

"I'm glad you didn't take long to make up your mind, Elayna,"

Heathron observed with a smile, and winked at Kathleen. "Your older sister left me dangling for months on end."

"How can you be so decisive, little sister?" Kathleen asked, giving Elayna a squeeze.

"He's handsome," she said simply, and then covered her face in embarrassment.

"You don't have to be shy. I think he's handsome too."

"Thank you, Your Highness," Heathron said with formal bow to the little girl. Elayna blushed all the more.

"You've grown up so much since I left. I don't remember you liking any boys before."

"She is growing up fast, we're not even allowed to call her 'Little Squirrel' anymore," Sam explained.

"What?!" Kathleen said, and rushed over to sweep her little sister up in her arms. She held her tightly and began to tickle her stomach and sides. "What do you mean I can't call you Little Squirrel anymore?" she said, as she tickled Elayna despite her sister's squeals of laughter.

"She refused to go to Horming," King Lukald explained. " I wanted her to go there to keep her safe, should the worst happen, but she refused. She hid somewhere in the gardens and wouldn't be found. Then she showed us all what she could do with stones...amazing."

"I thought she was an Artist, I had no idea she was a Builder," Kathleen said, flashing a look of pleasant surprise to the girl.

Elayna stood a little taller, proud of the approbation she was getting from the adults in the room, and especially her big sister.

"She may be an Artist as well. You should have seen the sand-castle she made," Girdy added.

Elayna beamed.

"If Elayna can help us keep the walls strong, I think we can hold off the invasion. We closed the city gates and are gathering as many men from the towns and countryside as we can. They are not coming as quickly as I would like, but they are coming," Lukald observed.

"Do you have food enough for all of them?" Kathleen asked.

The king looked at Sam and then to Girdy. "We will have to manage," he said with some apprehension. "Our stores have not been built up to their normal levels but the people are willing to tighten their belts a little more if that is what it takes."

"He means we don't have enough food for everyone here. The people will likely be hungry, but we need them to fight in order to defend the city," Girdy intoned.

"If Elayna can help mend the walls, allow me to do my part as well," Kathleen said.

King Lukald looked at her with a confused expression on his face.

"I am a Green Grower, Father. In this time of great need, may I not use the Talent I have been given to help feed my people?"

Lukald's face softened. "Whatever small effort can be made will help. I suppose we must all work together, I just wonder what difference it will make. If it helps you to feel better, Kathleen, I am sure a few extra ripened fruits, here and there, will help to cheer the men. I just don't want you overdoing it. Elayna seems to do her work effortlessly and Melva warned me of the danger overuse of her Talent might bring," he said.

Kathleen nodded. "Father, walk with me to the garden just outside," she said. Then turning to the servant, she said, "Sam, will you bring four measures of grain from the kitchen?"

"Of course, Princess."

The group walked with Kathleen as she led them to the royal gardens. After she had passed the royal menagerie and stepped outside, she was comforted by the scene she had grown to love as a child. This had always been place of refuge for her, a place of sweet serenity when all the world seemed to turn against her. This was one of the places she missed the most while shivering in the dungeon at Tyath. The day was warm, not unlike the first day she met Jared, those many months ago. It seemed like decades, now.

The garden showed signs of being neglected. It was not surprising, given the difficulties of the past year. There were weeds growing along the paths, and the fruit trees had not been pruned as meticulously as she might have liked. Errant branches hung unevenly from the older, larger ones.

Kathleen took a few tentative steps into the garden and paused to look around.

"It's not been maintained," King Lukald murmured. "I told the servants to leave the gardens alone once I got the news that..." the king trailed off. He shook his head, his voice trembling now.

Kathleen looked at her father.

"I wanted to preserve it—as you liked it," he finally explained.

Just then, Sam arrived with the wheat in a large wooden scoop that he handed to Kathleen.

"Father, a garden, like a life, cannot be saved by ignoring it, or freezing it, or shutting it up in darkness. The only way to save a person, or a garden, is to allow them to grow," she said gently. Then she took a few steps over to her father and kissed him softly on the cheek. The others remained silent, respecting the reverence of the moment. "Nevertheless, I appreciate the gesture," she added, then turned to look back at the garden her mother had established. Kathleen felt joy rush through her. Her heart expanded as she realized what she was about to do.

For the first time in her life, she would demonstrate her Talent to her father and her people. She would show others the beauty of what she could do without feeling shame, or fear, or guilt. She was not being compelled to use her Talent. She wanted to Grow and it would be a gift for all of them.

Each person gathered here loves me, she thought and her soul seemed to expand to fill her body and beyond. She felt a tingling sensation that spread warmth throughout her chest, arms and legs. Kathleen looked at her hands and they seemed to glow with a light of their own. The air immediately surrounding her glowed, too.

"Kathleen, are you okay?" Elayna asked. The sound of her sister's voice made Kathleen smile all the more.

"I have never been better," she replied. She placed her hand on a branch of the nearest tree and felt for a moment the sweet sap flowing inside the living wood. She could feel the urgency the tree endured as it grew close to the garden wall, shaded part of the day by the larger trees outside the walls. It wanted to bend to receive more of the light

"I remember you, little one," she said and gave the tree encouragement with her Talent to grow and produce. In her mind she hummed the tune that always called to her when she first began to Grow plants, but now she no longer needed to vocalize the notes. The branches of the small cherry tree began to shake gently and with each movement; to and fro it thickened and grew taller. The central limb reached upward at a steady pace and the horizontal branch bloomed, set forth buds and then became heavily laden with ripe red cherries. They hung in large clusters, succulent and round.

"Those are beautiful," Girdy said in his gravelly voice.

The others nodded in agreement.

"The soldiers will be most pleased," Lukald added.

"I can do more than a few cherries," Kathleen said.

She walked to the center of the garden where the wind had swirled the fallen leaves from the previous year into a moldering pile. She used her foot to spread them out a bit and stood in the midst of them, then took a handful of the wheat berries and held them up, examining them. They were dry and hard, and so she tightened her fingers, closing her hand a bit as she allowed the music of her mind to act with her desire. The seeds became swollen as Kathleen activated them, turning the seeds on to the needed germination. They became swollen in her hand, pregnant with potential. She gave them another push with her Talent as she cast more handfuls into the air, with the practiced arc a sower might use to seed the fields of the highlands.

As soon as the wheat berries touched the nutrient-rich humus, they spread roots downward into the soil and shot blades of green above. Kathleen bent down and brushed her hand along the tops of the bright green shoots. The wheat immediately responded by growing taller and putting on heads of grain that were thick and full.

When she turned to look back at her small audience, Kathleen stood waist deep in a thick, healthy stand of wheat that was just becoming golden, almost ready for the sickle.

Heathron beamed. Jared watched her with his head somewhat bowed in awe. King Lukald had his hands clasped as if in prayer while Sam and Girdy seems to lean on each other, nodding approvingly. Melva squinted her wrinkled face in satisfaction. Elayna clapped her hands and ran to her, wading through the new wheat and hugging her waist.

"That was amazing!" she exclaimed, "Can I—May I have some cherries?" she enquired, correcting herself and gesturing to the bowl she had carried from the table.

Kathleen nodded, lifting Elayna up into her arms. She held Elayna's cheek close to hers.

"We can all have some cherries," she said happily.

37

RETURN YOU MUST

"If you do not return, I will never forgive myself," Heathron said as he planted a kiss on Kathleen's lips.

"I am coming back. Hopefully with a treaty of peace," Kathleen replied and then she kissed Heathron in return.

"There is something different about you, Kathleen. Do you *really* want to marry me?"

"We are in the middle of a war for my homeland, Heathron. Forgive me if I seem a bit distracted. I do love you." She added another kiss to his forehead but the prince placed his hands on her cheeks and brought her face level with his own.

"I am not a fool, Kathleen," he said to her. "I must admit that I do not relish the idea of you running off with…him."

She began to reply. She wanted to tell him the the Sīhalt Guardian was no longer pursuing her, but Heathron placed a finger to her lips, silencing her.

"I know that you must do this for your people. And I know that the best way I can help you is by remaining here to support your father. I have decided that since I cannot control your heart, I will stop trying to. If you are meant to be mine, you will come back to me."

"We just need to speak with the leaders of this pirate fleet. I will survive this."

"It is not death that I fear could separate us," Heathron said.

Kathleen looked deep into his eyes.

"I understand," she replied.

Heathron pulled her closer and instead of placing a kiss on her mouth, he pressed his lips to her forehead and kissed it twice as she had just done to him.

"Now, go and I will look after your family here," he said.

3 8

PARLEY

Kathleen looked across the water see how the enormous pirate ship might respond.

"Run up the flag requesting a parley," she heard Channing order from the helm, and then watched as Jared rummaged through the heavy leather chest of multi-colored signal flags, seemingly unsure which one communicated a request for parley.

"It's the white one, with black trim!" Channing added impatiently. after a few seconds.

Jared found it eventually and then took no time to fasten it to the line. A few tugs later and the flag was rippling at the top of the mast.

"Good! Now we wait!" Channing shouted over the whip cracks of air as the flag caught a crosswind.

The ship in the distance was strange, Kathleen thought, studying it now. It was tall and had multiple decks. But even from here she could tell that the millwork on the vessel was ornate, with wood exquisitely carved in a style she had never seen before. Some of the carved details mimicked scrolls around the edges, with golden paint, picked out by the sun, that highlighted the depth of the detail. Strangest of all, were the many open windows built into the side of the ship. The windows looked more like eyelets, formed of black tubes that protruded slightly beyond the hull. They couldn't have had so many cabins there, and anyway, behind it everything was so shadowy. There were flickering movements behind each, as if sailors were dancing around in there. Kathleen could see men scurrying around the borders of the window as the black eyelets were withdrawn into the ship. The boat did not have long banks of oars, nor did the prow look as if it could sink enemy ships, which was strange. Instead, the boat had four masts and more sails than Kathleen thought was possible to stack onto a vessel. It was hard to see from this distance, but most of the pirates wore white. She could see some that wore splashes of red, yellow, and blue. *Those must be the officers*, she thought. Compared to the thunderous sounds of the ships she saw near the city, this one seemed calm—almost peaceful.

"Have they responded?" Channing asked after a while.

Jared looked across the water with no need for the aid of the looking glass. His Sensor eyes were perfect.

"They just raised a red flag. It also has black trim," he said.

"Blood and serpents," Channing swore.

"A red flag? What does that mean for us?" asked Maxwell, who was perched on the rigging like a spider, half tilted as he stretched his neck as if it would help him see more clearly.

"They are telling us to keep our distance. The red is for danger. They don't want to share their waters with us. And it's clear that they consider them *their* waters..." Kathleen said ominously and in a low tone.

"Are you ready, Lilly?" Jared asked, "If Kathleen is right, we may need you get us out of here with your swiftest speed if they start to swing towards us."

"I'm ready," Lilly confirmed, brow furrowed, as she tightened the rope about her waist at the prow of the *Marine Escape*.

"Good. Now remember, we don't want to get into a fight. We just want to talk to them, if we are able," Jared reminded the crew.

He was cut off by Kathleen, whose curiosity about those black eyelets she had mused on was now maturing into something more akin to fear.

"What *are* those strange black circles they have lined up on each side of their ship?" She pointed off toward the vessel, and all eyes squinted to make out what she was indicating, as the pirate ship turned fully to expose its broadside to the *Marine Escape*.

"I was wondering the same thing. Some of them are drawn in and others are sticking out more, as if long flutes are coming out of them," added Maxwell.

Jared held up his hand to the others in a gesture of quiet. He cocked his head and listened.

"They sound fairly animated. The officers are yelling at the men...telling them to...'ready the guns'." He raised his eyebrows inquiringly. "I am not sure what that means. Have you heard of that term, Channing? Guns?"

Channing frowned and shook his head.

"Doesn't sound like any nautical term I know of. Lilly?"

He turned to the dark-haired guardswoman, but she shook her head as well.

"Are you sure you heard them correctly?"

Jared listen again, turning his ear to the wind.

They are in a mad scramble now. 'Aim for the mast' they are saying."

"Well we know what that means," Maxwell chimed in. "If they are saying 'aim', they mean to shoot something at us. But they are much too far away to hit us with any arro—"

Maxwell's words were cut short by an explosion, and then the thunderous smoke that belched from the first of those little black eyelets. Kathleen flinched at the sound that now rolled across the water. She ducked along with the rest of those on the *Marine Escape* when a strange whizzing sound passed close overhead.

"What was that?" Maxwell said, as something hard and heavy fell and pierced the silver skin of the sea just shy of the *Marine Escape*. A large spout of water erupted from the surface.

"I don't know, but they are going to do it again!" Jared shouted, moving to protect Kathleen with his body.

She saw the flame and smoke again, and the pirate ship rocked with the force of the explosion.

Instead of a humming sound that passed overhead and the sound of something piercing the water, the plume of smoke was immediately followed by an explosion of wooden splinters. She heard it before she felt it. The sound echoed in her ears before the rail next to her, as well as a portion of the deck, was shredded into a million pieces of wood. Lilly screamed in pain as she threw her hands up to cover her face. It caused a separate explosion of its own, as the shower of wooden splinters shot out like arrows. The *Marine Escape* bucked like a colt as a second blast shattered the main mast this time. The upright timbers tilted and then began to twist at an angle, as the vessel made a sickening groan like a wounded animal. Jared crouched low with Kathleen, his hand gripped to the back of her neck as he pulled her under him protectively, turning them away from force of the shattered mast.

Kathleen's ears were still ringing, so she could not make out the faint distant cheer that rose up from the pirate ship when the main mast of the *Marine Escape* finally succumbed and came crashing to her deck.

There were no further blasts. Channing turned to aide Lilly, while Maxwell must have taken flight, or worse, for he could no longer be seen on the deck. The boat tilted toward the side where the mast lay over the rail and the sails were lapped by the waves.

Jared drew his sword and cut the ropes that remained and the large beam creaked as the boat shifted and the mast rolled over into the water.

39

TORN ASUNDER

C hanning stood with his ears ringing. He looked where the mast had fallen to the deck, then at what was left of the ship—tilting as the heavy timber pressed on the rail, and finally at the torn and limp sails that lapped the sea water.

"Blood and filthy serpents!" he swore.

Kathleen, under a pile of light wreckage, stirred and pulled herself free. She was cut and bruised in places, and the pain stung lightly all over her body. But nothing was broken. She was lucky. But Jared lay prone alongside Lilly near the broken mast. The Sīhalt had managed to push her clear of it before it fell, but some of the ropes had entangled him and the parts that remained of the mast now lay across both of them, pinning them down.

Channing stumbled across the deck strewn with splinters of wood and bent to try and lift the beam.

"Jared...Jared...?" he said, trying to stir the Guardian while lifting the beam only an inch or so before its heavy bulk heaved back. Kathleen helped too, but it was no use.

Jared didn't stir. He lay unconscious on the deck, next to the fallen Water Witch. Lilly's black hair was matted to the side of her head where she had been struck, and blood soaked her dark locks.

Far above them the scream of a rock eagle sounded shrill in the sky.

"They're coming closer," Kathleen said, looking where the pirate ship circled. Channing spun to look over the wreckage of the *Marine Escape*.

"We ran up the flag of parley!" he shouted, hailing the pirates as they advanced towards them, and jabbing an angry finger to where the white flag with black trim fluttered in the breeze.

A few minutes passed until the enemy vessel reached them.

"Don't you know what that means?" Channing demanded, continuing his protest. But the pirates aboard didn't answer Channing as their ship came alongside. There were row upon row of these ordered sailors, each of them holding aloft their swords and spears in victory.

Seeing them so closely now, Channing was shocked at what he saw. He hadn't known what to expect exactly, but he had imagined a wild and spiteful horde of shabby seafarers. *Yet these are the cleanest, most disciplined pirates I've ever seen,* he thought, as if in answer to himself.

Still, the anger burned within his heart, but there was no use. This duel had already been won. The *Marine Escape* lay broken in the water and their party was outnumbered by far.

They threw boarding hooks across the space between the ships and pulled them side by side.

"We warned you not to come close," one of the pirates finally said in an accent that sounded long and drawn out. His presence among the rest of them quickly pointed to him being the admiral of this ship. Another pirate next to him, however—muttering to himself—spoke rapidly, the words sounding clipped and fast.

Channing leaned over some of the splintered rail to examine

the eyelets of the enemy ship, and the dark flutes that stuck out from them. Their black metal and heavy wheels intrigued him.

"I am certain your ship has nothing that I want," the admiral, chin in the air, said as he stepped aboard and looked around, his gloved hands laced behind his back. He wore a dark blue uniform —different from the many sailors clad in white. A number of his crew trailed him with an air of menace and with their swords drawn. Others held spears and Channing held his hands up, showing that he had no weapon in his hand.

The admiral pointed to the princess, "You, woman with red hair, you will come with us. You will come with us too," he said, pointing to Channing.

"Now wait a minute," Channing said, "I have friends pinned down under that mast and unconscious. Let me stay here to care for them,"

The pirates did not speak or move any further.

"If your purpose isn't to kill us, then allow me to help them."

The admiral approached Channing. He was at least a head shorter than the man of Marth, but his straight black hair and fierce eyes held no hesitation in challenging him with a glaring look.

"You will not tell me what to do," the man said. "I am Admiral Yamatsu of the Sulian Navy."

The admiral drew his sword with lightning speed. Channing had little time to respond. He barely got his sword out and brought it up to meet the blade of the admiral, but just as quickly the admiral had delivered six strokes and knocked his sword from his hand.

Channing had never seen moves like that with a sword. Even the sword the admiral held was strange to him. The man held his sword level, his front leg extended, back leg bent as he shifted his weight to the back foot. Channing waited, the man could easily have cut him to pieces.

"I have defeated you," the admiral said, looking at Channing's sword lying on the deck.

Kathleen stood up to her full height. "I would say that you defeated us before you stepped aboard. Your weapons of thunder gave us little chance."

Admiral Yamatsu grunted and looked from one face to another, trying to determine who was the leader.

"We came to talk with you to parley, as we say. My father, King Lukald of Candoreth, King of Sundiland, has sent us to negotiate," Kathleen added.

Admiral Yamatsu frowned at Kathleen, looking her up and down. "Your people...they send women to negotiate?"

"Sometimes, yes," Kathleen replied.

The admiral shook his head. "We do not negotiate with women," he said derisively.

At the same time, a taller man wearing a three-cornered hat and a strange heavy belt holding wooden and metal objects stepped forward and spoke to the admiral—whispering in his ear.

The admiral's eyes went back to Kathleen, and he approached her. Kathleen stood still, watching him as the admiral circled her with his sword drawn.

"My friends need my help," Kathleen said. "Please let us go."

"No. As I have already decreed you will come with us," the admiral said to Kathleen.

When she hesitated, two of the pirates grabbed her by either arm and began to walk her toward the pirate ship. "You, too," the admiral said to Channing, pointing his sword at him.

"But I can't!" he begged, and gestured at Jared and Lilly. "They'll die. Someone must stay to help them."

The admiral paused to think about this, then nodded. "Fine. You battled well and lost with honor," he said. "I will leave you here to tend to your wounded."

He approached Channing then, and reached up to remove his hat. His gloved hand grasped at the long white plume and pulled it off. He tossed it to the man trailing him in the three-cornered hat, who promptly flung his own hat at Channing and placed the new one on his head.

"Take care of it. That's my lucky hat," the tall pirate said in his strange accent, nodding at Channing.

Channing creased the edges of the triangular shaped hat and placed it on his head. "Likewise," he growled.

He bit his lip, and balled his hands in restraint as the admiral left with his sailors, hopping back over the wreckage and onto their ship.

Channing watched as Kathleen was brought among the sailors. Many of them looked at her with awe.

"Be brave, Highness," Channing said to Kathleen as she left. As she was ushered onto the enemy ship, she glanced over her shoulder.

"Help Jared and Lilly!" she cried, and then she vanished down a ladder into the enemy's cabin.

Channing ran to Lilly. She was warm to the touch, and as he moved her she moaned and opened her eyes. "What...happened?" she asked.

"We were attacked. Are you okay?"

"Oh, my head aches," she said, placing one hand on her forehead.

"I'll get you some water as soon as I can. Jared needs my help."

Then Channing ran to the mast. He put his arms beneath it and lifted with his legs, but the massive wooden beam would still not move.

Channing grabbed his sword. He cut some of the ropes, hacking them multiple times. Then he placed his arms under the mast again and lifted, the wooden beam budging a little bit, rocking back and forth against the strain of Channing's effort, but still it could not be lifted or moved. Channing began hacking at the wooden beam with his sword. Chips of wood flew in all directions. Then he looked down and saw Jared's sword on his hip. He tossed his aside and drew the Sīhalt's *impla*. He swung the sword down at the beam and the blade of the impla buried itself halfway through the wood. Channing's eyes grew wide with astonishment.

"Now that works better," he muttered.

Then he moved away from Jared so as not to cut through the wood and accidentally harm the Sīhalt. He brought the sword down again once, then twice, and was through the beam.

The ship drifted forward and the mast began to rotate with more of the weight in the water the cut end rose and shifted leftward. Channing easily cut through the remaining canvas and ropes that were tangled against the *Marine Escape*. He rolled the heavy portion that remained away from Jared and knelt beside the Sīhalt Guardian. Channing placed his hands on Jared's face and rocked his head gently back and forth. "Jared," he said, "Lord Sīhalt, can you hear me?" Jared didn't respond. Channing ran to grab a bucket with water and threw it on Jared's face. The splash of the cold brought the Sīhalt Guardian back to his senses.

"Wh—What are you…doing?" he said, stirring at once.

The sound of air whooshed through wings, and the screech of the rock eagle was shrill on the air as the great bird landed on the broken yacht. The Sīhalt, just gaining consciousness, winced and placed his hands over his ears.

Channing pointed toward the pirate ship that was sailing away.

"They've taken Princess Kathleen," Channing said, breathless.

The words seem to cut through the fog in the Sīhalt's mind. His eyes opened wider and then narrowed. He struggled to get back to his feet.

"Where?" he said.

Channing pointed to the pirate ship as it began its escape toward the horizon.

40

BROKEN MAST

J ared looked across the water. The ship was moving away from them and there was nothing he could do to stop it. Soon it would be too far to swim…and Kathleen was on that ship.

"Maxwell!" Jared called.

The Shifter came and stood beside his friend.

"I'll do it if you really want me to do it, I will," the Shifter said, anticipating his thoughts.

Jared swallowed the lump in his throat.

"No, you cannot attack by yourself," Channing said.

"There is no use. You would be killed," Jared agreed.

"I will go, if want me to," Maxwell assured him.

"I know," Jared said, watching the ship move further away from their broken vessel.

"You love her," Maxwell said.

Jared shook his head at the bitterness of the situation. His head throbbed and the sunlight hurt his eyes. He had not fully recovered from the impact of the mast.

"She will need to be resilient until I can find a way to free her," he said, as he choked down the loathing and shame he felt at having lost her to the enemy.

But as he said this, and felt for the first time that he had truly lost her, he shaded his eyes and saw, in the distance aboard the enemy ship, a slim, female figure climb onto the rail. Squinting harder, he made out her pale arms, outstretched and elegant, as she balanced high above the water. It was Kathleen! The sails of the ship were reefed and it slowed. Even at this distance, he thought he could see the determined set of her jaw as the pirates began to approach her.

"She's going to jump!" Jared said.

"These waters are dangerous. This is the season where the mottled sharks come to feed among the islands," Channing warned.

The *Marine Escape* listed, smoldering in the distance. Kathleen imagined she could see Jared standing on the broken deck, looking in her direction.

She could swim to him, if only she could get free.

"Unhand her, boys. The princess isn't going anywhere," Captain Dagger said.

Admiral Yamatsu nodded his assent and the Sulian sailors let her go.

Kathleen darted to the edge of the deck and climbed the wooden rail. She looked out over the blue-green water. Jared's white shirt billowed in the wind as he beckoned her. Captain Dagger shook his head in short movements.

"These waters are filled with sharks," he laughed.

As if stirred by these words, deep green dorsal fins suddenly pierced the silver skin of the sea, churning the surface hungrily.

Kathleen looked away.

"Where are you taking me?" she asked frantically.

She remembered the pirates who had ambushed her on Turtle island. Girdy had saved her then, but she still ended up in the dungeons of Tyath.

"I will never be Lord Balfoest's slave again!" she shouted, almost losing her balance as the ship slowed.

"Do not let her escape," the admiral commanded.

The one called Dagger nodded to the man and made a calming gesture.

A few of the pirates began walking toward her. They spoke in calming tones, with hands raised as they approached. One of them held a rope behind his back—as if she couldn't see it.

"You don't want to do that, missy," said a voice unaccustomed to speaking in tones that were soft or kind. The sound grated on her ears like the sharp teeth of the sharks.

"Don't jump. You will regret it," Captain Dagger said.

Her fear was stoked by memories of the torture she'd endured under Lord Balfoest's power. No sunlight, no freedom, no food—it was more than she could bear.

"I'd rather die than be his prisoner!" she said, turning her beautiful face toward him.

"What's this all about? We don't work for any Lord Balfrost or whoever you say," Captain Dagger said, in a smooth, deep drawl. He held out his hand for her, but Kathleen arched her back and dove backward, plunging toward the freedom and dangers of the sea.

Kathleen fought off the panic, and moved purposefully as she swam. She tried to breath evenly as she kicked her legs and reached out with her arms to pull herself through the waves.

A drum roll sounded across the water. Oars slid out of the black ship. One side rowed forward while the other reversed. Like an enormous black beetle, the pirate ship began to turn.

Then something brushed against her leg. It moved quickly. Another came, soon after. A dorsal fin broke through the water, and rough skin brushed her arm. The stark unfeeling eye of an enormous shark passed her. The cold-blooded gaze pierced her heart like a bamboo stake. The shark turned and gave a swish of its tail, circling her.

Kathleen dove deeper, holding her breath. She prayed it might pass. Instead, the beast came on. Water rushed around the angled nose. It opened its mouth, presenting row upon row of sharp, triangular teeth.

~

J ared saw Kathleen leap from the rail and dive in a graceful arc, into the water. She began to swim away from the black ship.

Mottled dorsal fins cut the water near the ship.

"She is in great danger," Jared said. Knowing he could not protect her made him want to dive into the shark-infested water himself, but she was so far away. He would never reach her. He looked around for any way he could rescue her.

"I'll help her!" Maxwell said, leaping over the rail and Shifting to a rock eagle and flew above the water. Jared watched as Kathleen began to swim toward them.

"Swim!" Jared shouted, even though she was too far for her to hear him.

Maxwell flew just over the water, his talons barely clearing the choppy surface. He flew directly toward Kathleen, on powerful wings. Jared could see the sharks circling. Her movements drawing them to her.

"Please hurry," Jared pleaded aloud as he watched from the deck.

Jared saw the rock eagle tuck its wings, as if it would dive into the water. The bird angled toward surface and Shifted its shape. The sleek lines of its beak, feathers, and avian eyes were replaced with the smooth curves of a dolphin.

K athleen did not see the shimmering shadow that quickly swam overhead. In a hopeless gesture of defense, she reached her arms out to stop the monster. A trail of bubbles rose from her watery scream.

Suddenly, a sturdy greenish blue mass slammed into the largest shark. Deadly jaws disappeared as the fish rolled to one side, passing Kathleen without biting her. Other sharks circled, but the largest now swam to the depths, blood trailing from the gill slits. Beneath the water, Kathleen heard cheerful clicks and chirping. Her heart filled with hope, and she began to swim toward the surface once more. A single dolphin blew bubbles in her direction and circled her defensively. Now it moved beneath her. Her new protector struck the remaining sharks if any ventured too close.

The friendly dolphin swam beneath her. Kathleen grabbed onto the vertical dorsal fin. The creature nosed its way forward with rapid movements of its crescent-shaped tail.

"Cast the nets!" a man called, as Kathleen broke the surface.

She had no time to take a deep breath before the dolphin dove again. Her lungs burned with desire for air even as she held fast to the dorsal fin.

A net, with stone-weighted edges, struck the water and descended like a dome. Kathleen let go and kicked her way to the surface. She saw the dolphin turn and come back to her pushing its rounded nose against her thigh. She hurtled toward the light above. Her burning lungs were crying out for air. When she surfaced, she gasped, sucking in the sweet relief.

"Swim away!" she cried pointing to the net closing beneath them like a purse of coins being cinched shut. The dolphin pushed its head above the water and seemed to smile.

"You have traded your safety for mine," she said to the creature.

The dolphin bobbed its head and opened its smiling mouth, rimmed by a row of rounded teeth. It made a series of clicks and chirps, as if it were laughing.

"You're lucky I turned the ship," Captain Dagger said in a deep voice.

The sharks were getting their fill among the lifeless bodies in the sea. Kathleen shivered when she saw groups of sharks fighting for their next morsel.

"She's the luckiest girl I ever laid eyes on. The green dolphin came to her rescue!" said a pirate.

The net was drawn to the side of the ship and began to rise. The dolphin struggled mightily in the net.

"Let the creature go!" Kathleen demanded.

The pirates only laughed.

"Dolphin is a delicacy. We'll feast tonight," Admiral Yamatsu said.

Kathleen wished she had her knife to cut the ropes. Jared has drifted out of sight. She hugged the dolphin and kissed the top of its green head.

"Bring her aboard," Dagger said, "and grab the gaff-hook for the dolphin."

41

SEA GRASS

The pulley above her creaked as the net began to rise from the water. Kathleen fell back against the ropes, still waist deep in water, and allowed her eyes to close. She took a deep breath.

She wished dearly that she could touch some plants; they had been her greatest defense in times of danger.

But the ocean is barren of trees or vines, she thought, looking to the west where the shore and her home lay. She looked back toward the *Marine Escape.* It was closer now that the pirate ship had circled back. She wondered what Jared was doing, how helpless he must feel on the sea, with no way to run to her rescue.

The presence of trees that might comfort her or provide for her protection were miles away and yet felt living green things about her. Yes, they were tiny, some of them miniscule. Others made up small strands that brushed against her skin in the blue-green water of the sea. That's it! It was called the Emerald Coast, not just for the trees on the shore line, but the richness of the waters too, she realized. Then Kathleen remembered the lessons from one of her teachers: *'The water is full of living things. The sun provides the energy for plants to live in the water. The fish and other creatures feed on it and each other...'*

Kathleen squinted up at the sun above her and then down at the water. The pirates mocked her and the dolphin continued to flop in the shallow water in the net. The rays struck the water, penetrating the waves and highlighting small strands of millions of tiny plants drifting in and on its surfaces and in the undercurrents just below—plants well within her reach!

The net inched upward as the pirates pulled. Kathleen acted quickly now. She spread her fingers wide and began to hum. The areas between her hands sprang to life with a thick ball of seagrass and algae. The dolphin bobbed its head and chirped as if encouraging her. Kathleen felt exultant.

She poured her Talent into the act of growing the mass of aquatic plants. The roots of the seagrass intertwined with the kelp and other plants in the richness of the ocean. They shot out new growth attaching themselves to each other . The plants became a dense mat of green surrounding both Kathleen and the net that held them. The net slowed it ascent under the new weight of the thick, wet greenery.

"Pull her up!" the admiral shouted.

"We must have caught some seagrass!"

"We're trying to haul it up but we can't," a sailor exclaimed thorough gritted teeth. His arms quivered with the effort.

"Help haul her up. Get that girl and that dolphin on the deck or I'll have you flogged!" shouted the officer.

The nets strained and the ropes twisted under the sodden, green mass.

Kathleen was out of the water now but the mass of green extended down all around her like the veil of a forest bride. It hung like a verdant curtain. She did not need to touch the water now to have the seagrass grow. The aquatic plant sent long runners out in all directions. They expanded and even climbed up the side of the ship, past the waterline. The dolphin squealed and flopped about on the seagrass within the net.

"I wish I had a knife to cut you free," she said.

As she spoke—and drew more nutrients from the water to feed the rapidly expanding plants—Kathleen watched in amazement as the marine mammal began to change shape right before her eyes. The dolphin rolled onto its back. The flippers began to elongate and the tail began to shrink. The nose of the dolphin became less rounded and began to grow fur along both sides.

The pirates clamored for more help as the ship listed to one side with the sagging weight of the plants Kathleen grew. The dolphin no longer made clicks but had begun to make noises that sounded more like a low growl.

Kathleen scooted as far to the other side of the net as she could and stopped Growing the plants as the dolphin changed.

A strange rumbling snarl arose from the dolphin next, as Kathleen scrambled away. The green form began to Shift its shape as it thrashed in the net. More thick brown fur sprouted from its body, and its flippers became powerful legs.

"Maxwell?!" Kathleen exclaimed.

The Wolvermink released a deep, guttural growl. A large weasel-like creature with powerful claws, heavily muscled shoulders and gleaming black eyes looked at her. For a moment she would have sworn it smiled like the dolphin. Then it tore a section of the rope netting free with shearing teeth and crawled through. The beast climbed the heavy rope, paw over paw.

"What in the name of the Scarlet Empress is that?" one of the pirates asked, pointing to the creature climbing up the rope toward the deck of the ship.

"Quick! Cut the rope!" yelled Dagger.

The men on the deck leaned over the rail out to get a better view of the monster. Its thick fur was matted and wet. The lips curled back to reveal angry teeth set in a mouth that seemed far too wide for an animal of this size.

"Where did that come from?" a Sulian pirate asked in amazement.

"That thing must have crawled out of the deepest sewers of Hell," an old Centian pirate said. "I thought never to have seen such a thing."

They stood transfixed by the Wolvermink that climbed the rope in front of them. It looked up at them and let out a hungry growl.

"It's not afraid of us, at all," Thomas Dagger declared, grimacing at the sight.

"I told you not to kill a dolphin. It's bad luck. Now the sea has sent a demon to punish us."

"I didn't kill the dolphin! It was right there!" said the pirate with the gaff hook. He lowered it, ashamed it was still in his hand but pointed down to the net where the dolphin had been.

"It was right there just a moment ago, before that ...thing came crawling out of our net."

"Cut the rope!" Admiral Yamatsu said at once. "Cut it! Cut it now!"

The two pirates scrambled over the deck, wielding their cutlasses like saws, and began to hack at the heavy rope while holding the net aloft. The large line frayed but did not fully separate as they swung their blades again and again. But before they could cut the remaining threads of the rope, the animal leaped toward the side of the black ship and sank its claws into the dark wood of the hull. Kathleen saw the beast struggle to cling to the slippery hull. He slowly began to slide down several feet toward the water, until with a hulk of its furry shoulders, it sprang up, using its rear claws for extra leverage. Then it began to climb as Kathleen and the ball of greenery fell with a splash into the water. The plants intertwined with the netting, allowing it to float. Kathleen crawled through the gap the beast left in the net. She stood up on the green matting she had created. It had surrounded the ship, growing up the hull of the ship as ivy on a stone tower.

She pushed down on the seagrass, but the floating plants rebounded under the pressure. She worked her feet into the plants and continued her efforts to strengthen the hold they had on the pirate ship. They may capture her again, but they would not sail off quickly—not wrapped in the dense layers of seagrass that Kathleen had sculpted.

She looked toward the yacht and smiled to see a small sail rigged up to the broken mast. The boat was moving, if slowly.

She called to him, and saw him wave in reply.

Kathleen directed all of her energy toward Growing. The torturous days in Tyath had tempered her. Lord Balfoest's tyrannical demands had made her stronger, and Kathleen felt the strength and ability of her Talent expand within her entire body. In this moment of need, she felt powerful and willed the plants to grow in the direction of her Sīhalt Guardian.

The roots rippled under the surface of the water, shooting out toward the intended target. The rich waters of the sea fed the plants and Kathleen felt them respond to her Talented touch. It did not drain her strength to grow this much vegetation at sea. The available nutrients in the water meant she found little difficulty in sending a swath of thick, floating seagrass toward Jared and Channing on the *Marine Escape.*

AQUATIC PATH

Jared leaned forward and willed the wind to carry them faster despite the broken mast. He wasn't sure what all was going on, but from what he heard across the water, Maxwell was having a time of it. The pirates had weapons new to Jared. He worried that Maxwell might be putting himself in greater danger than he realized.

"Keep going, Channing. They aren't sailing anywhere yet."

"It's like the pleasure of a day trip!" Channing replied. The makeshift rig was working, even if the yacht moved slowly.

"I have to ask," Channing continued. "What is the plan once we reach the pirate ship?"

"I'm not sure yet, but I think it's fair to say our peaceful negotiations are over."

"I assumed as much," Channing said, not sounding afraid at all.

"I'm glad to have you with me, Channing," Jared said to the man of Marth. Channing looked over his shoulder and nodded his head in appreciation.

"You don't want to die alone?"

Jared smiled. "I haven't been released from my sworn duty to keep her safe, and if I remember correctly you swore a similar oath to her, about me. None of us is dying today."

A guttural growl sounded across the waves. "I can't say the same for those pirates though. Sounds like Maxwell decided it's Wolvermink time."

Then Jared heard Kathleen call for him. He stood up to look and waved. She stood above the swells, her red hair pulled to one side. She pointed to the water in front of him and shouted again.

"I can't hear her. What did she say?" Channing asked.

"She said to run on the grass," Jared replied, then smiling broadly and dropped his foot over the edge.

Channing looked around.

"What grass?"

A thick ribbon of vegetation wound its way though the water and spread itself on both sides of the yacht. Jared lowered himself over the rail of the boat, testing the support beneath his feet with the heels of his black boots.

"This grass," he said ,and spread his arms to show he no longer needed to hold on to the boat to keep from sinking. Channing turned around, looking at the thick sea grass mat surrounding the boat.

"Do you trust it? The sharks…"

"I trust Kathleen," Jared replied, and then turned and began to sprint across the floating carpet of green, his cloak flying out behind him as streams of water squished out from beneath his boots with each step.

J ared came running toward her. Kathleen's heart leapt. He ran swiftly, sword drawn, not looking to the right or left as he ran on the verdant path she had created for him. He did not hesitate to run to her and protectively place himself between her and the black pirate ship.

"You are a darling," he said, "I can't believe what you've done!"

"I don't think they can leave even if they wanted to," Kathleen said.

There were shouts of consternation coming from the deck and they heard a few booms aboard that Kathleen had come to recognize as the sound of Centian weapons. White smoke rose into the breezy air and was swept away across the water. The smoke smelled of sulfur.

Jared looked at her intently, his grey eyes questioning.

"I wasn't harmed," she said and hugged him fiercely. He returned her embrace with one arm, keeping his sword at the ready with his other.

"If we can walk on these plants, they can too," he cautioned. "Let me get you back to the *Marine Escape* with Lilly. She is recovering there."

Channing made his way to toward them, waving his hand, beckoning them. The turmoil on the ship had not abated.

"Go with Channing. I need to help Maxwell."

Jared's statement was punctuated by a small clap of thunder coming from the deck of the ship. The three of them winced.

"What strange weapons are those?" Channing asked.

"I do not know, but I believe Maxwell needs my help." The growls above them continued but now seemed to be more defensive than simply enraged.

"We will go together," Kathleen replied.

Jared paused for just a moment, then nodded his head. Very well, let's climb aboard.

Jared tugged hard on the rope. It resisted, so they scaled the ropes left dangling from the side of the ship.

The Sīhalt Guardian led the way, followed by Channing and Kathleen. She mimicked the movements of the men as they used their feet to hold the rope firmly and reach higher for another hand grip. Jared got his footing on the wooden ledge at the top of the hull and moved to the right, letting go of the rope and allowing Channing and Kathleen to do the same. All three of them held onto the railing without going over, onto the deck. Instead they remained hidden, peering through the stout balusters of the ship railing, watching the scene unfold before them.

43

A MAN

Maxwell, as the Wolvermink, crouched in a defensive posture, surrounded by sailors holding long spears with gleaming narrow tips. A number of the pirates lay dead on the deck. Still a few others were wounded and dragged to safety by their friends. It all happened so fast for him. But that was not his biggest problem. He had not counted on the thunder sticks being so effective. His shoulder burned with searing pain, and the white bones of his elbow protruded though his bloody hide. Even as a Wolvermink, Maxwell's mind was clear enough to understand that an escape through the air right now was out of the question. He could not fly with a shattered wing. So he maintained the formative posture of a wounded Wolvermink and made a noise that was half growl, half scream.

The pirates had been more organized and doughty than Maxwell expected. He hoped his attack gave Kathleen time to escape, but when the pirate pressed his strange weapon into Maxwell's forelimb and discharged a white hot pain into his shoulder, the tide of the battle had changed. Now the Shifter considered what he might do. A leap to the water would be difficult. He was cornered near the cabin, and he could not use his right front paw to run as he normally would have. They would pierce him many times as soon as he tried to run. More than the spears, Maxwell's concern focused on the taller pirates who held more of the strange metal tubes wrapped with a wooden handle. The men holding them seemed supremely confident, given how close they stood to a wounded Wolvermink. The other pirates cheered them, and a few were saying, "Stand back so they can shoot him again."

Maxwell didn't see any arrows, so he was not sure what would be shot at him. But he understood 'again,' and that meant more of the searing pain, broken bones, and blood being spilt. He could do without more of that, especially if it was his blood being spilt. He bristled all the more and rolled back his lips to reveal the shearing, dangerous teeth.

A whistle blew and the pirates dressed in white pants and no shirts retreated with their spears and formed a double line on the deck.

Now we are getting somewhere, thought Maxwell.

"Line up!" came the command, and most of the pirates obeyed immediately.

The closest pirate dressed in dark blue rolled his eyes at the command. He seemed tempted to comply, but held the weapon extend toward Maxwell, angling his body the way a swordsman might do to present a smaller target to his enemy. However, the man's sword stayed in his belt.

He must trust that little weapon a great deal, thought Maxwell.

"Thomas Dagger, if you cannot obey my command, how do you ever suppose you will rise in the ranks again?" The question was posed by Admiral Yamatsu. He wore his crisp dark blue uniform and held the golden knob of his walking cane.

"Sir, the men call this thing a demon. Surely you do not want it to get away," Dagger replied.

"It isn't a demon. It is clearly a … dog," the admiral said.

But he said it without certainty and the expression on the faces of the crew showed that they too were not certain of a canine category for the snarling beast aboard their ship.

Dagger furrowed his brow but kept his weapon steady.

"I don't think so," Dagger said.

"Stand down, Captain Dagger!" Admiral Yamatsu said angrily.

"Well, Admiral, it's nice to know you do think of me as Captain Dagger." His long curly black hair bounced in the breeze. He tossed his head to get it away from his face. The admiral reddened.

"This is no dog. I saw it as a dolphin in the net and then it turned into this…thing. So, I don't know what it is, but I don't think we should take our guns off the thing. It already tore up five of your men and Cutshaw won't be right after today."

"Cutshaw wasn't right before today. He never has been right!' another pirate dressed in blue added with a crooked grin.

"Shut up, Seco. I can hear you just fine, even if my ear is torn off."

Dagger smirked at the exchange, but kept his attention directed toward Maxwell.

"See! This is what you do," said the admiral. "You undermine discipline. Why are your men laughing at this serious situation?"

"Cause it's funny," admitted Cutshaw as he held the remaining portion of his arm together.

"I do not know if I will ever understand you Centians," the admiral said.

"You don't have to like us, but we need to work together. We've got the guns and you've got the men so we need to make some headway with the idiots in Desnia, or we are all going to have bigger problems."

The admiral reluctantly agreed. "True. Just kill that rabid dog and throw him overboard." He turned, his face pinched as he looked around. "Where did our captive go?"

"She used her…" He hesitated, struggling to find a word to convey what he had just seen, before saying, "..skills, to tie our ship up with seaweed, and after she had done that she escaped. She can't have gone far, but now we know what she possesses and who she is: she is a wild witch!"

Some of the men shivered at the word, *witch.*

"Don't kill the animal."

The men standing at attention with their spears stood straighter and even those of Centia turned to look in the direction of the soft feminine voice that had contested the admiral's order. Yamatsu wheeled round to slash this mutineer in two, before seeing who it was who stood before him. After wrestling his features into softness, the admiral bowed as the slight form of the Sulian lady took small, rapid steps toward him on the deck.

"Your Imperial Highness, we are sorry to have disturbed you," the admiral said.

Maxwell saw Captain Dagger roll his eyes again.

She nodded her approval to the admiral and continued walking directly toward the snarling Wolvermink.

She stopped, just behind Dagger, peering curiously at the wounded animal.

"You say it was a dolphin and then it turned into this thing?"

"Yes, Highness,"

The princess nodded. "It is not a dog."

"No, Highness"

"It is not a dolphin either…this is a man."

Dagger looked at her. The corner of his mouth drew back in disbelief.

"A man?"

She nodded. "He is not to be harmed any further. Bring the Healer," she said.

44

A SHIELD

Maxwell backed up on his haunches and snarled.

"It is called a Shifter?" Thomas Dagger asked, looking closer at the enraged beast.

Maxwell considered lunging at his face, but something made him hold back. The slightly built woman dressed in scarlet bent toward him.

"I do not recognize this form," she said, "It must be an animal common in Desnia. However, this form is not its true shape. Look at his intelligent eyes. This is a man," the princess stated confidently.

"Those eyes don't look intelligent to me, only pissed," replied Dagger.

The princess winced at the crude language.

"Sorry Highness," Thomas added, "but I wouldn't get too close to it."

The princess stepped forward and extended her hand to the Wolvermink. Maxwell growled low and wrinkled his nose.

"Who are you?" she asked, "Who were your parents?"

The question surprised Maxwell. He felt the sincerity of the

Sulian princess's words. She seemed kind and, although reason told him to escape, he found himself wanting to speak with her.

"If that is a man, then you might as well call me a pelican! That is no costume he's wearing. That demon tore the throats out of our men and bit clean through Merv's leg bone. He won't walk again except to have a peg for a leg and Gary is going to wear a hook for a left hand from now on," one of the Centians said.

The two maimed pirates, Gary and Merv, sat with compression bindings over bloody stumps. They shook their heads in disapproval that the animal was still breathing.

Maxwell gnashed his teeth and swallowed dramatically as if to add unrepentant emphasis to what it had done to the men's extremities.

"I would not go near it, Princess," the admiral said in agreement, his voice low and serious.

The princess paused, cocked her head, and looked intently at Maxwell. Her face was a picture of serenity, her expression calm except for the questioning eyes. Maxwell felt as if she could see through him. His Wolvermink form was no disguise to her, and he knew that nothing would be. He was enchanted, as if her were swimming in her dark brown eyes. He shook himself, trying to break the spell, and growled again. Instead of jumping back in fear, the princess reached out with her delicate hand and smacked him on the snout.

Maxwell let out a surprised yelp and pulled back, confused at her audacity.

"You change back into a man!" she said, pointing a slender finger at him and speaking in her heavy Sulian accent, "or I will have my men tie you up and choke you, until you pass out. Then I will see who you *really* are."

Maxwell was amused at the threat—he was sure a few more of her men would die before that happened—but he was intrigued even more. How did she know that it worked that way? He always reverted to his native form whenever he went unconscious, not matter his Shifter form. Maxwell had questions of his own and his arm was hurting badly. He looked at the distance he would need to cover to escape and then at the pirate holding the - what did he say it was again? A *gun*?

He decided to take his chances.

Maxwell began to revert to his natural shape. His torso elongated, his brow softened and the thick fur all over his body dissipated. His hands replaced the paws with their sharp claws. All the while, his eyes never left those of the princess. Finally he knelt in a crouch, naked, holding his arm where the bones protruded.

"By the Lord of the Sea, it is a man!" exclaimed one of the Centian pirates.

Maxwell stood slowly, maintaining eye contact with the princess. She held his gaze confidently, but Maxwell noticed a slight widening of her almond-shaped eyes when he stood before her with no disguise.

"You've met people like me before," he said.

"The Imperial House of Sulia knows many things," she replied haughtily, then turned and spoke to the admiral. "Have the ship Healer bind his arm. Keep him under constant guard, with spears at the ready. I will speak with the Shifter at dinner. If he is allowed to escape, the guilty will hang from the mast."

She turned and began walking back to her cabin.

"Don't you want to know my name?" Maxwell asked after her.

The princess did not acknowledge him in the least. She kept walking across the teak-wood deck as if what had just happened was as normal as anything.

"You are the strangest woman I have ever met!" he said, as she walked away. Still, she ignored him.

Maxwell was perplexed.

Then suddenly, Maxwell saw Jared DeTorre leap over the rail of the ship with his knife drawn. His feet landed softly on the deck and he grabbed the Sulian princess, holding the blade to her throat.

"No one make a move, or she dies!" Jared shouted.

The Sulian pirates immediate lowered their spears in Jared's direction. They advanced a few steps until Jared pulled her tighter with an arm around her waist. He pressed the knife closer to her throat and she winced, making the men retreat.

"I wouldn't do that if I were you," Maxwell said to the Sulian pirates.

"Now let my friend come over here," Jared said.

"You!" the admiral exclaimed in disbelief.

"That's right, admiral, you took my princess, now I've got yours."

His face turned red with anger. "What shall I do, Princess Shīanya?" he asked.

"Listen to the barbarian," she replied, looking down at the shining blade held to her throat.

The admiral bowed crisply at the waist and commanded the men. "Stand down!" he said, and they fell back, returning to their lines and standing at attention.

"Well, this just got a lot more interesting!" Maxwell said. He held his broken arm as he strolled barefoot, naked and nonchalant between the two lines of white-clad pirates. A few of the Centian pirates held their strange weapons at Jared, but they did not seem ready to fight, only watching carefully.

Jared motioned with his chin and Channing and Kathleen both climbed over the rail.

"You came back? Why would you come back after you escaped?" the Centian pirate called Dagger said.

"Maxwell is my friend. And you were going to harm him," Kathleen said. She walked toward Jared and the exotic girl he held with his knife.

"Well, look what he did to our crew," Dagger replied gesturing to the dead bodies that lay sprawled on the deck.

"He is very protective of his friends," Kathleen replied as if that explained everything.

"This is going to need some attention," Maxwell said, wincing as he looked at the compound fracture.

"There will be no flying for you, until we get Melva to take care of this."

"We can't sail the *Marine Escape*—the mast is broken."

They looked around at each other and then at the ship. Then they turned their eyes toward the pirates armed and ready for combat.

Maxwell quickly surmised the situation.

"Jared, I don't see an easy way out of this. We have their princess, and they have everything else."

"The best move in *Chendris*, when a valuable captive is all you have, what do you do?"

Maxwell thought about the game, "That's easy, you retreat—with the captive."

"Exactly," Jared replied.

He began to move toward the cabin door behind him without turning his back on the pirates. They held their spears in his direction.

"Shall I take a shot at him? I'm rather good with a pistol," one of the fancily dressed taller pirates asked.

"No!" the princess said, "Do not risk it. I can escape whenever I need to."

"We'll see about that," Jared replied, walking backward with an arm placed firmly around her neck. His other hand held the *impla* defensively.

Kathleen and Lilly went in the cabin and Channing helped Maxwell to bar the door. Once it was secure, Jared released the princess and allowed her to sit at the small table.

She smoothed her hair and resumed her regal demeanor.

"Good," the slight woman said. "Now we can talk privately."

45

THE HEALER OF SULIA

Maxwell held the bones of his arm to his torso to try to keep them from moving. He winced with the pain, but did not cry out.

"We need to get you bound up," Kathleen said. "I wish Melva was here to Heal you." Jared came over and examined the wound. After a few moments, he shook his head. "That's a compound fracture, Maxwell. I worry about infection."

"I'm just worried that I won't fly again," Maxwell replied, almost dismissing the risk of infection against the fright of not feeling the thrill of riding the wind once more. "With a broken wing, there's no more soaring in the skies for me."

Princess Shīanya looked from across the room. She sat primly, her lips tight, her eyes calculating. "Just have the ship's Healer come and Heal him," she suggested, and when she did all eyes turned to the Sulian princess.

"Wait, you have a Healer on the ship?"

Princess Shīanya nodded. "I am sure if you make the demands, they will send the Healer to help."

Jared and Kathleen looked at each other.

"Why didn't you say this sooner?" Kathleen asked, wondering if there was a trick.

"You didn't ask," Princess Shīanya said demurely, fixing her with an unreadable smile.

"There is little else for it. I'll call for the Healer," Jared said, and walked briskly toward the hatch to climb the ladder back on deck.

The Sulian sailors stood with spears at the ready outside the door. Some of the Centian pirates pointed their guns at Jared. He still had a difficult time reconciling how innocuous the small metal tubes appeared. They didn't seem as menacing as a sharpened blade, but he had seen the damage they had wrought on the *Marine Escape*, and knew now never to take them lightly.

"Call for the ship's Healer," Jared commanded.

No one moved.

"Call for the Healer. We do not wish to harm your princess."

An officer turned to his man.

"Go get the Healer," he said.

Moments later, a short sailor dressed in white approached the door. In his hand, he held a leash, the collar of which was fixed to the neck of an old woman. Her gray hair hung down in long straight strands and her eyes never reached above the teakwood deck.

"This is our Healer. She has been fed," the sailor explained.

He approached Jared warily and handed the end of the leash to him. Jared was confused. Never in his life had he been handed a leash with a human being on the end of it.

He felt a Tamer's bond pass to him

"What is this?" he asked in disgust.

"That is our Healer. She is very good," the sailor said.

"Why is she on a leash?" Jared enquired.

Now it was the Sulian sailor's turn to show looks of confusion.

"You cannot let a Healer walk free. All of the Talented people must be Tamed," he said.

"Tamed?" Jared replied. "Like a beast?"

The sailor shrugged his shoulders. "Would you allow the Talented to walk free?" he asked, incredulity in his voice.

Jared accepted the leash and shook his head. "Stay away from the door. Your princess will pay the price if you seek to attack us."

The officer in charge of the men at the door nodded curtly. Jared closed the door and walked with the old woman toward Maxwell, where he was seated at the small table.

Jared still stood with the end of the leash in his hand. It felt dirty to hold, so he grabbed the old woman's hand and allowed her to hold the end of the leash.

Again, she didn't respond as he expected. Her fingers closed softly over the leather cord and she stayed with her head bowed, almost as if she were asleep. The bond that Jared felt between the old woman and himself felt empty and hollow. She was a shell of whatever woman she might have been, void of many of the emotions he expected in a woman of her age, with her life experiences.

"They treat their Healers like this—like dogs? Kathleen asked.

"They treat all the Talented like this, I think," Jared said with disgust. He pointed to Maxwell's broken arm, trying to get the old woman's attention. "He needs to be Healed. Can you Heal his arm?"

Jared reached up and unlatched the collar from the old woman's neck. She immediately began to whimper, as if she were in pain. She whined and tried to put her head back through the loop that made up the collar.

"What is she doing?" Maxwell asked.

"She's like a sled dog that wants the harness," Jared replied.

In order to keep her from crying, Jared replaced the collar around her neck and the woman settled. The old woman approached Maxwell, and without looking at his face, examined the broken arm.

Her wrinkled, old hands gently felt the skin above and below the wound.

"Stretch out your arm," she mumbled.

Maxwell complied, but he fought the pain that came as she shifted the bones that had been shattered. A small clicking noise was heard and beads of perspiration sprang up from his forehead as the leashed Healer probed the wound. Channing offered Maxwell a piece of wood on which to bite and the Shifter accepted it gratefully, sinking his teeth into the wood.

"What is this?" the Sulian Healer murmured, and a piece of soft gray metal worked its way out of Maxwell's arm. It fell with a thud on the table.

"The bullet was inside," the Healer mumbled to herself.

As the old woman held his arm in her wrinkled hands, she began to chant softly at first, a cadence different than Jared had ever heard, and yet the result was the same as with Melva.

The bones knit together and the inflammation began to subside. The tear in the skin began to mend with light pink skin, and finally, with the scar tissue that fully enclosed the broken arm. When she finished her incantation, Maxwell breathed a sigh of relief. His hair had grown longer. When the older woman was done, she released Maxwell's arm and her hands once again hung limp at her sides, her shoulders hunched forward, neck bowed.

Maxwell bent his elbow, trying out the joint's repair. He rotated his arm in a circle at his shoulder and flexed his bicep, moving his fingers in clawing motions at the air.

"Oh, that feels a lot better," he said. "I think that'll do nicely."

"How long have you been a Healer?" Kathleen asked her.

The old woman opened her eyes without looking up at her.

"I have served in the Navy since I was a child," she said.

"Who did this to you?" Kathleen continued.

She didn't respond.

"Is that when they first put the collar on your neck?" he asked.

The old woman nodded. "I am a Healer," she finally said, "This is the purpose of my life."

Kathleen shivered, looking at the woman. "If this is how they treat all the Talented people, we can never allow them to land in Desnia."

Jared looked at her.

"She's been Tamed—like an animal," he said.

Kathleen nodded and swallowed, remembering her horrors of the dungeon once more.

"To try and take away someone's free will is the most evil a person can do," she said.

Jared agreed with her.

Princess Shīanya sat watching quietly from the corner of the cabin. She didn't offer her opinion.

Jared turned to look at Shīanya. The woman did not seem the least bit afraid—only curious.

"Your people do not Tame the Talented?" she asked.

"No, we don't," Kathleen stated, "and I am sorry we even had to take you captive."

"Yes, well, I wanted a chance to speak with you alone, too. I saw the parley flag you raised but Admiral Yamatsu and Thomas Dagger fired upon you before I could intervene. And, do not feel guilty. I *allowed* you to take me captive," the woman said.

"Well, that was really convenient, because it looked to me like the Sīhalt Guardian had a knife to your neck just moments ago," Maxwell said with a smirk.

"Could he hold you captive?" she asked the Shifter.

"Me?" Maxwell said, pointing to his own chest. He laughed. "Jared has tried to hang on to me. I always get away," he said proudly.

"Because you are a shape-shifter?" Shīanya asked, pointedly.

"That's one of the reasons," Maxwell admitted, as if he had a litany of reasons Jared was no match for him.

This woman is very strange, Kathleen thought. Shīanya was slight of build, with straight black hair and pale, almost cream-colored, skin. Her hands were delicate and soft - they looked accustomed to holding a paintbrush or a quill. Her dress was made of a brilliant red with a long fabric belt tied snugly about her narrow waist. She seemed to have wisdom beyond the years of her youthful face.

"Who are you?" Kathleen said.

The woman turned her almond eyes toward her. "I have many names, but you may call me Shīanya. My parents rule the Empire in Sulia from the Crystal Throne."

"And why have they sent you here?" Kathleen asked next.

The woman hesitated, as if gathering her thoughts. "I came to Desnia for the adventure and the freedom," she said tactfully.

"Do your parents know you are here?" Kathleen asked, sensing that the princess was not revealing everything about her reasons for being in Desnia.

Shīanya hesitated again.

"She ran away from home," Maxwell said, slapping his thigh as if he had it all figured out.

"Let her speak, Maxwell," Kathleen snapped at the shape-shifter.

Shīanya rounded on him. "I did not *run* away from anything. I *chose* to leave with the fleet," she said.

But Maxwell was in his element now. "What's the matter? Was Daddy going to make you marry one of his friends?" he said theatrically, a barely restrained chortle cutting through his words.

The woman furrowed her brow and looked at Maxwell with a curious gaze.

"My reasons for coming to Desnia are my own, but I believe my father will be glad that I have come. He did not know that any Shifters lived among the colonies." She stared at Maxwell, leaning close to him, her eyes moving around his form, studying him. "Your eyes are wide, like the Centians, and yet you do not look like them either."

Maxwell pulled away.

"I'm not sure what you are talking about. What colonies?" Kathleen said.

"Desnia is one of our colonies," Shīanya replied simply.

"You mean the continent? All of the land of Desnia?" Kathleen asked.

The woman nodded. "From north to south. Yes, our family sent settlers here centuries ago. We did not know if they survived, but now that we know the land is somewhat settled, the Crystal Throne will want their taxes, I am sure."

"Of course they will," Channing said, sarcastically. "And they will want to tame everyone who raises a shout of defiance."

The group of friends looked at each other, considering the new information.

"We don't even know of the Crystal Throne," Kathleen said. "Our empire's capital is in Tyath, the Golden City."

Shīanya nodded in understanding. "You have not traveled beyond the Sea of Storms, have you?" she asked.

Kathleen looked at her in consternation. "We haven't even gone all the way through the Delathrane lands. Most of our travels are along the coast—north and south. The Sea of Storms can't be crossed but through a miracle or extreme luck—or so we are taught."

"That at least is true. I did not think we would survive the storms. The wind was so strong and the water came over the ship in very high waves. Many times I thought we would go under. But the storms finally abated and the sun shone again. Unfortunately the fleet lost more than half of its ships."

"You had twice as many boats as the ones we've seen? This group of ships is already the size of the Tyathian Navy, or larger," Channing said.

"Most of our fleet is made up of settlers. The Tawins fled their island home when their rebellion was finally brought to an end, and the Centian privateering ships were commandeered in the process." She looked around the cabin, examining the ship's interior. "They are very good ship-builders, and they have guns. That was how the Tawins made it past my father's imperials."

"What are these *guns?*" Jared asked.

"The weapons, used by the Centians—they make thunder, fire, and smoke. It spits out a stone or metal ball, moving very fast. It destroys whatever it strikes. They are a clever people, the Centians—always making something new."

"Those taller men with beards and hats, they are Centians?" Jared asked.

"They look like us," Channing said.

Shīanya nodded. "They are big, they do not smell clean, and their eyes are too wide," she added.

Channing frowned and raised his eyebrows, but didn't reply.

"No offense," Shīanya added, "but for a people that are so few, they do well for themselves. There are Centian merchants and traders all over the Empire. Now, however, they will be expelled for joining the Tawins in their rebellion."

"These people plan to settle here? Permanently? We thought at first they were just pirates," Kathleen said.

"The Tawins are desperate and Admiral Yamatsu will land his people here. They do not have enough supplies to continue or wait. They need to find a new place to live."

"I see," said Kathleen.

"Some of the Tawins are loyal to me. Others despise my family, because our local agents were too harsh with the people. Admiral Yamatsu's family is from the mountains of Tawin—I suspect he has no love for the Crystal Throne."

"We should speak with him. Perhaps we can work out a peace," Kathleen said.

"What will you do with so many people? Can your home accommodate the Tawins?" she asked.

"We could fight and kill each other, but why? Desnia is large and there are many places that are unsettled. If these subjects of yours must establish a home here in our land, I would rather help them than fight them. Enough people have died already."

"You are kind. How does that serve you as a princess in Desnia?"

Kathleen considered the question. She looked to Jared and he smiled. "It hasn't always been that helpful, but I do not want to change that about myself. I should be more kind, not less. A ruler can be both kind and wise. My betrothed, the Prince of Tyath is like this."

"May we speak with him?" Shīanya asked.

"He has been deposed by an evil man in the Golden City," Kathleen said.

"I see. The ruthless ones gain power at the expense of the rightful ones?" Shīanya said.

"This is the struggle among all peoples, is it not?" Jared replied.

The Sulian princess nodded.

"It is good that your future husband is both kind and wise. I wish I had such a match," she said sincerely.

Kathleen's thoughts turned to Heathron. She wondered how he and her father were doing, defending Candoreth. She pictured Heathron's smile.

"I am very lucky to have him," she said, refusing to glance at the Sīhalt Guardian. "One more thing, Shīanya," Kathleen added, "a condition of my help for your people to settle peacefully here in our empire…"

"Is what?"

"The Talented people of Desnia," she said, flicking a glance over at the old and bedraggled Healer. "They must be allowed to remain free."

46

DEAD IN THE WATER

The Centian flagship named *Enmity* was bound in plants that clung tightly around the hull and rudder, suffocating it like the tentacles of some predatory octopus. She could not be moved until the vessel was cleaned and set free of the vegetation.

If a Desnian vessel finds us now, it will be catastrophic, thought the admiral.

He needed to see how his ships were doing near Candoreth. Had they smashed the harbor walls? The walls... Just how were the Desnians managing to repair them so quickly?

Instead of leading his fleet in destroying these durable walls once and for all, Admiral Cyril Yamatsu was trapped here, drifting in the shadows of the Turtle islands.

The admiral scribbled a note and handed it to his messenger. "Take it to the Desnians. Tell them I am ready to negotiate," he ordered.

The sailor saluted, took the note and ran the short distance from Admiral Yamatsu's quarters to the cabin where the foreigners held Princess Shīanya. The sailor approached the door and knocked, whereupon the door opened and the half-clothed brown-eyed man answered.

"Hello. How can I help you?" he said.

The sailor extended the note to him.

"Oh, Why, thank you. Is this an invitation to a dinner party?" the man said.

The sailor furrowed his brow. "Admiral Yamatsu is ready to negotiate," he said in clipped speech.

"Oh well, thank you very much." The brown-eyed man began to open the message. He spoke over his shoulder to the group inside the cabin.

"Guess what? Admiral Yamatsu has given us an invitation to parley," he said, holding up the paper.

"It's about time," Jared said.

"Please be advised that if Admiral Yamatsu is harmed in any way, none of you will leave this ship alive," the messenger added.

"We would expect nothing less," replied the Shifter. "And please convey to Admiral Yamatsu the certitude that if any of our party is harmed, Princess Shīanya will not survive. He is to arrive alone, to our cabin."

The messenger bowed at the waist, in acknowledgement, then climbed back onto the deck.

"Admiral Yamatsu is a skilled negotiator and a very capable leader of the navy," Shīanya said.

"Is he the one who can get this thing turned around?"

"Perhaps," Princess Shīanya said just as a knock was heard at the door again.

"Admiral Yamatsu of the Sulian Navy requests entrance to discuss the terms of our parley."

Maxwell opened the door.

"Come on in, Admiral. We don't have a lot to offer you in the way of food or drink, but please come in and be seated."

The admiral lowered his head to pass through the door and stood erect within the cabin again.

He looked at Jared and Channing, then to Kathleen. He bowed at the waist and Jared inclined his head. "Have a seat over there, admiral. Thank you for coming to speak with us," Kathleen said.

"You may relax. There is no need to fear violence while I am here. You have my word."

Jared leveled his eyes at the admiral.

"Okay," he said, folding his arms without losing eye contact.

"Are you the one with whom I negotiate?" he asked. Jared gestured to Kathleen.

"This is Princess Kathleen Delunt Dal Sundi of Candoreth. It is her home that you have threatened. You will speak with her. I am her Sīhalt Guardian."

"This is Channing Dur Ruston, a nobleman from the Island of Marth where your people have begun to invade. His ancestral home and lands have been taken by your people. You may speak with him."

"And this is Maxwell—a friend, a warrior, and one who could carry a message for us if need be."

Kathleen turned to Princess Shīanya.

"Are you to speak for the Sulian people as well?"

"I do speak for my people," Princess Shīanya replied.

"Then Admiral Yamatsu, if you could be so kind, please take a seat next to Princess Shīanya so that we don't need to look in both directions." The admiral rose to his feet and moved his chair to a position next to the Sulian Princess. "There, now, we can sit across the table and discuss this like civilized people."

"It is customary among my people to partake in tea while they negotiate. Would it be okay with you if we brought the tea?" the admiral asked.

"That would be fine. Could you have them bring some crackers as well?" Maxwell asked."

"Yes, we will have them bring tea, crackers and sausage."

"Oh, that sounds good," Maxwell said. Opening the door he called out to the sailors outside,

"Hey guys, your admiral said to bring some tea and some crackers with sausage. Bring some biscuits too, I'm hungry."

The sailors peered through the door trying to catch the attention of the admiral. When the man nodded towards them, they saluted and left briskly. Maxwell closed the door again.

Thomas watched from the upper deck as Admiral Yamatsu entered the cabin. He wondered what was being said inside that cabin.

"I'll not sail with a demon on board, I can tell you that," Merv said to the other Centians gathered about him..

Thomas Dagger placed his hand on the shoulder of the man in a show of empathy.

"We wouldn't sail with any of these Sulians either if we had our choice," he reminded them.

The men grumbled agreement and milled about on the foredeck.

"We need to stick together. It don't matter what ship we served on before, we are all of Centian blood. And if we want a chance to ever return home with our hides intact, we'd better listen to Captain Dagger!" Gary said, gesturing with the stump that no longer held a hand.

"He's the one the Sulians are willing to deal with, and that is fine with me. We may know the secrets of powder and ball, but they outnumber us and the sneaky Sulians are watching our every move each time we load and fire. I caught one of them on the cannon deck just the other day," another said.

The men murmured their shared concern over this fact and Thomas saw his opportunity.

"What about the powder? How much do we still have?" he asked.

"We have eighteen casks aboard right now. That will last us for a bit," a gunner said.

"We can't resupply in Desnia. So if we run out of gun powder or they learn the secrets we hold, how long do you expect us to survive?" Thomas asked.

"They'd use us for bait in their nets. We aren't worth the food they feed us, if the guns aren't working."

Thomas Dagger nodded gravely.

"The truth is, we are up against it, boys. We are outnumbered, sitting in the waters of a strange land. We have little food left, and foreigners who have shown they are willing to fight to keep us out."

"So what are you saying, Captain?" a man asked with a gap-toothed twist of his mouth.

"I'm saying that we are not going to be left out of the dinghy when the ship is sinking."

"Is the ship a'sinkin?" Merv asked.

Gary slapped Merv up side the head with his remaining hand.

"No, you blowfish, the ship ain't sinking. Captain Dagger is just saying we don't want to be left going upstream without a paddle."

"But you can't use a paddle now, Gary, look at you! That Desnian demon done ate off your right han—."

"Shh, quiet down," Thomas said to the two.

He looked around the deck to make sure their gathering of Centians had not drawn undue attention.

"We are with you, Thomas, if you can get us through this," a burly pirate said. "I gutted Matheson and threw him overboard after I caught him double dealing —sharing our secrets and the like."

"Only because you beat me to it," Thomas assured the man.

"I'd do the same to you, if you fail to look out for our interests."

"And I would expect nothing less," Thomas agreed.

They watched as Admiral Yamatsu was welcomed into the cabin where the Desnians held the princess prisoner.

"I need to join them and find out what is being discussed. Then, we can make a plan," Thomas said.

He descended the stairs that led to the cabin, then adjusted the smooth wooden handles of his pistols before he knocked on the door.

47

TEA CEREMONY

"The party keeps growing," Maxwell said, as he opened the door.

"My name is Captain Thomas Dagger, I represent the Centians of this fleet."

"Have a seat at the table, Captain Dagger," Kathleen said. They shuffled their chairs to make room for him around the small table.

"Let us begin without delay. Why are you here? Why have you brought violence to my nation?" Kathleen began.

Admiral Yamatsu raised a hand slowly.

"If you do not mind, we prefer to have the tea first."

Kathleen slammed her hand down on the table. "And I prefer to have my people protected! I prefer to have my city in one piece. Do you know that I returned to find my home burning?"

Princess Shīanya looked at her without betraying her emotions, and Admiral Yamatsu took a deep breath and turned his eyes towards Kathleen, bridging his fingers together.

"By our custom, it is a dishonor to not partake of the tea before we begin…" he said calmly.

But Kathleen was not to be manipulated. She mimicked his

gesture and brought her palms together, too. "And it is very rude of *you* to show up uninvited to our shores. To begin killing...and burning...and destroying."

Jared placed his hand on Kathleen's thigh in an attempt to calm her. She relaxed a bit at his touch, sinking back into the chair. Jared leaned forward slightly over the table and fixed his eyes on the admiral's.

"Princess Dal Sundi is rightfully angered at the unprovoked aggression. Her people had no dealings with yours. No offense was given. No reason for the attack," he said formally.

"So, what do you say, Admiral? I demand that you call a stop to the bombardment of my city," Kathleen added, unable to stay quiet for too long.

The knock came at the door, and Maxwell opened it. A sailor came in carrying a tray with small cups and a teapot. On the tray were stacked crackers and a plate of salted pork, the indulgent scent drifting across the room. Maxwell lifted the plate of meat and crackers off and gestured for the sailor to set the tray on the table. He had a cracker and piece of meat in his mouth before the sailor could leave. Maxwell turned to Channing. "Do you want some?" he said with his mouth half full. Channing held up his hand.

"Perhaps later."

"There may not be any left," Maxwell replied, still chewing.

"You need it more than I do," Channing said, looking up and down the lean body of the Shifter.

Princess Shīanya reached forward and lifted the tea pot. She poured the dark green tea into the porcelain cups, as graceful as a swan. She placed a cup before each of the people at the table, then poured another for Channing, who accepted it but preferred to stand. Admiral Yamatsu ceremoniously picked up the cup and took a sip. He set it down and waited. Jared gestured for Kathleen to take a sip as well, and he grabbed his own cup and lifted the hot liquid to his lips. It tasted green, like the spongy bark of a juniper shrub chopped fine and soaked in hot water. The tea had an earthy taste as well, bitter and gritty, one that made him think of new grass in the springtime.

He sipped the tea and felt a clarity in thought and calm wash over him. He looked at Kathleen, and by her expression, a similar occurrence was happening with her.

"The tea helps us to think with less emotion," Princess Shīanya explained.

Jared nodded and took another sip, as did the others.

"We came to your shores," Admiral Yamatsu began, sighing as if this was a tiresome act, "because we had nowhere else to go. The people in my fleet are refugees from our land across the ocean. Your father defended his realm as I expected him to do. We fought back. That is all."

"And this is your princess?" Kathleen asked, gesturing to Shīanya.

"She is honored by many of our people," the admiral replied, circumspectly.

"I am the heir to the Crystal Throne in Sulia," Princess Shīanya declared in a soft, mystical voice. "I am betrothed to the Premier of Dorgund. Many of the sailors are loyal to my parents."

"Even after the betrayal?" the admiral said, his mouth downturned.

"There was only one path they could follow!" Princess Shīanya replied hotly.

"Then why did they send you to torment us?" the admiral asked in sharp clipped words, pain and frustration evident in his voice, despite the calming effect of the tea. "Why does the Dragon House choose to hunt the very people who sacrificed everything for them?"

Princess Shīanya bowed her head.

"They did not send me to spy on you. I escaped and made it to your fleet before they knew I was missing. They do not know I am here. You are safe."

Admiral Yamatsu shook his head and laughed ruefully.

"You disappear the same day the fleet leaves Sulian waters. How hard will it be for your father and your future husband to put two and two together? Have you communicated with them since you left?"

"No," she replied. "I will never to speak with them again." The princess seemed to choke on these last words.

Kathleen felt a sudden wave of empathy for Shīanya wash over her. She knew what it was like to desire to run away, to have a life mapped out for her beyond her wishes. But Admiral Yamatsu looked at her with derision and narrowed eyes.

"You have communicated with no one—in Sulia?"

Shīanya looked at her hands.

"I brought four birds. One of them I released when we made it through the storms. I have three left."

"And who will retrieve your dove in the palace?" he asked.

"My handmaid, Tomoko," Shīanya said.

The admiral stared at the princess for a few heartbeats, his eyes glittering with doubt.

"If that be so, then we are still lost. We will be wiped from the earth, when it is discovered that you are among us," he said with only barely concealed fury.

"I'm not sure I understand," Kathleen said.

"The Dorgund, her fiancé, is a very prideful man. He will not rest. His honor will not stay him if he believes we have stolen Shīanya," the admiral explained.

"But you didn't escape with her, she's a stow-away," Maxwell replied, confused.

The admiral scoffed. "It will not matter. The Sea of Storms is no barrier to him, no matter how many ships and men he may lose. The colony of Desnia is not far enough to hide from the sword of the Dorgund," Admiral Yamatsu said with resignation.

"Perhaps there is a solution to our troubles," Jared grasped hopefully.

All of them turned to the Guardian.

"Does this include sending another bird to tell her parents that she's okay?" Maxwell asked.

Jared shook his head.

"Allow me to recount what I have gathered from our interactions today." Jared stood and looked at each of them for a moment. His grey eyes roved, sweeping from face to face as he seemed to measure each of them, weighing them against their words. He put his hands together as if he might pray and pressed the tips of his fingers to his lips in thought.

"You believe the Dorgund of Sulia will come with countless ships to demolish all of your fleet? That if so, not one of you will be left alive?" Jared asked.

The admiral nodded solemnly. "I believe he will seek to regain his honor or die trying. The Dorgund is like a force of nature...a cruel force of nature."

Jared turned to Shīanya.

"And you are his betrothed, but do not wish to return. You were willing to leave your mother and father—never to return again, in order to escape a marriage you despised?"

The princess nodded, but less resignedly than the admiral; she did so more in clear-eyed, faint hope.

Next, Jared turned to Thomas Dagger.

"You, your ships, and your countrymen were pressed into service to make this voyage. You hold the secret of the guns. Do you have no desire to be here other than to save your own lives?"

Thomas didn't delay with his answer. "I want my ship back," he said firmly. "Then I will turn for home. It's true that the storms are deadly, but I'd trust my fate to the sea, rather than wait for the Dorgund."

The Sīhalt nodded and stroked his chin in thought before asking, "Does the Dorgund have...guns?" The word still felt strange to him, but as a warrior, he knew the world had changed in the face of this strange new weapon.

Thomas Dagger and Admiral Yamatsu exchanged looks. "No," Thomas replied. "He only hires Centian ships as needed. The secret of the guns and its black powder remains with us."

Jared nodded with relief. "I see a possible solution to our problems. But there is one other aspect of our circumstance that must be determined before I go on..." he said, and pointed to the old gray-haired Healer still standing in the corner with a leash around her neck. "If you are welcomed into Desnia, you must be willing to allow all people to be free—Talented or not."

Admiral Yamatsu wrinkled his nose and then frowned deeply. "Is that not dangerous?"

"It is a long tradition we have kept," Jared replied.

Princess Shīanya spoke next. "If the Talented among us must go free so that we may be welcomed into Desnia, I will accept that. This is a wild land."

"I don't care much if the witches go free," Dagger said. "The concern I have is in getting more gun powder. Our supplies are limited and we will need to replenish it at some time."

"Not before we obtain a peace treaty between us. My people are dying as we discuss this!" Kathleen cried.

"Your people will be in a worse condition when the Dorgund arrives, if we are not prepared," Admiral Yamatsu warned.

"That is little comfort to me, Admiral, while your ships continue to attack. You must send word to cease at once."

There was a pause as no one spoke. The silence stretched, and Admiral Yamatsu's eyes never wavered from Kathleen's. Eventually, the admiral pulled a piece of parchment from his jacket and unfolded it over the table.

"Let us determine the terms of our peace then," he said. "These are my terms."

He pushed the document across the table to Kathleen and he began reading intently along with Jared.

"I will allow you time to discuss the terms without my presence," Admiral Yamatsu said, getting up from the table.

He bowed and departed, closing the door behind him.

Maxwell bolted the door as he left.

"Just in case," he said.

"The admiral is just being courteous," Channing said.

"We'll see. I trust him about as much as I'd trust a Delathrane," the Shifter replied with a suspicious eye on the door.

Jared cocked his head and listened.

"I believe you are right, Maxwell. It is possible that they have a plan to rush us and they have a friend of ours."

"They found Lilly," Kathleen said, her fingers almost crumpling the parchment in front of her as she stood.

Soon they could hear the commotion beyond the door.

"What do you mean?" Shīanya asked.

"I can hear the excitement among the crew. There are ships approaching, and they are not friendly to us."

48

NO COMPROMISE

Maxwell opened the door, and as the daylight shone into the small cramped cabin, the Sulian crew lined up in neat lines. The sound of drums signaled the approach of two additional ships, flying the flags of the pirate fleet.

Admiral Yamatsu looked at them and, despite his stoic demeanor, Kathleen detected his satisfaction. The plants that held the pirate ship so secure would mean nothing now that two more of his fleet had arrived. Tethered to the broken yacht by bonds made of living things, the ship had stood immovable in the water. That had been a bargaining chip in their discussions. There would be no movement until discussions were complete. Now that they were out-numbered, damage to the existing ship was not out of the question. They could light it on fire and still not worry about the consequences.

"I worried what might become of us if they gained reinforcements," Jared admitted.

The newly arrived ships cast ropes across the divide and brought their ship alongside.

The captain bowed deeply to Admiral Yamatsu.

Quick orders were followed by moving feet, and the men began to load provisions onto the ship.

"Give up the princess! You have lost. If the resolution is to be peaceful, you will agree to our terms," Admiral Yamatsu said.

Shīanya stepped forward, "They are no longer holding me against my will, Admiral. I wish to be with them. You are committing treason and will be held accountable."

A sailor walked up to him, holding a small bamboo cage with three rock doves inside. Her own rock doves—the last link with home.

"You wouldn't dare!" she exclaimed.

Admiral Yamatsu opened the cage and removed one of the birds. It cooed softly. The bird warbled as the admiral stroked the soft white feathers of its back.

"I will not allow you to send the other birds back to the Crystal Throne. I pray the one you sent will not make it. Only silence can save our people."

"Stop!" Shīanya cried.

But the admiral's strong hands moved deftly, pinching the neck of the dove between his calloused fingers and twisting the small head until a subtle pop could be heard. He released the bird as if to let it fly eastward, but the lifeless body fell. It sprawled in a contorted shape on the deck.

"You have chosen your course, and so have I."

"He must not be allowed to kill the other birds!" Shīanya shrieked.

The birds were her last connection to home. The fear of losing that link brought images of her parents to her mind. Shīanya could see the thin mustache of her father, and her mother's soft hair arranged high atop her head in a tight knot of complex braiding.

There were leagues of water between her and home. The birds were her last remaining link. Shīanya pictured her mother crying herself to sleep when she did not return. It pained her and she wished to explain, even if that explanation were only a short message sent by the homing doves she had treasured since childhood.

"Call out the sailors loyal to the Dragon House!" the admiral said.

From the even lines of Sulians, a number of men stepped forth. They stood as if they were about to be honored, and yet many of them must have known the consequences of their devotion. Despite being condemned and pursued by the Throne, these men of the waves cast their allegiance on the mercy of the Sulian Princess—Daughter of Dragons.

When Admiral Yamatsu called out to them, they shifted their feet and turned their heads in unison, now facing him in perfect order. Shīanya looked at him and then back at the birds.

"Do not harm my birds," she said. Her voice sounded fierce and reverberated like someone speaking into a chamber. The echo shaded the words with power, but the admiral pulled his sword from his sheath anyway.

He extended his arm with a sweep of his elbow, the tip of the sword now pointed at an angle to the sky.

"Don't do this," Shīanya pleaded.

The admiral turned on his heel, and severed the head of the closest allied sailor. The man dropped with a thud. Immediately the remaining sailors were brought down with flashing arcs of Sulian blades. The officers followed the example of their leaders. Shīanya almost cried out when the last of the men crumpled before her.

Jared moved to protect Kathleen as Maxwell stepped forward, shocked by the sudden actions of the admiral.

"They must never know you were on this ship. If the bird you foolishly sent home died on the way, we might have a chance. I cannot be found to have the Daughter of Dragons here among us.

"An alliance with the wayward colonies of Desnia cannot be tolerated. My only hope is to bring Desnia back under the rule of imperial law. If we deliver the colonies, to their rightful masters with no sign of you ever having been among us, we might be extended mercy."

"Don't do this," Shīanya cried to the remaining sailors. The tall, bearded Centians stood talking amongst themselves, trying to make sense of the new circumstances. Their nervousness was betrayed by the hands Shīayna saw resting on the butts of their guns. Thomas Dagger walked toward them and began to speak in whispered tones.

"Where do *you* stand, Centian?" Admiral Yamatsu demanded.

Thomas Dagger stepped forward and leveled his pistol at the chest of the sailor holding the birdcage.

"Give the birds back to her," he commanded.

Admiral Yamatsu remained silent.

When the man holding the cage began to shake his head, Thomas Dagger squeezed the trigger.

An explosion of fire and smoke rolled from the barrel and the Sulian man was blown backward by the blast. Maxwell quickly gathered up the bird cage and brought it back to Shīanya . The white birds fluttered their wings, but soon settled as she held the cage.

"So, you are with them?" the admiral seethed, fury creasing his brow.

" We've all seen the Dragon Girl, or whatever you call her, our lives are as much at risk as the rest of these sorry fellows. You get rid of her first, destroy the crew once those other two ships arrive, then blame all this bloodshed on the Desnians. It's a good plan, but I don't like it because it leaves me and my boys at the bottom of the deep blue ocean. We didn't come this far to take a swim right when we're in sight of a new land."

Admiral Yamatsu looked across the distance to the oncoming ships. He was running out of time. The new arrivals could not be allowed to witness the princess aboard his ship—she would ruin everything he had worked for.

"I do not believe the old stories. The House of Dragons is not our master . We want freedom! We want to eat the fruit of our own labors, not send it all to the crown while we watch our children and neighbors starve."

"That's understandable," Dagger replied, "but we have our own desires. We want to live, too."

Admiral Yamatsu glanced toward the oncoming ships, then back again at the pistol Thomas pointed at his chest. The other Centians watched the exchange. They drew their weapons and stood alongside Captain Dagger.

"They will retreat to the cabin. We'll close the door and no one on those two ships will see her," Dagger said. "You can leave us on this broken ship without seeking our death."

The admiral twisted back and forth, weighing his options— mentally clawing for a solution.

"I will leave. Stay where you will not be seen," Yamatsu said, and motioned for them to move back into the cabin. He signaled his men and gave quick orders to gather what they needed to take with them.

Shīanya and Kathleen retreated while Maxwell, Jared, and the others followed. They closed the small cabin door but kept a look out through the cracks in the wooden boards as the Centian pirates took up guard.

49

SULIAN SHIPS

When the Sulian ships got close enough, coils of rope sailed through the air as they were tossed from one ship to the other. The ends were made fast and then the vessels were hauled closer together, the ropes creaking and water sloshed between the ships as they were tightened.

"This is a risk. I don't like being trapped like this," Jared said as he looked out from the small opening.

"We don't have many options right now. It seems they are leaving peacefully," Shīanya observed.

The Sulians worked feverishly. The second ship was signaled to wait at a distance as the supplies were loaded. The red sail and fan rigging marked the ship as Sulian- made. The other ship sported gun ports and the curving lines of a Centian-made vessel.

"It had to be the *Temptress*. She's one of the gun ships," Dagger said.

When the last of the sailors had made their way across the divide, the admiral had them untie the ropes that connected them.

"How many more men do we need to ready the guns?" Dagger asked the Centians.

" We've enough if they stay on one side," came the reply.

"Take twelve men down to the gun deck and ready the cannons. We're trussed up like a fly in a spider's web with all this seaweed wrapped around us and won't be able to move. . But we can give them a few departing shots if they want to play that way," Dagger said.

"Yes Captain!" the men replied, saluted, and left at a brisk pace.

A smile creased Thomas Dagger's face.

"That's more like it," Jared heard him say under his breath.

The Sulians cast off and pushed away with long poles. The hooks were turned away, but instead of being used to draw closer they heaved against the hull and the red-sailed Sulina vessel slowly began to turn.

Jared could see the immaculate deck clearly. Admiral Yamatsu accepted the salutes of the officers on the ship. He barked out quick orders and all the men he'd brought aboard once again lined up in two lines. He began to yell, accusing some of the men of cowardice. The sailors who joined the admiral in his departure stood at attention, receiving the verbal lashing without a reply.

Jared watched as the admiral became more animated, commanding the men to unstrap their swords and deliver them up. The sailors who were armed bowed their heads in obedience, and offered their swords and spears to the new crew.

"He's taking away their weapons," Jared said.

"Of course he is. That is what a tyrant does when he wishes to freely kill the people."

As if on cue, the admiral gave another order. Jared was not familiar with the term he used, but the result was one he had seen often in his duties as a Sīhalt when punishment was dealt to criminals of the highest order. The two lines of Sulian sailors crumpled to the deck as they were struck down by the swords of their new crewmates.

"He didn't waste any time, did he?" Thomas Dagger stated with disgust in his voice. "Poor lads," he added.

"What's his next move?" Jared asked.

"He'll signal the *Temptress* to fire upon us. He can't leave us alive. We're sitting like a seal on a rock with a hungry blackfish circling," Dagger replied.

A flag rose above the red Sulian sail and the *Temptress* opened her gun ports.

"Here it comes!" Dagger said and rushed down the deck, calling out to his own men. "Hold your fire until you see them plain in your sights!" he shouted.

The Sulian ship rocked as the guns belched flames from its belly. The projectiles smashed into the *Emnity* and made her shudder. They had no way to turn the ship, no way to bring their enemy within their sights. The plant-bound ship took one blast after another, the crew ducking for cover as chunks of wood exploded between the decks.

Admiral Yamatsu stood on his deck calmly, enjoying the carnage. His lips were held in a stern line and his brow was slightly furrowed as he watched the destruction unfold.

"Can you free the ship from the sea grass?" Jared asked as another shot struck the ship.

"I'm not sure how fast I can do it, but I'll try!" Kathleen shouted above the booming.

"If we can maneuver, we can return fire. We will be sunk if we do nothing!" Dagger said.

Jared ran with Kathleen to the far side of the deck and helped to lower her down. Her feet landed on the sodden mat of floating vegetation. Jared leaped down to stand guard beside her, splashing water as he landed. He drew his *Impla* and began to cut away the clinging water plants with broad strokes of his narrow sword. Channing looked down from above and jumped down to help.

Kathleen grabbed the nearest plant and tugged, but while Jared easily cut through the vines, the ship was still shrouded in greenery.

"This is taking too long!" Channing said, swinging his cutlass to free the hull from the plants.

The cannons of the *Temptress* continued to pound the *Enmity* and the red-sailed ship of Admiral Yamatsu moved around to the starboard side. Archers took aim and released arrows as they tried to free the ship. Jared moved Kathleen out of their range and kept cutting with a frenzy at the plants that entangled the rudder. .

Suddenly a swell of water lifted them, almost toppling Jared as he fought for balance on the moving grass beneath his feet.

He looked at Kathleen and she pointed to the battered *Marine Escape*.

"Lilly!" she said excitedly, and looked toward the broken yacht still tethered to them by a string of green. It bobbed in the sea, the broken mast outlined against the sky.

Across the ribbon of green, Lilly walked with purpose. Her head was bound in strips of white linen and her arms were spread wide as if to embrace the whole scene of destruction before her. To Jared, she looked serene. Pieces of wood that had been blasted from the *Enmity* continued to rain down on the water between them, but the guns were momentarily silent. The powerful wave emanating from Lilly bounced all the ships as if they were toys floating in a bathtub of a giant.

Jared could hear Admiral Yamatsu calling orders to his men on the exposed side of the ship. Soon they would fire again.

"Who is she?" Shīanya asked, a note of concern in her voice. She looked at Lilly walking across the waves.

"That's Lilly," Channing replied. "She's a Douser, or what you would call a Water Witch."

"We should get back on board," Jared said.

The sea beneath them began to swirl with powerful undercurrents. The *Enmity* began to rotate with the moving water, and the plants that held it fast began to twist and break with the movement.

"She will free us!" Kathleen said.

Lilly waved to Kathleen.

"Climb aboard!" she called, gesturing to her friends.

"She's telling us all to get on the boat," Jared said.

Maxwell helped Shīanya get up the rope ladder.

Channing lent a hand and gave Shīanya a lift up as well, and then both men climbed up afterward.

"We're coming around!" they heard Captain Dagger call to his Centian sailors. "Fire at will!"

The turning of the ship was accented by the popping and breaking of a thousand stems of green. The clinging vines sagged as the water beneath the ship swirled and broke them free.

The ship slowly rotated. The guns began to fire. One, two, then three more guns joined in the explosive refrain. Jared saw water spout upward as the cannon balls landed missed their target.

"Steady your aim!" shouted Dagger as he paced up and down the deck. His order was repeated down the line and through the gun decks.

They were rewarded with a cry from the other side, when a blast caught the Sulian ship, shredding the sails and a portion of the deck. Sailors were scattered, their screams drifting across the water.

"Yamatsu won't leave us alive," Captain Dagger said "We will fight to the death."

A BRUISED LILLY

L illy's head still hurt. The linen cloth binding was just tight enough to staunch the bleeding. She could open her eyes against the sunlight now, but even though she squinted it seemed almost too bright. When she woke up beneath the shade of the broken mast on the *Marine Escape*, it took a few minutes for her to make sense of her surroundings. At first, she'd imagined she was a child again, aboard her father's fishing vessel, the boat rocking as he pulled in the nets. The blue sky above could have been a piece of her sky at home. But the gulls circling overhead had wings and tails trimmed in black feathers, and Lilly knew she was not dreaming nor was she home. Struggling to kneel, she placed a hand gingerly on the side of her skull and winced in pain. Her hand came away crimson. Lilly looked around at the water and saw the trail of sea grass sagging like a verdant ribbon between the vessels.

"Kathleen," she said to herself, and found the strength to stand. She steadied herself by placing a hand on a rope that was stretched across the deck when the mast toppled. She held onto the rough surface of the rope using it to help regain her balance.

Lilly was alone. The others must have gone to the ship in the distance. Her memory was foggy, but images of the preceding fight came back to her. She shivered at the flashing image of the splintering wood, explosions, fire, and smoke.

All was quiet now, except for the sound of sailors moving on the deck. Lilly saw the same type of strange pirate ships with rows of shuttered windows above the waterline. They approached the plant-bound ship and seemed to be maneuvering to board it in order to stop it from progressing.

"Is anyone here?" Lilly called out, looking around the broken yacht.

Only the creak of timbers and lapping of waves answered her call.

The pirate ship on the other end of the trail of plants was heavily entwined with seagrass and all manner of aquatic vegetation. Lilly smiled.

Kathleen must not have wanted them to leave. I hope they aren't too mad about that, she thought to herself.

Lilly tried to listen to the shouts coming from the ship. She saw the oncoming vessels draw near and men crossing the planks from one ship to another.

"What's going on here?" Lilly said under her breath. She took a timid step down to the floating seagrass. and sank midway to her calf before putting her full weight down, but found if she was careful she could walk on the watery green path.

She saw the ships part once men and supplies were exchanged. Lilly even caught a glimpse of her friends, talking with the pirates on the deck. Kathleen didn't seem to be in danger at the moment —she stood on the deck with the Sīhalt Guardian and others close by her side.

Lilly saw the group react with anxious movements as the pirates cut down their own men.

What is going on?! she thought.

Lilly almost threw herself down in the water when the closest ship retreated, only to turn the cannons and blast the Sulian vessel where her friends stood. The wood erupted, shards flying in all directions. Thunderous shocks rolled past her and Lilly was reminded of the explosions that disabled the *Marine Escape*.

She regained her balance and took a few steps forward, her ears ringing and her head throbbing painfully with the loud noise. Lilly knew she must help her friends. She allowed herself to focus on her Talent,not easy in her injured state; but she was no stranger to hardship. She had devoted her life to defending others, whether with a sword or with her gift for moving water.

First to free the ship so they can at least defend themselves, she thought.

With that, Lilly walked further along the floating pathway. She sank to her calves with each step, as the vegetation had dispersed some since its original growth, but the green mat was still supportive enough for her to continue walking.

Lilly recalled a tune from her childhood and began to sing snatches of it. Her bare feet remained in contact with the waves as she strode forward, her Talent flowing through her body and into the water around her. She sent a wave toward the boat where she had last seen Kathleen. Then she sent a twist of water that swirled like an eddy at the edges of a rock in the path of a river. The swirling water was enough to grab the entire ship and rotate the vessel as if it were being pulled around by cables. The plants growing on its side tore loose, and Lilly beamed as the wounded ship turned and fired at their attackers.

The feel of her Talent comforted Lilly even as her pain increased. She touched the bandages that encircled her head, and realized she was bleeding again. Perhaps she had overdone it. The Sulian ship had taken a serious hit, but it turned away from the wind and began to circle back around. Kathleen's ship was in motion, sailors scampered up the ropes and adjusted the sails, the ship not yet completely free of the plants. As the ship slowly rotated, Lilly could see much of the aquatic vines were cut away. Soon the vessel would sail free again.

Lilly staggered forward, a hand to her head as she moved her feet through the swirling blue-green water. A wave of nausea came over her and she paused to double over and empty what was left in her stomach.

"Lilly!" she heard Kathleen call across the distance.

The guardswoman looked up to see her friend waving frantically from the ship.

"Maxwell will drop you the rope!" the Sīhalt Guardian shouted. His words were pierced by the screech of a rock eagle, its metallic green wings pumping forcefully in the air, a heavy rope clutched in its claws. The bird swooped low and released the rope, the looped end falling close to where Lilly stood. She put the loop around her torso and made it snug. Walking a few steps further, she came to the point where the plants were torn free and the green path of floating vegetation no longer extended into the water. Twisted shoots of green danced like applauding hands. Lilly took another step forward and plunged into the sea.

Beneath the waves, Lilly could hear the groans of the wooden ships as they moved on the surface. The sounds were muted, and for that Lilly was grateful. Her head still hurt but she kicked her legs and moved her arms to rise back to the surface. The rope about her tightened as she was being hauled in by men on the deck. Lilly raised a hand to let them know she was okay and a cheer arose from the men.

"Lilly! You're okay!" Kathleen exclaimed happily.

"Haul the drowning flower in before she wilts!" a tall pirate said. He tipped his hat to her as she was drawn closer to the ship.

"They are turning around to attack," Lilly told her friends, gesturing toward the Sulian ship.

The pirate captain nodded rapidly.

"Admiral Yamatsu will not let us live. But I have enough powder to hold him at bay. Get onboard and we'll be off!" he said.

Lilly saw a dark-haired young woman dressed in scarlet

peering over the rails. Then the young woman looked anxiously at the circling ship and spoke in a strange accent.

"The other ship's advancing. We'll be caught in their crossfire."

The other ship plowed through the waves as the sails turned toward them.

"If we can be free of the vines, I'll show them what the *Dagger* was made to do," the tall pirate growled. He paced the deck, calling out orders to the men under his command.

Lilly's head hurt, but she wanted to help while she still had contact with the sea. She lowered herself into the water, the top of her torso rising above the surface. She rose until her waist and even her knees were above the waves. The rope grew slack as the men who pulled it slowed their efforts, watching Lilly's movements.

Standing above the waves, Lilly bent down and dipped both of her hands in the water, palms up. She thrust a surge of her Talent into the water and grasped at it like it was a sheet she was spreading across a bed. She snapped her wrists as she brought her hands over her head and let them fall once again to her waist. The sea responded to her instruction. A great wave began to travel away from Lilly in the direction of the oncoming ship, the added distance allowing the swell to increase in size as it arched toward the Sulian vessel. Lilly watched as her efforts reached their full potential.

The Sulian pirates on the ship began to cry out in alarm. The sudden wall of water that came toward them overshadowed the ship and men screamed as the impact of the monster wave smashed into them. The ship nosed up into the air and was whipped to the side as it was struck along one side by the wave. Men were washed across the deck and into the sea as the ship bucked and sought to right itself.

"They have a Water Witch!" the Sulians cried. The closer ship began veering away, having seen the near disaster that emanated from Lilly's position.

The men aboard Kathleen's ship made motions as if to ward off evil. They looked fearfully at Lilly as she was brought aboard.

"Captain Dagger, at your service," said the tall pirate with dark hair. He bowed to Lilly and removed his hat. At least he seemed at ease with a Talented person aboard.

"My name is Lilly," she replied.

"You have given us our escape," Captain Dagger said. "But more importantly, you have given me back the *Dagger*."

The sails filled their bellies with the wind and the ship moved away.

Admiral Yamatsu's ship began picking up the sailors who struggled in the water.

"He got away and not a soul aboard his ship knows you are here," Maxwell said to the Sulian girl beside him.

"He can chase us to Candoreth if he likes, but with Lilly on our side he'd better be careful," Kathleen said.

"I'm afraid I won't be much help for a while. My head is hurting badly, and I'm feeling very hungry," Lilly informed them.

"You were already depleted before you moved that wave. You need to rest," Kathleen said.

"Do you have anything to eat?" Lilly enquired. "I will make sure we arrive in Candoreth well before the Sulians."

Thomas gestured toward the cabin where the old Sulian Healer stood silently—almost as if in a trance.

"She can Heal you," he said.

The old woman with stringy gray hair and a simple dress swayed a bit with the movement of the ship. Her hands hung at her sides.

"Healer," Shīanya called, "come help our friend."

The old woman shuffled softly toward Lilly and placed her wrinkled hands on the bandages wrapped around her head. She murmured a few words and Lilly's eyes grew wide with appreciation.

"Thank you," she said to the Healer. "What is your name?"

The old woman bobbed her head gently and moistened her lips, but didn't respond. She bowed her head again as if to go to sleep again while standing up.

Lilly looked to Kathleen.

"What is wrong with her? At first she reminded me of Melva, but not like this."

Kathleen shook her head sadly.

"They treat the Talented like slaves. She's been Tamed, like an animal," Kathleen said.

Lilly recoiled.

Thomas shook his head. "I'm not much for witches. I try to avoid them, but it never seemed right to me to take away a person's free will."

"Breaking the siege of Candoreth isn't the only reason we must fight the Sulians," Kathleen added.

"We will put a stop to this in Desnia," Jared intoned.

Kathleen pressed some dried meat into Lilly's hand.

"If you are going to help us sail to Candoreth, you will need to eat," she said.

51

CEASE FIRE

"She is the *Enmity* no longer. The *Dagger* sails the seas once more!" Thomas Dagger said.

A sailor dangled from a rope with a bucket of paint in his hand. He dipped the brush and painted the golden letters carefully on the stern of the ship.

"Isn't it unlucky to name a ship after yourself?" one of the Centian pirates asked.

"I have luck enough to spare," Thomas Dagger replied, smiling crookedly, then seized the rope nearest him and launched himself into the air. He landed on the railing that enclosed the open hatches in the foredeck, balancing easily on the wooden rail. "I've traveled around the wheel of fate—been run over by that wheel a few times, too, if I'm being honest. But now I'm back on top!"

"We need more supplies and gunpowder if we are to *stay* on top," muttered another of the pirates.

"Help me defend my home, and you will have all the gratitude and resources our people can muster," Kathleen said.

"Even in war? Is your city so well-provisioned that it can spare enough food for us?" Thomas asked.

"I am Talented. I can grow the food for you," Kathleen explained.

"A Plant Witch can be a princess in Desnia!" one of the men exclaimed. This brought a round of rough laughter from the Centian pirates.

Jared placed his hand on the hilt of his sword and stepped forward. Channing touched Jared's shoulder in an effort to calm him. He stepped forward and spoke to the pirates.

"You saw what she did—entangling the ship in sea grass. Have you ever witnessed such a display of the Growing Talent? She will grow the food you need for your journey home. Help us, by defending the city and we will help you," Channing said.

"Give us food and send us on our way? What chance do we have of surviving a voyage back across the Sea of Storms?" Dagger asked

Kathleen saw the pirates furrow their brows and murmur to each other. The prospect was not a fair one.

"It is even more difficult crossing the sea sailing eastward. We will need more ships. We need to free more of our countrymen from the Sulian fleet in order to man them," Dagger said.

"Admiral Yamatsu will not allow you to sail away. He is likely already spreading word of your betrayal," Jared added.

The Centians considered this. They huddled in a group and spoke quietly amongst themselves.

"Food isn't enough for us! We want treasure as well," she heard them say.

"To sail halfway around the world, through the most dangerous seas, and return home with naught but a bag of vegetables? That will not make the wife happy."

"Or the girls at the tavern!" another exclaimed, to a round of approval.

More of them spoke, expressing concerns and doubts. Thomas watched them. He stood apart, having made up his own mind but intent on their discussions.

"Can we trust them?" Kathleen asked Jared.

"We need to go back to Candoreth and stop the attack by the Sulians. If these Centians pirates could help us do that, we can take the next step once Candoreth is safe. We will have a stronger position from which to negotiate."

"At least the Centians are proper pirates. They're not intent on stealing our lands—just treasure," Maxwell expressed.

Thomas looked toward Kathleen and then around to his newly restored officers. He approached her with open hands, upturning a black horn he wore on a sling over his shoulder. From it he poured a small pile of black, sand-like material. The wind caught some of the particles and blew them away.

"This is the magic I am most adept at using." Thomas shook his hand, allowing more of the dark grains to sift into the wind. "It can sink a ship and level a battalion in an instant. It can transport hundreds to the Land Beyond, just like that!" He snapped his fingers. "It keeps knaves honest, and kings humble. But I need more of it! Food isn't enough for us, Princess. This ship is the mother of this rebel armada. If I sail into Candoreth harbor, I can stop them. There isn't a ship in the fleet as swift or as dangerous as the *Dagger*—not with me as her captain."

"We do not know how to make this black powder," Jared explained.

Thomas eyed him, measuring his integrity.

"Argh, it couldn't be that easy, could it? In six hundred years the Desnians still haven't made use of the gun," Thomas said, dusting the black powder from his hand.

"Old Fester was the other man who knew the recipe best, and he was killed in that fracas with the admiral," a pirate stated. He pointed to the water where the bodies of the dead had been allowed to sleep.

"If we offer you food and treasure, freedom, and more of your explosive powder, will you join us? Will you fight by our side against the Sulians?" Kathleen asked.

Thomas Dagger tucked his thumbs into his broad brown belt and tilted his head to one side.

"Highness, if you can deliver all of that I will gladly offer you my services—as well as that of my men. We would fight the Great Serpent himself if you can deliver that. Am I right?" he added, turning toward the Centians who listened intently.

They gave a hearty cheer and a few made lewd comments, but reaffirmed their willingness to do anything to please the princess —as long as their needs were also met. Jared's face tightened at some of the remarks, but he remained tight-lipped. Maxwell slapped a few of the men on their backs to welcome them, but the pirate with a stump where his hand should have been frowned, and recoiled from the Shifter. Maxwell moved on to congratulate others on their decision to unite.

"How do you propose to get them more powder?" Channing asked quietly.

"I know a man in Tyath—a man of learning, with a laboratory. His name is Father Overbook. He might be able to determine what is in the powder and teach us how to make more of it," Kathleen replied.

"Our wise men have not discovered it yet," Shīanya said. "My father has offered to pay the Centians handsomely for the knowledge."

"Give me a sample of the black powder, Captain," Kathleen requested.

Thomas poured from the horn again. This time he placed the powder in a piece of paper and rolled it into a cylinder, twisting the ends tightly to close them. He handed the small package to Kathleen.

"I have enough for now. But when I'm done with Yamatsu, I'll need more." He smiled devilishly.

"Maxwell, will you take this to the Golden City and deliver it to the priest named Father Overbrook? He works beneath the

Great Library in Tyath and is a friend to Heathron. He can help us learn how to make it."

Maxwell examined the small roll of paper.

"This thing isn't going to explode while I'm carrying it, is it? he asked.

Thomas laughed. "Don't mistake it for a roll of smokleaf. Fire will set it off. And don't get it wet. Water will ruin it."

"No fire, no water—got it," Maxwell said.

"Could I go with you?" Shīanya asked. "I would love to see a place called the Golden City."

Maxwell swallowed, and seemed to blush at Shīanya's offer.

"Tyath is not that great—not with Lord Balfoest in charge. Besides, I'm *flying* there and there's no way for you to keep up," Maxwell said.

Shīanya looked disappointed. She lowered her eyes and bit her lower lip in frustration. She didn't seem deterred.

"There is no time to lose. Admiral Yamatsu will return for us when he has gathered reinforcements. We sail for Candoreth immediately and liberate what ships remain in King Lukald's fleet," Channing ordered.

MASTER SHIP

The *Dagger* cut through the wave as its name implied it should. Swift as a blade it divided the waters, the wake flowing behind the vessel in a long blue arc of bubbles pointing toward the Emerald Coast. Thomas was in his element, born for moments like these. Even far from his home in Centia, he felt at ease. His ship and the sea were his lovers—beautiful and yet dangerous. One cared for him and the other threatened his life, but he felt he could face any challenge with the two of them close by. With the Douser on board, pushing his ship through the waves, Thomas felt truly invincible. The sails were full, but even if the wind slacked they would still fly toward Candoreth like a wagon rolling downhill.

"These are the Turtle Islands," Channing explained to Thomas, pointing to the mounds of earth that rose above sea. "My home is called Marth. It lies to the south—the largest of the islands. Candoreth is eastward from here."

Thomas Dagger nodded. The man from Marth knew his way about a ship and was familiar with the waters on the shores of Desnia. Thomas could use a man like that to serve with him.

"Is he ready to go?" Kathleen asked.

The Shifter stood shirtless on the deck of the *Dagger*. He spoke with Shīanya, throwing his head back in laughter at something she had said.

"Those two seem to be getting along well," Kathleen observed.

"I thought he would have left already. I am not sure why he is delaying," Jared replied.

"At the rate we're sailing, Lilly will have us in Candoreth by nightfall."

"Maxwell will need a day to fly to Tyath. He should get started."

"I do hope he's able to find Father Overbrook," Kathleen said.

Jared placed a comforting hand on her arm. "He will find him, and we'll defend your home," Jared said.

Maxwell caught sight of them approaching.

"Shīanya, keep an eye on Jared for me. Don't let him do anything stupid while I'm gone," he said.

Shīanya frowned.

"Stupid? I am not familiar with this word. Is it a term for warfare?" she queried.

"Maxwell is very familiar with it. And yes, it is a word related to warfare. Maxwell battles with it daily," Jared sniped.

The Shifter closed his fists and raised both of his smallest fingers at the Sīhalt Guardian. When Kathleen turned to look at him he quickly hid them behind his back.

"I saw that, Maxwell," Kathleen said.

"Sorry, Your Highness; I just wanted to wave goodbye to my good friend," the Shifter replied. He tossed the paper packet given to him by Captain Dagger, and caught it again.

"Goodbye, Shīanya. I'll see you soon."

Maxwell waved to the Sulian princess and sprang into the air, leaving his clothing on the deck. His powerful wings caught the air and lifted him above the ship.

Jared eyed Maxwell as he flew upward. The rock eagle swooped down close to the water, allowing its talon to skim the surface of the ocean. It turned one way and then the next, screeching as it climbed higher and then dove down again.

"He's showing off for you," Jared said.

Shīanya looked puzzled.

"He's trying to impress you," Kathleen clarified.

Shīanya watched the bird as it finally flew out of sight.

"I wish to go with him," she said. "Isn't Tyath where your enemy reigns?"

"Maxwell will be fine. Trust me, he knows how to care for himself," Jared said.

"Maxwell is unique in his abilities," Channing agreed.

"I have never met a man more courageous," Shīanya replied with a longing gaze.

Jared and Kathleen glanced at each other with a smile.

"He will be back within a few days—you'll see," Jared said.

"If he isn't, I am going after him," the Sulian woman said resolutely.

FIX THE WALLS

"Once you finish your lessons, I will go with you to the gardens," Heathron promised.

He had taken to the role of teacher with gusto. He established a routine for Elayna despite the pirates' attack on the city. Candoreth had never fallen and the walls were strong. The little girl was very bright and excelled in mathematics, history, and music but her handwriting was atrocious. Each composition looked like a crayfish had been dipped in ink and allowed to crawl across her paper. They would need to work on that.

"We did this last week," Elayna said, frowning to show her discontent, but it was superficial. The underlying expression for the little girl was one of sincere joy—she smiled almost constantly and couldn't hide it with a momentary frown.

"I want to go to the beach," she insisted, trying to change the subject once more.

"You know we are not going to the shore," Heathron said. "The pirates have to clear out first."

Elayna harrumphed and folded her arms across her chest, tossing her red hair dramatically.

She looked like a miniature version of Kathleen, and Heathron found himself laughing.

"What's so funny?" Elayna asked, not wanting to miss out on the joke.

"Finish your lesson," Heathron replied, trying to redirect Elayna to her studies. She was trying to get him off track again.

Since being tapped as one of Elayna's protectors, Heathron had become her de facto tutor as well. Seth was always there, silent as a shadow and it was easy to forget about the Sīhalt Guardian and his ever-present blade, but Heathron was glad of it.

Since his abduction in Tyath, Heathron found himself feeling uneasy whenever he walked the halls of Candoreth Castle alone. He doubted his ability to protect the little princess even as he swore to himself that he would However, his mind and heart still bore the scars from his time in Tyath. His confidence was broken somehow. He no longer walked with the arrogant steps of youth, but treaded with caution and was glad to have Seth DeTorre with him as a Guardian.

There was a loud *boom*, and the room shook. A few flakes of plaster floated down from the ceiling.

"It's starting again!" Elayna said with frustration. She put her face in her hands and shook her head, mimicking the antics of an exasperated adult.

No doubt Elayna has seen that look often, Heathron thought with a smirk.

The prince had developed a great admiration for her spunk. Yes, she tried to pull one over on him now and again—hiding beneath the table when he left the room, copying from the text when she was supposed to compose her own words, and asking a thousand questions that had absolutely nothing to do with the subject at hand. The pirate thunder-ships made it all the more difficult.

"I need to go fix the wall," Elayna said.

"You need to finish your lesson," Heathron replied calmly.

The girl leveled her eyes at the prince. Heathron felt the strange sensation that prickled the back of his neck when Elayna spoke with a certainty unlike any child her age.

"The soldiers need me to fix the walls," she stated.

Heathron smiled. "I've seen you fix the walls, Elayna. It doesn't take you very long. Despite the war, your father asked that we maintain some sense of normalcy for you. We will go take a look as soon as you finish your lesson."

A handful of plaster fell to the floor with the next explosion.

Elayna did not take her eyes off of Heathron. She interlaced her fingers and placed her elbows on the table, leaning forward to press her lips against her thumbs.

She waited. Heathron did, too. He was not going to be bullied into doing what this little girl wanted. She could be very headstrong at times!

In the distance, Heathron thought he could hear screams.

"How many of our soldiers will call for me before you let me go?" Elayna asked calmly.

The Sīhalt moved closer to the window to peer toward the harbor wall. He shielded his eyes with a hand to his brow, squinting against the bright southern sun.

"Can you hear them?" Heathron asked Elayna and the Sīhalt Guardian.

Seth nodded.

"And see them," Elayna added with the same tranquility of emotion that rested upon her when she first insisted that she must fix the wall. However, her eyes went not to the window but flicked around the room as Heathron might do at a party, taking in the crowd. He felt a chill run down his spine, but he did not feel fear. Only urgency.

"Just write the last sentences and we can go," he said just as the doors to the library flew open.

One of the lieutenants of the Candorethian Army almost fell to the floor as he stopped to salute and give his request.

"They have doubled their attack," he said breathlessly. "More ships have arrived. The walls are broken at the seam and many of the men on the walls have died. Can you bring Princess Elayna to help us?" he asked desperately.

"Yes, of course," Heathron replied, closing the book in front of him immediately.

"Come, Elayna. We are needed," Heathron said, extending his hand to the little girl.

She turned to the empty room as he spoke.

"Don't worry," she said to her invisible audience. "I will fix the walls. Your families will be safe."

A CHILD TO THE RESCUE

They turned and dashed out the door of the library, with Seth in the lead. Heathron sprinted down the polished floors of the castle, holding Elayna's hand. They ran so quickly she could barely keep from tripping.

"I can't run this fast!" she said as he pulled her along with steps three times as large as hers.

"Then I'll carry you," Heathron said, and without slowing his pace he turned and swept her up into his arms. .

In any other moment, Elayna would have enjoyed being held in Heathron's arms. The prince was strong and handsome and he always smelled nice.

Right now, he was breathing hard. The blue-eyed Sīhalt Guardian ran in front of them, clearing the way of servants and citizens alike.

"Make way for the prince and princess!" he called in a loud voice.

When they ran outside, past the columns of the long veranda, Elayna could see the thunder-ships anchored close to the harbor wall. Black smoke and fire belched from the tubes that protruded from the open hatches cut neatly into the ship above the waterline.

As soon as one row finished, another row began. Fire spewed from the tubes and a sharp crack could be heard as enormous blocks of stone crumbled under the onslaught. A section of the sturdy harbor walls crumbled and slid into the water, creating a wave that expanded and crashed against the remaining ships of the Candorethian Navy.

"Elayna," Heathron said as he ran, "what did you mean in the library when you said, 'Your families will be safe'?"

Elayna held tight to Heathron's neck and, despite the bouncing of his rapid pace, answered him.

"Other people can't see them, but I can. The soldiers who died on the harbor wall—they came to ask me to help rebuild it. They were worried about their wives and children," she explained.

"Do you mean those who were wounded and died today?"

"They were not wounded when I saw them in the library—just sad," Elayna said.

Elayna saw Heathron look at the Sīhalt Guardian the way adults often did when she explained what she could do.

"I'm telling the truth!" she said.

"Oh, I believe you, little one," Heathron said.

"Please don't call me that," Elayna said. "I'm seven years old."

"That must be why you're getting so heavy." Heathron put on a smile and pretended he would drop her. She rolled her eyes but gave him a small smile.

"It is just a traditional way of speaking in the North. I didn't mean to offend you. I should remember your proper title."

"It's okay, as long as you believe me."

"We do," the Sīhalt Guardian said as they moved along. "Do you see the dead every day?" he asked.

"As often as I see the living," Elayna said, glancing at the people looking over the veranda. "Some of the people watching the ships are living, but most of them died a long time ago," she explained.

"How do you know?" Heathron asked.

Elayna looked at the many people who stood watching. Some of them were faint and the light passed through them. They were dressed in clothes of an ancient style, appearing to have stepped right out of her history book.

"They are quieter, and they don't make as much of a shadow in the sunlight," Elayna explained.

Cracks of man-made thunder rang out from the pirate ships. Black tubes belched smoke and fire, rocking the ship in the water as it set broadside to the stone wall.

Violent fissures spiraled outward in every direction as chunks of stone fell down into the water.

Shields and helmets in place, Candorethian soldiers hurried to surround Heathron and Elayna. The prince sat Elayna down on the pathway.

"We must be careful from here on," he said as they crept closer to the area of attack. "How close do you need to be?"

"I'm not sure. If the stone is joined closely I might be able to work from a distance, but it will be easier if I can put my hands right on the rock that needs to be repaired," Elayna replied.

"Go whenever you are ready."

Elayna took a deep breath and wrinkled her brow. She knew she could not wait any longer.

"Wait!" a cry rose from behind them.

Sam hurried with Melva as they bent at the waist to hide behind the broken parapet wall.

"You can't expect a child to defend the whole city," Sam said breathlessly.

"No one is making me," Elayna said. "I want to help. I promised them I would."

With that, the girl scampered over the broken stone scattered atop the wall.

Her movements were reminiscent of those in a simple playground game. Balancing on one foot and jumping to another piece of rubble, she moved forward to land again—balancing as a bird might, on one foot.

Elayna finally slid to her belly when she reached the breach.

She touched the wall where a devastating seam had opened up from the explosion. It began to close as Elayna worked. It was as if the stones were being Healed.

A murmur rose from the men who watched. Soldiers of Candoreth and the pirates of Sulia all spoke in excited tones. The stones creaked as they shifted and settled into a new pattern of ordered construction. The invaders could no longer access the breach. It was closed, and the smooth vertical height was beyond what any man could scale. Elayna lay with her eyes closed as if she were straining against a great weight. Her small hands pressed firmly to the stone as she hummed despite the furious shouts from the pirates below. Beads of sweat formed on her brow as she struggled to finish her work.

Heathron heard the pirates. Their accents were strange, and a few words were unknown to him, but he understood them for the most part.

"Reload the cannons!" they called. "We did not sail across the Sea of Storms to be beaten by a wild little Rock Witch. Send a signal to the other ships to concentrate their fire here. We made a breach, and we can do so again."

"Yes, sir!" came the shout from the men onboard.

Flags ascended the signal poles, and other ships began to turn toward their position.

"Aim for the top of the wall! Give that little witch the Centian thunder!" the officer shouted.

Heathron started toward Elayna. Seth was by his side, but they were stopped by a barrage of fire and shattered stone filling the air around them. Seth threw his cape across his face as he was blown back by the blast. The Sīhalt fabric crackled loudly as chips of stone struck it. Heathron threw up his arms to protect his face, but doubled over as he felt the burn of small chunks of stone ripping through his clothes on his left side and tearing at his face and neck, leaving him bloody. The soldiers of Candoreth were blown off the wall by the concussion. Screams barely escaped their lips before they impacted the earth below.

"Get back!" Heathron shouted. He turned to see that Melva had crouched behind a large stone, but the servant Sam was no longer beside her.

Trebuchet arms made an arc through the sky as they launched stones the size of a pumpkin or pots of burning pitch toward the invaders. Most fell to shore damaging the ships.

Heathron watched as Elayna got up from her position at the edge of the wall. She turned to look at him; the red dress she wore swirling about her knees, her eyes filled with fear. He motioned for her to come to him.

A barrage from the warship shook the foundations of stone and Heathron fell to his knees. Another slab of the wall, blasted and broken, fell with a crash to the harbor below.

"I need to close the harbor so no more ships can come in," Elayna said.

Heathron shook his head.

"No, Elayna! " he shouted about the fray.

He watched as Elayna knelt and placed her small hands on either side of the parapet wall, her brow furrowed in deep concentration. The child closed her eyes and her lips moved, but Heathron could not hear her words.

The wall began to shake and the water of the harbor nearest to Elayna bubbled like a pot being boiled.

A column of stone rose from the water, like the eruption of islands in the south. Heathron watched in awe as pillar after pillar of natural rock was raised to the level of the highest wall. The ships within the harbor bobbed and pitched like toys in a child's washtub. Sailors on both sides of the fight dove into the water in fear and swam for the closest shore. The erupting stone wall cast a long shadow on the pirate ships that approached, sealing them outside the harbor. Elayna walked barefoot and with each step another enormous column of stone was thrust through the surface. With a great moaning and shattering of stone, each pillar slid into place beside the previous one. The sound was deafening, but Heathron could hear snatches of a song the beautiful child sang as she continued onward—closing the entire harbor.

"We'll be cut off from the sea!" the pirates shouted.

The enemy ships returned their focus to Elayna.

As soon as her next step fell, the stonework beneath her feet erupted. In slow motion he saw the projectile from the ship impact the stone. Heathron screamed as the white stones of the wall were pulverized and Elayna disappeared in the blast, her body thrown with the raining stones to the far side of the wall, where a pile of debris was mounded from previous blasts. His ears were ringing and he fought to stay conscious, staggering toward where Elayna fell and then collapsing.

A cheer arose from the pirates below. A sheet of stone broke free from the wall, and like ice thawing on the Adisfall glaciers in springtime it slid into the harbor. The harbor remained open to the sea.

55

CLARION CALL

Melva stood on the remains of the harbor wall. The stones were shattered to rubble and the smoke that filled the air burned her lungs. She stumbled forward, going down on her hands at times to feel her way forward.

Prince Heathron reached down to help her stand up amidst the swirls of smoke and dust.

"Where is she?" Melva croaked in a raspy voice.

Heathron wiped his face with a tattered sleeve, the fabric covered in blood. The skin on his face was injured from the blast, but she could not worry about that.

"She's gone," he said, voice empty. "Struck by the blast of the ship."

The ship in question lay on the water, still rocking from the destruction it dealt, wreathed in white smoke.

"Show me the body," Melva said, refusing to accept Elayna's death until she'd inspected the body herself.

They stumbled over the broken blocks of the wall, almost falling to the ground where the stones were cut at a sharp slant. Heathron steadied Melva, helping the old woman onward.

"She was right here," he said, looking around at the corner of the wall where the embattlement widened.

The giant stones that made up the top of the wall had tumbled down. A rift had opened in the harbor wall where the assault had focused, and pirates were pulling on oars to land below them. The land assault was now in full swing.

"They will pour through the wall. Nothing will hold them back now."

"I will defend the top of the wall for as long as I can," Seth said. He made his way to the narrow point where the pirates would have to climb if they were to ascend the wall.

"We asked too much of a child. Elayna tried, but the defenses of Candoreth have failed," Heathron lamented.

"There she is!" Melva cried, pointing a withered finger in the direction of a jumble of stones.

Only a few locks of red hair and a small foot stuck out from beneath the stones. The small toes were stained with blood.

"Uncover her," Melva said.

Heathron frantically bent to lift the chunks of stone that covered the body. He threw them aside one by one, working as fast as his exhausted muscles would allow. He felt numb, as if he were living a horrible, impossible dream.

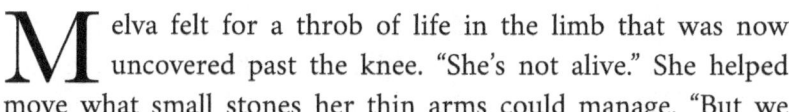

Melva felt for a throb of life in the limb that was now uncovered past the knee. "She's not alive." She helped move what small stones her thin arms could manage. "But we must do what we can for our loved ones—even in death."

Heathron strained against a heavy block that lay across Elayna's hips. He had removed most of the rubble. The little girl's face was bloodied from the blast that had taken the wall. She did not move, even when Heathron rocked the largest stone back and forth, trying to get it off her.

"She didn't deserve this. It should have been anyone, anyone but her."

"Leave it alone now, Heathron," Melva said. "I wish to talk to her."

Heathron collapsed beside Melva, his strength spent.

"I don't want Kathleen to see her this way," he sobbed.

"None of us can be insulated from the pain. Sit down and listen for a moment. Forget the pirates, and the smoke of battle. Listen to the wind."

Melva began to hum.

"I can't, Melva," he said. "I can't hear the wind."

She didn't respond to him but continued to hum, holding Elayna's hand in hers— caressing the delicate arm of the child as she knelt beside her.

Melva felt for life within the girl. She closed her eyes and entered the realm of unconsciousness. Elayna's body was a dark dwelling, familiar in the blackness but lacking in the warmth of light.

Elayna! Melva called silently as she hummed.

She walked through the corridors of the girl's physical existence, searching for a spark of spirit that might still be found within the millions of parts that made up her body.

Melva began to search the head and neck, but found no light. She searched Elayna's airway, feeling for a flutter of breath—the slightest change in pressure as air might move in and out—but felt nothing.

Elayna! she called out again into the silence of her mind. *Come back to us!*

Melva moved down her spine from the shoulders. She felt no pulse in the major nerves. Even the larger ones, made to command survival, were silent.

She eased toward Elayna's heart, ready to accept the final demise of the child she loved as her own.

A Healer can only Heal that which is still living, she heard her own mother say as she trained her, so many years ago, in the Talent.

If I can just find a spark!

Melva called out loud to Elayna's spirit, "Come back to us!"

And then she felt it, the smallest twitch in the fibers of the muscles of the heart. Melva stopped her searching and focused on that smallest movement. She could feel the spark of energy—of life!

The old woman hummed all the louder, almost breaking into song. She gathered her strength and pushed it down her arms, through her hands, and into the girl's body.

She vaguely heard Heathron speaking. She saw him draw his sword and turn toward the steps where the pirates surely would climb, but she felt no distraction, no fear. The only thing that mattered was Elayna and coaxing the eternal spirit of the child to return to her body. In order for that to happen, Melva knew that she must mend the terrestrial frame that lay broken by the rock. She felt for the broken bones and the muscles that were torn. Melva mended the vitals that were bruised from the powerful concussion. She soothed the hemorrhage on the brain and helped to dissipate the blood that pooled within the skull.

"She is badly broken," Melva said to herself, "but I will do what I can to save her."

~

Heathron watched as the pirates poured into more boats and rowed to shore. They were not a disorganized rabble like he had seen before. The men moved with precision and followed the commands of their leaders without hesitation. Now that the defensive catapults no longer threw stones or fire pots, the pirates wasted no time in coming ashore.

Heathron crouched down, hiding behind what remained of the parapet wall, while Seth concealed himself on the opposite side of the breach. He glanced over at the Healer, still kneeling beside Princess Elayna.

Can she truly bring back the dead? he wondered.

The little girl was broken, having been crushed beneath heavy stones. Surely only grief inspired the old woman to try and Heal her. Nevertheless, Melva deserved time alone with the child. Die if he must, Heathron would not see that precious moment interrupted by pirates or anyone else. He tightened his grip on the hilt of his sword, gritted his teeth, and wiped the blood from his face, all while swearing silently that he would defend the narrow walkway at the top of the steps—the only way to the top of their section of the enormous harbor wall.

They cannot swarm us, and I do not see archers among them. We should be able to hold them off for a while, fighting man to man.

Heathron took a deep breath and readied himself. He saw Seth take a breath and close his eyes.

A bronze gong sounded, alerting them of an enormous ship sailing into the harbor. Heathron shook his head, not wanting to believe what he saw. The master ship of the fleet had come to finish the attack. The men aboard the great vessel struck a large gong that was positioned near the mast, the sound resounding deeply across the harbor. Again and again it came.

Heathron exhaled in relief. The pirates on the shore, like ants returning to their hill, begin to retreat to their ships.

56

MELVA'S PROOF

Heathron went quickly back to Melva as Seth remained as a guard to their flank. He did not know why the Sulian fleet had called off the attack, but he was thankful.

"I can find some food. Doesn't that give you strength?" he asked, kneeling before her. He did not have any food, and wondered if Seth could run to the castle and return in time to save her.

"Do not fear, Heathron," Melva said to the prince. She smoothed his dusty hair and looked down at him with compassion.

"Kathleen will be lost without you, Melva," Heathron said. "She will never forgive me for allowing you to die."

"You have done your duty, and I have lived a good, long life. Take my cloak...for her," Melva said, gesturing to Elayna who was sleeping peacefully on the stones a few paces away.

Melva removed her outer garment and handed it to the prince. He laid it gently over Elayna, the dark brown fabric contrasting with her smooth, white skin.

The ancient woman stood like the essence of a sunrise just

before it breaks through the clouds. She seemed to glow golden in the failing light of the day. In her flickering image Heathron saw a youthful visage of the Healer that had saved them all.

"Kathleen will be inconsolable if you go," he said.

Melva's voice dropped to a whisper: "Tell her," she began, and then took a deep breath. She was growing more faint and Heathron could almost see through her. She would not last much longer.

"Will you say these words to her?" Melva asked.

"Of course, dear woman; I will give her whatever message you like," the prince promised.

"Say to her, 'I have loved you, but now I must let you go.' Can you do that for me?" the Red Grower whispered.

Heathron held her hand and nodded, repeating the words to himself.

I have loved you, but now I must let you go.

"I will tell her," Heathron promised, and added, "she loves you, too."

"Tell her, 'I will take care of Elayna'."

"I will tell her," he said, "Thank you for bringing Elayna back to us."

"What is a mother for, if not to give life to her children? I have never had a child of my own, but now I do," Melva said, looking at the place where Elayna rested.

"And she is beautiful and good," Heathron replied reverently.

Melva nodded and smiled. She fixed her gaze on the sleeping young woman. Heathron turned to look at her. Then he could no longer feel Melva's hand on his. When he turned to look back at the old woman, she was gone. Like a whisper, the wind swept her dress out to sea and her wooden beads made a soft clinking as they fell to the ground.

Heathron felt a tingle up his spine and bowed his head, amazed at what he had witnessed.

"Do you think she would mind if I wore her necklace, too?" a womanly voice asked. It had the playfulness of a brook and the softness of nectar.

Heathron turned slowly, looking over his shoulder.

Elayna sat on the stones where she had died, but she was not dead. She was alive and she was whole. She held Melva's cloak about her and sat gracefully, surrounded by shattered stones and the remains of the ramparts.

Heathron looked at the miracle that sat before him and almost collapsed to his knees.

Elayna's red hair fell past her waist, shimmering in the sunset. She held the Healer's rough cloak closed at her neck, and her cheeks shone with a perfect complexion—quite unlike the destruction of stones that surrounded her.

Heathron swallowed.

"Do you think she would mind?" Elayna said again.

Heathron wavered, blinking, trying to take in the moment.

The woman extended a hand to him.

"Will you at least help me stand?" she asked with a smile.

Heathron blinked. He gave a subtle shake of his head and remembered his manners.

"Melva would not mind if you wore them. I am sure of it," he said softly.

Elayna nodded. Then Heathron picked up the wooden necklace from the ground and offered his hand to Elayna. She took it and for a moment he thought that perhaps he was in the presence of an angel, that he might be dreaming, or have died himself. He felt as if he, too, were being Healed, simply by feeling her fingers against his own.

When Elayna stood, she was able to look him directly in the eye. Her piercing blue gaze made him take a deeper breath. He brushed the dust from the necklace and placed it over her head. She held the cloak closed as Heathron moved to one side and lifted her hair so that it fell over the necklace and the brown cloak she wore.

"You are barefoot," he said, seeing the sharp stones scattered about.

"I don't know where my shoes are," Elayna said, looking down at her feet.

"They wouldn't fit you now anyway," Heathron remarked.

She smiled at him and he immediately felt a great sense of comfort.

They looked back toward the castle and could hear the faint voices of those who sang for the dead, the mourners using complex harmonies to express their sadness.

"We lost a lot of people today," Elayna said quietly.

"Without you, there would have been many more."

The outer wall she'd built arched across the harbor to a narrowing, where the waves still managed to disturb the smooth surface of the water within.

"It looks like a row of giant candles, don't you think?" Elayna mused, and tilted her head, examining her handiwork.

"It saved us," Heathron replied.

"I could have made it a lot prettier, if I had not been in such a rush," she added.

Heathron smiled. Not all of her childlike innocence was gone. There was a sadness, perhaps from the terrors of the day, but Elayna stood before him as a woman in the prime of her youth—full of beauty and vigor. He was pleased that she maintained the spark of laughter that had seemed to color all her speech when she was a child.

"You are injured," she said, touching his cheek.

"It's nothing. I don't want you to cut your feet. Can I carry you?"

Elayna smiled again. "You almost dropped me this morning. How will you manage to carry me now, Prince Heathron? Are we not the same age?"

She laughed, and the sound of it made Heathron want to sing. His exhaustion fled at the sound of her voice.

"I will not let you fall," he said, lifting her into his arms.

The weight of her body was no burden. He felt strong and alive.

"I fear I already have fallen," she replied, placing her arms around his neck and pulling herself close to him.

Heathron's heart drummed.

He moved toward the castle, his boots crunching on the sharp bits of stone that lay in their path.

THE OVERBROOKS

Eldin Stellat bowed toward the altar before exiting his pew. Father Overbrook had given a good service, even if it was sparsely attended. Instead of leaving the Grand Cathedral by going out one of the smaller side doors as he often did, Eldin made his way to Father Overbrook. The old priest had given a homily, and in those words Eldin had found hope that the old man might remain an ally to his cause.

"Father," he said quietly.

Father Overbrook didn't respond.

"Father," he said again, with a little more volume.

The old priest with the white beard looked up, his watery eyes gazing in Eldin's direction, and then lit up when he recognized his face. The priest tapped Mother Overbrook on the arm.

"Mother, look who's come to visit us! It's Eldin Stellat." The elderly couple hobbled over to speak to him.

"How is your family? I have not seen your parents for quite some time."

Eldin looked down.

"It's true. They are worried about visiting the city."

"Do you mean now that Heathron is gone?" Father Overbrook asked.

Eldin nodded, wishing the priest would speak more softly.

"Heathron's absence is only part of the problem. Lord Balfoest has tightened his control here and Mother and Father fear to leave our estate for too long. I've not been to the cathedral in months, so I thought I would risk it today. How are you?"

Father and Mother Overbrook looked at each other and then back at Eldin.

"How are we?" Mother Overbrook asked. She seemed hesitant to answer.

"We're fine," Father Overbrook replied, in an obvious attempt at optimism.

"We still get to serve the church now and again."

The pews were sparsely filled on this Tuesday mid-morning.

"They don't allow you to lead the worship on the holy days, do they, Father?"

The old man shook his head. "The Luzian priests have taken over everything. They don't honor the old ways," he intoned. There was sadness in his voice.

"They're even trying to shut down my laboratory!"

"It's out of the way, far down past the main stacks in the cellar. There are more hallways than you could ever discover down there, and we keep our work tucked away," Mother Overbrook added in comfort to her husband.

Eldin couldn't tell if she was explaining how they continued despite opposition, or giving a reason why they should be left alone in the first place.

"That's such a shame," Eldin replied. "I enjoy all that you taught me when I was your student. I even set up a laboratory of my own! You should come and see it."

"They've given me an ultimatum," Father Overbrook told him. "They told me that if I don't stop with my experimentations I'll be defrocked, stripped of my right to minister!"

Eldin was shocked.

"That cannot be," he said softly.

The old man shook his head gravely. "I do not jest. There's no humor in it."

Mother Overbrook patted her husband on the elbow.

"It's okay. We're getting older now, and he probably shouldn't be messing around with potions, fire, and glass."

"Oh, Mother, hush," he said, turning to her. "You enjoy it as much as I do."

Mother Overbrook reached into her pocket and pulled out a handkerchief. She dabbed a tear that welled in the corner of her eye. "It's true, Eldin. There's so little that we enjoy together, but that's one of the few things. Without being able to serve fully in the church, and without our research, where will we be? We didn't have any children of our own; the students were our children, and now we're not allowed to teach either."

"Why won't they let you teach?" Eldin asked.

"They said we're 'professors emeritus'. That means no time in the classroom."

"I actually sought you out, Father, because I wanted to invite you to minister at our estate for a time. I worry that Mother has not been to the worship for so long."

"Oh?" His white eyebrows rose in interest. "I do enjoy your mother's company. Would your parents agree to this, Eldin?" the old priest queried.

"They would be delighted to have you for a season. And I could show you my laboratory."

The elderly couple looked at each other, considering the invitation.

"I would like to see his laboratory," Mother Overbrook told her husband.

"And I could deliver a full service in their chapel," Father Overbook added.

"It's settled then. You must come without delay."

"We will make our way to your home. Perhaps by Thursday?"

Eldin leaned in closer and held them with the intensity of his expression.

"Is there any way you could leave *today*?"

Father and Mother Overbrook exchanged glances again and then looked back at Eldin. There was a moment of hesitation, but they saw the seriousness with which their former pupil beseeched them.

"Yes,. we will leave today," Mother Overbrook replied.

"Very good," He turned to go, and noticed that from the balcony some Brothers of the Luzien Order looked down from hooded cloaks.

"I cannot come here again. I will see you at my home."

Eldin left the cathedral and quickly climbed into his carriage.

"Let's go," he said to the driver.

The carriage wheels turned and the horses' hooves clattered on the flagstones that lined the street. Eldin bit his lower lip and prayed again, this time in the hopes that he would make it out of the city without being stopped, and that Father and Mother Overbrook would actually show up at his estate tomorrow.

HOUSE STELLAT

Eldin smiled as Father and Mother Overbrook made their way into the House Stellat enclosure.

He liked the look of their vintage carriage. Even with chipped paint and faded curtains, the thing was a work of art. Few carriage-makers gave the same detail to the embellishments nowadays—no amount of gilding could compete with the carriage's decorative wooden scrolls and layer upon layer of detailed millwork.

"Nice carriage!" Eldin called to the old man sitting behind the faded velvet curtains.

"Don't encourage him, Eldin. He bought this carriage as a young man, sometimes I think he loves it more than me," Mother Overbook opined as she patted her husband's arm.

"Nonsense, Mother. I couldn't love an *object* more than you. Besides, I bought this to impress *you*, don't you remember?"

"I'd take that carriage over any girl I've ever met," Eldin said, and he almost meant it.

"Now I just need to get a better team to pull it. These old nags don't do the carriage justice," Father Overbrook stated.

"Be careful, dear. Willy and Tom might hear you."

"Those two horses can't hear any better than me. Either that, or they've gotten so belligerent that they just aren't listening."

"I suppose your trip from Tyath was uneventful?" Eldin said, glad the couple had been allowed to leave.

Father Overbrook waved his hand.

"They didn't even try to stop us. Of course, we hid our extra luggage inside."

A servant opened the carriage door and extended a step for the passengers. Eldin could see a dark wooden trunk was placed opposite the couple on the seat facing rearward.

"I brought some supplies for your laboratory!" Father Overbrook informed Eldin.

They stepped down from the carriage and embraced Eldin.

"I'm glad we didn't have to travel any further—my bones wouldn't handle that so well," Mother Overbook exclaimed. She placed her hands at the small of her back and stretched her bent posture. Her petite build seemed so delicate to Eldin, almost like a bird.

"We have rooms ready for you," Eldin said.

A servant girl curtsied, then led the couple to an arched doorway leading from the courtyard while the footmen carried the luggage.

"Be extra careful with those! I hope we are close to the laboratory, Eldin," Father Overbrook said. "We are looking forward to resuming our experiments "

"Of course, your rooms are right beside the laboratory," Eldin assured him.

The old couple nodded their gray heads and smiled.

"Thank you for sharing your home with us," Mother Overbrook said.

"Mother and Father are honored that you accepted my invitation," Eldin replied.

"Master Eldin!" a young guard called. He wore the green livery of House Stellat and ran toward them.

"What is it?" Eldin asked.

"There are riders on the horizon. Shall we open the gates?" the servant asked.

Eldin climbed the stairs to get a better vantage point. He could see out to where the land leveled toward the Clearwater Sea and in the distance a number of riders. One was in front of the others, his black horse churning the dust of the road as it made its way quickly to their gates. Eldin recognized the horse as the one that belonged to the Sīhalt Guardian—the great black horse of the Windstall Hermitage.

"Have the guards open the gate," Eldin instructed.

The great chains began to lift the exterior gates of House Stellat's fortifications, opening with a creak. The great timber gate was bound by iron and reinforced with bars of metal running both vertically and horizontally.

Lady Stellat arrived and stood beside her son.

"That must be Dallin Sarkkand," Eldin said to his mother. Lady Stellat shaded her eyes to see into the distance.

"This cannot be good," she replied, her tone fearful.

"You should have invited the Sarkkand family to join us for a month or so. It's not too late to have them stay with us. Our fortifications are stronger than theirs, and it's farther from the city," Lady Stellat offered.

"I doubted they would accept," Eldin replied.

"Certainly the mood in the city and the region's roundabout is different since Heathron is gone," Lord Stellat said as he limped forward, favoring one hip.

"A change in the mood is one way to say it. I just call it tyranny," Eldin said.

'Now, dear," Lady Stellat said, laying her hand on her son's arm. "Be careful what you say. There's no need to jump to conclusions. I'm not entirely pleased with the leadership Lord Balfoest is providing in the city, but times do change and the noble houses must adapt when circumstances dictate," she intoned.

"Circumstances aren't independent from those who rule," Eldin said. "It's the Steward of the Golden City causing the upheaval."

"What shall we do?" Lady Stellat asked, the firmness in her voice challenging both her son and her husband.

"There's no need to go to the city," Eldin replied. "I've checked with our quartermaster and our stores are full. Our men are loyal, and there's no reason to go to the city except for amenities, and perhaps entertainment."

"We won't be seeking entertainment in the city," Lord Stellat said. He shook his head. Eldin could see the concern on his father's brow.

"You say that's Dallin riding our way?" Lord Stellat asked his son.

Eldin nodded. "He was taking care of Sīhalt's horse."

The black horse was closer now, running with great strides toward the gate, further ahead from the group of riders that followed. "Now that they're closer, I think I can see that they're Tyathain Guardsmen," Lord Stellat said.

Eldin squinted his eyes, trying to focus on them at a further distance.

"You're right, Father. The pursuers are wearing gray uniforms."

"Shut the gate as soon as Dallin's inside," Lord Stellat commanded.

"What if the City Guard requests entrance?" Lady Stellat enquired.

Eldin's father turned to his wife. "They're not welcome in my keep."

"So it's come to this," his wife replied. Her face was grave.

"What else can we do, Mother?" Eldin asked.

"I have reached out to the other houses that are allies with us, to find out what they plan to do next," Lord Stellat said.

"Can I attend the meeting?" Eldin asked.

"Yes, you have studied ledgers and supply lists long enough. I want you there tonight."

"I'm ready, Father," Eldin replied.

Lord Stellat put his hand on Eldin's shoulder and squeezed. The weight of his father's touch and the new opportunity to participate in the discussions of the men made Eldin feel proud. He stood with his shoulders back as his mother always reminded him to do.

Eldin's mother wore a tight smile, but her eyes were kind—the worried face of a loving mother.

"Your father trusts you more than you know. He loves you. He just has a hard time expressing it."

"I know," Eldin said.

It was enough. His mother leaned in and hugged him, surprising him with the suddenness of her affection . He placed his arms around her.

Eldin watched as the black stallion galloped through the gate and was brought to a stop.

"Hello, Dallin," Eldin said with a wave. Dallin heard the call from Eldin and looked up to see them on the wall above him.

"That was quite a ride! We will close the gates on the Tyathian Guard. They don't have jurisdiction here," Lord Stellat said.

The gates began to close.

"Lord Balfoest killed my parents," Dallin Sarkkand said. The words almost stopped Eldin's heart. He placed his hands on the stonework to steady himself. At a closer look, Dallin's face was smeared with dust and sweat. His eyes were red and his mouth was set in anger.

"They destroyed everything. Wild Northmen from Addisfall are living in our home."

"I can't believe it!" Lady Stellat exclaimed.

Eldin descended the steps to the courtyard, followed by his parents.

"The Steward of the city had my parents hanged in the orchard," Dallin said through clenched teeth.

"I'm sorry," Eldin stammered.

The gray-clad men of the Tyathian Guard were galloping onward, but began to slow as they realized they would not be allowed inside the walls.

The sound of the heavy gate impacting the stone as it sealed itself shut gave Eldin some comfort amidst the shocking news.

"He sent the Guard after you?" Lord Stellat queried.

"Without Steed, they would have taken me," Dallin said. He was shaking as he patted the horse's sweat-drenched neck and swung down from the saddle. The great black stallion bobbed its head, as if affirming Dallin's anger.

"I was able to get word to House Aviella, and they promised to let Coronado know as well. They aren't safe. None of them are safe. We need to join together to resist," Eldin said.

"I am already planning to meet with the heads of houses tonight," Lord Stellat said.

"I hope they make it, what with the guards patrolling everywhere," Dallin said.

"Will you come, too?" Lord Stellat asked.

Dallin swallowed, leveling his gaze at Lord Stellat.

"I am the head of House Sarkkand now. I'll be there."

ONLY EMOTIONS

L ars Balfoest watched as Iskabel bent over the plants that were growing in neat rows. She felt stronger after the months of working as his Plant Witch. Of course, he still kept her hidden and chained. Iskabel knew that this was done to prevent the news from getting back to her father. If he knew she was a captive in the Golden City he would move the mountains of the west to rescue her—if he only knew. Iskabel missed the red-haired woman named Kathleen. She had taught her how to deal with Lars Balfoest.

Iskabel went about her work efficiently. She decided to find joy in her labors, sometimes kneeling down in the warm dirt and placing her hands around the tiny leaflets of Kabris shoots. Other times she would look up at the ceiling of glass when she worked late into the evening and would glimpse a moon or a few stars come out. She wondered how far away her father and clan must be, looking at that same moon and stars.

Iskabel hummed softly to herself to coax the little plants to take deeper root, then she gently teased them forward, lifting them from the ground as they grew, obeying the Talented gift that flowed from her fingertips into the small plants. She could feel the small veins expanding within the leaves, drawing the nutrients from the soil.

Iskabel resisted partaking of the sacred dream plants for herself like the warriors of her clan who used them for their vision quests. She'd come to know the plant intimately with her work, feeling its ability to alter the mind, to expand creativity and sometimes enhance horrific aspects of the human psyche.

She did not dislike the plant for what it was. It was fulfilling what generations of this same plant had done before—seeking sunlight and a chance to propagate itself. She did not hate the plant for the harm it caused those who abused it. Nor did she feel any guilt knowing that the stacks of dried Kabris leaves would be ground into powder and given to the growing number of people enslaved by its properties.

"Have you finished your work?"

Iskabel was down on all fours. She looked back at the man standing in the lamp-lit doorway, his skeletal frame propped at an angle.

"I'm almost done," she said, wiping her hands on the front of her dress and rising to her knees. She brushed back a few of the long, black strands of hair that obscured her face.

"Finish that row and come and be fed," Lord Balfoest said. "The caretakers are ready for you."

"Yes, Lord Balfoest," Iskabel replied, her voice retaining a thick Delathrane accent. He didn't close the door and leave as he often did. Instead, he stood watching her.

Iskabel bent back down toward the plant and spoke to it. "It's time to grow, little one. No more resting as a seed. I will raise you to a small tree," she said, and then with her gentle humming placed both hands around the base of the small plant and lifted it, encouraging the plant to grow. She stood as the plant increased in height and lifted her arms high above her head, extending to her full height.

Iskabel was no longer a little girl. The multiple Healings of the

Meat Witch had ensured it. It had taken some time, but now she felt comfortable within her matured frame. She felt that her body was hers, and not something she had borrowed from an older person.

Lord Balfoest watched her as she raised her arms above her head, reaching the full extent of the final plants in the row. Out of the corner of her eye, Iskabel kept watch. He did not observe her the way Iskabel knew some men looked at women. Instead, Lord Balfoest looked at her like a dog, or a beast of burden.

"Come now, Iskabel," the rasping voice of Lord Balfoest said.

Iskabel walked obediently on bare feet between the rows of the Kabris plants, beneath the glass ceiling. The plants would be harvested tonight and begin drying in the morning, and a new crop would be ready for the next day, as it always was.

Iskabel approached Lord Balfoest with her head bowed.

"Look at me," he said.

She raised her eyes to look into his wrinkled face. It was like an old drum left out in the rain—skin stretched across a bony frame. She wondered if he, like the Kabris plants, was only doing what he was designed to do. Did this man have a choice? Was he carrying out the disposition of his evil ancestors in his current form? The thought gave her a pang of empathy for the man. Did this man, who was once an innocent baby, have days when he slept against his mother's breast as she caressed him? Iskabel remembered her own mother, and felt the love of that stolen relationship.

And just as she was feeling so, Lars Balfoest reached out and ran his fingers through a lock of her tangled, dark hair. His fingers brushed along her ear and his eyes widened.

"Iskabel," he said, "did I sense that right?" He still had the manner of a predator, but he leaned closer and looked her in the eyes, this time reaching out a hand and placing it around the nape of her neck.

Iskabel didn't recoil in terror, as she had when she was first his captive. Nor did she fear as much as she once did, knowing that her Talent was valuable to him. She was, after all, the only Plant Witch who ever came to the secret garden within the palace walls. Iskabel knew that Lars would be killed if her father ever found him, and yet there was a note of sadness she felt towards him as she tried to understand what made him do what he did.

His long, dry fingers touched the back of her neck and he turned her head so that she would look again into his eyes.

"Do you love me, Iskabel?" he said. "Is that what I'm feeling from you?" He let go of her and his grim countenance smiled. "Oh, my. You are a strange creature," he said.

Iskabel was confused, but she had long since learned to keep her face placid, to betray no more of her emotions than was absolutely necessary. He certainly seemed able to draw them from her. "You see, Iskabel, I can tell what you're thinking. I can understand your every thought. There is nothing you can hide from me," he said.

And yet Iskabel knew that he did not speak the truth. She knew, because what she felt for him was not love. It was a desire to understand. It was empathy. Perhaps it was love—as one might love a plant.

Iskabel remembered helping her mother weed the garden of squash and corn they planted every spring. She did not want to remove the little plants with their bright, blue flowers. "But they're so beautiful, Mama," she remembered saying, as her mother directed her to pull the weeds.

"Yes, they are beautiful, daughter," she replied, "but they choke the plants we want for food and so we must remove them." She put her hands around the base of the plant and ripped the roots from the ground.

When Iskabel did it, she remembered feeling the pain of the plant as she destroyed it and it made her wince, even though the sensation was very slight. She felt similarly for Lord Balfoest. Not love, really, but rather a sadness in knowing that he must be plucked up from his existence, his life broken and extinguished, if good was to come about in her own life.

He does not know my thoughts.

The realization was sudden and Iskabel fought to keep her face placid. A smile forced itself onto her lips.

He knows my feelings, but he does NOT know my thoughts, Iskabel thought with excitement.

"Don't get your hopes up," Lord Balfoest said over his shoulder as he turned away. "I can't remember ever being interested in a woman—at least not for many years."

Iskabel watched him go then knelt again beside the garden of Kabris plants. A small weed had begun to grow in the crevice of the stones at the edge of the garden. She held the small plant gently between her first finger and her thumb. Then she squeezed and ripped it out along with its roots.

LADY ALLISON DAL AVERY

L ukald heard a knock at the door of his study.

"Come in," he said gruffly, not in the mood to speak with anyone. The door opened slowly, and the auburn hair of Lady Allison del Avery peeked inside.

"Is it okay if I come in?" she asked, hearing the tone of his voice. Lukald immediately smoothed the front of his shirt and straightened himself.

"Oh, come in, come in," he said, speaking more sincerely now. It had been a long time since he'd seen Allison—years, it seemed.

"I thought I would visit and ask if there's any way that I could help."

Lukald wasn't sure what to say next. His relationship with Allison had become strained ever since he married Renata. And now that she was gone, he wondered how things might change for the better. "Renata's gone," he said.

Lady del Avery nodded. "I know; I heard she left last week. I've spent the past few days thinking of what I might say, or how I might approach you," she added.

"Am I that difficult to approach?" King Lukald asked. He smiled, and she returned the expression.

"We've been friends for a long time. Would you be willing to accept my help?"

"How so?" Lukald said. He brushed his fingers through his curly red hair. He'd been running through the calculations of men that he still had in reserve, as well as the ships that had been sunk by the pirates. It wasn't looking good. Thankfully, the city had held. Elayna had come to the rescue of them all, but the war was not over.

"I wasn't sure how you felt about the use of the Talents," Lady Allison stated.

Lukald glanced at her, wondering how much she knew of how the city was saved. "The Talents?" he asked.

Allison del Avery nodded slowly. "I spent some time speaking with your daughter, Kathleen, before she left for Tyath."

The king huffed. "They're not married yet, but Prince Heathron is here and I'm very grateful for the support he's given us."

"As am I," Allison agreed. "But since he's arrived, no shipments of food have come from Tyath. The pirate blockade has further strained our people. Even so, the culture has not favored those of us who have a Gift," she said.

Lukald nodded. He heard the underlying meaning.

"I loved Anneliese dearly. Her Talent was a blessing to us. I don't agree with where things are headed—telling Talented people that they must restrain themselves and not use the gifts given to them by Abbath."

"I'm glad to hear that," Allison replied. "I've taken the liberty to gather those who are willing into a Society of Succor."

"Go on," the king said, willing to hear her explain.

Lady del Avery closed the door behind her.

"We've been practicing. I have some Green Growers, and some Red Growers, too, of varying ability."

"What do you propose?" Lukald asked.

"Some of my Green Growers are no better than a gardener

with an especially green thumb, but some of them have real ability that I think could be developed."

"You mean like Kathleen's? Like yours?"

Allison del Avery looked around, making sure there were no ears to hear what she would say next. She placed her hands on Lukald's desk and leaned forward, speaking earnestly.

"Some of them are really good. Some of them could have been inducted into the Talented Academy back when we were younger."

Lukald raised his eyebrows. "How many people do you have, Allison?"

"Fifteen," she said with excitement. "Some of them are very young, but others are as old as seventy-five."

The king huffed and sat back in his chair.

"We could make a real difference," she said.

"What do the Luzian priests know of this?" the king asked.

"They don't know anything. Most of the Talented that I have gathered are female, but I have some boys, too."

"Does the Talent run stronger with the ladies?" Lukald asked.

"That is what they used to teach in the Academy. Except the Tamers, who are almost always male," Allison explained.

"We run a risk using the Talents. Some of the people will not like it, no matter how dire our circumstances."

"With fifteen of us we could make the fields grow, Lukald! We could feed the people and Heal the wounded."

"I personally have no hesitation. This is a crisis and we should bring all of our abilities to bear," the king mused.

"Lukald, there are young men crying out for their mothers in the field hospitals set up on the castle grounds. Think of the work going on day and night to try and save their lives. Think of the battles we have in front of us. Candoreth still does not have the advantage," she said.

"I would love to have the help. I believe most of the people would accept your Talented work in the spirit in which it is offered," he replied.

"Do you think our Society of Succor would be in danger by revealing ourselves to the public?" she asked.

"Our whole nation is in danger either way," Lukald said. "You heard about what happened to Elayna, did you not?"

Allison shook her head. "No, how is Elayna? Was she harmed?"

Lukald stopped. He paused and bit his lip, considering the words he might say. "She was harmed," he said slowly. "But Melva was there…"

"Oh, good," Allison said. "She's Talented. She's a very good Healer."

"Elayna was injured badly," the king explained. "It took everything that Melva had to Heal her."

Allison's eyes widened. "*Everything* she had?"

The king nodded solemnly, "Melva was a constant in my life, and a comfort to me since I was a child. She was like a grandmother to me… and the girls. She's gone … but Elayna is alive because of her sacrifice."

Allison reached for Lukald's hand and placed hers on top of his, giving it a comforting squeeze. "At least you still have your little girl," she said.

Lukald smiled at Allison. "She's not little anymore.We should go see her. I think she's in the library."

He led Allison down the hall and slowly opened the double doors. Maps and charts of the surrounding islands and the terrain were laid out on the table. The Sīhalt Guardian named Seth was there, along with Prince Heathron and Princess Elayna. Elayna looked up and saw her father.

"Father," she said. "Heathron and Seth have an idea. We think we've found a place where we can face them head-on."

Lady Allison del Avery stepped from behind the king. When she laid eyes on Elayna, she took in a sharp breath and turned to Lukald.

"And I thought Kathleen looked like her mother!"

Elayna stood up and walked towards the woman, extending her hand in friendship. "Hello. I don't know if we've met."

Allison del Avery wiped a tear that sprang at the corners of her eyes. "Oh, we've met, but it was years ago and you were just a baby. I held you in my arms the day your mother brought you into this world."

Elayna smiled. "What's your name?"

"My name is Allison del Avery. I've been a friend of your mother's since childhood. We were in the Talented Academy together."

Elayna smiled. "She's spoken to me about you."

A questioning look came across Allison's face. "She did? How can you remember it? She died shortly after your birth."

Elayna shrugged her shoulders, tossing her long red hair. "It wasn't so long ago," she said.

"You are beautiful, like your mother," Allison replied.

Elayna smiled and laughed. "Yes. Everyone thinks I'm Kathleen's twin. I can't wait for her to see me when she returns."

"It's a pleasure to meet you, Elayna. Thank you for what you've done for the city. I heard how you mended the walls."

Elayna nodded."It's my pleasure to do what I can to save the ones I love."

Lukald saw her glance at Heathron when she said it.

"Your father and I were just speaking of how we might be able to use those within Sundiland, or at least those here in the City, to help to Heal the wounded and Grow food for the hungry. I have a group of people who are willing to use what we've taught them to help us win this war."

"That is very good of you," Elayna replied. "I'd be happy to meet with them."

Allison looked back at the king. "May I bring them to the castle?"

"Please do, and give them my regards for their willingness to take this risk. The pirates have been relentless. I see no stopping their desire to take from us what is ours. Unless we can negotiate a peace, I fear there will be even more bloodshed and more hunger in the days to come."

"I'll bring the Society here this afternoon," Allison said.

"Very well," said King Lukald

He hugged Allison del Avery, and in that embrace he felt a comfort that he had not felt for many years.

6 1

DRAGON SHIPS

Enderick Farson leaned against the rudder of his longship. Two hundred men pulled at the oars as his enormous dragon ship sliced into the harbor, the sail quartering into the wind.

Enderick indulged himself in a way that was uncommon for him—he smiled. It was not the smell of fresh caught fish, or the ease with which they had entered the territorial waters of the Golden City with so many ships of war that brought a smile to his rugged face. No, it was the prospect of riches beyond anything he could have hoped.

Tyath had long been the coveted jewel of the Adisfall Northmen. So when the invitation came from the Steward of the City inviting them to dwell within the shining walls, few of the men of Adisfall or the surrounding islands delayed. They joined the ranks of those ships willing to go into the Clearwater Sea and form an alliance to help fight off the expected Delathrane Army. Soon they would be within the very heart of the capital.

He spied the emissary sent out to meet him on the edge of the harbor wall. Enderick was not impressed. No matter how many fine robes, thick city walls, or displays of wealth these people showed, he could tell that they were as soft as they had ever been. *Why do warmer waters make men soft?* he wondered.

The cadence-giver barked a command and the men at the oars stopped pulling. They raised the oars as the dragon ship slid in between the boats moored near the city. The width of his ship was larger than most longships, and it required the expert hand of the men to ease his vessel to the edge of the dock.

Enderick signaled and fifty of the strongest men hoisted their shields and fell in behind him. As the dragon ship came to a stop along the side of the harbor dock, Enderick was already running. He sprinted down the length of his longship, cleared the wooden rail, and felt his feet hit the hard stones of Tyath. The men followed behind him, battering their shields with their swords and leaping to form a shield wall beside him.

The portly nobleman sent to welcome him to the city took a few steps back, his face creased in fear. The man might have been athletic in his younger years, but wealth and security had taken their toll. He was soft, and Enderick could see that his hands no longer carried the calluses of the sword or spear. Instead, Tyathian Guardsmen dressed in gray leveled their spears and began to circle the nobleman defensively. Enderick Farson gave a shout of jubilation. His wide eyes, painted face, and crazed look made it difficult for his enemy to discern whether he was happy, angry, or crazy. With another signal to the men, their shouts and shield battering stopped. The shield wall parted and Enderick took another step forward. He raised his hands with his weapons and shouted to the nobleman, "My name is Enderick Farson. You called me here!"

"I am Lord Albodris," the man stammered. Enderick laughed, seeing the fear melt into relief. He wouldn't have been surprised to see a yellow puddle at the nobleman's feet.

"Lars Balfoest, the Steward of the City, sent me to welcome you."

"So welcome me!" Enderick said.

He looked at his men and grinned fiercely, his red topknot swinging back and forth.

"Where is the mead hall?" he asked, eyes wide and teeth clenched in an unnatural smile.

The men with him murmured their agreement. A mead hall was just what they wanted.

Even the men still at the oars in the longship shouted their approval.

"These men have been at the oars and the chill wind of Adisfall for too long, Nothing like a drink to warm the heart and hearth," Enderick said.

"That can be arranged. Lord Balfoest welcomes you to Tyath. We're grateful for your assistance."

Enderick looked around at the commerce going on, ships being loaded, merchants moving their goods. It wasn't as impressive as his imagination had led him to believe, but what wealth! He turned to Lord Albodris. "We didn't come here on a charity mission," he said. "There'll be riches to be had before it's all over." If it sounded like a threat, let the man interpret how he pleased.

"How many Northmen will be coming to our city?" Albodris asked. "Lord Balfoest asked that I get an accurate number,"

"The men are my men as long as they desire to be my men," Enderick explained. "I don't know how many dragon ships will cross the Clearwater Sea but we will put the word out. This is the first wave." He looked behind him. Dozens of ships moved among the fishing boats, sliding across the water toward the harbor.

"So what is the chance we could have 100 ships?" Albodris asked.

Enderick looked around at his men. "I don't command the other Northmen. I make suggestions and they choose whether or not to follow. I'm sure many more ships will arrive. This is the Golden City, after all."

The nobleman smiled, as if he had shared a joke.

"Where are the barbarians? We heard there were Delathranes,"

Enderick asked, looking around as if he would see barbarians walking among the merchants on the harbor.

"They promised to return. We are preparing the defenses and training new soldiers from among our people," Lord Albodris replied.

"We want to fight some Delathranes. So where are they?" Enderick asked.

"They were here last year. They will return—we are sure of it."

"Hmm, I hope so," Enderick said. He slid his sword into his sheath and hung his shield on his back. He folded his arms in front of him, contemplating the situation.

"So where *is* the enemy? We came to fight," Enderick said.

"I will take you to Lord Balfoest. He will explain more of what you must do."

"Come here," Enderick said, motioning for the nobleman to approach him.

The Tyathian Guardsman tensed as the nobleman approached the Northmen. When he was no more than a pace or two away, Enderick suddenly lunged and grabbed him by his rich robes. In the same instant, Enderick pulled his knife and held it crosswise across the man's throat. The nobleman was tall, but not quite so tall as Enderick. The Northman lifted the nobleman off of his feet so that he was standing on his toes. The city guards had their spears leveled at Enderick.

The captain shouted "Unhand him!" but Enderick paid them no mind, trusting that they would hold steady while the dagger was at the nobleman's throat. A hostage could do that for a man.

"Let's get one thing straight, man of Tyath," the Northman said, gritting his teeth as he spoke through his red beard. "There is nothing that I *must* do for Lord Balfoest, or any other man. Do you understand me?"

Lord Albodris nodded his head against the sharpness of the blade at his neck.

"It is only a manner of speaking," he uttered.

"Well, make sure that we understand the meaning of your words and mine," Enderick said. "Now tell the City Guard to back off before I have them slaughtered by my men," Enderick threatened.

"Captain Bastion, stand down with your men," Lord Albodris ordered. The dark-haired, dark-eyed Tyathian captain nodded and told his men to stand down. They drew back their spears and stood, holding them vertically.

Half a dozen more longships landed while they discussed the nature of their relationship. Men from Adisfall were unloading by the scores and walking among the families and business people on the Tyathian harbor. The people from Adisfall were taller on average than those of Tyath, their skin somewhat paler. They wore rough fabrics and thick furs common to the North. They were boisterous and shouted in harsh voices to each other across the distances between them. Some of them embraced old friends they hadn't seen for years as various ships from the North met at the Golden City.

One Northman grabbed a piece of fruit from an apple cart and the merchant called out in dismay at having been robbed. The large Northman flipped him a coin from a purse tied to his belt. The amount would have purchased the entire cart and all of the apples with it. The nonchalance with which the Northmen engaged with the people of Tyath told the story of how they viewed the people here. Men of Adisfall, for the most part, were masters of themselves. In this new setting of abundance, they clearly viewed themselves as masters of the city as well. A large group of them followed Enderick Farson and his initial warriors being led by Lord Albodris through the city, escorted by men of the Tyathian Guard.

A PASSING FRIEND

"How did you make it back?" Heathron asked Kathleen.

"There were pirate ships everywhere, but Channing took us to the south and we came through the river delta and then north," Kathleen explained.

"I'm so glad you are back."

Heathron's face was torn in a horizontal wound that began at the left line angle of his forehead and extended to his jaw on the same side. It gave a fierceness to his boyish looks. Fierceness was a part of him she knew existed, but now it was written on his expression.

"I was too close to the stone wall when it was struck by one of those thunderous explosions—a gift from our pirate friends," Heathron said, and brought his right hand up to gingerly touch the scabs that were forming in long horizontal lines. The broken skin looked like a saber-toothed cat had raked its claws across the prince's face, from the corner of his eye and cheekbone to his ear.

"So many have been harmed in this fighting," Kathleen said. She took a step closer and put her arms around Heathron's neck and pulled him into an embrace.

"If those end up as scars, you might be able to rival the Serpent King," she said with a smile.

"Careful now," Heathron winced, "this extends down part of my torso as well."

"I'm sorry!" Kathleen exclaimed, retreating.

He opened his jacket and revealed a linen bandage that had been wrapped around his stomach, chest, and upper left shoulder.

"Oh, Heathron!" Kathleen said. "Why wouldn't Melva just Heal you?"

Heathron winced again, and Kathleen realized it was not from the pain in his side this time.

She felt a void opening up within her.

"Where is Melva?" she asked.

"Why don't we sit down and talk," Heathron suggested softly.

Kathleen felt herself growing faint.

"I don't want to sit down," she said, resisting the terrible truth that worked its way into her thoughts. She put her hands to her mouth.

"Where is she?" she asked again, her eyes filling with tears.

Heathron reached out to Kathleen, steadying her as she wavered on weak legs.

"I don't think I can stand," she said.

Heathron placed his hand on her wrist and put her arm around his shoulder, offering his support.

"I would carry you, but I don't think I can," he said.

Kathleen collapsed onto one of the benches spaced evenly along the covered causeway. She sat with her back against the wall and her head on Heathron's shoulder, and cried with sobs that released the tension of weeks. He held her and she surrendered to the strength he offered.

Heathron gave Kathleen a handkerchief, for her nose ran along with her tears. She sniffed and looked at the ornate piece of silk with intricate needlework displaying the Fox and Acorn.

In the painful moment she felt it strange to think, *Where in all of Desnia did he get a personalized hanky?*

She looked at it through her tears and then looked up at Heathron.

"This may seem like a strange question," she said, wiping her nose, "but how do you have a white, silk handkerchief with your House emblem on it? Lord Balfoest took everything from us."

Heathron continued to gently run his hand over her head, smoothing her hair.

"That is a gift from one of your countrymen...or women, rather."

"That's nice," Kathleen said.

"I joined your father in leading the army to victory on the Southern Beach," Heathron explained. "The people were very glad of that."

Kathleen put her hand on Heathron's thigh and pulled herself closer to him.

"I am so grateful to have you," she said, closing her eyes and resting her head against his chest. She could hear his breathing, steady and strong. She needed that from him at this moment.

"Melva gave me a message for you," Heathron said quietly.

Kathleen's heart was broken, even as her mind was swimming to find an answer to the loss. She had so many questions.

"What did she say?" Kathleen asked.

"She said, 'Take care of Elayna.'"

"Of course I will," Kathleen said in a voice that was half crying, and half laughing. She took a deep breath and wiped more tears as they streamed from her eyes.

"And also, 'Let me go,'" Heathron said.

"Melva devoted her life to me and my family and saved us on a number of occasions. She was so tireless in her charitable service. I could not ask for a more loyal servant."

Kathleen paused.

"I am just sorry it took me so long to see her for what she truly was—a loving friend," she added.

"Melva is an inspiration," Heathron agreed. "She was brave and good to the very last day of her long life."

"I have no memory of my biological grandparents but she was a grandmother to me," Kathleen said through more tears.

"We would have never made it out of the dungeons if it were not for her," Heathron said.

Moments passed and they sat in silence. The ocean breeze tossed the wispy drapes that blew along the causeway.

"My mother always used to hang drapes like those on the causeway. I haven't seen that done for years," Kathleen said.

"I think your father ordered them to be put out. That was how he wanted to celebrate the victory," Heathron explained.

"Mother always did that for him."

"He seems to be filled with a new vigor," Heathron said, watching the white drapes dance in the Sundiland wind that pushed them back and forth along the long curve of the causeway.

"What will we do now?" Kathleen asked. "We will need to plan a funeral.."

"The people of Candoreth really pulled together. I've not seen this sort of unity in a city in all my life. I think I have a lot to learn from the people of the Southern Realms," Heathron said.

"Really? That's wonderful!" Kathleen said.

"I heard the Luzian priests even joined with the others to help Lady Allison del Avery's Society of Succor to administer to the sick, hungry, and wounded."

"The church working side by side with Talented people? I did not think I would see that in my lifetime," Kathleen said happily.

"There are more of you than you might imagine," Heathron said.

"I can't wait to meet them," Kathleen replied.

"There is one lady who was especially helpful in defending the city," Heathron said slowly.

Kathleen leveled her eyes at Heathron.

"Did she make the handkerchief for you?" she asked coyly.

"No, but you will want to meet her," Heathron said.

His tone made Kathleen sit more erect.

"Oh?"

"She is a woman of amazing wit, beauty, and grace," Heathron said.

"So she reminds you of me?" Kathleen said playfully, still looking through bleary eyes.

"Actually, she does remind me of you. The two of you are very much alike."

"Really?" Kathleen said, finding it strange that Heathron would share not only the absolute tragedy of Melva's passing, but assume she would be in the frame of mind to make new friends.

"Is she part of the Society of Succor?" Kathleen asked. "They are all Talented, aren't they?"

"I don't know, but I am sure this lady would happily join Lady Allison's efforts."

"You seem taken by her, Heathron," Kathleen said. "I'm glad she was not the one making you silk handkerchiefs."

Kathleen was surprised to see color rising in his cheeks.

Who is this woman? Kathleen wondered.

"I want to introduce the two of you. I believe she is in the library right now. Do you mind if we walk there?" Heathron said.

"Now? In our library?" Kathleen asked, suddenly smoothing her skirt. "You want me to meet her right now? This may not be the best time."

Heathron held Kathleen's hand and led her up the steps of the causeway, toward the castle.

"You seem really excited for me to meet her," Kathleen said, furrowing her brow as they walked across the polished marble floors, approaching the heavy wooden doors of the library.

"I suppose I could tell her that now isn't a good time, if that is what you wish," Heathron said.

"We are already here," Kathleen replied, gesturing to the doors. "We might as well go in."

Heathron nodded and took a deep breath.

"You seem more nervous than I am. Who is this woman?" Kathleen asked, puzzled at Heathron's demeanor.

"Allow me to introduce you," Heathron said with a nervous smile and a twinkle in his brown eyes.

Heathron opened the doors of the library. At a distant window, positioned to look out over the ocean, stood a woman with her back to them. Her hair was like fire.

MOTHER'S IMAGE

Kathleen took a tentative step into the library. The slender woman with red hair the same hue as her own turned from the window when she heard the sound of the doors opening. Kathleen gasped. It was as if she was looking at a living memory of her mother. The woman had the same jawline, the same curve of her neck. Her shoulders were about the same width as Kathleen's, and her deep green velvet bodice tapered to a narrow waist. Her long red hair, longer than Kathleen's, fell to the middle of her back. She stood with the grace that the Queens of Sundiland always managed. Her eyebrows were outlined perfectly against creamy white skin. This living image of Kathleen's memory relaxed. Her expression held lips that were full and perfectly balanced with the wide set of her bright eyes. Kathleen looked at Heathron, wondering if he too saw the person in front of them. The prince looked at the woman with his eyes shining brightly, a smile on his face. He could see her, too, and yet her mother had died when she was just a child.

In an instant, the woman who looked like Annilese Dal Sundi broke into a delightful smile. Her straight white teeth sparkled, and from her mouth came the sound of a voice that was as soft and sweet as Kathleen remembered.

"Katie," the striking woman said, opening her arms, welcoming an embrace. Kathleen slowly began to walk towards the woman.

"Mother?" Kathleen said tentatively.

"Katie, I'm big now," the woman said.

Kathleen blinked. She stopped and tried to make sense of the statement. Realization dawned suddenly. This was not her mother standing before her, this was Elayna.

"Sister!" Kathleen exclaimed.

They fell into each other's arms. Kathleen embraced Elayna, and the sisters held each other close.

"What happened?" Kathleen asked as she held her.

"Melva's gone," Elayna said, "but she saved me." Tears fell as both women embraced, and Heathron nodded his head in somber reverence.

Kathleen pulled back, holding her baby sister by her shoulders and looking into her eyes.

"Tell me what happened," she said through tears.

"I look like you." Elayna said, almost breaking into a laugh.

"You look like Mother! You look *so* much like her," Kathleen sobbed.

"That's what Father says," Elayna replied.

"I should let you two be alone," Heathron offered.

"Oh no, Heathron. Stay with us," Kathleen said, pulling a chair out from one of the sturdy library tables. Heathron nodded his assent and joined the sisters.

"What happened?" Kathleen asked. "Tell me everything!"

Elayna recounted the defense that she had initiated in repairing the walls that were battered by the pirate ships. At times she would look to Heathron, and he would fill in details.

"I was trying to keep her safe," Heathron said to Kathleen, "but your sister can be...insistent."

"I can't imagine a Dal Sundi girl ever being strong-willed,"

Kathleen said with a smile. "So where did she go? You said Melva's gone."

"I was struck," Elayna said. "I have no memory of it, but Heathron told me the weapons of the pirate ships smashed the rocks and I was hurt severely. Melva was there, and she used the last bit of her strength to save me."

"She used too much of her Talent. You must have been wounded horribly to lose so many years," Kathleen said, leaning forward and brushing her hand down the side of Elayna's face. Memory of Girdy's wounds and Melva meeting them at the docks seemed so long ago.

"She was crushed beneath the rocks," Heathron confirmed.

"And then Melva *Healed* me. After that Heathron carried me back here, to the castle." Kathleen saw Heathron reach over and touch Elayna's hand, comforting her as she recounted the memory. In that small, subtle gesture Kathleen felt a pang of understanding.

The touch was gentle and soft, not lingering, but filled with love and consideration. Heathron had touched Kathleen like that before, but her reaction had never been as forthright as Elayna's. Her sister returned his caring look with an expression that spoke of devotion—not the child-like devotion she might have expressed a few weeks before, but the deep, all-encompassing devotion of a woman in love.

Kathleen swallowed. She felt a mix of shock and confusion at what she was witnessing.

"I wish I could have protected her better," Heathron mumbled, staring at his hands in his lap.

"I'm sorry you lost so much of your childhood. It isn't fair," Kathleen said, trying to smile as she held her sister's hand.

"I am happy to be alive," Elayna replied.

"Tell me. Where has Melva gone?"

Elayna cast her eyes toward the floor and Heathron furrowed his brow.

"Melva gave me everything she had. When I was injured and broken, she placed her hands on me and brought me back to the land of the living. She traded her life for mine," Elayna explained.

"I saw Melva wavering like a phantom in a flame before she finally left. There is no trace of her," Heathron said solemnly.

"She had few material possessions. The people she loved were her treasures, so I want to give you this," Elayna said.

She held up the beaded necklace. "I don't know the significance of these beads, but she made a new necklace as soon as she came home."

Kathleen extended her hands and received the wooden necklace. Each bead was round, smooth, and shiny. She'd chosen wood of different colors—dark Ebony, Purple Heart, and Hickory. She saw the smooth light-colored grain of Cherry wood. The sound of the beads, with their dull clinking, brought the memory of Melva back to her, and Kathleen closed her eyes.

"We don't need a funeral for her?" Kathleen asked.

Heathron shook his head. "There was nothing left; not physically anyway," he told her.

"I haven't heard from her spirit, but I am certain that Melva will visit me when circumstances allow," Elayna said in an effort to comfort her sister.

Kathleen smiled gently.

"I'm sure she has a lot of catching up to do on the other side."

Elayna nodded.

"She missed her family, and lived longer with ours than I ever thought she could. She lived a good life. I will miss her dearly," Kathleen added.

"I may be old enough to accompany you and Larissa now, don't you think?" Elayna said, offering her presence as a comfort to her sister.

"Of course you can. You are a lady now. Although, there's probably a few things we should explain to you about being a woman."

Elayna smiled with understanding in her eyes. Every now and again she would seem wise beyond her years to Kathleen, but to have her seated in front of her—fully mature and radiantly beautiful—made Kathleen feel in awe of her. Kathleen noticed how Heathron's eyes rarely left Elayna's face.

Is he in awe of the miracle, or in awe of my sister's beauty? Kathleen wondered.

She felt a tinge of jealousy and defensiveness at the question.

"I can see that you have been devoted to her, Heathron. Thank you," Kathleen said.

Heathron faced Kathleen and she detected a flush in his cheeks.

"It has been an honor," he said.

AUROCH HUNT

Cedric lay on his belly, deep in the green grass. He crept closer to the edge of the rise,.surrounded by the generals that he had chosen from among the Delethrane. Finally, they had found the herd. "Look at them," he said, his guttural voice and split tongue making him sound like a serpent king. "The great herd of the Aurochs. We'll be well fed soon men." His generals nodded, holding their heads low in the grass. None of them wanted to be spotted by the great horned beasts. Not until they were ready.

"Each warrior will bring down one or two," Grawn said.

"IWe will dry and smoke it, so we have enough food for the journey to the Golden City." Cedric was glad, not for the first time, that he had gained the alliance with Grawn Verda. The man was wise, and he commanded the respect of the other leaders. Cedric was glad that Grawn respected him, too, despite his youth.

"We will send warriors on horses through the trees to the far side. If we can turn the herd, they'll begin to run and we can run them in circles."

The others nodded.

"I will take a dozen or so with me," Kalt offered.

"Good," Cedric agreed. He turned to the leader of Clan Ermine. "You will go north over those hills. You will need plenty of spears." The slender man nodded, licking his lips in anticipation. Their supplies had grown thin as the host had increased with many of thousands of warriors who had gathered together. The grass needed to feed the horses and the meat for men was great indeed. Wagons followed as women and children came along to join the procession of the Serpent King.

Now we will see what the iron-sharpened arrows and lances from our Delver will do. He smiled, proud of the good that he had done for his people. Cedric felt more confident. Plate armor covered his shoulders, while a new breastplate fitted his torso perfectly. He wore sheets of metal against his shins that had been formed by the Talented hand of the Delver. And although he still wore the soft leather shoes, when he climbed into his saddle his toes were able to work themselves deep into the sockets of metal that had been formed to protect him as he rode. Even his horse wore armor on its neck, shoulders, and head.

So many of the Delethrane had benefited from this work of the Delver, and yet there was more for him to do. Today, however, they would hunt. They inched their way back down over the slope from where they had looked upon the Auroch herd. They made their way to their horses, checking their lances. When the signal was given, Cedric led the charge through grass that stood as tall as his horse's saddle. They moved like a black blanket, like fog rolling across a river. They roiled like a storm cloud on the grasslands, and yet they were not the cloud. They were the Delethrane and they had found the herd they were looking for. The bulls, which stood like sentinels for the herd, raised their heads at the sound of the thundering hooves. Their tails rose and their ears flicked forward. The bulls bellowed a call of warning, and the cows and the calves began to move in the opposite direction.

The Delethrane had trained their horses for this kind of hunting. The men used their knees to steer their horses while holding bows or long lances as they rode. The bladed spear tips glistened as the Delethrane galloped over the hill.

Cedric heard the whoops of the young men as they raced each other to be the first to reach the wild cattle. Some of the bulls did not run, but instead lowered their heads and tossed their wide spreading horns, pawing dirt and kicking it up so that clumps of sod landed on their own backs. These bulls were angry, and set to defend the herd.

The glee of battle rose within him. Cedric encouraged his horse to run faster and used the reins in his left hand to guide the horse along the path that the bull had run, trying to defend the herd. Cedric rode alongside a cow. He used the sword in his right hand and, riding behind her, passed the cow and swung his sword backward, catching the cow in the neck. She crumpled as she ran, tumbling over, rolling in the grass and spraying Cedric with a burst of red mist. He inhaled deeply and opened his mouth wide. His severed tongue curled, and he let out a cry of exaltation. He used the flat of his sword to slap the flank of his horse, and the sturdy Delethrane pony charged onward.

Cedric saw a bull with head and shoulders that stood high above the rest of the herd. It had a hump on its back between the shoulders and the base of its horns was twice as thick as Cedric's arms. The bull bellowed and tossed its head, watching Cedric in pursuit. The hide was a reddish brown with spots of white scattered across its shoulders, and a line of gray marked its spine. Like Cedric, the bull was in the prime of its strength—the height of its vitality.

The Delathrane chieftain rode his horse alongside the bull and stabbed downward, aiming between the ribs. The bull turned quickly, dipping the tip of its horn and catching Cedric's pony under the chin. The bull then savagely threw its head upward. The mount screamed and Cedric was thrown into the air. The sturdy pony collapsed in the grass with a broken neck as Cedric came spiraling downward, right on top of the bull. The tip of a horn caught Cedric's arm and he lost his sword. He managed to grab the hair of the bull's forelock with one hand and threw his arm over the massive horn to keep himself from being crushed under the powerful hooves.

Cedric slid his feet to the ground. He bent his knees and rotated his weight, using his hips and shoulders to spin and create extra weight on one side. The long horns worked as leverage for him, and he pried the bull in the direction that he wanted to go until his feet touched the ground.

Cedric torqued the horn downward, the tip digging into the sod. The magnificent Auroch bull bellowed as the horn dug deep into the ground, bringing the animal's head to a halt as the momentum of its body upended the animal. Rolling over, Cedric kicked his feet to the front and rotated his body to avoid being crushed. When the bull landed on its side, Cedric pulled his knife and plunged it deep into its windpipe, ripping upward. The beast bellowed one last time, struggled to regain its feet, and then collapsed in death.

Elated Delathrane warriors rode past Cedric, cheering for him and shouting their praise of the Serpent King. The hunt was successful. Many of the men made kills of their own and were beginning to butcher the meat. Cedric stood over the bull at his feet. He was breathing hard. He extended his arms, examined both hands, and looked down at his legs. To his surprise, nothing was broken. He took a deep breath and looked up at the expansive blue sky. It was a good day to live. It was a good day to hunt. It was a good day to be a Delethrane.

Cedric walked back toward the larger group where the women and children had brought the wagons up and had begun the process of skinning the aurochs and cutting the meat into strips to hang on racks. Cedric sought a new horse, one sturdy enough to hold his bulk and fast enough to carry him the way he desired.

As he walked by the horses, he saw some young Delethrane boys in a circle shouting. It was a game he recognized. One of the auroch calves stood in the middle of the circle of cheering young warriors, bawling for its mother. Despite its size, the animal was little more than a suckling. Its horns were barely nubs that stuck out on either side of its head, and its legs were gangly.

The boys took turns sneaking up and slapping the calf on the rump or kicking it to make it run to the opposite side of the circle. The animal bellowed and lowered its head to try to ram one of the boys but they just laughed and jumped aside. The calf kicked, trying to connect with its tormentors. But again, the warriors dodged the hooves.

Cedric knew how the game would end. The young calf would make a delicious meal. The animal stood with its head lowered as Cedric approached the circle. For a moment, the long-lashed eyes connected with Cedric. Its face was half dark, the fur as black as night, while the other half was a pale cream color. The hair on its face faded to gray as it reached the crown of his head, but the area between the eyes down to the nose, and even on the nose, was divided into two colors, the lightest pigment contrasting with the dark.

Something in that image, something in the way that the calf looked at him, made Cedric swallow hard. One of the warriors stood up with a spear and walked forward, preparing to end the life of the calf. "Hold up," Cedric commanded. The young man looked to the Serpent King, who was still covered in blood from the hunt. Cedric held up his hand. "Don't kill this one. I will trade you," he said.

The young man furrowed his brow, confused that the Serpent King would give such a command. "I killed a great bull. You men have done well today. You take my bull. I'll take the calf." The young man smiled and tossed the spear to Cedric.

"Serpent King, we are honored." Cedric pointed to the great mound that protruded from the grass where the carcass of the bull lay. "Go and enjoy. The hump meat is sure to be good on that bull." The young men cheered, clapping Cedric on the back as they ran away.

The calf didn't run. It was exhausted. It stood still and looked at Cedric, unable to move. Cedric took a few steps closer to the calf, placing his hand on its head. He could feel the sweat in its light and dark hair. "Will you always remember this day?" he asked the calf. The animal stood panting, standing on shaking legs. Cedric walked to the side of the animal and reached down to wrap his enormous arms around the four legs of the calf and raised it off the ground. He pulled the legs over his shoulder, squatted, and lifted the calf onto his shoulders.

The animal kicked, trying to escape as it was raised off the ground, but Cedric secured the hind legs tightly and bent the calf across his shoulders to still the struggling. He took measured steps back to where the encampment was being established. His tent was already set up, and he staked the calf in front of his tent with instructions to his servants to bring water for the calf and to find a cow that had milk so they might feed it.

DELATHRANE ARMOR

I will show you how he does it," Grawn said as he led the way through the encampment. Cedric towered over the Delathrane warriors who moved briskly among the clan. They had been enriched by the talent of their Delver.

Cedric saw blankets spread out with piles of pointy steel arrowheads. He saw knives and spears, and even coins that bore the mark of the Delathrane clan. He'd never seen coins before— not among his people. Cedric's heart leapt, knowing that this could certainly even the odds between his army and the one he would face.

"How long does it take him to make a suit of armor?" Cedric asked. He had visions of himself wearing the full plate that he had witnessed among the Handri.

"The Delver can make the armor in minutes, but he has a sour attitude. I think it has something to do with the fact that he is handicapped and will never wield any of the weapons he makes. He has no need of armor himself. The man has never fought in a battle."

"There he is," Grawn said, pointing to a group of people who swarmed around a central point in the market.

"Stand back, stand back!" called the men already dressed in armor. They had protective helmets that reminded him of those from Horming. His father had traded for one that had been captured in battle. When he was a child he had put it on his head, and been beaten for it.

"Stand back. There'll be plenty of opportunity to trade or make purchases," the man said. Cedric saw people from many different clans here among the hills. Word had spread. He was glad that he had left his enormous host outside before he came to the marketplace.

When he saw the Delver, Cedric immediately noticed the crippled hand that hung useless at the end of a limp arm. .

"So you're the Serpent King?" the Delver asked, when he saw Cedric's hulking frame looming over his work space. The man sized him up, glancing from head to toe. "What might I make for the Serpent King?" the Delver asked.

"A suit of armor," Cedric said.

"Turn around," the Delver replied.

The people made room for Cedric to walk into the circle. Cedric spread his arms and turned around.

"It's going to take a lot of metal," the Delver mused.

Cedric scowled.

Some of the younger warriors in the circle chuckled, impressed at the size and strength that Cedric presented.

"Do you want a helmet as well?" the Delver asked.

Cedric nodded.

"What style?"

"Make it like the Horming helmets, but with a serpent."

The Delver pursed his lips and looked at the exposed rock before him. The hand that still functioned reached forward. He extended his fingers and placed them on the stone. The Delver began to chant.

He passed his fingers back and forth across the stone, and a quiet descended over the crowd. His chanting rose and two of the assistants came and stood close by the Delver, wearing aprons of leather and holding black tongs at the ready.

Cedric was confused. He saw no sign of any fire or any hot coals, and yet there were burn marks on the leather aprons of the assistants. As the man chanted, Cedric watched as the stones before him appeared to melt. Red liquid bubbled up like molten silver as refuse fell away into a pile that cooled to a dark gray.

With movements of his hand, the Delver shaped the metal brought forth from the rocks. In a moment, Cedric could recognize greaves made to fit his forearms, a chest plate, and armor for his legs as well. One of the assistants stepped forward and lifted the new pieces of armor with his tongs. He thrust the greaves into a vat of oil and a hiss was heard as it cooled. The assistant began to polish the piece with a cloth and charcoal. Cedric saw the metal begin to gleam.

When the helmet was formed from the liquid that glowed red, the Delver waved off his assistants. He picked up his own pair of tongs, both shorter of handle and stout. He grabbed the helmet by the crest and turned it around for the first time, showing it to Cedric. The central crest rose to form a viper, its mouth open and fangs extended and the metal spread outward like a widened hood.

"Why did you give the serpent wings?" Cedric asked.

"The metal has a will of its own. I only guide it to see if it is willing to become what I wish," the Delver said as he motioned for his assistant to polish the newly made piece. When it gleamed with a silvery light, the Delver moved with difficulty to bring the helmet to Cedric. The man's legs were imperfect as well. He bowed before Cedric and then raised the helmet as if to place it upon Cedric's head. Now Cedric knelt before the Delver, bowing his head and closing his eyes briefly to receive the helm. It fit perfectly. The smooth edges within rested comfortably on the crown of his head. There was no need for adjustment. It was as if he had worn it forever. The place where his face looked out was the open mouth of the snake.

"May the Serpent King of the Delathrane bring our people honor and dignity so that we can regain our eastern lands." With that, he placed the helmet on Cedric's head.

When Cedric stood again, the Delver's crew began placing the elements of his plate armor over his leather clothing. He shook it to remove any excess oil, then brought it to Cedric and clasped it on his forearm. The greaves were all made of one piece and the metal flexed as the assistant fastened it to Cedric's arm. No sooner was it in place than the next one was shaken from the oil and placed on his other arm. In moments, Cedric was being covered with the kind of armor he had always dreamed of wearing.

"You need to try it out," the Delver said, even as the people shouted their support and raised their weapons and cheered for the Serpent King.

"May I use this?" Cedric asked, lifting a slender battle axe from a pile of weapons the Delver had made. The people made room as Cedric prepared to test the armor. There were rows of wooden targets set up to allow the warriors to test their weapons which Cedric began to run toward. The strength of his body was not slowed by the well-formed armor, instead it was lighter than he imagined.

Cedric leapt over a pile of arrow tips. When he landed on the ground, he tucked his head and went into a forward roll, the articulating joints of the armor allowing him to move freely. He brought the battle axe up and swung it with all his might, using both hands as he finished a forward roll. At full height, he released the axe expertly and watched it spin in the air twice before burying itself deeply in the wood, splitting the target.

Another cheer rose at this display of martial prowess, but Cedric was already moving forward again. He retrieved the long handle of the slender battle axe and spun it horizontally above his head. He used it to sever the handles on several spears that had been placed upright in the ground. He then just as quickly tucked the axe back under his arm, coming to a stop before the Delver.

"It will stop most blades and arrows," the Delver said.

"I will make good use of this in the coming battle. You will join me in my travels to the East," Cedric insisted.

"Without these hills I am useless. I need the metal ore found in these rocks," the Delver explained.

"I will show you new hills, my wounded brother; even mountains from which to draw the many metals we need."

The Delver cracked a smile.

"I'll join you."

WESTERN OCEAN

C edric took off the horse-hair-crested helmet and moved the strands of his long black hair away from his ugly face. Despite his gruesome appearance, the Delathrane barbarian smiled. His wide lips parted and the expanse of his mouth grew even wider. The thick scar running perfectly vertically on his face remained a whitish shade against his sun-darkened skin. Cedric threw back his head and began to laugh. He had made it to the Western Sea, and gathered or defeated every clan he met.

Grawn Verda stood beside him like the father he wished his own had been.

" I never imagined I would see this," the older man said. Cedric watched as Grawn's eyes grew distant and the gnarled Delathrane chieftain clasped his hands in front of himself.

"Iskabel would have loved this," Grawn said.

Cedric turned to him, his eyes alight with the golden reflection of the setting sun.

"I swore we would make it here. The Sīhalt Guardian insisted that we wait for his word. I have been patient and grown stronger for the waiting. You shall have your daughter back—or satisfaction in blood from those who stole her away."

Grawn clenched his jaw. The muscles in his cheeks flexed from the pressure.

"Now we see with our own eyes that there is a limit to how far our people may retreat," he said. Surveying the expanse of water, he continued, "There is not always another mountain, or another valley, to which we may flee. The grasslands end, and so do the pine-covered hills."

Cedric nodded his agreement. He was glad to have Grawn as a trusted general. He agreed completely, although he did not believe he would have said it so eloquently.

"There is a limit to how far we may run. Our people must stand before the press of the *Handri*. We must fight them and defend our lands, or risk losing everything." Cedric said in his deep, guttural voice.

"Have the warriors bathe in the sea. Then we will turn our great host back toward the Golden City. We will root out the *Handri* devils."

"A baptism for battles to come!" Grawn growled.

Cedric climbed the dune that obstructed the view of the men. His boots made imperfect footprints in the fine sand. From his vantage point he could see the vast host that he had assembled. Behind him the sea rolled in constant motion. The men did not shout at seeing him as they once had. Each company leader held his men in silent thrall, and at this momentous occasion Cedric held them all. Only when he raised his sword to salute them did they shout a cry of respect for their leader.

Rise, Serpent King!

Rise, Serpent King!

Rise, Serpent King!

Cedric gloried in their fervent adoration.

Their travels in the western lands had solidified his leadership. No tribes resisted now. They joined him in throngs that flowed from the mountain peaks to the river valleys. The newest warriors accepted their training as men fit for a unified nation of Delathrane. Those who broke the oaths they swore after joining would never perpetuate a bloodline of weakness and lies. The Serpent King made sure of that.

His men were no longer a force of brave but undisciplined barbarians. When they hunted, it was with the rapidity and precision of a flint-knapper's strokes. But none of his people used flint anymore...they used steel-tipped arrows and gleaming swords. There was a blade for every hand that desired one, and even plates of armor to protect the heart and lungs of his people.

"Bathe in the sea,. wash the blood of your Delathrane brothers from your skin. We no longer fight one another. We stand united as one people. And we will once more have the land between the oceans as our own. I have seen it in a vision. The Delathrane will reside in their old lands—even those taken by the *Handri*.

"We will stop their advance. We will break their walls. We will take back what is ours and will fill ourselves with the glut they have created. We will hammer their coin into armbands and tear down their great Golden City!"

"Rise, Serpent King!" they shouted again, the vastness of the voices like an echo of the crashing waves.

Cedric held up his hand and the voices quieted.

"No longer say, 'Rise, Serpent King,'" he insisted in a quieter tone. "Instead say 'Rise, Delathrane!'" he bellowed.

The Delathrane host cried out until their throats were hoarse. With a gesture from Cedric the men moved past the dunes, onto the beach, and waded into the water. They splashed the water to wet their dusty faces and slapped each other on the back exultantly. They carried their weapons into the sea and bathed them as well. The cutting edges of their knives would no longer be soiled by that of their brethren. These weapons would only be used against the *Handri*.

COMMUNE WITH MELVA

Sīhalt Girdy Frast could feel it. As he watched Kathleen and Elayna talking and laughing with each other, he knew his time in the home of King Lukald Dal Sundi was coming to an end. So much had changed in the years that he had served King Lukald and his beautiful wife, Annalise.

Their daughters had grown rapidly—faster than he expected. Neither Kathleen nor Elayna needed him for the protection that he had always offered. He ran his wrinkled hands through his long hair and white beard.

"Where are you going, Girdy? Will you say goodbye to the girls?" King Lukald asked.

The Sīhalt Guardian turned to the king.

"I need some time alone. I would like to commune with Melva."

"We miss her, too," Lukald said.

Girdy nodded.

"Be careful. Not all of our enemies have been brought to an understanding," the king said.

Girdy patted the *impla* at his hip.

"I'm not without my defenses, Your Majesty," the old man said with a twinkle in his blue eyes.

The king smiled in return, but his face was somber.

"I am told you will soon leave for Windstall."

"My years have grown short," Girdy replied.

"And my daughters have grown tall!" King Lukald added.

Girdy looked at the young women, full of vibrancy and potential.

"Yes, they have," Girdy observed, feeling a deep tenderness and gratitude within his chest at the sight of them.

"You sail with the tide?" the king asked.

Girdy nodded.

King Lukald approached him and placed both hands on the old Sīhalt's shoulders. He looked directly into the watery blue eyes of the Guardian, and pulled the older man forward, slowly, until their foreheads met.

"How can I ever show you the depth of my gratitude?" Lukald asked.

"You shared your family with me. They became my own," Girdy answered in his rough voice.

"You always have a place with us," Emotion swelled in his voice.

"This is not a final farewell, as there is more we must do," Girdy said as the king let his grip loosen.

"You have fulfilled your duty, Lord Sīhalt," Lukald said respectfully, using the honorific title for the Order. The king pressed a letter into Girdy's hands.

"Give this to Master Tove. It is a response to a letter I received from him."

Girdy held up his hand, not needing to know the contents of the letter.

"It expresses my profound gratitude to you and the Sīhalt Order. We will send the sons of Candoreth and all of Sundiland to be trained in the ways of the Sīhalt Guardians if you will have them. I pray that perhaps a few will have the mettle to keep the Windstall Hermitage strong for another generation."

Girdy nodded in appreciation.

"Thank you, Your Majesty," he said with heartfelt sincerity.

He turned and walked down the long corridor, across the gardens and into the glade where an estuary fed the sea. It was a place he and Melva had often walked, sharing their time and thoughts. The tide was high, so he followed the narrow path that wound around the gentle stream that made its way to the ocean. He watched as small crabs scuttled among the marsh grass, dipping into their holes as he approached. Girdy paused at a prominence, the wind tossing his white beard. He took a deep breath and looked out to sea, and then back toward the Emerald Coastline with palm trees and vines and vegetation that was rich. He always feared the day when the Healer woman could no longer walk with him. Now that day had arrived and, like a fool, he had remained silent about the depth of his affection for her. They were from two different worlds, with duties that remained their first allegiance. Yet, they had shared the same household for many years and had come to love the same family and finally each other.

"Melva Al'Cantas," he whispered to the wind, using the full name of the Healer that few people knew. No words came on the wind, and yet he felt as if she would appreciate the message he would share.

"Your adopted daughters are grown and I am now old, even though you are young again." He smiled.

Her brown skin and eyes, her dark black hair… she must be beautiful in her youthful soul, he thought

He kept walking, reaching as he might've done in the days when they were younger to grasp her hand, to help her along the path. He smiled, remembering how much more he needed to hold her hand than she needed his stabilizing arm. He needed the opportunity to be the protector, to be the Guardian. Melva always understood that. He recalled overhearing her explain to Kathleen:

"…a man must have his pride. Don't try to take that away from him."

Girdy recognized the wisdom in her teaching, even if he, too, was a man with pride in need of cherishing.

"I plan to go back to my home in Windstall," he told her. His words carried softly from his lips on the wind. "My years here have been good, and now I am an old man." He looked at the wrinkled skin of his hand and flexed his fingers. Still feeling the strength within them, he recognized that he was well into the winter of his mortal life.

"If you had not sacrificed yourself for Elayna, you would still be here with me. But I am thankful that you did it. I would have given my life for hers. She's beautiful and good. They both are."

"We now have a daughter from the realms across the sea, in the Old World. Her name is Shīanya. You would like her, I think," Girdy said, smiling.

"But she represents a change in Desnia. A change that is coming that may not be all for the good. We have seen our land pass through the Great Sickness, and now the Old World comes to clash with the New. Just as you always said, 'Interesting times make for interesting people.'"

Girdy wiped a tear that began to brim from his lower eyelid. "You were the most interesting woman I never told you that I love you."

The rustle of dried palm fronds whispered along the glade and Girdy looked into a pool of water, its surface reflecting the blue sky and white clouds above.

"But I think you knew."

He pictured Melva's wrinkled face and broad lips smiling.

"Yes, you knew," Girdy said again to the sky.

"I will go back to Master Tove. I'm looking forward to his companionship. I feel a longing for the walls at Windstall."

Girdy walked beneath the sweeping branches of an ancient beech tree, lowest touching the ground. Their girth supported where they rested on the earth. He stepped over an enormous branch and walked in the cool shade of the tree, looking up at the moss that hung from the pendulous branches. "Do you remember when we kissed here?" he reminisced with a smile. He ran his hands along the bark of the ancient tree. "There is no memorial built to you, woman," he said, "but you have constructed an enduring memorial in my heart. This tree remains as a monument to our friendship, and the love that we shared."

Girdy took out his knife and knelt down beside the tree. His weathered hands found the grooves on the smooth gray bark, where he had first touched it with his knife. He renewed the marks in the tree—G & M—refreshing the initials and the heart shape that surrounded them. The wind blew through the branches and Girdy thought that he heard the lilting sound of youthful laughter and the faint clinking of wooden beads.

BLACK POWDER

"I can tell you everything I know," Captain Dagger said in his Centian accent. "But I don't know the exact recipe for the black powder."

"How will we fight them without your guns?" The word felt strange on Jared's lips, but the importance of this weapon was not lost on the Sīhalt.

"What makes the guns work is an explosion within the metal barrel," Captain Dagger explained and then held up his hand, allowing the small black grains to slowly fall onto the table. They looked like sand from the icebound beaches of some of the islands near Adisfall. Jared rolled the black grains beneath his finger, feeling the irregular shape of the grains.

"This is needed in order to make them fire, correct?" Jared surmised. He used the tip of his finger to pick up some of the black grains on the table. They were hard and gritty, almost like corn meal that had been burnt but did not smell of smoke. "Do you know of anyone who might discover how this is made?" he asked Heathron.

Heathron looked closely. "You say it is fire that sets it off?" he asked.

"Fire of any size. Small sparks will do. Candles must be kept away."

"I don't know where we would even begin to discover how this is made. This secret of the Old World has never arrived in Desnia," Kathleen said.

"This may sound strange," Captain Dagger said, "but I believe it has something to do with chicken manure."

"Chicken manure?" Maxwell repeated. His face held an expression of comedic delight—he simply hadn't thought of a way to include this bit of information in his next statement yet, but Jared knew it was coming.

"In Centia, the navy buys wagon loads of chicken droppings from farmers. By right of the crown, the military has first right of refusal on the material it is so important to the process."

"Your military uses chicken manure as their most powerful weapon? That's nothing to crow about!" Maxwell said. A smirk lingered on the Shifter's face and Jared offered him the desired recognition with the smallest twitch of his lip. Maxwell grinned as if he was the most clever man in the world.

"I know of perhaps *two* people who could figure it out," Heathron said.

They all turned to look at the prince.

"The first one is Father Overbrook. The second one, if I had to put my money on someone who could reverse the recipe and discover the ingredients, would be Eldin Stellat."

Larissa nodded her head in vigorous agreement.

"He was the best student in our alchemy classes. He's brilliant. His parents even allowed him to set up a laboratory in their home. After a few explosions, they moved it to a reinforced building on their estate. He showed *all* of it to me when I visited," she explained.

"Where can we find him?" Captain Dagger asked.

"He lives close to the Golden City, on the Southern shore of the Clearwater Sea."

Then they turned to Maxwell.

"I'll take it to him," Maxwell said reluctantly.

"You will want to write out your instructions—if you have any specifics," Jared said to Thomas.

Captain Dagger dipped a quill pen into the ink bottle on the table. He scribbled out a few lines of text.

"I know how to use the black powder in battle; I have never created the stuff, but I will share what I know," he said.

"I wish we had more of it," Heathron said as they poured the remaining grains of the black powder into a small wooden container and closed the lid.

"You should seal that with wax," Dagger said. "If it gets wet, it will be ruined."

Jared used melted wax from a nearby candle to coat the joint of the lid,

handing it to Maxwell.

"Never thought I would be asked to fly chicken poop to Tyath. I swear, my talents are wasted!" Maxwell said as he reached out to take the container.

"Thank you," Heathron said.

Kathleen laid her hand on Maxwell's shoulder. "We don't thank you enough for all that you do in the cause for our freedom."

"Well, when you put it like that, don't mention it," Maxwell said. "I've been keeping a tally, though. You'll make it up to me eventually, once we get these kingdoms back on their feet and your butts back on the throne." He winked and walked out the door, then a loud screech of the rock eagle resounded in the air and they watched it fly into the distance.

~

Maxwell circled the Stellat estate on wings of metallic green feathers. His keen eyes looked down into the courtyard, where he saw a number of people moving about. He landed on the high wall, pumping his wings to slow his descent. He saw Eldin Stellat and Dallin Sarkkand waving to him. The young nobleman squinted his eyes against the sunlight and shaded his view with his hand. Maxwell opened his curved beak and let out a screech of recognition, holding the canister in his talons.

Maxwell flew from the high wall and landed softly on the flagstones in the courtyard. He shifted into the form of a man, knowing that he would cause shock and perhaps some indignation among the people, but there was little he could do. Being a Shifter meant he never knew when he might have his clothes or not.

"Take my cloak," Eldin said as he approached, offering the garment to Maxwell.

The Shifter stood to his full height and wrapped the fabric around his shoulders.

"What word do you have from the South?" Eldin asked.

"Your friends need your help," Maxwell said. "And from the looks of it, you could use some help as well. I saw a number of rough-looking fellows outside the walls. What are they doing here?"

"Lord Balfoest sent his goons to try to intimidate us. They haven't attacked us, but that doesn't take away the feeling that we are under siege. None of us have left the walls of the estate since they arrived," Eldin explained.

"What can we do to help you?" Dallin asked Maxwell.

"There are sand-like granules in this container. Prince Heathron said we need you to help us make more," Maxwell replied.

"What have you got there?" Eldin opened the lid and poured a bit of the contents into the palm of his hand.

"It flashes when set to flame, and it is the secret to the weapons of the Centians who have joined us."

Eldin's eyes narrowed and he examined the black grains closely.

"I will begin immediately." A light in his eyes and the crack in his voice revealed the excitement Eldin felt at the challenge.

"Heathron said that Father Overbook was the other man who might discover how to make it," Maxwell added.

Eldin smiled and looked at the Shifter.

"Of course, both Father and Mother Overbook will help us determine how to make more of this."

THE SICKNESS

During his flight back to Candoreth, Maxwell felt his mind wandering. In the clouds above the earth he often felt at peace—more so there than any other place he knew. Today, however, he found his thoughts drifting in a most concerning direction. Shīanya had said something to him before he left, and she had touched him on purpose. His mind was not clear, and the muscles in his chest seemed tight whether in the form of a man or a bird. He grew more concerned as he glided back down to the capital city of Sundiland. His friends would be there, but so would she. Maxwell was determined to speak with Jared and Seth, they would know how to help him. He flew directly to the tower where they would be meeting at early morning light. He landed on the stone sill and hopped to the floor inside, shifting back into his natural form.

"I think I'm sick," Maxwell said, passing his hand over his heart and spreading his fingers wide at the left side of his chest. He furrowed his brow in concern. The day was dawning and the Sīhalt Guardians were going through their morning rituals.

"What do you mean, Maxwell?" Jared asked, examining his friend closer. "Was your flight difficult?"

"My flight was fine. I got the black powder to Eldin. But my mind was not clear," Maxwell explained.

"What is bothering you?" Seth asked.

"I'm not sure I should be around the Sulian lady," Maxwell said vaguely, his voice full of concern. He swallowed and looked off into the distance, as if he were afraid to say what was on his mind.

"You mean Shīanya? Why?" Jared asked.

"What's happened?" Seth added, feeling the depth of the Shifter's emotion.

"She cast a spell on me," Maxwell said seriously.

"A spell?" Channing repeated, his voice rising.

"I've not been right since the day I met her, but just before I left I think she cast a spell on me," Maxwell said.

"Is it your arm? Were you Healed properly?" Channing asked.

Maxwell moved his hand from his heart to his elbow and flexed his arm, moving the joint as he evaluated it.

"My arm feels fine. I just…"

"What is it?" Jared asked.

"I just feel so distracted and unable to focus," Maxwell admitted.

"And you think that is a new problem for you?" Seth replied.

Jared gave a brief glimmer of a smile when he caught Seth's eye. The Shifter was known to both of them as an energetic, if somewhat distracted, seeker of adventure. Maxwell saw the expression between the brothers, and turned his head away with bruised pride.

"I'm serious!" he said, his hand drifting back to his chest where he rubbed it in concerned circles.

"What is it?" Jared asked more seriously.

"I don't feel right—I feel sick," Maxwell said.

"How so?" Channing asked. "Do you feel as if you would vomit, or are you having a hard time maintaining your balance? There are many troubles that can afflict a man."

"You look okay, if somewhat melancholy," Seth added.

"I think she poisoned me. That's it! She must have given me something dangerous in my drink or put something in my food," Maxwell said, looking off into the sky to reason out the mystery.

"First you accuse the Sulian Princess of casting a spell on you, now you are saying you think she poisoned you. I am beginning to worry," Seth said.

Channing stood in front of Maxwell and lifted his chin in the direction of his gaze.

"Look at me," the captain commanded.

Maxwell looked at Channing. The man raised one eyebrow and stared deep into Maxwell's left eye and then the right. Then he held up two fingers and passed them in front of Maxwell's face.

"How many fingers am I holding up?" Channing asked.

"Two," Maxwell replied, then rolled his eyes.

"He wasn't struck on the head, was he?" Jared asked.

"No," Maxwell confirmed.

Next, Channing took him by the shoulders and looked him up and down.

"You brushed your hair," Channing observed.

"No I didn't," Maxwell replied, passing his fingers rapidly through his straight brown hair.His brown complexion was tinged by a rosy blush that was just visible in his cheeks.

Channing tilted his head and looked at Maxwell like a bird examining a shiny object of interest.

"You did brush your hair this morning!" Channing stated.

"Like I said, I'm not feeling normal," Maxwell said.

"You said you are feeling sick," Jared replied.

Maxwell looked from the face of the two Sīhalt Guardians to Channing, and then at his own hands.

"I've eaten the same food you have. Are any of you feeling strange?" Maxwell asked.

The other three men looked at each other, shaking their heads in response.

"I feel wonderful," Channing said, stretching his arms, "but I think I may have an idea of what your problem might be."

"I can't stop seeing her in my mind!" Maxwell exclaimed. "I can't sleep at night without thinking of her. When I do sleep, I dream of her." He was clearly exasperated.

He looked forlorn, pleading with his eyes to each of his trusted companions.

"Is she doing that to any of you?" Maxwell asked.

Now Channing wore a broad grin.

"No, she's not doing that to me at all," the captain said.

Maxwell glanced around, fearful that someone would overhear the conversation. He moved his hand, motioning for the others to be quiet. He looked to the brothers he had known since childhood and they, too, shook their heads.

"I'm afraid it's just you," Seth remarked, patting Maxwell on the shoulder.

The Shifter passed his hand over his face, feeling desperate for a different answer.

"You are sick," Jared said. "Love-sick."

"No I'm not!" Maxwell insisted.

"It's a malady that is not easily overcome," Channing began. He puffed out his chest, confident that his experience and perspective in this area would be helpful to his little friend.

"She did cast a spell on you, my boy." Channing dusted his hat, lowering the brim to disguise what he would say next. "But it isn't the work of a witch. It is a power that *any* woman might hold over a man, if she so desires."

"Well, I wouldn't say *any* woman. That might be true for you, Channing, but most of us are a little more discriminating," Jared said.

Seth chuckled at the comment.

"You're making sport of weakness," Maxwell said. "I'm overwhelmed. What should I do?"

"What do you *want* to do?" Channing asked.

The question brought a far-off stare to Maxwell. It seemed a perfect blend of wistfulness and terror.

"I don't know," he said, looking off into a dream-like place.

"Yes you do," Channing said.

That brought Maxwell back to the present. He shook his head.

"You see what I mean?!" he exclaimed. "I'm not right... I think I'm dying. I just keep thinking of things I can do for her, to make her happy."

"Or *to* her...?" Channing teased.

Maxwell scowled.

"You are in love with her," Seth said. "All the symptoms you are describing fit the truth perfectly."

Maxwell recoiled at the comment.

"I am sorry for your suffering, but Seth is right. You are in love," Jared said.

"And the only cure for love-sickness is to embrace it. It's like the flu; you have to feed it," Channing said, his eyes blazing. He stroked his chin, evidently remembering past episodes when he did such a thing.

"I don't know if I agree with that completely," Jared said.

"Does she know how you feel? Does she feel the same?" Seth asked.

"I don't know!" Maxwell wailed. "I'm just trying to deal with my feelings, I have no idea how she feels towards me."

"Have her eyes lingered on yours as you've laughed? Has she found reasons to touch you when there was no need? Even a brush of her hand across yours as she reached for something? Every gesture could be a sign. An innocent approximation of your elbows as you sit at dinner, a laugh that springs to her lips all too suddenly as you jest... all of these smallest signs will tell you what you need to know," Channing said, his voice growing a bit deeper as he explained the clues of attraction.

Maxwell sat rigid, seemingly unable to move.

"Take it easy," Seth said. "It is normal to feel the way you are feeling. Just take a deep breath and go about your day. If this thing is meant to be, it will progress naturally."

"What *thing?*" Maxwell asked, unable to conceal his concern and confusion. "What do I do now?"

"You wait for a moment when she is alone and you strike!" Channing said. "Tell her how you burn for her. Tell her that she is the wind beneath your wings as you soar as an eagle toward the setting of the sun! Profess to her how your reason is completely unhinged at the depth of her beauty and the desire you feel in your loins—"

"Say nothing of your loins," Jared cut in. He held a hand up, defending Maxwell from the well-meaning advice Channing unfurled.

Seth nodded his ascent, then added, "Don't say anything right now, Maxwell. You need time to think and consider the future."

Maxwell looked to him in fear.

"The future?" he said.

Channing spread his hands wide.

"I warn you. You will regret it forever if you allow this woman to fly away with your heart, never telling her that she has wounded you eternally because of the love she has kindled within you."

"It is truly a powerful moment when a man falls in love," Jared agreed.

"It has happened to me at least two dozen times. And it doesn't get any easier," Channing added.

Both Seth and Jared looked at Channing as if he were an enigma. They shook their heads and turned back to the Shifter.

"Maxwell, keep your feelings to yourself for now. We need to work out some negotiations with the Sulians and Centians alike. It will not do to throw your passion into the mix. It could ruin everything. Shīanya is their princess after all."

Maxwell nodded and swallowed, accepting Jared's advice like a drowning man being given a life-line.

"But you aren't dying, and you will be fine… in the end," Seth said.

"As long as she returns your love," Channing added. "If she doesn't, then I guess then you'll suffer."

The small amount of tranquility in Maxwell's face drained at the prospect of Shīanya's potential indifference to his ardor.

"Be quiet. You aren't helping," Jared said to Channing.

The captain bowed with a flourish. "As you command, Lord Sīhalt. But I remain ever at the service of Maxwell, my brother-in-arms in the greatest of battles, even the curse and blessing called love."

"Thanks," Maxwell said. "I think I'm going to need all the help I can get. We are all going to need help."

"What did you see Maxwell?"

"I saw Northman longships moored in Tyath harbor."

Jared's face fell.

"How many?"

"Hundreds, and more coming," Maxwell replied.

Seth shook his head. "Our countrymen must have been offered a great reward," he said.

"Y We need you to fly to the Delathrane lands and tell Cedric we are ready to meet him at the Serpent River west of Tyath. Also, you must go to Windstall and warn Master Tove of all that has transpired here. He surely knows of the arrival of those ships from Adisfall."

"After you meet with Cedric, return to Tyath and retrieve the recipe for the black powder from Eldin. I just pray he has discovered it!" Jared said.

PIRATE MAIDEN

Later the same day, Kathleen went to the harbor and boarded the *Dagger* as she had promised. She was accompanied by Shīanya, Jared, Seth, Lilly, and Heathron. Larissa had begged them to come and see the ship once more before she departed. Kathleen wouldn't have missed it. Girdy planned to return to Windstall Hermitage, and Kathleen needed to see him off. Channing was there. He waved to Kathleen as she crossed the narrow plank that joined the vessel to the shore. Sailors scurried about the ship, coiling ropes, moving barrels, and tightening the complex system of pulleys and ropes.Once aboard, Kathleen saw her friend moving in her direction.

"How do I look?" Larissa asked.

"You make the perfect pirate maiden," Kathleen said.

She walked the width of the deck, placing one foot in front of the other. She wore a tan dress she had adapted for life aboard a ship. The front hem was cut into a wide arc that revealed the high leather boots, while her white blouse was gathered tight to her waist by a broad leather belt that matched her boots. She had a cutlass in a sheath hanging from the belt, and one of her shoulders was bare. Atop her head was a three-cornered hat, similar in make to Thomas', but she wore hers with slight tilt. The final element of her costume was the strange Centian weapon in its own little sheath on her right hip. Golden curls fell down past her shoulders, and even though Larissa had aged from their ordeals in Tyath, she looked more youthful and vibrant than Kathleen remembered in a long time. Each of her steps crossed over the other, making her hips sway. She twirled when Channing extended his hand and whirled her about. Her blonde curls, held back by a band of red silk, tossed energetically around her shoulders and framed her heart-shaped face.

"You don't need me to tell you that you look amazing," Captain Channing said.

"I know," Larissa said, then laughed. "But that doesn't mean I don't like to hear it."

"How many girls in Desnia are like this one?" Captain Dagger asked in his thick Centian accent.

"There aren't many. Believe me, I searched long enough for this one."

"I'm sure you have!" Larissa said as she pranced about in her high boots.

"Captain Dagger promised to teach me how to use one of these," she said, pulling one of the strange Centian weapons from the leather holster at her hip. She lifted the small tube, pointing it toward Thomas. He quickly raised his hand and deflected the weapon toward the sky.

"The first thing you need to learn about pistols is to avoid pointing it at someone you do not wish to kill," he said.

"Oh, I'm sorry," Larissa replied, looking down at the barrel and staring into the depths of the cylindrical projection.

"Nor should you ever point it at your own face," he added.

Thomas placed his hand around Larissa's, firming the grip and extending her hand in the direction of the water.

"Point your pistol out to sea and then pull the trigger, if you must practice," Thomas instructed.

Larissa aimed the weapon at a piece of driftwood that floated on the surface and used her finger to activate the small metal lever positioned on the underside of the pistol.

A small explosion erupted from the end of the weapon and the wooden target jumped as the air around Larissa filled with smoke.

"I hit it!" she exclaimed.

Kathleen had to smile. Larissa had much to learn about being a pirate.

"This is a good weapon," Lilly said. "With one of these, Lana would still be alive. No man is strong enough to withstand this! Even a child might slay a warrior with one of these."

"I was thinking the same thing," Channing said. "I'm glad some of the girls in Candoreth didn't have one of those. I wouldn't be around if they had."

"Well if this helps you to be more of a gentleman, that's a good thing," Larissa said, returning the weapon to the small holster at her hip.

"Old George offered to teach me how to use it if we ever get any extra powder," she said.

"I bet he did," Thomas replied, looking at Larissa from top to bottom.

"No threat of danger in the world is going to change my ways, Miss Albodris. But when a beautiful pirate maiden such as yourself captures a man's heart, what can he do? He would die a thousand times just to be in your presence," said Channing.

Larissa smiled, and Channing seemed happy at the effect of his words on her.

"You are so sweet. Still, I plan to practice with my pistol," she promised.

"Without more black powder, there's not a lot of practicing we can do," Captain Dagger said. "But still, it does complete the uniform," he said, appraising her.

"The women of Sulia would never wear such clothes," Shīanya observed.

"The women of Sulia would never look so good in them," Channing replied.

Captain Dagger laughed, and Shīanya frowned in displeasure.

"We have our own gifts," the Sulian princess said.

"Oh yes, without a doubt," Captain Dagger agreed. "They just don't look like those."

His eyes drifted toward Larissa as she tossed her golden curls, batted her eyelashes, and placed her hands on her hips as she spoke with Kathleen.

"We're going to go and see if we can find the *Marine Escape*," Larissa explained. "Maxwell said he saw it drifting further out to sea, so Thomas promised to take Channing and me to the broken yacht. If we can salvage it, he will allow us to join his fleet."

"My fleet," Shīanya stated curtly.

Thomas Dagger bowed to the Sulian monarch. "Of course, Your Highness. *My* ship and that of Captain Channing will join *your* fleet."

"You fight well, Captain Dagger," she replied.

He bowed again.

"I'm not truly part of your navy, Highness. But I can hold my own in a battle on sea or the land," Channing stated.

"Because you are a pirate?" she said.

"I prefer the term privateer, if you don't mind. It has a more legitimate ring to it. Once we get the *Marine Escape*, I'll go back to Marth and gather what ships we can. I am sure the men will be itching for a fight."

"Just keep them away from the Sulian settlers and sailors; I don't think it would go well if they were mixing so soon after the invasion."

"You're right. But if you point them in the right direction, with their honor injured the way that it is, you will rarely have seen men who are more talented on the water."

"We will restock the ships and organize them according to their crews. Sulians, Centians, and Desnians," Thomas said.

"I told the men of Marth that Lars Balfoest is to blame for the invasion. They want a chance to settle the score, and now that I have a ship to sail, they are ready," Channing said.

"Take your ships to the Straits of Windstall," Jared said to Thomas. "At the Hermitage you will find a friend in Master Tove. I have prepared letters of introduction."

Jared handed the sealed letters to Thomas. The former pirate accepted them gratefully and placed them in his jacket pocket.

"May I request the services of the Water Witch?" Thomas asked.

Lilly looked toward Seth. Kathleen noticed.

"I travel with Princess Kathleen," Lilly said.

"We could use her Talent. Without the powder, we are at a disadvantage," Thomas explained.

Kathleen considered the request.

"It does make sense for Lilly to be among the ships at sea, where she could do the most good," Kathleen agreed.

Lilly's face fell. Her usual stoic expression revealed her disappointment at being separated from her, but Kathleen was sure her crestfallen demeanor had something to do with being separated from Seth as well.

"Will you do this for me, Lilly? We need you to use your Talent where you may."

"I live to serve," Lilly said as she bowed her head.

"I ask for your willingness to protect me by helping our navy make it to the harbor of the Golden City."

Lilly raised her eyes and Kathleen was surprised to see moisture in her eyes.

"I will," she said aloud, and stepped forward to hug Kathleen. In her ear, Lilly whispered, "Protect him for me."

"We will meet you in Tyath," Kathleen replied.

"This is going to be exciting!" Larissa said.

"Be careful," replied Kathleen. Her long-time friend seemed to have forgotten how harrowing sea battles could be.

"I've got Selene," Larissa said, and pulled the old Healer of Sulia forward. Her thin gray hair was no longer hanging limply at her shoulders, but had been cut and curled into a neat style. Her face, though still pale and gaunt, seemed to have a light Kathleen had not seen before.

"Her name is Selene?" Kathleen asked.

"Yes, and we are going to become close friends. She is the only other lady on the ship."

The Healer had a spark of self-awareness in her eyes that Kathleen had not noticed before.

"Watch over her, Selene," Kathleen said. "Larissa can be fun but foolish. Make sure she behaves as a lady."

The old Healer nodded slowly, seeming to take a moment to slowly register the commands Kathleen had given her.

Larissa laughed.

"Now *this* is a chaperone I can agree with!" she said as she clutched Channing's arm.

Kathleen shook her head.

"I will look out for her," Channing said seriously.

"I will protect her as my own sister," Lilly added.

At this, Channing's eyebrows rose.

"Now, Lilly is a more appropriate chaperone," Kathleen said with a laugh.

Larissa's expression fell to a coy pout.

"Don't worry, Larissa. I'm just promising to keep you alive. Whether or not you are virtuous is completely up to you," Lilly said.

At this, Larissa was at a loss for words, feigning a truly scandalized expression.

"I'll meet you both in Tyath, Abbath willing," Kathleen said.

Sīhalt Girdy had remained silent through all of the exchanges.

He stood with his white beard mimicking the billowing movement of his black cloak.

"We will miss you, Girdy," she said.

The old Guardian embraced her.

"Katie," he said. "You are in good hands. I take my leave of Candoreth and House Dal Sundi, proud of the people I have known and loved. I will see you in Tyath before long, or you may visit me in the halls of the Hermitage. Either way, we will not be forever parted."

"You deserve some rest," she said.

Girdy laughed in his gravelly voice.

"That I do, I suppose. I want to see Master Tove and reconnect with my brothers of the Order. There are very few of my generation left,"

Tears sprang to Kathleen's eyes.

"I hate goodbyes," she said.

"You have been a blessing to me," Girdy told her.

They stepped apart and their hands finally released their hold on one another. Kathleen walked with the others back to the harbor walk and waved as the sailors cast off.

"I hope they have success in gathering the men of Marth. We will need those ships if we are to defeat Lord Balfoest," Kathleen said.

MY POWER

L ars Balfoest turned and walked down the hallway, shaking his head and speaking to himself.

"I shall never cease to be amazed," he said, thinking of the little Delathrane girl falling in love with him, of all people. The irony of it struck him as humorous.

He was joined in his walk by one of his underlings. "Lord Balfoest, the men from Adisfall have arrived. They're making their way into the city, and unfortunately there have been some events that did not go as planned," he said.

"Speak plainly with me. What did the stupid ice-fools do?" he asked.

The man winced and looked around. "Please do not call them ice-fools to their face. They call themselves Northmen."

"I don't care what they call themselves. Tell me what have they done?"

"All manner of destruction. In the short time since they've arrived there have been seventeen unexplained deaths, a number of establishments along the harbor front burned, countless brawls, and the Tyathian Guards' ability to keep the peace has been brought into question."

"Where is Enderick?" Lord Balfoest asked.

"He's making his way to the throne room as we speak."

"I'll meet him there," Lars said, and continued on his way.

Lars had barely settled into the throne before the large doors were thrust open and the growling voice of Enderick Farson echoed through the chamber. "The men were just having a bit of fun," he said, holding his thick tattooed hands up in a show of innocence. His manner was one of complete disdain for the symbols of power the throne room represented. The Northman belched and reached toward the back of his neck, trying to scratch the middle of his back. In doing so he revealed an exposed armpit with more hair than a red squirrel in winter. The Northman moved with a prowling ease that was untempered by any refining customs—all raw power and staunch individualism.

It was refreshing to Lars, in a way. Here was a man who would not easily bend to his will. He enjoyed a challenge.

Jarek Bastian entered the throne room after the Northman.

"You cannot allow your men to do this in the Golden City. We have laws for the order and good of the people," the captain was saying.

"I was invited here as a guest. We were all invited," Enderick said, his arms spread wide. This allowed his fur-lined vest to open, revealing a massive chest and more tattoos. The three missing teeth in his upper arch were visible as he threw his head back and laughed when Captain Bastian tried to explain the damages that needed to be reconciled.

"Take it up with Lord Balfoest, the ruler of your city," Enderick said.

"Lord Balfoest is not our ruler, he is our Steward," Captain Bastian corrected the man.

The Northman just laughed again.

"What has happened?" Lord Balfoest demanded. His voice remained even as he prepared to navigate the differences between the men.

"My men were feeling rambunctious after a long voyage," Enderick said. "It is nothing at all. We made it here, they wanted to have some fun. The locals did not want to share their drink with them."

"That's not the way it was reported to me," Captain Bastian said.

"One thing led to another and they took the fight out into the street," Ederick said, waving the situation off with his large hand.

"Five men died at that tavern," Captain Bastian said. "Three from an axe to the head." He turned toward Lord Balfoest, seeking support.

"And two of my men were stabbed," Enderick said, as if that was enough of an explanation.

"Because they raped two of the women who worked in the weaver district! Why were your men even there?"

"They wanted to trade in some cloth," Enderick said, the explanation a pitiful excuse.

"Are all the men from Adisfall this difficult to control?" Captain Bastian asked.

Enderick chuckled to himself, his deep voice rumbling. He coughed and spat on the floor of the throne room and looked at Lord Balfoest, rubbing his hands together. "First, we make something understood. Men of Adisfall are not to be controlled. Each one is a man free in his own right. A free man in Adisfall is a man who owns lands and carries a weapon. We are all free men. I lead them because they choose me. They choose me because I lead them to victory," he said with a smile.

"Nevertheless, the enemy is outside the city walls. Not inside," Lars Balfoest said to the hulking man who stood before him.

"That is what we were told. But we have not seen them yet. Where are the barbarians? Where are these Delathrane?" Enderick asked.

"I have reports that they are moving eastward," Lars said. "There is much that we must do to prepare for their arrival, and it will not do to have the Tyathians angered because the men of Adisfall are trampling on their livelihoods. And their daughters," Lars added.

"The men are excited to have the dream powder in unlimited supply," Enderick said. "We sprinkle it in our drink and it does wonderful things to a warrior." His eyes widened even more, revealing the shrunken pupils and a crazed grin.

"Then maybe I should cut your supply short for a little bit. We need you sane in time for the battle to begin. Then, if you wish to go *berserk*, as you like to say, that is fine with me. But it needs to be aimed out there." Lars pointed beyond the city wall. "Not in here."

Captain Bastian nodded, his frown fixed and his arms folded. He seemed to appreciate the support that Balfoest was giving him, even though he despised the presence of the Northman.

"Oh, it will be a sight to behold," Enderick said. "Seven-hundred more ships are coming tonight and more within the week. You will have the support for your Golden City, as you like to call it."

"Have them moor their ships north of the harbor. The Delethrane are not a seafaring people. They will attack by land."

"Yet they ride horses?" Enderick asked.

"They are agile on their ponies, but they also run and shoot with the bow."

"Wait until they experience a Northman's shield wall. They will find what it means to be stopped cold," the man said. He fingered the handle of the long-hefted battle axe that was looped in his belt.

"Let's shake on it," Lars said. He stood from his throne and extended his long, skeletal hand. Enderick Farson took another step up toward the throne and grasped Lars' hand with his massive fist. Lars poured empathy through their grip and drew out the sensation of the emotions the man was feeling.

Enderick looked him in the eye with crazed delight. "We are brothers," he said. " Brothers in this fight."

Lars reciprocated his grip, tightening it. He delighted in the emotions of the man. A beast such as this would cause devastation once he was released from his chain.

SOCIETY OF SUCCOR

Kathleen and Elayna climbed into the royal carriage, while King Lukald climbed into the saddle of his white horse.

"Lady Allison Dal Avery started the Society of Succor," King Lukald explained, "and she's excited to show me all that she's accomplished."

"We are happy to visit with her," Kathleen said to her father.

"I would love to meet with her," Elayna added.

King Lukald gave the signal and the guards led the way as the carriage began to move beyond the gates.

"Did you notice that Father put on his ceremonial armor? He is gleaming and seems ready to crow like a spring rooster," Elayna said, as the sisters rode together.

King Lukald sat proudly in the saddle.

"He's been like a new man since Renata left. Right after Mother passed away, I used to dream that Lady Dal Avery could be our mother. But she stopped coming around as soon as Renata had formed an attachment with Father," Kathleen explained.

"I don't remember any of that," Elayna said.

"You were too young," Kathleen said, patting Elayna on her knee.

She couldn't help but be amazed at the growth that had taken place. Elayna's knee was no smaller than her own. Her baby sister who, weeks before, had been building sandcastles and running around with a dirty face now sat regally beside her, even surpassing her own beauty. However, Elayna still leaned toward the window to catch the breeze that came through the curtains, just as she had always done when she was a child.

The gusts of wind tossed her beautiful red hair and she directed her bright blue-eyed gaze to Kathleen, accompanied by a smile.

"I do love the feeling of oncoming summer," she said. "If we can establish peace, do you suppose we can enjoy long days on the beach together again?"

"Of course we can," Kathleen said.

She felt a pang of loss, realizing that she would never again see the tiny footprints of her sister's bare feet in the wet sand.

"I was just thinking about your feet," Kathleen said. She slipped off her slipper and held her foot beside her sister's. "Look at that. We're the exact same size."

"Now I can wear all your nice clothes," Elayna said as she wrinkled her nose at Kathleen.

"I don't mind. You don't have many dresses that will fit you now."

"Maybe I can use some of the gowns Renata left behind." She seemed to be seriously considering it.

"Only if you want your thighs and bosom exposed!" Kathleen exclaimed.

"I hadn't thought of that," Elayna replied, furrowing her brow and looking down at herself.

"We'll need some sturdy clothes for the journey to Tyath. We can't delay. Soon I will have Candoreth completely repaired and refortified," Elayna said. Kathleen shook her head in amazement at her sister.

"I knew you had a Talent, but I always thought you might be an Artist. I didn't know my little sister would be a Builder."

"I don't know. It's just the way it worked out," she said, shrugging her shoulders.

The carriage drew up into the marketplace and the guards formed a perimeter. A guardsman opened the door and offered his hand to assist the two princesses down to the street level. "Thank you," Kathleen said to the man. Elayna echoed her as she, too, stepped down from the carriage. Lady Alison Dal Avery stood before them in a purple dress with scarlet trim. Her dark brown hair was curled and arranged neatly around her shoulders. A small wisp of gray could be seen in her hair. She bowed low.

"Welcome, Your Highnesses. Thank you for accompanying your father today. I'm excited to show you what we've accomplished."

Kathleen could not help notice that the noblewoman seemed to have taken extra care in her appearance and the king's eyes never left her as they walked together.

The long, covered stalls of the marketplace were lined with people. Women in clean, light blue dresses with white aprons scooped measures of grain into baskets and sacks—anything the people could bring. The lines, although composed of bedraggled people, were orderly. A murmur and then a hush fell upon the crowd as the royals came closer.

"This is wonderful, Lady Dal Avery. You have it so well organized."

"I couldn't have done it all myself. Allow me to introduce to you the Society of Succor." Lady Dal Avery curtsied, then swept her hand in a gesture that encompassed a group of people working to unload another wagon.

The men and boys who helped wore clothing that matched that of the women measuring grain.

People in line to obtain food were using crutches, or had bandages around their head or shoulders. Some people walked with a limp or were helped between the arms of another. Many of them looked dirty and soot-stained.

"The ravages of the battles with the Sulian pirates have taken their toll," King Lukald said.

"But the people look hopeful," Kathleen observed.

"Among this group of citizens of Sundiland, I've identified nine Green Growers of varying ability and seven Red Growers as well, whose talents span the entire spectrum from people who can Heal almost as well as Melva, to those who just seem to have a healing touch as they bind up the wounds of the injured," Lady Allison Dal Avery explained.

"Who gave permission for this?" Kathleen enquired.

"I'm sorry, Your Highness. I did not receive permission. I took it upon myself," Lady Dal Avery replied.

"It's okay. I'm very glad. Look at this. It's wonderful, Father."

Lukald surveyed the service that was being done for the people of his realm.

"Allison, I didn't know the Talent existed among so many of our people."

The people of the Society of Succor bowed and curtsied as one.

"Thank you, Your Majesty," Lady Allison replied. "There is so much we all need to learn. It's sort of haphazard, but we are alleviating the suffering and feeding the hungry."

"I can see that," King Lukald intoned.

"Did you find any other Builders?" Elayna asked.

"So far, you are the only one. We questioned many people, and it seems that we might have a few of the minor Talents here as well."

"I don't know what you mean," Kathleen said.

"Oh, that's right. You didn't attend the Academy. It was closed before you were of age. There's so much I wish we could share with you. There are minor Talents that can be used to help as well," Lady Dal Avery answered.

"That is as it should be. Allison, you do our nation proud," King Lukald said, nodding his head in agreement. He then stepped forward and Lady Dal Avery offered her hand to the king. He took it gently and kissed the back of it, holding it to his lips. "I wish that our great city and nation had more women of your dignity and valor," he said.

"You do me great honor, my liege," she told him. Elayna and Kathleen looked at each other and Elayna began to grin.

Turning to the surrounding gathered citizens, King Lukald spoke in a loud voice. "Lady Allison Dal Avery has my support, and whatever she wishes to implement to alleviate hunger or injury. Please hearken to her. Our people will be better for it. And may Abbath's blessing rest upon you all."

He raised his hands in support and the people cheered.

Lady Allison Dal Avery mouthed the words, *"Thank You"*

73

A RETURN TO TYATH

Behind closed doors, Kathleen leaned over and watched as Elayna fused two stones together. She did it easily, in an almost distracted way. Kathleen picked up the stones that were now made into one and examined the joint.

"That is amazing. You didn't even need a tune. I always needed to hum a tune when I was new at Growing"

"I am stronger than I was," Elayna said.

"You should be. You are an adult now," Kathleen replied.

"Melva once taught me that you can do too much with your gift. You can wear out your strength. A Talented person can become a phantom if she pushes herself too far."

"Is that why you look older?"

Kathleen suffered a smile at her little sister. Elayna still had some things to learn about diplomacy as an adult. Her mind would catch up with her body soon, but Elayna would need to be careful in the meantime. There was no substitute for experience and Elayna, in many ways, was still child-like.

"I have come close to injuring myself by doing too much. I look a bit older because Melva had to Heal me so many times in Tyath."

"You were hurt?"

"Lord Balfoest is a wicked man. He tortured us and forced me to use my Talent for him."

Kathleen didn't want to get into the details; she felt herself wanting to protect Elayna from the truth even though she was no longer a child.

Elayna studied her sister closely, tilting her head to one side and pursing her lips in understanding.

"We can't let that man stay in the Golden City," she said.

Kathleen nodded her head in agreement.

"He must be removed from power. He is a tyrant and a usurper."

"Do the people support him?"

"Some of the noble Houses despise him; however, he has enough support to keep them quiet," Kathleen explained.

"Heathron is the rightful king. The common people would rise up to help him regain the throne. He's a good man." Elayna said.

"Good men do not always get what they deserve," Kathleen said.

"Neither do wicked ones, it's about time we changed that," Elayna said with an edge to her voice.

Kathleen was surprised by the hardness she sensed in Elayna's voice. Maybe her little sister was maturing emotionally faster than she thought.

"I will accompany Heathron back to Tyath. He will need a wife if he is to have legitimacy," Kathleen said.

"I will go with you this time. I can help to rebuild what has been destroyed."

Kathleen considered this. She didn't want to leave Elayna again. She sensed that she still needed her, and having maturity happen so quickly might leave her feeling confused and vulnerable.

"I would like that," Kathleen said, and placed her hands on

Elayna's. She then leaned forward and kissed her sister on the forehead.

Heathron entered the room, accompanied by King Lukald, Lady Dal Avery, and Shīanya.

"You both have a satisfied look on your faces. What have you been discussing?"

"Just how you need to go back to Tyath. Candoreth is secure; we have a larger navy than before and the Sīhalt Guardians say there will be a Delathrane army on the march toward the Golden City," Kathleen said.

"I wonder what is happening there. I look forward to Maxwell's report," Heathron said.

"He *is* taking a long time to return," Shīanya stated.

"Don't worry. Maxwell is very resourceful," Kathleen assured the Sulian woman.

"Father, I want to go with Kathleen this time," Elayna told the king.

King Lukald held up his hands. "Come now, Elayna, how could I stop you? After saving our city, we owe you a debt of gratitude. Besides, I don't want the two of you to part any time soon. You both are so beautiful, so capable. I couldn't be more proud. Look out for each other. We have won the peace here, but Tyath is another story."

Lukald looked to Heathron, and Lady Dal Avery stepped closer to the king.

"We plan to stay here with our people," she said.

"Very well. I will go to Tyath and the soldiers you are sending with me are greatly appreciated."

"They all volunteered.," King Lukald said, and Heathron could hear the emotion in the king's voice.

"I know they have already been through great trials. I will seek to lead them valiantly," Heathron said.

King Lukald placed his hands on Prince Heathron's shoulders, leveling his gaze to meet that of the younger man's.

"My men are under your command. I trust you. Protect my girls," the king instructed.

"I will," Heathron replied. The marks he carried on his face added a fierceness to his reply

The king released his hold on Heathron's shoulders and reached for Lady Dal Avery's hand.

"Send letters often," she said.

Kathleen and Elayna both nodded agreement to the request.

Jared strode into the room, followed by Seth. They bowed to the prince and the king—their Sīhalt formality returned as peace was once again established.

"We have the men assembled and ready to march," Jared told them.

"And Kathleen's carriage. Is it ready?" Heathron asked.

"The smiths are placing the last of the iron plates on the exterior, so it should be ready to go within the hour."

"Elayna will accompany her sister on the journey," Lukald told the Guardians.

"The carriage is a confined space. Will there be room for another person?" Seth asked.

"I don't plan to ride in that metal box. I will ride on horseback," Kathleen said. She appreciated her father's concern, but she felt it was a little much to expect her to ride in what amounted to a prison cell on wheels.

"If you are attacked, will you and your sister at least go inside?" Lukald asked.

"Not if there are rocks or plants close by!" Kathleen said.

"Still, I want you to have it," the king stated.

"Thank you, Father," Elayna said. "I will ride in the armored carriage as long as it isn't too hot. I wouldn't want to roast like a pig in a Wintertide oven."

That brought some laughter from Kathleen.

"We are gathering a fighting force so that when we arrive at the Golden City we have numbers with us," Kathleen said.

"We have asked the people so much already," Elayna countered. "Can we ask them to do more?"

"I am their king," Lukald replied. "I know the people have suffered much, but we must ask for them to sacrifice even more."

"We will meet up with Cedric. He has plenty of men behind him," Seth said.

"We need the people of Horming and the others to join us, too," Jared replied.

"If we show up at the gates of the Golden City in front of a hoard of Delathrane, without the loyalty of our own people, we're asking for failure. We will go by the King's Road, along the river," Kathleen said.

What do you hope to do?" Lukald asked his daughter.

She was quiet for a moment, then locked eyes with her father. "I plan to feed them," she said. "I've been aboard a ship or behind the walls of this stronghold for most of the war. And yet when I was in Tyath, I learned to Grow. I can feed the people."

Lady Dal Avery nodded her agreement.

"We could help," she said, a light burning in her eyes. "The Society of Succor could help, Your Majesty," she said. King Lukald placed a gentle hand on her back, comforting her in the gesture.

"Take care of Candoreth," Kathleen replied.

The woman nodded vigorously.

She will be a good match for Father, she thought.

"Do you believe I will be safe in the presence of the Serpent King?" Heathron asked.

Seth looked to Jared for confirmation.

"I believe if we are both with you, and share with him the circumstances of our battle, he will accept you as a brother-in-arms."

"And if he doesn't?" Heathron asked.

"If he doesn't, then it really doesn't matter if you retake the Golden City. You will immediately be at war again," Seth said.

"He has a host of warriors following him, and I don't believe there is any way to placate them. We must find a solution that works for the Delathrane without murdering the innocent citizens of Tyath," Jared said.

"My people are caught in the political workings of Lord Balfoest. Nevertheless, if they fear an attack the people will rally around Balfoest and the Council of Nine. They will gather their defenses and launch every stone, arrow, or ship they have," Heathron said.

"Channing is gathering the remains of our fleet at Marth before heading north," Lukald told them.

"And we will need every one of them. Maxwell reported that several longships are docked at the harbor in Tyath," Jared said.

"Longships?!" Heathron exclaimed. "What are the Northmen doing in the Clearwater Sea? My father signed a truce with them."

"The truce appears to have been broken—at the invitation of Lord Balfoest."

Heathron clenched his fists in anger. "Many of my friends died to establish that peace."

"The might of the Delathrane will be at our backs," Seth said.

"What can I do to help?" Shīanya asked.

The slight woman spoke softly, but with a confidence that belied her age and appearance.

"You are welcome to stay here in Candoreth with us," King Lukald said. Kathleen noticed that her father used the term "us" and believed that he meant Lady Dal Avery and himself, not just the people of Sundiland.

"Many of the Sulian sailors still follow me, but I have transferred the authority to Captain Dagger. Our sailors will obey. They don't take their commitments lightly," Shīanya stated.

"Why have we not yet heard from Maxwell?" Shīanya asked Jared.

"I expected him back more than a week ago. I can't imagine he's in any danger, but it is somewhat disconcerting that he hasn't returned," Jared admitted.

"What if he *is* in danger?" Shīanya asked.

"Well, I suppose he'll have to get himself out of it," Seth said with a smile. "Maxwell has a habit of getting himself into trouble, but he's especially slippery when it comes to any danger he might face."

"I am, as you say, slippery, too," Shīanya said.

"I am sure you are," agreed Kathleen. "I don't know much about the Sulian Court, but I imagine it requires grace and diplomacy. Why don't you travel with us? It certainly couldn't hurt to bolster our case if we had a Sulian in another nation, even if it is one to whom our people are not familiar."

"The Prince of Tyath, two princesses of Candoreth, two Sīhalt Guardians, and a princess of the Old World, that will make an impression on the common people and the noble Houses. Even the nobility from Horming and towns in between here and the Golden City will be impressed. It will help us gather the army we need to defeat Lord Balfoest. But it will be dangerous," Kathleen opined.

"I am not afraid of danger," Shīanya said. The woman did not appear as someone who could well endure the rigors of the journey on the road.

"Since Elayna has fortified the city, I'm not worried about the defenses. I plan to send the majority of the men-at-arms of Sundiland to join you. I'll send messengers to Hestin, asking for their help, too. Certainly the merchant kingdom has an interest in Heathron regaining the throne. I'll ask the King of Horming to send as many knights as he can spare," King Lukald said.

"We don't have any time to spare. The sooner we can go among the people, the better. Just a year ago I left Candoreth, on my way to meet you," Kathleen said to Heathron. "And now I'm leaving again."

"And you still are not married," Elayna said.

She didn't mean it as a dig, but Kathleen felt a pang in her heart. Elayna was now fully grown, and all of Kathleen's dreams of love and marriage were still unfulfilled. Their people enjoyed neither peace nor prosperity, but at least their city was still their own.

"What did Melva always used to say, Elayna? If at first we don't succeed, we should try again."

Elayna smiled at her sister.

"We will go to the Golden City and free the people there. Heathron will sit on the throne," Elayna said confidently.

Heathron smiled at Elayna in a way that made Kathleen feel kind of lost. She swallowed and tried to smile confidently as well, but the room felt small and restrictive. She wanted to leave.

"Then let us not delay. Cedric will be marching east. I want to meet him before he crosses the Serpent River. He will need a few days to understand and come to agreement with the plans that we've laid. We need to be prepared to travel quickly," Seth intoned.

"I'll send messengers throughout the city and beyond. It won't take long to gather the soldiers of Sundiland," Lukald said.

An avian cry pierced the air.

"It's Maxwell!" Shīanya said with excitement.

The green rock eagle swooped down and landed on the wall of the courtyard. It flapped its wings and came to rest on the ground. As Maxwell shifted back into the form of a man, Jared stepped forward and wrapped his Sīhalt cloak around his friend.

"We were worried about you," Shīanya said to Maxwell. He furrowed his brow and let out a huff. "Worried about me?" he repeated. "What for? I can take care of myself."

"See what we mean, Shīanya? Nothing to worry about!" Jared said.

Maxwell pushed out his lower lip, folded his arms, and nodded in a self-satisfied way.

Shīanya inclined her head slightly, acknowledging Maxwell's ability.

The Shifter beamed and held out the container in his hand. "I've got it," he said with a smile. "Eldin and the old priest did it. They gave us the recipe for the black powder."

"Captain Dagger promises this will make the difference in our war," Elayna said.

Jared took the container and twisted off the end that had been sealed with wax. He pulled out two sheets of paper that had been folded carefully. On one he saw instructions for the manufacturer of the black powder. On the other, he read a letter written by Eldin. "It's for you," Jared said, handing the letter to Heathron. The prince accepted the note.

"What does it say?" Kathleen asked.

Heathron held up the letter and began to read.

Your Highness,

I hope this letter finds you well. I'm glad you are alive. Had you stayed in the city, you certainly wouldn't be. Dallin, Michael, and Hannah have joined my parents and me at our estate, with their families. But Balfoest has placed a guard around our estate. We're under siege. We have food sufficient for months and water aplenty, too, but I do worry that they would bring siege engines. Our little redoubt was not created to withstand the full force of Tyathian siege engines. Maxwell said that you plan to return, and I hope you do so soon, but carefully. All is not well in the Golden City and the lands about it. Maxwell tried to explain how the black powder would be used. I do have some understanding based on his description, but I hope it makes the difference. Please hurry.

Your friend,

Eldin Stellat.

Heathron closed the letter.

"They're under siege," he said.

A somber feeling pervaded the room. The thought of their friends being held captive by Lars Balfoest made Kathleen feel even more sick.

"We will want your full report within the hour," Jared said to Maxwell.

The Shifter nodded.

"Notify the troops that we will leave before first light," Heathron said.

74

MOTHER'S SON

The Serpent King walked in front of the line of captives. He examined the recent acquisitions. The Delathranes did not keep slaves as pets, and they tolerated none that were weak or sick. Only the strong survived among his people. These captives were strong. They required little sleep and little food and they worked constantly in the service of their masters.

They stood in a line as he approached. Cedric passed by the men and the boys, the younger females too, and paused only when he came to a middle-aged woman. He grew tired of looking, but something within him compelled him to keep searching. The Delathrane woman stood with her hair in braids. She looked as if she might spit at him. Cedric smiled.

"I did not come here to demean you," he said to the captive, "Nor did I come here to lengthen your servitude."

His ability to speak with a severed tongue had increased and very few people had difficulty in understanding what he was saying. Cedric raised his voice over the sound of the wind that swept across the grasslands, down from the mountains.

"I come to bring peace to our people, not war. War is what we will wage on the *Handri* when we return across the great river! We will destroy the Golden City."

The slaves turned their faces toward him. Cedric felt the apathy of their circumstance. Many had lost their fire. It had been crushed when they entered a life of servitude.

"You may join our fight and become free, or you may return to your homes. Either way, there will no longer be any slaves among the clans."

A murmur rose from the gathered slaves, and from their masters as well. The slaves dared to hope, while the masters feared losing their property.

"We will not keep each other as slaves."

He motioned for his men to come forward. They struggled under the weight of a large wooden chest.

"I will buy the freedom of every man, woman, and child. Slavery will have an end. We will not be keepers of our sisters and brothers."

The men opened the chest and revealed a trove of precious metals. Cedric ran his hand through the nuggets of gold. It seemed to him such a small trade for the life of a person. He reflected for a moment on how much he had changed since his Healing. He was still willing to take the life of any man who stood in his way, but he felt strongly that the captives should go free. He ordered the men to distribute the riches. They placed the treasure into the hands of the slaves and they wore expressions of shock, unwilling to believe this strange circumstance.

"You will trade these riches for your freedom," he instructed. The slaves began to pass the wealth to their masters. Cries of joy rang out as the captives hugged on another and fell to their knees in gratitude to the Serpent King.

"What if we are not willing to accept your bargain? I want to keep my slaves," a man said from the multitude.

Cedric paused and let the words drift away. He slowly turned to look at the man who had dared to challenge his command. A hush fell over the people as they waited to see what the exchange might bring.

The man was tall and lean. He had a confidence and fierceness in his demeanor that spoke of leadership. This was not simply a fool or a drunkard speaking out of turn. The man shouted the challenge for all to hear. Cedric could not deal with him privately. This demanded a public response.

"I offer you payment," Cedric said.

The man spat on the ground.

"I joined you for battle, not to have stolen what is rightfully mine."

The man moved closer to a slave woman who was handsome of feature. She stood tall beside the others in the line of captives.

"If you are in love with your slave, marry her. For she will be free along with the rest. I will take no slaves for myself, and I forbid my people from having them from this day forth. The choice is yours."

"You say the choice is ours? You say, 'Join me or die'. You say, 'We will fight the Handri and free the lands between the seas'. How are we to believe this?" the man demanded.

Cedric walked toward him, drawing his sword. The man, seeing the Serpent King striding toward him, drew his sword as well.

The first strike was blocked by the man as he parried Cedric's blade. The man was strong, but Cedric was stronger. He attacked again and followed his series of thrusts by doubling his fist and smashing the jaw of his opponent. The man crumpled to the grass like a deer felled by a stone from the sling. Cedric grabbed a fistful of gold from the wooden chest, held up his hand for the multitude to see, and scattered the gold onto the chest of the man lying in the grass.

"What is your life worth?" he questioned in a loud voice. "I hereby ransom the slaves. From this day forward we serve one another at will. The services of another person will be for paid or traded for. We will abide no slaver living among us," he said.

A chant rose that had become common in the mountains and plains of west Desnia: *"Rise, Serpent King! Rise, Delathrane!"* they cried.

Some of the slaves trembled as they fell to their knee. Many of them cried in joyful disbelief.

However, one slave woman stood still. Her hand held the gold she would trade for her freedom. Hard lines were chiseled into her cheeks and at the corners of her eyes. Her skin was toughened by years in the wind and sun. She caught Cedric's attention because she did not cry. She showed no emotion on her face. The woman was so covered in scars he could barely tell that she was *Handri*, but the tattoo on her wrist bore symbols of the Tyathian variety.

Cedric approached her.

"What is your name?" Cedric asked.

The woman looked at him with fierceness.

"What does it matter to you?"

"You are not one of us. Are you not happy for your freedom? You may return to your home."

"I have no place to which I may return," she said.

"Tell me your story," Cedric requested, intrigued.

The woman who did not cry looked at him and furrowed her brow, staring off into the distance, trying to remember.

"The Delathrane have taken everything from me," she began. "I was a common girl in the city. I moved with my family to the countryside when new farmland was offered to those of us willing to settle the land.

"We cut trees and dug stumps to clear the first pastures and fields. We created a life worth living."

The corners of her mouth drew back as she considered the memory.

Cedric watched her, listening. She was not made of stone. He could see the current of emotion the woman hid beneath her shield of stoic resolve.

"Our farm was just east of the Great Serpent River. King Raldric came with his warriors and took me away from my family as I worked in the fields. Four children I had—three daughters and a son."

"You said it was King Raldric who took you? Were those the only children you had?"

The woman nodded. "They were the only ones that I had during that part of my life with my husband—before I was taken."

"Your life has been nothing but bitterness with our people," Cedric said.

"After I was taken captive, King Raldric kept me as his own. I had another child—a little boy, with big dark eyes."

Cedric's heart beat faster. *Could it be?*

"But I was sold to another clan. King Raldric tore my baby away from my breast because he was small and pale and did not grow quickly. I wish he could have lived."

"What was the name of your child?" the hulking barbarian asked, leaning closer as her voice trailed off in softness at the memory.

"I named him Cedric," she said.

The Serpent King almost stumbled forward. He steadied himself and reached out with an enormous hand to place it gently on the shoulder of the woman who stood before him. She raised her eyes to look into his own.

"I am Cedric," he said.

The slave woman blinked her fierce eyes.

"How can that be? My son would only be a youth of twelve, maybe thirteen years, if he were still alive. Surely he was left for the dogs when King Raldric's encampment moved on," she said.

Cedric nodded.

"Your child was sick and weak. He was treated horribly, but he was not left behind to be eaten by dogs. Being half *Handri*, he was made a spectacle of laughter and derision—until the day he was Healed."

Cedric pointed to the vertical scar that divided his face.

"I sustained this wound two years ago. It nearly killed me. The Meat Witch named A'zrah took many years of my life as she Healed me. I was left with this mark to remember it."

Then he held his massive arms wide. "And this stature with which to regain my honor, and that of my people."

"And your father?" the woman asked.

"He died the night I was wounded."

She swallowed.

"Woman who never cries," Cedric said, "behold your son."

She held her hands, trembling as they were, in front of herself and looked at Cedric in a new light. She seemed uncertain, as if this was just another cruel trick.

"Are you really my son?" she asked.

"They told me you didn't want me," Cedric said.

The woman put a hand to her mouth.

"I fought for you. That's why I have these scars. I never stopped hoping that Abbath would protect you," she said.

"I do not know the God of the *Handri*, but now I know I have a mother. And that is enough," Cedric replied.

He put his massive arms around her shoulders and felt the frailty of her body. She was strong of spirit, but his mother felt small in his arms.

"What is your name, Mother?" he asked as he held her.

She looked at him and passed a hand over her face as if to wipe away the dust of her memories. She seemed to find it difficult to recall her own name.

"It was so long ago. My family called me Riley, when I was a child. My name is Rilsa Anterro."

"You have no need to fear, Mother. We are together again," Cedric said.

He squeezed her gently in his powerful embrace. And then he saw the tears begin to flow from Rilsa's eyes.

"Take me back to the Golden City," Rilsa pleaded.

"I will," Cedric promised.

The End of Book Three

STAY IN TOUCH

I hope you enjoyed this installment of the Sīhalt Series. I expect to release Book 4 in 2023. It will conclude this story arc. I plan to continue to write in the world of Desnia. Thank you for reading.

Stay in touch by emailing austin@austinrehl.com